TOWER *of* STRENGTH

TOWER *of* STRENGTH

A Novel

Annette Lyon

Covenant Communications, Inc.

Cover image: *Manti Temple* © Al Rounds. For print information go to www.alrounds.com;
Monarch © William Whitaker. For print information go to www.williamwhitaker.com

Cover design copyrighted 2009 by Covenant Communications, Inc.

Published by Covenant Communications, Inc.
American Fork, Utah

This is a work of historical fiction. Some of the characters, names, incidents, places, and dialogue are
products of the author's imagination, and are not to be construed as real.

Printed in Canada
First Printing: March 2009

16 15 14 13 12 11 10 09   10 9 8 7 6 5 4 3 2 1

ISBN-13: 978-1-59811-694-6
ISBN-10: 1-59811-694-0

To Marvin and Vicki Lyon, who have loved and accepted me as their own daughter. I am grateful for so many things they have given not only me, but also my entire family over the years. They are truly some of the most genuine and generous people I have ever met, and I am blessed to have them in my life. I owe a great debt to them on many counts, but perhaps the greatest is for raising the son who became my husband.

ACKNOWLEDGMENTS

A huge thanks to historian Darrin Smith for his patience with my queries along the lines of, "Hey, Darrin, here's another question" about Cache Valley, Logan, or Brigham Young College. There's no way to describe his generosity but with *wow*.

A special thanks to Michele Paige Holmes and H. B. Moore for going over the entire manuscript for me and to Jeffrey S. Savage and Lu Ann Staheli for their critiques. Also to Lynda Keith and Richard Metcalf, who became my go-to people for all things equine.

Finally, I'm grateful to Sharon Metcalf and Shauna Andreason for sharing with me the story of the real Mantia. Although I took significant creative license with my version, their experience provided the inspiration.

PROLOGUE

Coalville, Utah—August 1877

FRED HEADED OUT FOR ANOTHER day at the mine before the sun crested the nearby hills. He strode through the chilly streets, feeling giddy and hardly noticing the houses and businesses he passed. For once the cold didn't bother him, and the walk to the mine flew by. Fred's mind whirled.

I might be a father soon. Already!

His wife Tabitha had just sent him off with that bit of news, and now his feet hardly touched earth. At twenty-eight, he was far older than most men when they got married. *But I had to wait for my bride to grow up.* He smiled. *And Tab was worth the wait.* They had a ten-year age difference, but somehow, when they were together, the years melted away, and he felt at home.

When he reached the mine, he went inside with the other men, holding a lantern in front of him to guide the way through the narrow passages. The stale air and dank walls met him like an unwelcome but oh-too-familiar friend. Regardless, he still wore a smile on his face that even the chilly tunnels couldn't erase.

Reaching the section where he was assigned, he set down the lantern and got to work. He was part of the team that constructed the interior supports, attaching beams together to hold up the walls and prevent cave-ins.

Holding a mallet in one hand, he rubbed the base of his back with the other. His muscles cried out in protest from yesterday's work, but his mind kept returning to home. If Tab was going to have a baby, they should move back to Sanpitch County right away. Her family would want them to be close by. And he'd find some way to keep his mother from meddling in their affairs and continually insulting his sweet wife. He hadn't realized it until after the wedding, but now he recognized that a good part of his mother's objection to Tabitha had probably resulted from the inheritance he'd received four years ago from his uncle, which had provided some money for his mother *until* he married.

No wonder no girl was ever good enough for me in Mother's eyes.

Except for Betty Hunsaker, a woman Fred had courted briefly when he was much younger, a woman who had been married for several years already. His mother always sang her praises.

"Too bad you missed out on marrying her," his mother said often. "*She* would have been a real catch."

He breathed out heavily and got to work. Would Tabitha be willing to buy that piece of land in Ephraim this soon? Even without a baby on the way, he didn't know if he'd be able to stand an entire year here in Coalville as they had originally agreed. Tabitha had wanted a full year far away from Manti—and from his mother. The days were long beneath the surface, with rarely seeing daylight—or his new bride. Leaving Coalville would be a welcome change.

But he wouldn't mention it quite yet; he'd wait a little longer and see how she felt. He'd stay as long as Tab wanted to. They had left Manti for a reason, and he wouldn't take Tabitha back until she was ready.

He finished shoring up the walls of one section of the tunnel and moved on to the next. In spite of himself, Fred kept checking his pocket watch. The hours crept by at a dreadful pace. He kept thinking about the light in Tabitha's eyes when she had told him she was with child. A grin would likely stay on his face until he went home that night, until he could hold Tabitha in his arms again and they could celebrate the new life growing within her.

"Hall, you got the end of that beam?" Joe asked. His voice seemed disembodied, coming from just outside the glow of the lantern.

"Coming," Fred said. He hefted the other end of the beam, and the two men carried it to the next spot on the tunnel wall that needed reinforcing. The two didn't need to talk to communicate as they worked. In unspoken cooperation, Fred held his end of the wood in place above his head while Joe hammered spikes into the other end, turning it into a crossbeam.

Suddenly the ground trembled beneath Fred's feet. The wood in his hands vibrated, and a shower of pebbles fell around his shoulders. A rumbling went through the earthen walls, reverberating throughout the entire tunnel.

A massive explosion boomed, sending a searing heat over Fred's body. The force of the blast threw him across the tunnel and smacked him into the wall. Heavy rocks and broken beams collapsed on him.

The lanterns had gone black, making the tumbling rocks and cries for help seem even louder. The air was thick and hot. It choked back any cry coming from Fred's throat. He tried to move; his body wouldn't obey. He needed to cough but couldn't get enough air through the strangling smoke and coal dust. Rocks and debris pinned his legs, which had gone numb. The sensation slowly crept uneasily up his torso.

After a few more labored breaths, Fred's eyes slowly closed on their own, and the world began to fade.

Tab, he thought. *Our baby. Oh, Tab.*

Then all went still.

CHAPTER 1

Seven Years Later
Logan, Utah—May 8, 1884

TABITHA CRUMPLED THE LETTER AS she walked down the street. Holding her son's hand and moving too quickly for his short legs, she muttered the first words of the letter.

"'Dear Tabby' indeed," she scoffed under her breath. "I am not a cat!"

The old nickname was really the smallest thing that rankled her about the letter, but somehow it was the only part Tabitha would let herself think about.

It was also the safest element of the letter to dwell on.

Tabby, she thought again, picturing a fat, multicolored feline. *It's Tab. Tab!*

As she marched down the road, six-year-old Will had to trot to keep up, and Tabitha was only slightly aware that she held his hand a bit too tightly. But what else could she do when the letter clutched in her other hand held information that might change the course of their future? When she knew all too well that her future intertwined tightly with her son's, that whatever she chose for herself, she chose for him?

And what, oh *what,* should she choose?

"Ma," Will said between steps, puffing, "why are . . . we going . . . so fast? I thought we were . . . going home."

She stopped at his words. Sweat dampened his hairline, and his brown eyes looked up at hers with total trust and obedience. She knew that if she were to ask Will to keep running for another hour— in circles—he would do it. *Sweet Will.*

"I'm sorry," she said, tousling his hair. "You're absolutely right—there's no reason for such a rush." She kissed the top of his head and tucked the letter into her waistband. It could wait. No sense in making him worry about such things yet. He deserved to have her full attention.

"Would you like to visit Chester before we go home?"

"Yes, let's!" Will said with a hop.

They turned around and headed the other direction. Tabitha's offer to visit the horse in Brother Merrill's stable wasn't selfless on her part. Visiting Chester—a horse she had helped birth and train—was something she did often when needing a spell away from the bustle of life. Somehow she felt as if she could think clearer when brushing his coat, talking out her problems in his stall. She could use some clearing of her mind about now, and Will would enjoy the visit; seeing Chester always cheered him up.

As if he needed cheering up. As if she had already decided to leave Logan and take the job in Manti. Move back to Manti after all these years.

Was that the right thing to do? Her left hand instinctively went to the letter in her waistband, and she drew in a breath. As they reached the stable, Will rattled on about his day at school and how he had won the impromptu spelling bee.

"Congratulations, Will. That's wonderful!" Tabitha said, grateful she had heard that much of his story. "You even beat out Eloise Spencer, then?"

"She messed up on *neighbor*," Will said, sticking his chest out, smiling widely with a tooth missing in front. "She put the *i* before the *e*."

Tabitha gave him a squeeze around the shoulders as they reached the stable. "Then maybe we'll find time to let you ride Chester for a few minutes."

She lifted the latch and pulled the heavy side door open. A whoosh of stale manure- and straw-filled air hit her full-on as she stepped inside. She raised her hem a few inches to avoid getting manure on the bottom of her dress.

She held the stable door open for Will and watched him go inside, wondering what it would be like to go home to Manti. She hadn't seen Fred's mother or siblings for a long time—hadn't seen his grave since the funeral.

Her years at Brigham Young College had been a convenient excuse for staying away. After all, even with the nest egg left by her husband, a widow needed a way to care for her son, and it was a matter of provident living for a widow to get an education. No one could argue that—least of all Mother Hall, who had held Tabitha's lack of education against her. And Fred's money wouldn't last forever.

She had done well for herself. At six years old, Will was content, and Tabitha was happier than she could remember being since her oh-so-brief marriage. Refusing to think about that now, she followed Will inside. He had become the center of her world. It was because of him that she had pulled herself out of the spiraling hole of despair and come to Logan to attend school.

She had enrolled in only a few classes at a time because of her little boy, so it had taken longer than normal to earn her teacher's certificate. Now she taught at BYC while Will attended school during the day. On the two afternoons a week that Will arrived home before Tabitha did, he spent the time with their landlady's children. All in all, it was the perfect situation.

Yet here she was thinking about leaving everything she had built for the two of them, thinking about taking Will away from it all. Of course, he had never known his father. And he knew his grandparents only from letters, a couple of brief visits her parents had made to Logan, and one visit to Provo two years ago when they had met up with Fred's mother while she was up north visiting family. Tabitha hadn't managed to go as far south as Manti since coming to Cache Valley. It was so far away. Hundreds of miles. Days of travel. Lots of money. At least, that's what she told herself.

If they went to Manti, Will would get to know his family. Yet doing so would take him away from the only home he had ever known.

The stable was empty of people. Hanging on the wall was the kerosene lantern she often used during her evening visits. She walked on, Will trotting at her side to keep up. She unlatched Chester's stall. They went inside, and Tabitha pulled the door closed.

"Hello, boy," she said, reaching inside a bucket that held sweet oats. Chester shook his mane and turned his head expectantly toward her voice. Tabitha stroked the horse's rust-colored neck, admiring his strong lines. With her other hand cupped, she offered the oats, and

Chester's lips opened and scooped them up.

She wiped her palms together to get off the last bits of oats, then lifted Will onto Chester's bare back.

"Woohoo! Ride 'em, cowboy!" Will yelled, pretending to lasso something in the distance. Mild-mannered Chester didn't seem to notice or care.

Laughing at his excitement, Tabitha leaned against a post and pulled the letter from her waistband. The envelope was thin and sealed with a blob of red wax. Inside was a single sheet of paper. When she had picked it up at the post office, she'd been pleasantly surprised to see that it was from old Brother Christensen back home. In her younger years, she had spent afternoons haunting his newspaper shop, watching him typeset the paper and work the press and cleaning up after him. In some ways he had been like an uncle.

But in all the years since leaving Manti, he had never written her. Why now? Even after reading the letter, she could still hardly fathom it. With a sidelong glance at Will, who was apparently chasing Indians at a frantic gallop while Chester stood there looking bored, she reread the letter, again bristling at the old nickname.

Dear Tabby,

I'm getting ready to retire from the newspaper. Trouble is, I've spent my life making the paper what it is, and most of the citizens in the county have said they don't think anyone else could possibly run it.

Your parents tell me you've got book learning in newspapering and a right smart head on your shoulders. They've given me some of your writings—newspaper articles and school themes—to read, and well, I'm impressed. You should know that I'm not one who gives compliments lightly. In general, I don't think women are the best choice for positions normally held by men, especially in business. Don't know if you still have an interest in these things the way you used to, but I've been looking around for someone to take over, and after chatting with your folks and reading your work, you've changed my mind. You're the best I've found, man or woman, and I'd be proud to turn my paper over to you.

So I'm hoping you'll consider taking over as the editor and publisher of the Sanpitch Sentinel. *At first, I want the transfer to be gradual so that folks here will still think I'm the one running it, 'til they realize that a woman can do the job just fine, as I suspect a good number of them will have stronger opinions than I ever did regarding the matter.*

I mean no disrespect, of course. Terms for buying the paper can be discussed when you reply, but I'm sure we can work out an arrangement pleasing to us both.

Please respond in a timely manner so I can make arrangements accordingly. If you do not wish to take my offer, I'd like to begin a search for another replacement as soon as possible.

Best regards,

Theodore Christensen

Feeling tired and a bit confused, Tabitha lowered the paper and tried to think logically through her options. If she stayed in Logan, she could continue to teach. She could continue to write for the *Utah Journal,* the local paper. Financially, she wouldn't be rich, but they'd get along. She'd been careful with Fred's money. They could get by on it for several years yet. But it was also probably enough to buy the newspaper.

The biggest question of all hung over her head. How would Will fare if she stayed in Logan? He would do fine.

But what would happen if she went back to Manti?

She wouldn't be teaching anymore. And she couldn't take any new classes. There would be other issues, things that had nothing to do with employment, and she had to face those, just like she would be facing the past again—everything she had tried to walk away from. She would have to think again about Fred's death, about becoming a widow at such a young age. Those events felt like they had happened to another person, another woman. Not her.

And yet she remembered all too well what it had been like to be eighteen and wearing mourning black as she looked across the grave and saw Fred's mother glowering at her. What could she say to this woman who blamed her for the accident? In a way, Tabitha blamed herself. If she hadn't been so all-fired eager to leave Manti, Fred wouldn't have been in that mine.

Maybe he would have been better off with Betty Hunsaker. At least he'd be alive today.

After the accident, Tabitha had returned to Manti while she waited for Will to be born. When she left shortly after his birth—to attend school, she told everyone—she didn't admit even to herself that she was really trying to escape. Just as she had escaped Manti with Fred. Only now could she begin to admit the real reason she'd left. But that didn't mean she was ready to go back and face the ghosts and pains of her past.

Tabitha took a deep breath and watched the bits of hay dust dance in the cracks of sunlight. *I'm no longer a child,* she reminded herself. *There are good things about going back.*

She forced herself to list those things. If she accepted Brother Christensen's offer, she could write and publish to her heart's content. She would be in charge of an entire newspaper, be her own employer. The very thought made her tremble with anticipation and excitement, and she almost hated to admit that to be in control of her future was what she had gone to school for. She wanted to be in the newspaper business. She wanted to *write* newspapers, not just *teach.*

And then there was the biggest question, the one she kept returning to. What about Will?

He would be close to all three of his living grandparents. He'd get to know some of his aunts and uncles and cousins—family he barely knew. That would be good for him. He would find new friends. Sure, leaving Logan would be hard. She looked out the window again, this time to the hill where the walls of the Logan Temple were nearly complete. The temptation to stay to see the building dedicated pulled at her, but she reminded herself that a near twin was being constructed in Manti. Staying to be near a temple certainly wasn't an excuse.

When it came down to it, going back to Manti *would* be best for Will. It might be the thing best for her, too, even if difficult.

She folded the letter and put it back into its envelope, then rubbed her eyes as she slipped it back into her waistband. "Will, what would you think about going to live with Grandma and Grandpa Chadwick for awhile?"

Will pretended to pull hard against the reins to slow down his mighty steed. He patted Chester's neck.

"Good boy," he said. "Living with Grandma and Grandpa Chadwick? That would be neat."

"Then I guess we're going back to Manti," Tabitha said. Will leaned down and wrapped his arms as far around the horse's neck as he could.

"Do they have horses?"

"They sure do," Tabitha said. "Two."

Will held out his arms, and Tabitha got him down. He snuck out of the stall, closing the door behind him. If Will had his way, he would be jumping off hay bales and trying to tie a real lasso.

When he scampered off, Tabitha leaned in to Chester and whispered, "I'm going home."

Home. The word brought a sting of tears to her eyes, and she suddenly had to bite her lips together. *I'm going home.*

All of the emotion that the word *home* implied bubbled up inside her again—childhood, mother, father, Fred, Will, security, love, hope, peace. Emotion filled her, and she didn't dare speak loudly in case her tears upset Will. Instead, she stepped closer to Chester and began stroking his face and neck.

"Thanks for letting me think in your stall," she said. "You always help." Chester nuzzled closer, and she smiled. She reached up to a shelf for Chester's brush. He nickered with pleasure as Tabitha worked the brush over his coat, smoothing her hand over his muscles.

"I have a lot of good-byes to make," she said quietly. "Leaving will be hard. I've made friendships here; this is the only home Will's ever known." She paused, thinking back to the young, inexperienced girl she had been when she'd arrived—scared, alone, and husbandless, with an infant son to care for. "It's almost as if I grew up here too," she added with a wistful smile.

At a sudden realization, Tabitha stopped brushing.

Chester must have sensed her increased tension, because he started shifting his weight back and forth. She held the brush between her hands and took a step toward Chester's face. She gazed into the horse's big brown eyes, with their long lashes, and put a hand on his neck. The brush dropped to her side. She leaned in and rested her cheek against his neck.

"I'll be leaving you too, Chester. I hadn't thought of that." He pushed her shoulder away as if she had invaded his space, and she laughed. "I'm sorry," she said, stroking his muzzle. Her fingers threaded through his mane—his beautiful, long mane. "And you're right. I shouldn't cry like this." She wiped her cheeks. "But I'll sure miss you."

CHAPTER 2

Manti, Utah

"SAM, WAS IT? I'M BROTHER Carlisle. Good to meet ya." The man stuck out his hand.

Samuel Barnett shook it and nodded, not correcting the man. He had never gone by the shorter version of his name. It sounded strange to his ears, but Americans tended to call him plain old "Sam" regardless.

"A pleasure," he said, looking around the fort, constructed of tall, cream-colored stone walls. He stood there, unsure where he was supposed to go or what he was expected to do next. Who knew that becoming Mormon could turn his life upside down and inside out? He had hardly any idea who or what he was anymore.

Not that he regretted it. Not at all. He just hoped that sooner or later he'd be able to predict what tomorrow would bring with a little more accuracy than he could right now. If someone had told him six months ago that instead of trudging beside Helen through the foggy streets of London to go to the factory, he'd soon be riding in a jolting wagon on a hot, dusty road through sagebrush to a city in the middle of nowhere, he'd have laughed them to scorn.

Manti. He silently tried the name of the town on his lips and shook his head, wondering exactly what he'd gotten himself into. A leaden ball seemed to form in his gut as he tried *not* to think back to the burial at sea where he had left Helen behind somewhere in the swirling black waters of the Atlantic.

Brother Carlisle took in Samuel's build, eyeing him up and down, then jerked his head backward and motioned with his hand. "Come this way." He led Samuel toward a barn, speaking as he walked. "You look like a strapping kind of fellow to me, and we've been looking for some help at the stable."

Samuel picked up his sack and bedroll and followed Brother Carlisle across the fort, trotting to keep up. A feeling of dread grew inside him with each step. While Brother Carlisle was right about Samuel being strong—he was broad-shouldered and could lift more than most men—he had only ever worked with heavy machinery. Not once in his life had he ever had to deal with an animal.

Stable work doesn't bode well for me, he thought, swallowing a sickening knot. A breeze kicked up, and with it, the smell of manure filled his nose. Bile rose in his throat, and he had to cover his mouth. *Don't let yourself lose your biscuits.* He clamped his teeth to steel himself and squared his shoulders. *Act like a man.*

"Stephen," Brother Carlisle called into the dark recesses as he opened the barn's side door. "I found you some help."

As they stepped into the barn, tiny bits of straw seemed to float everywhere. Samuel wiped the bottom of his nose with the back of his hand and tried not to sneeze or breathe too hard at the dank stench of livestock. He looked at his boots to see what on earth he had stepped in. They scarcely made a sound on the dirt floor, which was actually more like mud mixed with straw and manure packed down into a thick covering.

Stalls lined one side of the building, and the other side held mostly tools and tack. The far end also housed animals, but he couldn't make out what kind they were. The only ones he could see right off were horses, some sticking their heads over the edge of the half doors of their stalls, some eating . . . whatever it was horses ate. A couple of tails flicked here and there, and chickens clucked and pecked off to the right.

Brother Carlisle grabbed a handful of oats from a nearby sack and walked up to a horse, letting it eat right from his hand. The animal opened its mouth and gobbled the food right off Brother Carlisle's palm, its tail swishing as it ate. Samuel watched it work the food, especially watching the jaws and teeth, which looked plenty strong to break a man's hand. He shuddered at the idea of feeding a horse from his palm.

"This one's named Molasses," Brother Carlisle said, then nodded to a shelf at Samuel's side. "Over there's some carrots. Grab one and feed her."

Samuel looked from the shelf to Brother Carlisle and back again, then at Molasses. The horse looked powerful strong this close. He pictured the beast breaking off a finger instead of the carrot. Suddenly Samuel had an urge to hightail it out of the building and get back on the wagon and from thence to Salt Lake City, where he'd catch the first train heading east. It was one thing to ride a wagon that was pulled by a horse and properly attached to a harness and controlled by a man who was trained in such things. It was quite another to see a horse with rippling muscles at this proximity—and with nothing stopping it from biting your hand off. All the way from Salt Lake City, Samuel had made a real point of keeping a good distance between himself and anything alive that had more than two feet.

"That's all right," he said with what he hoped appeared to be a lighthearted shrug. "Let's see if we can't find . . . what was his name? Stephen?"

"Oh, of course," Brother Carlisle said, patting the horse's face and moving on. "Where is he? Strange. He's usually in here at this time. Maybe he took a longer dinner break than usual."

As they moved farther into the building, Samuel wondered what other animals were housed in there. After a few steps, they passed the chickens he had heard before. Were there other creatures like goats or sheep—or something bigger? *Buffalo?*

How many animals would he personally be caring for? What would his jobs be? He imagined all kinds of options. From the end of the corridor came a low moo. Samuel's step came up short.

Cows. Land sakes, will I have to milk cows? What in tarnation have I gotten myself into?

* * *

The hired wagon took well over a week to travel to Manti from Logan. As they went south, first leaving the Cache Valley canyons behind, then Salt Lake City and Provo, they saw fewer and fewer signs of civilization. Tabitha felt as if they were venturing into the wilderness, with drab yellow hills and scrub brush in all directions, leading right up to the bluish mountains in the east. She could have pressed the driver to go farther each day, saving her both time and money. But she justified the expense. Surely young Will tired easily, she told herself. There was no need to push either of them to exhaustion.

The real reason, of course, niggling in the back of her mind—and in her middle—was that with each step of the horses' clomping hooves along the dusty road, the more she dreaded reaching their destination.

This is the right thing to do, she had to keep reminding herself as the wagon jolted over the bumps in the road. *It is.* But she had never been one to welcome change—especially not since Fred's death, which had upended her life—and this was the biggest change in her life since then. In some ways, it was also a change that seemed to be an attempt at bringing things back to the way they were.

But life could never be the same as it was when she married Fred nearly seven years ago. She wasn't sure she could face the town without him, the boy she had admired and had eyes for since she was a girl really too young to be noticing boys. But how could she *not* have noticed the handsomest boy in town, even if he had been so much older?

The wagon drove southward on the long road that would eventually bring them into Manti. A hill in the distance was as far as she could see, but it merged into other hills, other colors and shades, and she couldn't make out anything distinctly. She had an arm around Will almost more for her own strength and reassurance than for his.

"We're almost there," she said quietly, not knowing if he'd hear, since he had slept the last hour or more.

Where there had been nothing visible but the purplish hills before, suddenly a brilliant white shape appeared on the horizon ahead. Tabitha studied it for several seconds before she realized what it was—the temple, with its rising walls of ivory stone. Her parents had told her about how big it was now, with sides more than fifty feet tall and the towers on each end about to rise even further into the sky. But to *see* it—to have that be the first thing Will laid eyes on when she came home—was something spectacular and unexpected.

She and Will jostled against one another along the road as they drew closer to the city and what was now clearly visible as Temple

Hill, with the temple getting larger and more distinct every minute. Tabitha took Will's hand in hers and squeezed it. They would pull into Manti very soon. He took a deep breath and lifted his head, blinking sleepily.

The city would be much as it had been when she left, with no place to look that *wouldn't* have ghosts of memories that she and Fred had shared. She imagined what some of those memories would be. Just seeing her parents' porch again would be hard. Fred had picked her up and dropped her off on those wooden steps more times than she could count. That's where he had proposed one rainy spring day.

Where would she and Will sleep? She hoped it wouldn't be in her old bedroom; she couldn't bear to sleep beside the window where she had sat as a young slip of a girl, staring at the stars, dreaming of what she had imagined would be her beautiful life with mature and brave Fred. Their future had stretched in front of her like a long, twisting road, and she had been so excited to see where the road wound, what lay behind all the bends. Who had known it would be short, with only a single turn?

The first of the ghostly memories hit her full force and much quicker than she had anticipated when the wagon hugged the road that edged Temple Hill. Will pointed to the right and asked, "Mama, what's that place?"

Tabitha's voice caught in her throat. "That's the cemetery."

"Is my daddy buried there?"

"Yes, he is," Tabitha said, trying to keep her voice even. "Do you see that line of pine trees on the far end? His is the tall white monument."

While Will searched the area, Tabitha gazed at Fred's headstone. It stood taller than she was and was made of the same off-white rock as the temple, which stood off to the left on the hill. She wished she could press her eyes closed and look away, but instead she could do nothing but stare at Fred's grave as the horses continued their trot. She remembered the day of his funeral—how much she had cried, the weak and frightened feelings that filled her very being, the accusatory stare of Fred's mother from across the open grave.

Tabitha wrenched her gaze away from the plot, finding her breathing had grown rapid. "And over there is the temple," she said, trying to avert Will's gaze—and her own attention—from the graveyard.

While it was natural to be weak and emotional at the funeral of one's husband, her pregnancy had only made her physical and emotional state worse. She hugged Will to her side as the scenes from the past crashed over her and the wagon left the cemetery behind. She raised her eyes to the temple and marveled at the work that had happened while she had been away. The last time she had seen the hill had been shortly after the site was dedicated, and nothing had been built there at all, not a stone atop another, not a piece of the four huge terraced walls that she now gazed on.

Those walls had been under construction when she'd left with Will; she remembered explosions shaking the air as tons of rock were blasted away. They were another reason she had wanted to escape— each explosion sounded so much like the one that had taken Fred's life that they sent her entire frame trembling and shaking. At times the noise made her retreat to her bedroom and sob from sheer fright.

But the work went on. The blasting allowed stone, sagebrush, and wild trees to be cleared, and in their place those four giant walls were constructed in terraces going up the hillside. Tabitha had heard about the size of the terraces, but seeing them herself was different. At a distance, they appeared to overlap, making them look like one mighty wall—a rugged fortress protecting what would someday become a house of the Lord. This close, the separate walls were more distinct, and she could see the zigzagging pathway that led from the top of the hill and through the walls to the street below on the west. So far, the Manti Temple looked like it would be close to the same size as the one in Logan. But the terracing here gave an entirely different feel to the hill.

On their wedding day, after they had left the crowd of well-wishers behind, Fred had stopped their buggy right here on the road and pointed to the hill. "Someday," he'd said, "we'll be sealed for eternity in a temple right up there." Tabitha had wrapped her arms around him and had gazed at the hill, planting her dreams of the future on the hillside as Fred clucked his tongue and moved the buggy forward. She had looked over her shoulder as they had driven along the road leaving Manti. Gazing at the hill, she had wondered what the temple would look like when it was complete.

Now as she skirted the hill, there it all was—the terraced walls layered one atop the other, and above them, four white walls rising into the sky. Her parents had told her in one of their letters that the towers on either end, one taller than the other, would represent the two priesthoods. Tapping, pinging sounds echoed as the stonecutters worked and formed white stones to the right shape and size.

She couldn't help but think back to when she used to walk up to Temple Hill on Sabbath afternoons—years before any discussion of a temple being built, let alone before the blasting and the terracing began—in search of trinkets with the other children. Not arrowheads and fossils—that's what the boys wanted. No, the girls sought for round, black rocks—Jack Stones, the girls called them—which they used when playing jacks. But her favorite thing to find was the round, white ones that looked almost as if they had fallen off a pearl necklace. At home in a small fabric pouch that she had made herself, Tabitha kept a small hoard of the pearly stones and dreamed of somehow making holes in them and stringing them onto a thread to make a necklace for herself. How beautiful she would look!

As the wagon rumbled past the hill, she rubbed her arms, feeling unwell and shaky as the rush of memories came over her. When she was a little girl, the hill was ugly and barren, nothing but rocks, weeds, and sagebrush. Back then you could still see the dugouts in the south side where, her parents often told her, some of the early settlers had huddled against the brutal winter their first months here. She looked back at the south side of the hill. All evidence of those days was gone with the blasting powder and the terracing.

The last time she had dared play on Temple Hill was when she was ten, so she never did get quite enough pearl stones to make that necklace, even if she had managed to come up with a way to drill holes into them.

That's where it happened, she thought, noting a spot on the near side of the southern slope where the top terrace and the one below met.

The day stood out in her mind as if she could see it happening before her all over again—a Sabbath evening when, as usual, the children and the youth congregated at the hill to talk and search for treasure. At the time, Fred was a man of twenty, so mature and grown up. Tabitha was sure he didn't even know she existed, but she definitely knew of him—and seriously disliked Betty Hunsaker, the girl he had walked around the hill with, picking wildflowers and giving them to her. Betty gathered the flowers into a bouquet and gave him shy looks and smiles that infuriated Tabitha in spite of the fact that Fred was so much older.

She had watched the two of them climb past her, and Fred stooped down to pick up a gleaming white stone to hand to Betty. Stomach roiling with envy, Tabitha glared at the seventeen-year-old beauty batting her eyes at Fred as she told him thank you. Tabitha balled her fists, wishing she had found that pearl stone for her own collection before Fred had given it away to Betty.

Tabitha stomped forward but then halted abruptly. Not two steps beyond Fred's boot was the biggest rattler she had ever seen. And he was about to step right on it. If he did, it would surely bite him, and—

Acting before she thought, she ran toward him as fast as she could, yelling, "Fred, stop!" He paused in his step just as she reached him. She grabbed his arm and pushed him backward. He stumbled, lost his footing, and landed on the ground, pulling Tabitha on top of him.

All these years later, she could still remember how strong his arm felt, the muscles flexing beneath his sleeve, along with the excitement and awkwardness of unexpectedly finding herself in such close proximity. Suddenly shy, she scrambled off him and to her feet.

"Silly, what was that for?" he asked with a smile as he sat up and replaced his hat, which had fallen to the side.

Tabitha was unable to respond at first for catching her breath. Instead, she just pointed several feet off where the rattler had disappeared under some rocks, then managed one word. "Snake," she panted.

Betty squealed in fright and backed away. Fred looked a little pale, but he smiled. "Thanks, Little Chadwick," he said, patting her shoulder.

Tabitha's heart began racing faster. He *knew* her name?

"That's your name, isn't it? Tab?" he asked.

She nodded, a giddy warmth shooting through her. No one had ever shortened her name to Tab before. She liked it.

"Then thanks again, Tab," he said, putting an arm around Betty, who was near hysterics, having abandoned both her wildflowers and the stone Fred had given her. He gently led her down the hill. Tabitha looked after them then defiantly picked up the pearly white rock and slipped it into her pocket before leaving too.

She never did go back to look for stones, telling herself she was too afraid of the snakes. But she did return several years later, her arm through Fred's as they walked together. They had meandered the hillside during the last summer before the workers had begun blasting and leveling the hill. The two of them reached the top, on the northwest corner of the future temple's footprint—although neither knew that at the time. There Fred picked a small spray of surviving wildflowers, this time for her.

"It looks like a castle, Mama!" Will cried with delight, twisting in his seat to watch the temple recede behind them.

Tabitha didn't turn around. "Yes, it does."

She shifted forward on the wagon's bench, looking away from the hill. In her mind's eye, she could see the day with the snake as if it were only a moment ago rather than nearly fifteen years previous. Just as she could picture the precise spot where Fred had plucked her bouquet—right there, where a worker was pushing a wheelbarrow.

As the wagon traveled through the town streets, she could almost see herself and Fred walking together, arm in arm, to a dance or a theater performance in a neighbor's parlor. The girl whom he had seen as nothing more than "Little Chadwick" before had now begun to grow up and had caught his eye. Fred was closer to thirty than twenty, and it was no secret that his parents wished him wed.

One night after they had been courting for a few months, they attended a recitation of Coleridge's *The Rime of the Ancient Mariner.* Under normal circumstances, she wouldn't have dared be so bold, but something about Coleridge's poetry moved her and made her more brave than usual. As they left the performance and drew away from any prying ears, she eyed him askance and asked airily, "So Fred, after all these years, have you simply sworn off marriage altogether?"

In all honesty, she yearned to know the answer but would never have thought herself capable of asking such a thing. But truly, what *did* he want in life? Betty had married a few years back, but there had been several other girls who would have happily become Mrs. Frederick Hall had he so much as uttered the question.

"On the contrary, I have the greatest affection for the institution of marriage," Fred said. He turned, took her hands in his, and kissed the tops. "I just had to wait for you to grow up."

Could that night have been less than a lifetime ago? Could it really have happened to *her*? Tabitha had thought the moment was nothing short of the most romantic thing to ever transpire anyplace in the world.

But what if Fred hadn't waited for her? What if he had married Betty or someone else when he was in his early twenties, when all his other friends were marrying? He'd almost certainly be alive today.

She smoothed her forehead with her fingertips, knowing that she couldn't live her life on "what if." But she had a feeling that after returning to Manti, it would feel like this everywhere she turned. No matter where she looked, she would be faced with one more "what if," and each one was horrendous to contemplate.

I saved him from death when he was twenty. But saved him for what? To die in a mine explosion when he was newly married?

A boom rocked the air, shaking the wagon, and Tabitha sucked in her breath. "What was that?" she asked, hating how much panic filled her voice.

"Just some stone blasting, ma'am," her driver said over his shoulder. "For the temple over yonder."

"Oh, of course," Tabitha said, sitting back. "How silly of me." The sound had been only a quieter version of the huge boom that killed Fred. She'd dealt with it after his death, too. If the construction workers still blasted stone regularly, she would simply have to learn to not hear the noise or react to it. Nevertheless, the memories of Fred, combined with the explosion from a moment before, made a torrent of emotions come back. She pressed her lips together tightly and looked away.

"Mama, what's wrong?" Will asked, reaching for her hand.

Opening her eyes, she put on a smile. "Just a sudden headache, that's all. Must be from the sun." She put her hand on his cheek and tried to smooth away his worry with her thumb. "Really, I'm fine."

But as she attempted to swallow the lump away, Will's mouth pursed to one side. He studied her face, remaining unconvinced. She laughed and kissed his hair. "I'm all right," she said, pulling him close and resting her chin on top of his head so he couldn't look at her. The young boy could practically read her soul. She held him tight and let tears fall silently down her cheeks as their driver continued down Main.

Was it part of God's plan for me to save Fred from the snake so we could have our child? she suddenly thought. *If I hadn't been on the hill that day, I might not have Will.* Tears stung her eyes, and she forced herself not to sniff, in which case Will would know she was crying. She held him tighter, grateful for the greatest blessing in her life.

"Farther this way?" the driver asked over his shoulder as they went past the Little Fort.

"Left after the fort, and then straight for a few of blocks," Tabitha said, hoping emotion didn't register in her voice.

She wouldn't let her mind continue straying to memories about Fred and Temple Hill. Not today. With brute force, Tabitha shoved such thoughts from her mind. She would see Mother and Father soon, and a sniveling daughter wasn't the first thing she wanted either of them to lay eyes on.

In no time, the wagon stopped before her parents' home—a pretty, pale blue house that sat on a corner lot with a flagstone walkway leading from the street corner to the front door. The path was flanked by shrubs that were much larger than when she was there last. Some of the plants were new. To the left of the porch stood a round, turreted room. Woodwork scrolling edged the gables and roof, while flowers and small bushes nestled at the base of the house. The maple out front was taller now, as was the line of stately evergreens along the right side of the house. The place felt smaller than the one in her memory, especially the round room, which she used to imagine as a castle tower.

The front door opened, and an excited voice emerged, saying, "Paul, they're here! Oh my goodness, they're here!"

Tabitha took the driver's hand as he helped her down, and then she reached for Will as he jumped off the wagon. She turned to the door, where her parents stood, smiling broadly. Father had more gray hair than he used to, especially in his brown beard. Mother's face had more lines, and both of their waistlines had grown by a few inches. Her father leaned on a cane, his shoulders not nearly as erect as they used to be. He looked so much like Grandpa Chadwick had before he died. When had her father grown old?

Seeing her parents brought another lump to Tabitha's throat. She took Will's hand and marched up the walkway, then noticed one more person standing in the doorway—Fred's mother. Sister Hall's face was unreadable.

"I didn't know you were coming today," she said evenly. Her voice still carried the same chilly bite Tabitha remembered. "I came by on a Church matter. But it's good to see you again."

The shock of seeing her mother-in-law so soon made Tabitha's step come up short. She swallowed hard and tried not to reflect her surprise. She hadn't prepared herself for this. What would she say? The woman surely still blamed Tabitha for marrying Fred and taking away her money, for making Fred move to Coalville, which had killed him.

Sister Hall, I still blame myself, too, she wanted to say but couldn't. As she and Will walked up the path to the door, Tabitha wished fervently that she had known Sister Hall would be present for her return.

Her parents came forward and crushed her and Will with hugs. Her mother kissed her cheek then pulled back, holding her daughter's hands out to the side as she appraised her. "Look at you! So grown up and ladylike."

Tabitha smiled in spite of her nerves. Of course her mother still thought of her as an adolescent, a mere girl. Just as Tabitha thought of her mother as the young woman she had been when all of the Chadwick children were small, not the grandmother with graying hair and lined face that stood before her now. Time had a strange way of playing games with one's memory and expectations.

Her father bent down with his hands on his thighs and looked right at Will. "And who do we have here? He's sure a handsome fellow. Must take after his grandfather."

Will looked from his mother to his grandfather, sudden shyness etched in his eyes, which had opened wide. Tabitha stepped beside him and put an arm around his shoulders, enjoying the banter. "Will, this is my father, your Grandpa Chadwick."

Her father stuck out his callused hand, virtually enveloping Will's small white one, and pumped it a few times. "Nice to see you. You're practically a strapping young man." He measured how tall Will came on him—just to his plump waist. "Your mother had better stop feeding you so much, or you'll up and grow taller than me, and that just won't do. Maybe I can squish you down a bit." He playfully pushed on Will's shoulders as if trying to make him shrink. Will's mask of shyness melted, and he burst into laughter.

"I'm *supposed* to be this big," Will said, stretching himself to his greatest height, jutting his chin into the air as if that would add another inch. "I was six in April, and I'm gonna keep growing."

His grandfather laughed. "Let's go inside and show you around." He put a hand on one of Will's shoulders, leading him into the house. At the doorway, he paused and said in a mock whisper, "Let's see if we can't swipe some of that cake Grandma Chadwick made today."

When the screen door clanged shut behind them, there was nothing left to delay speaking directly to Sister Hall. The ease Tabitha had felt a moment before evaporated. She nodded and said quietly, "Good to see you again, Mother Hall. I hope you've been well."

"Likewise," Sister Hall said with the slightest tilt of her head.

It was strange calling her "Mother Hall," but the moniker was something the woman had insisted upon after the wedding. Perhaps the name—the title—would have seemed natural by now if the two had spent time with one another over the years, but using it felt stilted and false. She had hardly known Sister Hall before the wedding, but not for lack of trying to create a relationship on Tabitha's part. But it was difficult to spend time with and get to know a woman who didn't think her son should marry "that Chadwick girl," as Tabitha had heard herself referred to during their courtship. Apparently none of her successes in becoming self-sufficient and raising Sister Hall's grandson had made a snit of difference in her opinion of Tabitha.

The woman's face was inscrutable, which made Tabitha's stomach turn over. For the last hour on the road, she had felt rumblings of hunger, but suddenly her stomach felt sour, and she had no desire to eat anything.

"Come, come," Mother said, ushering Tabitha inside like a hen. "Let's get you settled." To the driver, who was still waiting patiently by the wagon, she called, "Come in for some refreshment, and then I'll send the men out to help with unloading the wagon."

Everything inside the house was smaller than Tabitha remembered. In spite of her uneasy middle, she graciously took a plate with cake on it and tried to choke down a few bites as Will sat with his grandfather next to the fireplace and laughed himself silly at his games and magic tricks. Will seemed perfectly at ease now, having no qualms about reaching up and pretending to steal Grandpa Chadwick's nose. Will let out a belly laugh over the capture, which turned into a delighted shriek when his grandfather began tickling him, demanding, "You give me back my nose!"

Tabitha let the plate rest on her lap and watched the scene with sudden contentment as Will reveled in his grandfather's attention.

For the first moment since she had left Logan, Tabitha felt happy, for the sake of her son, even with Sister—*Mother*—Hall peering at her over her own cake plate. The road ahead would be bumpy at best—especially if she were to make peace with her mother-in-law. But somehow, as Tabitha settled into her chair and enjoyed watching her son play, pure joy on his face, she knew she had made the right decision. For Will at least.

CHAPTER 3

SAMUEL ROTATED HIS SORE SHOULDER as he left the stables late one night. As June approached, the daytime heat intensified. He wasn't used to such a dry climate and at times yearned for a good, cleansing rain or damp fog. He smelled of grime and muck, and blood spatters covered his trousers from helping with the birth of a calf. Finally, all of his work was done—at least until early morning, when it would start all over again. He groaned and tried not to think that far ahead. Working in the spring had to be worse than any other season. If one more animal gave birth, he felt certain he just might lose what little of his mind remained. He exited the Little Fort by the east entrance and continued heading that direction, toward the boarding house he stayed at, located just south of the rising temple. When he got there, he'd wash up and sleep.

Sleep. The single word felt like a dream.

He had spent the last couple of weeks since his arrival working in the stables with Brother Carlisle and felt no closer to understanding the strange creatures he had to take care of than he had when he'd started. Granted, he'd learned a few things about stable life. Some lessons had come the hard way and some because other workers, like Stephen, had generously shared their knowledge. But he still had so much to learn, and most of the other men seemed to assume Samuel knew more than he did because *they* had grown up with animals. It must never have occurred to them that other men might have lived in a bustling city their entire lives, or that until he arrived in America, Samuel's only contacts with livestock had been passing horses in the streets of London as they pulled carriages or riding behind them on buggies—always a good distance away from them and certainly never handling them himself.

One of the lessons he learned on his own was to never walk behind the ornery cow Dolores in the far stall when going to milk her, because she kicked backward at noises. Also, thanks to a young man named Horace, Samuel found the trick to holding a shovel without getting blisters all over his hands as he mucked out stalls. *That was a lesson that came a bit too late, alas,* he thought, looking at his palms. Several popped blisters were healing, and he was getting calluses on the bases of his fingers.

He hated the stables and their sickly smell of manure. He despised getting filthy and covered in animal waste every day. At times he feared the stench would penetrate his very pores and he'd never get it out. *I wasn't made for working with animals.*

Before long, he reached Mrs. Mirkins's house, where he was boarding—a two-storied, white-brick home built in an L-shape. A covered porch nestled in the corner of the L, with pretty woodwork framing the edges of the porch roof. A decorative railing with thin spindles lined the enclosure. For some reason, every day when he returned from work, Samuel felt compelled to see the temple. He walked past the boarding house, which sat on the corner, then stood in the street and looked north. There, not more than a block or so away, was Temple Hill, looking regal with its ivory walls. The huge terraces climbing the hillside made it look protected, safe.

Crickets chirped somewhere in the darkening evening as he took that short moment to pause and look at the building.

It's beautiful, he thought, then lowered his eyes and went to the front door of Mrs. Mirkins's house. The simple act of seeing the temple usually calmed him—something he had no explanation for. But tonight it brought up unsettling feelings. One day marriages would be performed in that temple, marriages for eternity.

If only she had lived that long. He closed his eyes tightly and headed for the door. As much for his own sake as for his landlady's, Samuel gripped a post and cleaned his boots on the scraper beside the stoop. Thick mud and manure caked the heels of his boots, and that fact bothered him more than almost anything else; he never knew when the red streaks on the heels would get worn completely off. He cleaned his boots carefully, then looked down, first at one boot and then the other, to ensure that the bright slash of paint was still visible on the sides of both heels.

The paint was there—fading, but there. He breathed a sigh of relief.

How many more days in the stables will the color last?

It seemed silly to care about a little paint, but it made him think of his wife. It made him feel that perhaps she wasn't completely taken from him. Shortly after they were baptized, Helen had bought a small can of bright red paint. With a piece of old rag, she had smeared a streak of paint on each heel.

"What in the world did you do that for?" Samuel had asked, grabbing one so he could wipe off the mess. "I can't wear them looking like this."

But Helen snatched the boot back, saying, "When I'm working on the weaving machine at the factory, I can't stop to look up and see you when you come in with the other men. I see you gents walking around fixing things, but all I see is your boots. For all I know, you could be monkeys walking around and I'd never know it." She looked at his boot, a slightly wistful look on her face. A shoulder lifted and fell. "I want to know when my husband is near me. If I can tell which boots are yours, I'll know."

"Surely you can tell when I'm there sometimes," Samuel said, softening.

Helen looked up and smiled teasingly. "Only when you smack your thumb with a hammer or catch your finger in a gear and let a curse fly."

Samuel was about to protest. He didn't curse *that* often, did he?

Before he could utter a retort, she pressed a finger to his lips and said, "But I won't know it's you from that anymore. Seeing as how we've found the gospel, you won't be cursing any longer . . . will you?" She smiled at him in the way only she could, looking almost innocent in her simple way of requesting a new standard.

He took the boot from her hand and grabbed the other one by the top, then leaned close and kissed her. "I'll wear them proudly every day. And that's the *only* way you'll know it's me. You have my word."

She had put a hand to his cheek and caught his eye. "Thank you, Samuel," she said softly, then lifted her face for another kiss.

Now as he went inside the boarding house, he found himself glancing at the red marks as he walked—something he did several times a day—as if doing so might help Helen spot him even from above. They were also the only thing keeping him from letting all kinds of words fly from his mouth as he worked day in and day out doing things far more frustrating than hitting his thumb with a hammer.

"Evening, Mr. Barnett," Mrs. Mirkins said as he stepped inside. She sat on a chair by the newly lit fire. Her voice startled Samuel out of his reverie. She was knitting what looked like a sock—likely for the temple workers, he guessed. She donated much of her handiwork to the cause.

"Evening," he said with a nod, meaning to proceed to the stairs around the corner.

Mrs. Mirkins set her work aside and followed him into the entryway. "I set out a candle for you," she said, stopping by a sideboard. "I thought your last one was probably burned down by now. Do you still have matches in your room?"

"I believe I do, thank you," Samuel said, pausing to take the new candle on its pewter holder.

"Would you like to eat downstairs, or shall I bring some supper up to you?" she asked, already heading toward the kitchen before he had a chance to respond.

"I'd prefer to eat in my room, please," Samuel called after her. "And thank you." He wearily tromped upstairs to his room and unlocked the door, grateful that she didn't seem to mind that he didn't usually dine with her and the two other boarders.

The door swung open, and for a moment he remained in the hall and stared into the room. In the dimness that dusk brought with it, the room looked more barren. The room was small and spare, five or six feet wide and twice as deep. It held a bed tucked on one side and an end table beneath a tall but narrow window looking southward. The ceiling had a peaked gable, so he could stand at his full height only in the center of the room. A washstand with a cracked basin barely fit against the wall. His traveling trunk stood at the foot of the bed and held all his earthly possessions.

This is the sum of my life, he thought, stepping inside and closing the door behind him. He set the candlestick on the washstand and lit it, then sighed. The flickering glow brought shadows as well as light to the room, which didn't lift his spirits any. His life was so different from what he'd pictured when he and Helen had first heard the gospel at his preacher's home one evening, or the days following when they had decided to be baptized.

She had scooted close to him under the patchwork quilt that night last January. Had it been only five months ago? Their room had been cold, and Helen's breath came in light puffs as she tried to keep warm. But he relished his new wife's closeness all the same. She looked up at him, and even now he remembered the moonlight from the window spilling across her smooth cheek, the brightness in her eyes.

"Isn't it amazing?" she asked, easing closer to him. "We've found the same church that Christ established during his life. And we *will* go to Zion—somehow. We'll find the money, I just know it. The Lord will provide a way." She took his hand and kissed it, then tucked it under her chin between her own hands in the way he had come to love so much. He kissed the top of her nut-brown hair as she went on. "The future holds so many wonders for us," she said, leaning her head against his shoulder. "I can't wait to see what changes the next months will bring."

Those months certainly brought changes, Samuel thought as he walked across his sparse room. He sighed heavily as he sat on the hard, narrow bed, which had space for just one. He pulled off one boot and then the other, tempted to throw them onto the floor. But because of the chipping paint, he set them side by side with care— orderly, just as Helen liked—not wanting to risk losing any more color from carelessness. He glanced at his solitary pillow and then the window, hating the fact that he had a clear view of the moon most nights. It always reminded him of that perfect night with Helen.

He stood and stripped off his dirty shirt, poured some clean water into the basin, and did his best to wash off the grime from the day. A knock sounded on the door, followed by Mrs. Mirkins calling, "Your supper."

"Thank you," Samuel answered through the door as he hurriedly put his shirt back on to be presentable. His stomach seemed to growl louder than his fatigue, and he eagerly opened the door. A tray of food lay on the floor, which he brought inside and quickly devoured, then put back outside with a few coins on it. His monthly rent paid for both his room and board, but he always felt awkward not paying something extra for Mrs. Mirkins's kindnesses, like when she brought up his food on the days he didn't come down to dine, so he tried to express his appreciation as best he could.

He locked the door and put on his nightclothes then blew out the candle. After a much-needed stretch—making his back crack—he collapsed onto the bed, nearly falling asleep as his head hit the pillow, when a passing thought stopped his eyes from closing. Helen never let him go to sleep without their nightly prayer.

I'm already in bed, he told himself. *But how many nights in a row have I forgotten to pray?* He fought against the thought. *I shouldn't have ended up in this room alone. She should have arrived in Manti with me.*

They were supposed to be here together. She was the one who had the most faith that they would find a way to come to Zion. She knew the gospel was true before he did. If one of them had to die on the sea voyage, it should have been him. But neither of them should have died. They had followed the prophet's counsel to gather, hadn't they? And here he was, instead of sitting around a cozy fire with his sweet wife's supper on the table, where he could tell her about his miserable day. Had she been here, Helen would have laughed with him about Dolores's latest orneriness, easing the tension and fatigue in his body and mind. Not even that old cow would be able to make him miserable if his wife were with him. But she wasn't. Instead, he lay in this tiny room alone, his entire body sore from work, his heart aching with loneliness as he stared into the darkness, trying to decide whether to pray.

Helen wouldn't be happy with me if I didn't get on my knees.

He pinched his eyes closed, hating the rush of emotion that thinking of her always brought with it.

Very well.

He rolled off the bed onto the wooden planks of the floor. His arms were folded, but as he prayed, he struggled to find something to say in thanks as the elders had taught. What was there for him to feel grateful for? Some days he wasn't even grateful to be alive. What he wouldn't give to be in heaven with Helen right now instead of smelling of dirty straw and Dolores droppings, with the prospect of facing the rest of his life alone. Alone, in a foreign land, among strangers.

Helen, I miss you so. Giving everything up for the Lord wasn't hard when it was with you. I didn't think I would have to give you up, as well.

The loneliness got the better of him, and soon one hand covered his eyes as he tried to ward off emotion.

Finally his heart simply poured out his greatest question. *Why am I here, Lord? Wouldn't she and I have been better off staying in England?*

CHAPTER 4

AFTER A LIGHT SUPPER, TABITHA and her family retired to the sitting room. Mother Hall had already left, refusing to "impose" on the Chadwick family dinner. Tabitha was too tired to contribute much to the conversation, but she enjoyed listening to her parents and Will getting acquainted. The talk turned to the early days of Manti, when both families had first arrived to settle the area with a few dozen others.

"I don't think we've had that brutal of a winter since that first one," her father said, clasping his hands behind his head. "Couldn't believe how many cattle died. Pathetic, really, with the surviving ones being so thin you could practically see through them. You know, it's a wonder any of us survived, considering we couldn't hardly plant crops in the spring because most of the plowing animals were dead."

Mother tsked and shook her head as she rocked in the rocking chair, Will in her lap. "To me it wasn't just sowing crops that nearly killed us. Don't you remember the rattlesnakes? It's a miracle no one got hurt."

Will, who had been nodding off in her lap, suddenly sat bolt upright. "Rattlesnakes?" he asked, eyes popping.

His grandfather laughed heartily. "You heard right. *Rattlesnakes.* Hundreds of 'em. Turns out they were living in the very same hill we had taken shelter in, only they weren't active in the winter. But when it warmed up, hooey! Those rattlers started coming out of their holes and slithering all around." He moved his hand back and forth like a snake, slithering it toward Will, who yowled with delight as his grandfather grabbed his leg and "bit" him.

"So what did you do?" Will asked, breathless.

"We spent days fighting 'em off with clubs and fire and guns. Killed dozens of rattlers."

"Did anyone get bit?" Will asked in awe.

"Nope, not one." Grandpa Chadwick said, and Will sank back, a little disappointed.

"One almost did," Tabitha said quietly. She wasn't born at the time, but she knew the story—although she hadn't thought of it in years.

"Who?" Will asked Grandma Chadwick. Tabitha and her mother exchanged sad looks. When they didn't answer, Will bounced in his seat and demanded of his grandfather, "*Who* almost got bit?"

Tabitha's mother reached around and settled him into the crook of her arm. He looked up with innocent eyes as she said, "Your father, Will. He was nearly bitten by one of the snakes when he was just a little boy."

"Was he younger than me?" Will asked.

"Much younger," Mother said. "Only about two, if I recall correctly."

"Did the snake get 'im?" Will asked.

Mother began rocking back and forth as she went on soberly. "He could hardly toddle around Temple Hill. All of the children played there, and there was little Fred, trying to keep up with the older ones."

Even though she knew the outcome, Tabitha shivered as she thought of what happened next. She took up the tale as if she were seeing the events playing out before her in vision. "Your father picked up a stick and poked it into some rocks. A rattlesnake came out, but he was too young to know of the danger. He even reached for the snake as if it were a toy, right, Mother?"

Tabitha's mother nodded quietly.

"What happened, Mama?" Will demanded. "Did he grab the snake? Did it bite him?"

His grandmother continued the story. "I was nearby gathering some greens for dinner, and I saw the snake. I nearly had a conniption fit when I saw how close he was to the snake. I dropped the bowl, scooped him up, and ran like wildfire down the hill to your Grandma Hall." A wan smile crossed her face. "He laughed all the way, thinking it was a game. Little did I know that I had just saved my daughter's future husband from an untimely death."

"Wow," Will said, leaning against his grandmother again. "I wish I could have seen it. Are there any more rattlers around now?"

Grandpa Chadwick shook his head. "Not many. We've seen a few here and there over the years, but nothing like that first spring."

Tabitha's gaze drifted to the window southward, toward Mother Hall's home. An ache gnawed in her middle. Fred had been spared—twice—in miraculous ways. No wonder his mother hated her for taking him to Coalville. Whatever his mission in life was supposed to be, she had probably cut it short.

Mother saved Fred from a rattler when he was just toddling on the hill. And I did the same when he was a grown man.

For what?

Her mother interrupted her thoughts. "It's getting late. Let's get you and your mother off to bed."

"All right," Will said reluctantly. "But Grandpa, tomorrow can you tell me more about killing the rattlesnakes?" He ran across the room and nearly bowled over his grandfather.

Grandpa Chadwick laughed and scooped Will into his lap. "Tomorrow I'll tell you about the night we spent setting snakes on fire and clubbing their heads and—"

"Paul, please," Mother said, putting a hand on his arm. "You're going to give him nightmares."

He winked at Will. "We'll talk later."

Will nodded in silent wonder, a silly grin on his face.

A knock sounded on the door, and when Tabitha answered, she found a short, elderly man on the other side. He tipped his hat in greeting, revealing a ring of gray hair. She studied his face and recognized an older, more wrinkled version of Brother Christensen than the one in her memory. He removed his hat and put out his hand, which Tabitha shook.

"Brother Christensen. What a pleasant surprise."

"Heard you were back," he said with a smile. "Wanted to see you straightaway."

Tabitha's mother chimed in. "Come in. We have some cake, if you'd like a piece."

"I'd be much obliged," Brother Christensen said as Tabitha and Will retreated inside so he could enter. Tabitha's mother brought the gentleman a plate with cake on it. He nodded and seemed to study the room. Judging by the businesslike look on his face, he had obviously come here for a reason, not just a social call. "I suppose you'll want a few days to get settled? Perhaps we can meet at the *Sentinel* office on Saturday?"

"That would be ideal, thank you," Tabitha said. "A few days would be nice to unpack and get Will into school. I know it's almost summer break, but it would be best to get him started anyway—help him make some friends and the like."

"Very good, very good."

"I don't have to go to school already, do I?" Will asked, suddenly perking up from his spot on his grandfather's lap. "Can't I just stay out of school until after the summer?

"We can't do that," Tabitha said. "Even with only a couple of weeks left, we can show the children of Manti what an amazing speller you are."

Will smiled crookedly. "Yeah," he said. "And I'll beat them all in spelling."

An uncomfortable silence followed with Brother Christensen eating a bite of cake and seeming to want to speak but never quite getting there. Tabitha's mother seemed to sense the awkward tension in the room and that their visitor was there on business with her daughter. She coughed and said, "Dear, would you come help me get Will ready for bed? I have a feeling he'd love to hear more of those snake stories."

"Of course," Tabitha's father said. "If you'll excuse us." He took Will by the waist and plopped him onto his feet, stood, then followed his wife out of the room, leading his grandson by the hand. He laughed and pretended to whisper, "See, I told you I'd be able to tell you more about the snakes."

When everyone had gone out, Brother Christensen said, "I'm mighty grateful that you accepted my offer."

"I think the move will be good for us," Tabitha said, suddenly nervous about his visit.

"I'll get the paperwork settled when you come to the office in a couple of days, but I just wanted to be sure that you understood that, well . . ."

When his voice trailed off and he didn't speak for several seconds, Tabitha prompted, "Yes?" He wasn't having second thoughts, was he?

His face seemed to color a bit. "If you recall what I said in my letter, I'd like to keep the arrangement quiet at first. I know a few people in particular who might cause a ruckus if they knew a woman's running the place—*owning* the place. That could be bad for business. So I was hoping you'd consider, well . . . whenever you write a letter from the editor or other announcement, if you wouldn't mind signing it with my initials like I've always done? Just for a little while, until we can find a gradual way to introduce you as the new owner. Once they adjust to you as the editor, we can tell them you're also the owner."

"I . . . I suppose I could do that," she said. *Theodore Christensen,* she thought. *T.C. Those are my initials, too.* At least, they were before she married. In a sense, she'd be signing her own initials anyway. "I do hope it's not too long before we can announce the change."

"No, no. Of course not," Brother Christensen said with a dismissive wave. "I'd like people to see how well you're doing before they know I'm no longer at the helm. When I told some of the brethren in my ward about my plans to retire, they gave me a lot of flak about it. Wanted to know who was taking over. They feel that the paper's the pulse of the Sanpitch area and that the wrong person would ruin it."

"I couldn't agree more," Tabitha said. "A newspaper can be a powerful thing, which is why I'll do my utmost to make it the best it can be, even if it means signing my name at first as *T.C.*" She smiled at Brother Christensen, hoping to ease his worries.

"I knew you'd understand." His cheeks spread into a smile. "Thank you kindly, Sister Chadwick."

Sister Hall, she thought, but didn't correct him, since he'd probably forgotten her married name altogether. Abandoning the rest of his cake, he stood and shook her hand. "I'll be going now. Perhaps we can arrange a tour of the building evening after next? Bring your son along. I think he'd enjoy seeing what his mother will be doing."

"Thank you, I will," Tabitha said. "I'll see you then."

Her parents appeared at the doorway as he left, and her mother headed for the kitchen to finish cleaning up from supper. Her father jutted a thumb over his shoulder. "You've got a fine young man in there."

"I know," Tabitha said, her heart warming.

"He's asking for you. I think he's a bit worked up from all the excitement. Not my fault, of course."

Her mother chortled from the kitchen. "Oh, no. His grandfather had *nothing* to do with getting him all riled up."

Tabitha laughed. "I'll go check on him." She headed to the new addition of the house, where she and Will would be staying for the time being.

She sat on the edge of the bed. Will appeared to be dozing, but the moment she touched the mattress, he sat right up.

"We need to say our family prayer together," he announced. His eyes were tinged with red; he was clearly tired.

"You're right," Tabitha said. *Sweet Will.* The extended family had held a prayer together after supper, but apparently Will didn't think that counted. Tabitha was grateful that he still saw the two of them as a family unit. "Would you say it tonight?" He scrambled off the bed, then wedged his way between Tabitha and the quilt. She clasped her hands around his then waited. He said a quick prayer of thanks, mentioning their safe arrival, his grandparents, and even the cake.

When he finished, he flopped back onto the pillow. "Sing me a song?"

"Of course." Sitting by the window and gazing into the Manti night felt strange; the last time she had spent a night in this house, she had been much younger. There were the familiar fir trees out back, the rounded tops of the foothills to the east—a view very much like the one from her old bedroom upstairs. She was glad they weren't staying in that room. This new addition her father had built included two small rooms, with plans to add additional ones in a second story when he had the resources. The plan was to let her older brother Nathaniel and his growing family inherit the place in a few years.

As she sang, rubbing Will's back while he drifted off, she gazed out the window at the soft, black sky, the stars looking like sharp points of light. *What will the future bring?* she wondered. She almost didn't dare imagine; last time she looked out on this same sky and dreamed, her predictions were horribly wrong.

"I miss home," Will murmured sleepily.

"I know," Tabitha said, a feeling of homesickness coming over her as well. She had a sudden hankering for a raspberry tart from Mrs.

Holmes at Brigham Young College—and one of the good long talks that always went with them.

Tabitha continued stroking his back as he dozed, thinking about everything she needed to accomplish in the next few days. Her mother had already arranged for Will to be part of one of the schools operating in town, taught by Henrietta Pierce, just a block east of the Little Fort. It was close enough that Will could walk.

When his breathing deepened, Tabitha leaned down and kissed his cheek, then retired to the rocking chair beside the window. She tucked her feet under her legs and stared at the night sky.

Being in her childhood home brought a feeling of when she was Will's age, making her feel as if she should be asking her parents' permission to stay up past her bedtime. She hugged herself and leaned her head against the back of the chair, remembering her girl-hood and the times she and her two sisters—one older, one younger—would stay awake in one big bed, warming their feet on one another's ankles and giggling.

Inevitably, Father would poke his head into the room and say, "Girls, it's time to go to sleep. Your mother will be getting up early, and she needs her rest."

"Yes, Father," they'd say in a properly subdued chorus. As the door closed, they'd hide their heads under the covers and try desperately to keep their uncontrollable giggles quiet.

No matter how well they thought they managed to muffle the sound, it still reached Father, and they'd soon hear a single word of warning through the wall as he said, "Girls . . ."

They'd hush up fast, biting their lips together, but doing so would only make the laughter bubbling inside worse, and inevitably they'd break out in giggles again.

The memory sent Tabitha laughing quietly. She had so much fun with Opal and Adaline back then. Father always appeared so concerned with Mother's sleep. Looking back, Tabitha had a sneaking suspicion that he probably was sick and tired of the girls' noise and wanted to get his *own* rest. In those days, he generally woke up a few minutes earlier than Mother did to stoke the fire and get out to the cows, but growling about his personal lack of sleep wouldn't have been as effective as pulling heartstrings regarding their mother.

Tabitha wished she could see her siblings, but they had all married and moved away—not only her sisters, but three of her brothers: John, Seth, and Wilford, too. The closest were Charles, the baby of the family, and Nathaniel, the elder brother who had teased her within an inch of her life when they were young. Both of them lived in Ephraim with their families. That wasn't too far; perhaps she'd be able to see them soon.

The exhaustion of the trip and the reunions washed over her. Tabitha closed her eyes and thought about her family, recalling joyful times when they were all young and at home. With memories of working with her family in the field, celebrating birthdays, and reading scriptures by candlelight, she fell asleep in the rocking chair by the glow of the rising moon.

CHAPTER 5

IT WAS EARLY MORNING, AND Brother Carlisle had given Samuel a simple set of instructions—to bring the six-month-old filly from the stable, out of the Little Fort, and across the street to the round pen owned by a Brother McCleve. She needed to start her training, and that was the best place to do it; the Little Fort didn't have room for a round pen.

After weeks of mucking out stalls, feeding horses that were big enough to kill him, and even helping to birth a calf—which nearly did Samuel in right there—this chore was something he felt he could handle. What could possibly go wrong with tying a rope on the gold-colored horse and leading it a pace down the road?

He secured the rope without trouble—he even remembered the correct knots and gave himself a mental pat on the back for it. The filly followed him out of the stable and into the early-morning sunlight, and Samuel breathed a sigh of relief when they reached open air. But not two yards out of the fort and onto the road, the young horse dug in its hooves and refused to move another inch. Samuel turned around and tugged at the filly's rope. The infernal animal dug its heels deeper into the dirt.

Samuel tugged harder, wishing he were dealing with a machine at a factory back in London. At least those things didn't have *brains*. You didn't have to try to figure out what language they were speaking or try to reason with them in some animal way. Just take a mallet or a screwdriver and fix the dratted thing.

"Come on, you dumb horse. You're supposed to come to the round pen with me. Over this way. Just *come*."

He pulled again. Once more the horse fought him, planting its rear feet into the ground as it resisted the rope and refused to budge. Its eyes went wild, rolling back and showing just the whites. Samuel felt a bit queasy looking at it. How a horse only a few months old could possibly be so strong—or so stubborn—he didn't know. Of course, this one was a female. *That counts for something,* he thought wryly. But wasn't it mules—or was it donkeys—that were supposed to be so set in their ways?

And hadn't Brother Carlisle said that mares always taught their young a bit of manners and discipline, sort of kept them in line? Sounded almost like human parents. Then again, Brother Carlisle had also mentioned that this mother was a first-timer and might not know how to teach her little one.

You can tell, Samuel thought with a grim set to his mouth, tugging on the rope again and wondering if he dared swat the animal's hindquarters and risk getting kicked. *How hard can a filly kick?* he wondered. Probably not very hard, but he wasn't sure he wanted to test the theory.

"Just come with me, you stupid horse."

A snigger came from the fence lining the street. Pursing his lips, Samuel let the rope go slack as he turned around to see who was mocking him. A young schoolboy stood on the lowest crosspiece, his arms folded across the top. He held his books and slate, cinched with a belt, in one hand, and they swung back and forth like a pendulum. A grin split his face in two, revealing a mouth missing several teeth.

Samuel pushed his cheek out with his tongue. "So, you think you can do better, do you?" He adjusted his hat so the morning sun didn't hit his eyes so directly. "What are you, five?"

The boy squeezed through the fence and hopped to the ground, still swinging his books. "I *know* I can do better." He dropped his books by a shrub, then rolled his eyes and sauntered past Samuel. "And I'm *six.*"

The boy, who scarcely came past Samuel's waist, took the lead rope, clucked to the filly, and said, "Come here, girl." The horse immediately stepped forward and followed.

"How in the—you didn't just . . ." Samuel reached forward and grabbed the boy's arm. "You *know* this horse, don't you?"

The horse paused as the boy stopped. He raised his eyebrows and rather snootily said, "I've never seen her before in my life. But I know horses. And horses know people." The boy leaned in. "You know, they can *tell* if you're scared of them."

Samuel folded his arms in a huff. "I'm not scared of a baby horse."

"Horses can tell," the boy said. "Look, I'm going to be late for school, and it's my first day. Show me where you want to go, and I'll take her there."

"Late, you say?" Samuel raised one eyebrow. "You were perfectly willing to be late a moment ago if it meant watching me be made a fool of." He waved at the fence where the boy had laughed at him.

"That's 'cause you were so funny," he said with a giggle. "I couldn't *help* but watch." The boy's mouth twitched, and he laughed.

Eager to get the job done—even at the expense of humiliation—Samuel motioned toward the round pen at the end of the block. "Over there. I'll show you."

The boy clucked again, and once more the filly followed without any trouble. Samuel couldn't believe how effortlessly the boy and the filly moved together. When they reached the pen, the boy led her inside, tied her up, and turned to face Samuel. "Well, there ya go, mister. I gotta go now. Have a nice day."

The boy nodded and hurried through the gate of the pen, grabbed his books, then ran down the road. Before he got too far, Samuel called out to him. "Wait. What's your name?"

"I'm Will. Bye, mister!" With that, he dashed off, his books trailing on their belt behind him. He left Samuel feeling less useful and less of a man than he had ever felt before. A six-year-old boy could do his job better than he could.

Could someone explain exactly *why* he was needed in Zion again?

CHAPTER 6

"AND THIS IS WHERE THE magic happens," Brother Christensen said the following evening as he led Tabitha and Will into the printing room. The sun was setting outside, casting orange and gold light across the wooden floor.

The pungent smell of ink wafted about them as they stepped inside, Tabitha breathing it in as she looked around in awe. Stacks of paper lined one wall. Along another, ropes were strung across the room like clotheslines. Large sheets of paper hung, balancing on a fold from the ropes as they dried. Near the window stood a desk for the tedious job of laying out the text in the frames.

Tabitha had never done typesetting before, but she had watched some of the men at the *Utah Journal* do it. They grabbed the reversed letters and punctuation marks nestled in their individual cases without more than a glance, knowing exactly where each letter belonged from reaching above their heads so many times. She remembered the workers consulting her text and then spelling out entire sentences, paragraphs, and articles in mirror image, and she wondered how the men didn't get headaches from it.

She noted the leading—strips of lead used to make extra room for spaces and lines. To one side were the clamps used for tightening all the letters together so that the ink could be applied and the entire frame then placed into the press. She surveyed the grand printing press itself, standing in the middle like a stately old gentleman.

She stepped further into the room and ran her hand against the press's smooth, silver surface, admiring its lines. There in the center is where the frame would go, where she would apply the ink, place a blank sheet, and crank the lever. A newspaper would be made out of what used to be only ideas. The entire process was nothing short of miraculous—an incredible act of creation.

And soon it would all be hers.

Gooseflesh broke out on her arms, and she rubbed them through the deep blue calico of her dress. "It's wonderful," she said, smiling as she turned to Brother Christensen. "Just wonderful."

He pushed his sleeves past his elbows, grinning. "I knew you'd appreciate it."

"What are these?" Will asked, running over to the desk on the far side. He pushed a chair into place and climbed onto it.

"Oh, Will, don't touch anything," Tabitha exclaimed.

"It's all right," Brother Christensen said with a laugh. "I don't usually let children in here, but Will's fine." He joined the boy, who now stood on the desktop. Brother Christensen pointed to the lined-up boxes the boy was looking at. "Those are where we keep the letters that we print with. Can you guess why there are two different sections—an upper case of letters and a lower case?"

"An upper case . . ." Will pushed his lower lip out in thought, then laughed with delight. "I know! The big letters are on the top, and the little letters are on the bottom?"

"Yep." Brother Christensen tousled his hair. "You got a smart boy here, Tabby."

"Yes, I do," Tabitha said with a smile, forcing herself to hold back the request that he not call her a cat. Brother Christensen looked so delighted over Will that he continued teaching him about the letters. He pulled one out of its box. "Can you tell what that one is?" he asked, squinting a bit and holding it up to the fading sunlight. Both of them leaned in close.

Will studied the metal piece and squinched up his nose. "Doesn't look like any letter I've studied in school. Looks like a backwards J."

"That's *exactly* what it is," Brother Christensen said, slapping his thigh with pleasure. "See, when you're printing, all the letters have to be backwards." At Will's confused expression, the newspaperman laughed and said, "Watch."

Will sat down on the desktop as Brother Christensen got a little ink on his finger from a pot on the desk. He rubbed the ink on the letter, then took Will's arm and pressed the metal letter onto his skin. "*Now* what does it look like?"

"Why, now it looks like a regular J," Will said with wonder. "Neat! Let's try that with some more!"

He reached up to the lower case of letters and pulled down hard to help himself stand. Before Tabitha could cry out a protest, the entire case pulled away from the wall. It seemed as if dozens of little boxes and thousands of metals pieces tumbled to the floor and clinked to the ground. Although it couldn't have been half so many, Tabitha cringed at the metallic clatter that seemed never-ending, the letters falling to the desk, then to the floor then finally—and mercifully—stilling.

Will's eyes were wide with horror, and Tabitha knew hers were no less so. She stood with her feet rooted to the floor and her tongue unable to form any words besides, "Oh, Brother—oh no, I—"

What had she been thinking, letting a six-year-old into a printing room?

Brother Christensen's previous happy demeanor fled. His face fell, and Tabitha could only imagine that he was calculating the time involved in sorting through the hundreds of little pieces and getting them back into their proper places, then securing the boxes back onto the wall.

With a sudden rush, Will jumped down from the desk and started scooping up the mess, dumping large handfuls into random boxes.

"I'm sorry! I'll fix it. I'll fix everything," he said, his voice frantic and his face bright red.

"No." Brother Christensen's voice was gruff, cutting off Will's movements. "Stop. Don't touch anything."

Tabitha knew he was trying to be firm, not mean, but his tone clearly frightened Will, who stood up and stumbled backward. His arms flailed, knocking a large tub of ink from the press to the floor. With a cry, he fell on top of the tub, then rolled to the side onto the thick, black goo.

He gasped in horror, and Tabitha struggled between the urge to race over to him and the reality that if she did, she'd destroy her dress, one of only three she owned. Will was reaching for her and crying.

"It's all right, Will. Just stay where you are, and *don't* move another inch!"

She turned to Brother Christensen, trying to keep calm and not let her own emotions get the better of her. "I'll clean everything up. You needn't worry." She did her best to smile, but as she looked at him, her heart pounded in her throat, and she couldn't read his expression.

Brother Christensen didn't say a word. Brow furrowed, he grabbed his hat from the edge of the printing press and clomped out of the room, trailing black boot prints across the floor. Tabitha closed her eyes and held Will's hand across the inky puddle, looking around to figure out how she'd clean up the mess.

Will whimpered, and she held his hand tighter. "It's all right," she said in what she hoped was a soothing voice.

"I'm sorry, Mama," he said, sniffing hard. "I didn't mean to ruin the cases. I didn't know I was that strong."

A strangled sob turned into a laugh in Tabitha's throat as she wiped her nose with the back of her hand. "I always said you were a strong boy, didn't I? I guess neither of us knew just how strong you were." She squeezed his hand again. "Try standing up, but don't step away from the ink or you'll track it all over the floor. And don't you worry, Will. It'll all be just fine."

He did as he was told, trying to balance so he wouldn't slip. Tabitha took a chunk of paper from one stack and spread the sheets over the floor. "Step on this," she ordered. As he obeyed, she steadied his shoulders, trying to avoid letting him touch her otherwise. Then again, she realized, as she cleaned up, she would likely do the dress completely in by morning. The skirt alone would be covered in ink after cleaning up this disaster. How—and where—in the world would she get another dress to replace this one? She only hoped that by sunrise the place still belonged to her.

Please, Brother Christensen, she thought as she gazed at his boot tracks, *don't change your mind.*

"You're doing wonderfully. Just keep still," Tabitha said, putting everything she had inside herself into sounding light-hearted so he wouldn't worry any further.

"Can I move yet?" Will asked, tears streaking down his cheeks as he tried to stay frozen in his movements. Her happy voice hadn't fooled him for a moment.

"Not yet, sweetheart," Tabitha said, heading once again for the wall with the paper. She lugged another stack off the top of one pile and began laying a trail of white sheets across the room, leading from Will to the door. "Just stay there for a few . . . more . . . minutes." She wrestled with one of the large sheets that kept trying to fold over.

With her paper trail complete, Tabitha set the remaining stack aside and rubbed her hands across her forehead, which had started to ache. She returned to Will.

"Careful now," she said, taking one of his hands but holding it far away from herself. "Walk along the paper so we don't soil the floor."

By now Will had stopped crying, but he sniffed and wiped his nose on his sleeve. Holding his mother's hand, he followed Tabitha along the white path and through the office area. She gently got him past the front door, which was white—and which she hoped to keep that way—before she fished inside her pocket for the key. She hadn't ever imagined these circumstances as the ones in which she would use her key for the very first time.

Vandals or theft were extremely unlikely, but when her future hung in the balance, she wasn't about to risk the newspaper being worse off when she returned than when she left it. The lock clicked into place, and she pulled the key out, turning it over in her fingers. How long would she get to keep this key? Had her trip home been for nothing? If Brother Christensen changed his mind and decided not to let her have the paper, what would she and Will do? She wondered if staying in Manti would be best or whether she should try to find a way to support them elsewhere.

She shook her head, realizing she was getting miles ahead of the situation. *I'm overreacting,* she assured herself. She plunged the key into her pocket, then turned to Will. "Let's take you home to get you cleaned up."

She took his hand again, and they headed for home. Tabitha figured that when they arrived, she'd bathe Will as best she could, and then her mother might be able to get him to bed while she returned to clean up the mess.

As they walked, Will kept glancing askance at his mother. Tabitha was too upset at first to acknowledge it, but finally her maternal nudges couldn't be avoided. When he looked over again, she squeezed his hand a couple of times as a comforting gesture. "This wasn't your fault, Will. You know that, right? I don't want you to feel bad about it. Not one mite."

"But it *is* my fault," he said quietly. He sniffed and lowered his head.

Neither said another word until they reached home, where Tabitha finally spoke, telling Will to stay outside while she fetched Grandma. The last thing her parents needed was ink tracks through the house.

Tabitha found her mother dozing in the rocking chair with her Bible open in her lap. At the creak of a floorboard, she opened her eyes and saw her daughter. Her eyes opened wider, and she wiped a look of fatigue from her face as she said, "Back already? How did it go? Goodness, is something wrong?"

Nodding shortly, Tabitha wearily rubbed at one eye. "There was an accident." At her mother's gasp, she hurried on to reassure her, glancing in the direction of Will outside as she did so. "It's nothing serious, but Will's covered in ink, and I need to go back to clean up the rest of it. I was hoping that—"

Before she could finish, her mother stood and marched to the front door. A hand came to her mouth as she chuckled. "Land sakes, Will, is that you? Let's get those filthy clothes off you."

Tabitha went to the door and found Will already shirtless and Mother rushing to the well for water. He smiled at his mother, showing startlingly white teeth against the black smears on his cheeks. "She said I look like an Indian with war paint."

Bless her for making him smile, Tabitha thought as her mother hurried back with a sloshing pail of water, an old dishrag, and a bar of soap—Mother's powerful, take-the-skin-right-off-with-the-dirt home-made lye soap. "Let's see if we can't get you scrubbed up and that war paint off your face," she said as she dipped the rag into the water and then rubbed it against the soap.

Will leaned toward his grandmother and said, "Do I really look like an Indian?"

"You practically look like Chief Walker himself." His grand-mother gave a melodramatic shudder. "You about scared the daylights out of me when I laid eyes on you."

Will giggled as she rubbed at the ink covering the back of his right arm. The sound lightened Tabitha's mood. She walked to her mother and kissed her cheek. "Thank you, Mother."

"You're welcome," she said. "I'm glad I can do something for my grandson after all these years."

"I'd better get back," Tabitha said. "Would you . . ."

"Will and I are just fine," Mother said. "Happy as two peas in a pod. Take care of whatever you need to." She gave a look that Tabitha knew meant she'd be expected to reveal the entire story when she returned.

"Good night, Will," Tabitha said. For the sake of self-preservation, she blew him a kiss in lieu of his regular bedtime hug and kisses.

"G'night, Mama," Will said, his face slightly strained as his grandmother scrubbed his cheek, making his skin rosy pink with the friction.

Tabitha hurried back toward the office, unsure what she'd do to fix the place up. How did one clean ink? Perhaps she could soak up as much as she could and then sand off the rest. The cases of letters could be sorted later, but the ink might destroy the floor if it sat there much longer.

She unlocked the door and hurried inside, where she looked around for supplies. The paper trail had soaked up a lot of ink, especially where they had walked, revealing dark splotches bleeding through the pages. That was probably the best thing to do, she figured—soak up as much ink as possible. She walked along the trail, back and forth, sliding her boots along the way to absorb the excess. She laid even more paper over the puddled area that had the biggest stain. She felt a little silly walking around and hopping here and there for extra pressure.

If someone could see me now, they'd think I'm doing a ridiculous jig, she thought.

The sun had set, and soon the light grew too dim for her to work. She found a kerosene lamp on a table, then searched for a means to light it. In the twilight it was hard to see much of anything—she had let it grow too dim before acting—so she had to search through drawers and under tables. Near the window she found a bag of sawdust. Tilting her head curiously, she hefted it, wondering what use sawdust would be in a printing office. But then her eyes landed on the paper-draped puddle again.

One of her eyebrows rose in sudden realization. The sawdust would soak up ink better and faster than paper, and she wouldn't be using up the stock of paper. Maybe that's why the sawdust was here, for spills like this.

The thought warmed her a bit. Perhaps this wasn't the only time such an accident had occurred. Brother Christensen might not be as angry as she thought. Before pouring out the bag, she looked around a bit more and found some matches that she used to light the lamp. The glow warmed the room, allowing the printing press to cast long shadows across the floor, making the dark spots seem even bigger than they were before.

But the light also revealed a stained patch she hadn't seen yet—one she was quite certain could not have been caused by Will's mishap, as it was on the other side of the press from where he'd fallen. She stepped toward it and bent down, rubbing her hand across the mark. It was dry to the touch and faded. Her lips twisted with a tiny hint of relief. Sawdust in a corner. A stain on the floor. Will *wasn't* the only one to have ever made a mess here.

Feeling hopeful for the first time since the cases crashed to the floor, Tabitha carefully stacked up the ink-covered papers and set them outside the back door. The knot at the top of the sack of sawdust gave her a little trouble, but with a little work from her teeth, it loosened, and she tossed the twine aside. After having worked for over an hour, her back was tired, but she still dragged the sack to the stain, lifted it into her arms, and shook its contents over the ink.

Just as the last bit of sawdust fell to the floor, she heard the squeak of the door hinges. With a surprised cry, she dropped the sack and whipped around. A shadowy figure stood in the doorway and stepped forward, making the floorboards creak.

Tabitha's heart nearly stopped as she waited to see the face in the light. "Brother Christensen! You frightened me," she said, grasping the front of her dress.

"Sorry. Didn't mean to startle you." Brother Christensen looked about the room and nodded with satisfaction. "Glad you found the sawdust," he said. "Works in a jiffy."

"That's what it's for, then?" Tabitha's heart was beating now. Brother Christensen didn't look angry, and that alone made her feel like she could breathe again.

"That's exactly what it's for," he said. "We don't have many spills, of course, but it does happen from time to time." He tilted his head in thought. "Granted, I don't think we've ever had one from a six-year-old boy, and we've never lost an entire case of letters before . . ."

"I'm so sorry," Tabitha began, but he just shrugged.

"This too shall pass, as they say. To be honest, I'm glad it's your young back dealing with the mess instead of mine doing it with my rheumatism acting up." He lifted his arms to show what he was carrying—a tool caddy in one hand and a basket with a cloth napkin covering its contents in the other. "Fetched my tools so I could fix the cases. The missus thought you could use some pie. I think she put a bottle of milk in there, too," he said, offering the basket to Tabitha.

"Thank you so much," she said, taking it and lifting the corner of the napkin. The smell of warm peach pie wafted over her, and her mouth began watering. "You don't have to sort the letters. I'll take care of that."

Brother Christensen chuckled. "To be honest, I wasn't planning on sorting them. My eyes aren't what they used to be, either. And it's your place now, right?"

"Right," Tabitha said gratefully. *It's still mine.*

"Is your son all right?" he asked as he crossed the room to the type cases. "I'm afraid I'm not used to speaking with children. I'm a businessman, first and foremost. I was worried about losing type pieces and tracking ink all over and such. Didn't mean to upset him."

Upset *him?* Tabitha was just relieved that the newspaperman wasn't livid.

"Will's fine. My mother is cleaning him up." She paused, looking at the basket as she tried to sum up her thoughts. "When you left, I thought that . . . You're *not* upset, then? You haven't changed your mind about my taking over the paper?"

He didn't answer right away. Instead, he looked about the room then shrugged with one shoulder. "Of course she's still yours. The whole thing did jolt me a bit, I must admit. It's hard to think of turning over your baby to someone else, hoping they'll care for it like you did, and suddenly seeing her get marred first thing out of the gate."

Tabitha's stomach twisted, but she said nothing. He raised a hand. "But don't you worry. I know it was an accident, and no worse, to be honest, than some of the things I've done in here myself over the years. Course, I don't recall ever having two major disasters within a minute of each other." One side of his mouth crooked up into a half-smile. "But I just needed a moment to cool off a bit and accept that it's not my job to worry about this place any longer. That's your job now."

Relief washed over Tabitha like a warm rain, but she couldn't quite let herself believe. "It's not mine yet, not really. We haven't signed the papers, after all, and if you're not sure . . ."

"It's a done deal, Miss Chadwick," he said with a pat on her shoulder. He headed for the injured cases. "And don't you dare try weaseling out of it."

CHAPTER 7

It was mid-June when Betty Hunsaker Tidwell answered the knock on the door, not knowing who would be on the other side but certainly not expecting Jeremiah Hancock.

"Well, hello," she said. "I didn't expect to see you today."

"I don't suppose you did," the old man said, holding a beat-up hat between his hands. He scratched his chin, which was covered in unkempt whiskers of gray and brown. "May I come in, then?"

After glancing up and down the street briefly, Betty gave a curt nod. "I suppose, but just for a few minutes. I don't want the neighbors talking."

Jeremiah took a step over the threshold but paused at that. "Still ashamed of your old man, are ya?"

"Please come inside," she said, begging. Her mother had died a few years back, leaving just her and Jeremiah as the only living people who knew her real parentage. She hoped to keep it that way.

Jeremiah came in and followed her into the kitchen. She knew he'd take it as an insult; welcome guests would be brought to the parlor. But she couldn't risk his muddy boots staining her rugs or furniture—not only destroying her belongings, but also announcing to the world that she had hosted the man in her house. Though technically a Latter-day Saint, he hadn't darkened the doors of a chapel since she was born. He was an old bachelor who lived alone in a ramshackle cabin and was known for yelling at people for looking at him wrong.

Having people know he was visiting her wouldn't . . . *look* right.

She gestured to the kitchen table, where he pulled up a chair. It creaked as he sat. She hadn't been this close to him for some time and suddenly wondered at his wiry frame. He didn't have a housekeeper to look after him. It was a wonder he hadn't starved himself to death. She sat opposite him and picked up her stitching.

"To what can I attribute your visit?" She pretended to sew but couldn't concentrate.

"I know something about you," Jeremiah said without preamble. "And I don't like it one bit."

Betty lowered the skirt she was mending and tilted her head. "Oh, really? Pray tell, what is it you know that has anything to do with me? Been listening to idle gossip, perhaps?"

"This ain't no idle gossip," Jeremiah said. He leaned forward on the table.

Betty instinctively pulled back. He looked as if he *knew* something. "Oh?"

"I saw something at Daggett's place a week ago."

"*Whose* place?" Betty looked up innocently, although she knew full well who Daggett was and where he lived. Jeremiah couldn't have found out . . . could he have?

"Don't play with me, girl," Jeremiah said, pounding the table. "It's not right what you done, and you know it."

Betty felt her cheeks warm. She swallowed, trying to ignore him as she made another stitch in the leafy design. "I don't have any idea what you mean."

"The constable will catch up to you eventually." Jeremiah paused as if waiting for her to respond. When she didn't, he leaned back, making the chair squeak. "You're one stubborn woman, you know that? I suppose you got that from me. But I also suspect you got yerself a bit of a conscience from me. Break the law, and you're gonna feel that twisty thing in your gut that's called guilt."

Her hands seemed to be paralyzed; she clenched the skirt, unable to make another stitch. He *did* know. And as much as she hated to admit it, he was right. Her insides had been riddled by guilt. She closed her eyes and took a deep breath.

"How did you find out?" she asked quietly. She stared at her handiwork as she waited for an answer, unable to look into his eyes. *No one* knew. So far not even Daggett himself seemed aware.

"I saw you," Jeremiah said.

Betty looked up in alarm.

"That's right," Jeremiah went on. "I was coming back from setting my traps in the foothills when you left his place with a sack under one arm. Middle of the night, no one at the door to send you away. You dropped the bag."

She swallowed hard. When the bag had slipped out of her grip, coins rattled and paper bills fluttered to the ground. If Jeremiah had been within fifty yards of her, he could have figured out easily enough that it was money she was shoving back into the sack. It had been late at night, and she'd thought that not a soul had seen her go in or out of the house. Apparently she'd been wrong.

"We're near broke," she finally said. "Yet Arthur is bound and determined to go through with that fool freighting business with Daggett, who has plenty of money of his own."

"It's business, Betty. You can't blame Daggett for your family's misfortunes."

"But Daggett doesn't need Arthur as a business partner. He doesn't need our money—he just wants to use our animals and wagons. But then he expects us to cough up money to boot." She smacked her mending onto the table and stood up in a huff. "When the business fails, what do we do? *Starve?*" My poor girls are wearing rags for dresses as it is."

"So Arthur doesn't know what you did?"

"No." She sat back down and picked up her mending, now ripping out a seam with feverish intensity.

"We can keep it that way, ya know," Jeremiah said after a pause. "I won't tell your husband. But ya gotta bring the money back. Ya just gotta."

Fear, guilt, and a wagonload of other emotions felt heaped upon her head. She wished fervently—too late—that she hadn't succumbed to the temptation and panic that drove her to sneak into the Daggett home and take the money from the hiding place she had overheard him reveal to her husband. She had crossed that final threshold days ago.

"I can't bring it back. They could throw me in jail if they knew what I did. What about my children?" For the first time, Betty looked into his eyes—really looked into them. What she saw surprised her. Compassion. It was deep down, but it was there. She thought she even saw a flicker of love for his only daughter.

"Does Daggett know he's missing the money?" Jeremiah asked.

Betty shook her head. "He and Arthur met this morning about their plans. Didn't say anything about it."

"Good. Then you gotta return it before he notices it's missing," Jeremiah said. "At some point, word will get out that your family's doing better, but with no reason. Arthur *will* figure out what's happening. If you let this go, you're far more likely to end up in jail than if you return the money."

Betty knew he was right and that even if she weren't ever caught, she'd feel horribly guilty until she returned the money. She had taken it in a fit of jealousy and anger that had since passed.

Jeremiah put a leathery hand on her shoulder. It was surprisingly comforting. "Would you be willing to give back the money if it weren't ever tracked to you? If no one ever knew you were the one who took it—or that it was even taken?" The harsh lines of Jeremiah's face softened as he spoke.

Tears sprang to Betty's eyes, and she nodded. "Oh, I would. It's been burning a hole into my dresser drawer ever since I took it. I haven't been able to spend a single penny."

"I'll return it for you."

"I don't understand," Betty said with a shake of her head. "If you return it, won't Daggett think *you* stole it?"

"Not if I go in at night like you did and leave it. No one need ever be the wiser. When Daggett finds the sack, he can think it was simply misplaced rather than stolen. Then *you'll* be able to sleep again, and *I'll* stop worrying that my own flesh and blood will end up behind bars."

Tears streaking down her cheeks, she opened her mouth in wonder. "You'd do that for me?"

Jeremiah cleared his throat and looked away. His eyes appeared glassy. "Yeah. I'd do it for my daughter. And I will."

CHAPTER 8

THE THIRD SUNDAY OF JUNE, Tabitha walked alone to the cemetery and stood before Fred's perfectly manicured headstone. She'd been in town too long without having paid her respects—nearly a month—and tomorrow she'd be publishing her third issue of the paper. Settling in and learning about running the business had kept her busy, but in a way, she'd also been avoiding this moment.

The stone stood several feet off the ground and over a foot thick, like a column rising from the ground. One of the flat sides bore a lengthy inscription that his mother had paid for to honor her only son. Why did Tabitha feel guilty about the fact that Fred had no brothers?

Because it made his death an even bigger blow.

She looked to both sides, avoiding what she had gone there to do, and noted how much the cemetery had changed since she was last there. The changes surprised her—the trees were taller, a section to the southwest had far more stones in it than she remembered, and a new shed had been built to house the groundskeeping tools.

A moment ago as she had walked to Fred's grave, she found several gravestones from the previous year, all with dates within days of one another—two in one family. Many of them from that spring listed diphtheria as the cause of death. Tabitha's parents hadn't mentioned a diphtheria outbreak, and she hadn't recognized any of the names on the headstones, but the idea of such a tragedy saddened her and made her feel even more disconnected from the city she had once called home.

She glanced about, afraid someone might be watching her, gauging her response, knowing that she had come more out of duty and other people's expectations than anything else. Fred wasn't there. And neither was the girl who had married him. The road leading into town ran right past the cemetery; anyone going or coming could see her clearly as they drove past. But for now, there were no sounds of buggy wheels rolling over stone and dirt, no hint of clopping horse hooves. Since today was the Sabbath, even the regular clinking and pounding of the stonecutter's tools from Temple Hill were silent.

I'm alone, she thought, and with a relieved breath she looked back at the words etched into the ivory stone of the monument.

Sacred to the memory of Frederick Clarence Hall
Son of Quincy and Wilhelmina Hall
Born February 23, 1848
Died August 17, 1877
To live in hearts we leave behind is not to die.

Tabitha looked down at the spray of wildflowers she had brought with her, a feeling of shame flushing her cheeks. They had lived as husband and wife so briefly, when she was so young. So much had happened since as she had matured into the woman she was now.

To live in hearts we leave behind is not to die.

After all the intervening years, Fred no longer lived in her heart like he once had. Did that mean he was more dead now than in the summer of 1877?

She opened her mouth and whispered, "Fred, how is a young widow supposed to feel after seven years?" She had no idea, but however it was, it certainly wasn't this—such emptiness. She clenched and unclenched her hands around the bouquet of wildflowers she had brought. It was a small token of the man he'd been, of how she'd known him, even a little. The small bouquet held some of the same flowers her bridal bouquet had. She bent her knees and placed the flowers against the grave. They seemed pathetically tiny as she traced her gaze up to the top of the huge stone, which seemed to tower above her from that vantage point.

Why was it that when she had first come into town and seen Temple Hill, it had made her so emotional, yet his grave brought up . . . nothing?

Perhaps it was because the hill represented so much more than his grave did. The hill held happy memories from her childhood and their courtship. It still held happy memories and hope of what the future might bring, while his grave held nothing but the end of something that hadn't even begun to start. It didn't even mark the place where he died, the place they had spent their few happy weeks.

"There you go," she said, standing and smoothing some dirt from her apron—acutely aware of the rising temple behind her, as if it were watching her instead of some townsperson. "They aren't much, but I remember how much you loved wildflowers."

Should she stay longer? Should she say something more?

Two months. That's all she had him for. It was a happy time, surely, but somehow when she thought of their marriage, the happy days were usually overshadowed by the day of the explosion. Thinking about that summer always brought two images before her mind's eye.

The first was telling Fred that she was expecting their child.

The second was the moment he was pulled out of the mine on a stretcher. The stars in her eyes had extinguished awfully fast.

Now as she gazed at Fred's gravestone, she sighed. It wasn't as if she regretted anything. It's just that she felt as if she hardly remembered her late husband anymore. She had been a blushing, innocent bride when they married, and he had been a grown man for a long time, a man with experience and maturity that she lacked. In hindsight, she realized that her love for Fred still had been that of the young girl, a girl who'd been infatuated with him ever since she had first picked up Betty's pearl stone.

Now that girl was gone.

So was the young one who had fallen apart at the seams when her husband was pulled from the mine covered in blood and soot, almost unrecognizable except for his wedding ring and one of his boots. The other had been blown off with a leg.

She had gone home to Manti after that in a daze, unwilling to speak to anyone or do anything, lying in bed for days at a time. Dreading the time that her baby would be born. How would she care for the babe? She couldn't, not alone, not like this. But somehow, when her belly started to swell, when Will's growing body kicked and prodded from within her, something changed. She knew her child needed a mother.

She shut off a part of her mind and heart, refusing to think of herself as a widow any longer—such thoughts only brought heartache. Instead, she was a mother. Not a wife. Not a widow. A mother. She hadn't allowed herself the luxury of self-pity—or rest, for that matter—since.

If it weren't for Will, I might still be lying in that bed, she thought.

Since then she had faced so much. She had grown up and become a woman almost overnight. She'd given birth, learned to take care of herself and her son. She'd pursued an education and raised Will for six years without anyone's help. And most significantly, she'd turned her back on her home so that she wouldn't have to be reminded of all the painful memories it contained.

And she had vowed to never, ever again fall apart like she had after Fred died. She had to be strong. Will needed her to be.

Standing here at the grave felt strange, as if she didn't belong—as if Fred's real wife were someplace else, and that by coming here, she was committing some kind of sacrilege.

Shouldn't I be weeping over his grave? she thought, wrapping her arms about her body. But how could she weep, when those newlyweds no longer existed? Their marriage could be counted in days. Ever since she had gotten out of bed for the sake of her baby, she had labored to build a full life for herself and their son—a life that, by circumstance, was completely devoid of Fred.

She strained to find tears, but they wouldn't come. Again she looked over her shoulder to peer at the road. Still seeing no wagons or horses, she hoped there wasn't anyone who might note the fact that she *wasn't* crying.

"Good-bye, Fred. Perhaps I'll bring Will next time." She kissed her fingers and blew on them. It was the most she had to offer. She sighed, then turned left and walked away, heading toward the pine trees.

It wasn't until she had walked several yards that the tears built up. She felt ashamed that they weren't for Fred. They were for the young woman who had died when he had, for the woman she had forced herself to become—strong and immovable, with a spine made of steel.

She raised the back of her hand to her nose, then gasped at seeing a man staring at her. He stood behind a pine tree and clearly did not look at all surprised for her to have stumbled upon him unawares. She stood stock still. Who was he? Had he seen her at the grave? She didn't recognize him. He gazed at her with something akin to recognition. Maybe it was just her tears that he understood. Surely he had come to pay his respects to a lost loved one and assumed her own loss was the cause of her tears.

"Afternoon, Miss," he said with an English accent as he touched his hat with the tip of a finger.

"Afternoon," she replied with the slightest curtsey as he passed her. She couldn't help but watch him retreat down the wide path between two sections of headstones. He glanced over his shoulder, and when he caught her staring, he nodded again and raised a hand in a wave. She turned about quickly, embarrassed to be caught staring and wishing the grass would open up and devour her.

He was watching me, she thought. *I know it.*

For some reason, the thought wasn't completely disturbing. She itched to hide behind the same pine and watch to see where he went, to observe another person pay their respects and not cry in the process. It might make her feel a little less like a bad person. She smoothed her hair and turned away but couldn't resist a final glance in the direction of the cemetery.

He was gazing in her direction. She felt a swooping sensation in her middle. Clearing her throat, she picked up her skirts and hurried to the main road *without* looking back.

* * *

Samuel watched the woman retreat. Who was she, he wondered, and was her sorrow as great as his? He hadn't meant to intrude on another person's private moment, but there was something about her that made him pause and wait behind a pine tree. She was young—likely only a few years his junior—her brown hair smoothed back into a bun. She had placed a small bouquet of flowers onto a grave—uneasily, he thought.

Now that he stood in the cemetery, he wasn't entirely sure why he was here. A strange peace came about him, like a wisp of air. He might never have the luxury of a headstone to stand before and grieve, but perhaps here he could find a slice of the solace he was looking for—here, where so many others' loved ones lay in the ground. Perhaps as he communed with past souls, he would find a bit of healing in some small way.

Samuel walked along the gravel-strewn path that led into the cemetery. Headstones stood on both sides of the path, some large monuments with elaborate engravings, some very small stones with nothing more than initials carved into them. Many were hewn from the same rock as the temple, like the tall one the woman had stood beside. As he walked among the stones, he couldn't help but wonder about the past lives of those resting beneath them. What were their stories? How did they pass on?

Who did they leave behind?

He paused before the stone the woman had been at, noting the bunch of flowers at the base. He read the inscription. The man buried here was described only as a son. Perhaps the woman was his sister.

I wish Helen had a final resting place, he thought. Part of the pain over her death was her burial at sea. She had no final resting place where she would be at peace. Ocean currents would do what they would with her body, tossing her to and fro. Who knew but what sea creatures might find an interest in her . . .

He shuddered and turned away, intending to go back to Mrs. Mirkins's home. After a few steps, he paused, his attention caught by the rising temple walls directly in front of him, the white stone surrounded by scaffolding like a cage.

I wonder if the temple feels trapped inside that. Does it know that someday it will be free of the shackles and stand beautiful, in all its glory? The thought flashed across his mind; he almost laughed at himself for such a silly thought. As if a building had feelings.

Even so, the thought had planted a seed of hope into his heart. Perhaps his feeling of being caged, of wearing shackles, would also be temporary. And not only temporary, but a necessary step toward his own freedom and ability to stand tall.

CHAPTER 9

"I THOUGHT YOU SAID WE didn't have much money," Will said, holding his mother's hand. They walked out of the tithing office in the Little Fort after Tabitha had picked him up from his last day of school.

"We don't have much money," she said. *Especially not after using so much of it to buy the paper.*

"Then why are we giving some of it away?"

"Paying tithing isn't giving away what's ours," Tabitha explained. "It's about returning part of what already belongs to the Lord."

She had just handed over her first offering since arriving in Manti. It wasn't much, but she wanted as many blessings as the Lord could possibly spare. Paying tithing, she hoped, would be a way to nudge those blessings closer. The sooner that happened, the sooner she and Will could be on their own, and—she prayed—the sooner she'd break free from the constant memories of the past that seemed to cling to her like gossamer cobwebs.

The bishop seemed pleasantly surprised that she paid in coin as well as with some product; money wasn't all that common, apparently, so most of the buying and selling going on consisted of bartering, with people paying in goods and services.

"We're always grateful to get money," Bishop Sherman had said as he recorded the amount in a ledger book. "President Young said the temple will be built solely with donations, and it's a bit tough to get everything we need when you're trying to exchange pigs for lumber and nails."

"I hope I can continue to pay in money, then," Tabitha said.

She already wondered how likely that would be. She had received several subscriptions and advertisements over the last week, and more than half were paid in kind. A woman could only use so many eggs or apples before they went bad, and while her mother appreciated the wheat, chickens, and other items Tabitha had been paid with, none of it was anything that would help Tabitha and Will create a future for themselves. Most of the inheritance money was gone now, but she had used some of the remainder to pay her tithing. She wondered how soon Manti would have its own bank. The residents didn't seem particularly concerned with having one, so she guessed it wouldn't be for some time.

Now as they walked out of the tall, stone walls of the fort onto Main Street, Will's forehead crinkled. "But if the tithing belongs to God anyway, why did He give it to us in the first place? Why not keep it and give us the rest?"

Tabitha patted his hand. "In reality, Will, everything we have belongs to the Lord. He's only asking for a little in return—He wants us to willingly offer a tenth to show our gratitude. It's a show of our faith that He'll continue to care for us. Does that make sense?"

Will seemed to be thinking hard about the idea. "I suppose," he said slowly.

A rumbling, booming sound shook the air, and Tabitha came to a stop. She unwittingly squeezed Will's hand until it had passed. The stone blasting for the temple sounded just a bit too familiar. At least these explosions were quieter. Maybe she'd get used to them. She shook her head and kept walking.

"Where were we?" she asked, putting on a wide smile. "Oh, yes. Tithing. You see, the interesting thing is that the moment you give something back, the Lord blesses you, so even if you try to repay him, you're always in His de—" She stopped suddenly when she heard another sound, this one like a pained animal.

Will twisted his head from side to side. "Where did that come from?" he asked with an anxious expression in his eyes as if he thought some runaway carriage might be barreling down the road.

"I don't know," Tabitha said, turning in a circle, "but it sounded like a horse, if I'm not mistaken."

The pained whinny returned—this time clearly a horse—and Tabitha found the direction it was coming from, several hundred feet to her right. Across a field to the west, the horse reared, pulling its head back against a restraining rope, then kicking its front feet sharply.

Unsure what she was seeing, Tabitha walked to the fence at the edge of the road.

"What is it, Mama?" Will asked.

"It *is* a horse, and if I'm not mistaken, it's hurt." She stepped onto the bottom rung of the fence in hopes of seeing better and shaded her eyes against the afternoon sun. A man appeared to be walking toward the horse.

"Oh, good," Tabitha said, relieved. "I think the owner is coming to help."

She gripped the fence as she stepped back down, only to hear the snap of a whip and the horse letting out a high-pitched whinny. She quickly stepped back onto the fence piece. The man appeared to be showering curses at the horse. Had Tabitha not been so horrified at how he kept whipping the animal—pausing here and there to throw what were probably rocks—she would have hurriedly covered Will's eyes. As it was, she stood there, immobile from the shock.

The man *wasn't* beating his horse. He couldn't be. *Could* he?

Another crack of the whip—and a terrified squeal from the pen on the other side of the field—sent Tabitha's blood boiling. Without thinking through what she was about to do, she gritted her teeth and climbed over the fence.

"Mama?" Will asked.

His voice brought her back to the present—barely. "Will, you stay here. Don't move. I'll be right back."

I think.

More curses and screams from the man cut through the air. Tabitha felt like growling as she clenched her fists and strode across the grassy field to the pen. As she drew nearer, she noticed the animal's condition. What should have been a body with strong muscles and a sleek chestnut coat instead looked matted and dirty.

As she reached the corral, she saw more. Its ribcage protruded from its sides as if the animal weren't getting enough food. Its hooves were overgrown and unkempt. She wouldn't be surprised if the hooves were split. Sores marked several areas, whether from whip burns or other mistreatment, she had no idea. Tabitha pursed her lips. How far did the owner's cruelty extend? The anger bubbling inside her rose to a boil. She fisted her hands and marched faster.

He didn't see or hear her even when Tabitha found herself climbing inside the enclosure. She marched over to him and grasped the end of the whip as he extended his arm backward. Before he managed to snap it forward, she yanked hard.

On reflex, the man pulled hard on the whip's handle, which sent the leather slicing through Tabitha's palm. She sucked air between her teeth just as he turned around and demanded, "Who are you, and what in the name of Betsy are you doin' on my land?" He was clearly unconcerned with her injury.

Tabitha cradled her bleeding hand and glared at the middle-aged man. His beard looked scraggly, as if he didn't intend to wear a beard but shaved only when it occurred to him. His clothes were so filthy she wasn't sure of the original color of his shirt, and his oily, gray hair hung in strands to his shoulders. But his hard eyes and the sharp edge to his voice made a cold stone settle in Tabitha's middle.

"I—I—please don't hurt your horse," she stammered, trying to ignore her stinging palm.

"I asked who are you, and what do you think you're doing on my land?"

"Please don't hurt him."

"It's a *her,*" the man snarled. "And I'm trying to break her proper like. So skedaddle already before *you* get hurt."

He turned away, clearly expecting Tabitha to obey and scurry off like a scared jackrabbit, but she stood her ground. She didn't know a whole bunch about breaking horses—let alone wild ones—but she had experienced enough while training Chester with Brother Merrill to understand that what she had witnessed wasn't right.

"I've never used a whip when breaking a horse," she said, shocked at her own boldness.

He turned on her. "Yeah, and how many have ya broken?"

Tabitha swallowed. "I've had some experience," she began, but he plowed over her.

"Hah. I doubt you've had one that's gone wild at three years old." He spat on the ground.

"N-no . . ." She had only been involved in breaking Chester as a young foal. And she had only *helped* at that, doing just what Brother Merrill instructed each step of the way. But she wasn't about to reveal that information to this atrocious man. "She's . . . wild?"

"Might as well be. The mother was bred by a local farmer. His wife spent months dying when it was born, so by the time he got around to training, it broke out of its pen and escaped. Couldn't catch it. The last owner is the one who finally caught it, but even he couldn't break it."

"Her," Tabitha corrected. Once she knew the gender of a horse, the animal ceased being an *it*.

He glared at her. "Until you've broken a wild one, leave me in peace. Go do some embroidery or whatever it is you women do to stay out from under foot." He waved a hand dismissively as he turned back to his horse.

Tabitha lifted her chin without moving her feet so much as an inch. "A good horseman never needs to hurt the animal, Mister . . ." The words hung in the air as she waited for him to answer.

With exasperation, he finally turned and groaned. "Didn't I tell you to git?" When he glared at her, she merely raised an eyebrow in challenge. He grunted. "It's Hancock, all right? Jeremiah Hancock. And do tell me the name of the *woman* meddling in my affairs." Judging by the way he said *woman,* he held females in about as high esteem as he did horses.

"I'm Tabitha," she said with a dip of her head, trying to decide whether to call herself "Hall" or "Chadwick." He wouldn't recognize her married name, and perhaps that would keep her safe from future ire. But everyone at church the other day had called her Sister Chadwick. In a strange way, she felt as if using her married name would be dishonest, as if she'd be hiding behind it. Hancock stared at her, and she tried not to notice—or flinch at—the bleeding welts on the horse's flank as the beautiful animal cowered on the opposite side of the corral.

"Just *Tabitha?*" He raised an eyebrow at her not mentioning a family name, then wiped a sleeve across his forehead and went on. "So are ya goin' to leave or what? I've got work to do with this here beast."

"I'm not leaving unless you promise to stop hurting her." Tabitha folded her arms tightly against her bluff. She couldn't very well stand there for hours, not with Will waiting for her across the field. But she also couldn't walk away, knowing that this man would continue whipping the horse. Considering the conditions the animal had been living in, such a victory would be a small one. Another tactic occurred to her. "What is it you're trying to do with her anyway? Any fool can see that you can't coax a horse by whipping it."

Jeremiah Hancock colored, scowling at her. "I won't be working out here any longer today—won't have a *woman* giving me grief over my methods." Without a backward glance, he threw the whip on the ground and stalked away.

She watched until he had gone inside the house and slammed the door, which made her jump. Then she let out a shaky breath, only now realizing how tense she had been during the encounter. The horse still stood on the other side of the pen, her ears flat against her head, hooves prancing nervously.

"It's all right, girl," Tabitha said in a soothing tone across the distance between them. "He won't bother you anymore . . . today."

"Mama?" Will's thin voice carried through the air, tugging Tabitha toward him.

"I have to go now," she told the horse—wishing the mare could understand her words and intentions. "I'll try to come back soon," she added, knowing that she meant it. She'd be back in spite of Mr. Hancock. She climbed back over the corral fencing and took several steps toward the field, then turned around again.

She simply could not imagine the horse staying there forever—or living long if she did. The thought made her ill. "Something must be done about that man," she said under her breath, holding her skirts up as she navigated the field. "That horse *cannot* stay with such an infernal master."

* * *

By midweek, the heavy gloom that had settled over Samuel the previous Sabbath had lifted somewhat. As he cleaned the chicken coop, fed the pigs, and otherwise dealt with all the things he hated about his new life, the burden didn't feel quite so heavy on his shoulders. At first he couldn't quite peg what had caused the shift.

Going to the cemetery helped, he thought as he dumped a bucket of slop into the pig trough. The fact that he hadn't spent much time there—or that most of the time was spent watching a woman at a grave and then wondering who she was—wasn't something he analyzed, or wanted to. *She looked a bit like Helen,* he told himself. *That's why seeing her made me feel better.* He still wondered who she was, since the marker didn't list a wife or children.

"Barnett," came a voice behind him.

Samuel set the bucket down and wiped some slop off a hand, then turned to Brother Carlisle. "Yes, sir?"

The stable manager held out a paper. "I've got an advertisement here—we need another stable hand. I'd like you to take it to the *Sanpitch Sentinel* office so they'll put it in the next issue." When Samuel took the sheet, Brother Carlisle fished inside his shirt pocket and produced two bits. "This should be enough to cover it. If you need more, let me know."

"I'd be happy to," Samuel said, which was an understatement.

Finally a job I can enjoy, Samuel thought as Brother Carlisle went to talk with Stephen about the feed. Samuel adjusted his hat and headed out of the barn. He walked past the tithing office and through the camping area where travelers could stay without charge, paying only for food and animal feed. Today there weren't many people there, only a man in a tent and two or three wagons.

At the Little Fort opening, he turned south onto Main, making a point to walk leisurely and enjoy the sun. The errand wouldn't take long, but for a few minutes at least he would be free from the stifling, nauseating smells of the animals. Even fifteen minutes of fresh air in his lungs would be a welcome respite.

As he walked along, Samuel decided to not completely disgust the newspaper editor by tracking manure into his office. He went to the side of the road, where he wiped his boots on some tall grass. A few particularly nasty clumps of straw and muck wouldn't come off, so he scraped the boot soles on a fence post and made a face. *Better.* Feeling at least somewhat presentable, Samuel brushed straw from his pants and shirt, removed his hat, and blew bits of straw and dirt off it.

It's everywhere, he thought miserably.

Putting his hat back on, he looked up. In a field to the right, a man held a rope attached to a horse. The horse bucked and whinnied, its ears flat against her head as it pulled against the restraint.

"Stupid horse!" the man yelled. At this distance, Samuel couldn't make out the man's face, just that he held the other end of the rope, but the owner yelled loudly enough that his voice carried across the field that separated them. The man raised his arm and suddenly brought it down, hard. A crack split the air, and the horse reared, tugging hard at its rope. With hooves in the air, it kicked, and when it just missed the man's head, he snapped the whip again. The horse fell to the ground, whinnying in pain.

Samuel stood there, stunned, realizing that the man had just whipped the horse. With nauseated curiosity, Samuel kept watching, unable to tear his eyes away. The man kept yelling at the horse, pulling at the rope and whipping the animal every time it didn't do what the owner demanded.

I don't know the first thing about animals, Samuel reminded himself, trying to control his feelings of disgust. The horse seemed terrified and in agony. It didn't appear to understand what the man wanted.

But what do I know? Perhaps this is how all horses are broken.

Samuel stood there for several minutes, trying to convince himself that what he saw wasn't torture, but he couldn't manage it—especially each time the whip cracked and the horse bellowed with pain.

Before Samuel knew what he was doing, he had vaulted over the fence and was striding across the field toward the man. At the edge of the corral, Samuel opened his mouth but was unsure what words he'd say.

"What—what are you doing?" he said. It was all he could think of.

The man wiped his forehead with a sleeve and grunted. "Breakin' this horse—what did ya think? But it's too stupid to learn; probably too old." He waved a hand to indicate the animal and tied the end of his rope on a fence post. He dropped the whip—several inches of which were tinged red—and climbed out of the corral. The horse, suddenly free from its owner's attentions, drew as far away as it could on the rope and, trembling, kept an eye on the men. It pawed the ground nervously.

The man reached Samuel's side and held out a hand. "I'm Jeremiah Hancock."

Samuel tore his eyes from the horse and shook the man's hand. "Barnett," he said warily.

"Good to meet you." Jeremiah nodded toward the horse. "That thing's too wild. I may have to give up on it. Not worth the trouble, if you ask me. I got her cheap from another farmer who couldn't break her either. Should've known better."

Samuel stood there speechless, wishing he knew enough to argue with the man about being cruel to a living thing, but his inexperience with animals kept him from voicing his concern.

"Sure is a pretty horse." In reality, the animal might have looked pretty if it were fed properly and if its hair weren't all dirty and matted. But Samuel didn't know what else to say.

"She's a good horse," Jeremiah agreed, tilting his hat back with a knuckle and admiring what could be seen of the chestnut-red coat. "That's one reason I bought her. I could see potential in her. Thought she'd make a good mare for breeding. But she's so wild, it's a wonder I got the rope tied to her today. Most of the time, she's liable to run off or trample you before she lets you get near her."

How would a person tame a wild horse? Samuel wondered. Was brute force the only way to bring it into submission?

"So if you're giving up, what are you planning to do with it?" Samuel asked, trying to sound casual. What did men do with undesirable animals? Abandon them? Kill them?

To Samuel's relief, Jeremiah said, "I was hoping to get someone else to buy her. That way at least I'm not losing any more taking care of her. I'd be happy if someone would pay what I did for her. Wouldn't mind selling for cheap, neither—never mind how much I've spent on feed so far. I just want to get rid of the beast. Let someone else deal with the wretched thing. You understand, I'm sure."

Samuel nodded vaguely at the comment—this man was one more in a chain who assumed he was a farmer, born and bred. In spite of hating his job at the stable—and the animals he was caring for—he wished he somehow had the money and the know-how to care for this one.

Pity, he decided. *That's all this feeling is. Pity for a hurt animal. I'll never love horses.* Regardless, he lacked the funds to do anything about the horse anyway. An idea struck him. Perhaps . . .

"It so happens that I'm heading to the newspaper office right now," Samuel said, acting on the idea that had jumped to mind.

Urgency burned in his belly; he couldn't stand to think of this poor horse being in the company of Jeremiah Hancock a day longer than necessary. "If you like, I can bring an advertisement for the horse's sale with me."

Jeremiah tilted his head curiously, as if he wasn't sure why a perfect stranger would offer to help. "That's mighty kind of ya," he said. "I don't suppose *you'd* be interested in her, eh? Nah, not after seeing how wild she is, right?" He laughed ruefully.

"If I had the means, I'd love to," Samuel said, surprising himself not only at how eager he sounded but at how sincerely he meant the words. "But since I can't, I can at least help you get the notice into the paper."

Jeremiah pushed out his lower lip in thought. "Yeah. Might as well. She's hopeless. If you don't mind sitting here a spell, I'll go write up a notice. Be right back." He left for the house—a small, ramshackle outfit with missing shingles and the general air of a place ready to collapse on itself.

Samuel waited restlessly, knowing that Brother Carlisle would be looking for him soon, but also knowing he couldn't just leave this horse without the possibility of freeing her from her master. Would his employer be willing to take the horse? Samuel suddenly wondered if he should hurry back to the stable yard and ask Brother Carlisle about it—then decided against it. To have another horse there, someone would have to foot the cost. Brother Carlisle couldn't do that, and Samuel doubted whether Church leaders would look too kindly on taking in stray animals into their stables, either. Start with a horse, and where would you draw the line?

A bit timidly, he walked around the corral, closer to the animal, and held out his hand. "Hey, horse," he said in a soothing voice. It shied away, eyes wild and ears folded back. Samuel dropped his arm against the fence and sighed. Who was he trying to fool? He didn't know a lick about animals.

Jeremiah returned, clutching a piece of paper. He read through his own script, brows furrowed, then nodded. "That should do it," he said, handing it to Samuel. "And here's a few coins to cover the cost. Let me know if it comes to more than that."

"I will," Samuel said. "And thank you."

"Why are *you* thanking *me?*" Jeremiah asked, shooting Samuel an odd look. "You're the one doing me the favor."

"Right." Samuel smiled grimly. "Well, you're welcome then. I'll see you around." He nodded and turned away, feeling increasingly uneasy about Jeremiah—and sensing that the man was staring at his back as he retreated.

When he reached the fence by the road, Samuel climbed over it and turned. Jeremiah was still watching, so Samuel raised a hand in a wave before heading down the road, trying to hide a scowl at the thought of everything he had witnessed.

Upon reaching the newspaper office, he paused outside to wipe his boots again, which had been soiled after being near Hancock's corral. He went to the door of the small, yellow building surrounded by thin, white trees with leaves that shimmered in the breeze. He had heard that they were common in the area, these quaking aspens. Pretty trees, they were, and they always seemed to grow in clusters, never alone, but in family groups.

As he reached for the doorknob, he hoped he didn't stink but knew the chances of that were about the same as Dolores being in a good mood for once. After pulling the door open, he walked inside to see a tall counter. He reached into his pocket and withdrew both advertisements and the money, expecting to see Brother Christensen behind the counter. Someone was working at a desk, but after stepping into the building, he realized that it wasn't a man after all, but a woman with light brown hair drawn into a loose bun. A tendril had escaped one side, and she absently pushed it behind her ear as she worked over some papers, not noticing him.

Seeing a young woman instead of the old man he had expected threw Samuel off guard. He coughed lightly to draw her attention and said, "Excuse me, Miss?"

Her head popped up from her work. "Oh, hello," she said, putting down her pen and standing. "How can I help . . . you?" Her voice caught in her throat, and she stared at him.

They both stood there, staring at one another, taken aback. She was the woman he'd seen at the cemetery, the one who looked so much like Helen. This close he could tell that her hair was somewhat lighter, but she had similar brown eyes, the same oval face, and a pleasant smile.

"Can I help you?" she repeated, taking a deep breath and letting it out. He noted a slight flush to her cheeks, and she avoided his eyes.

This time Samuel coughed for real and looked away. He couldn't believe he was comparing a woman to Helen—and finding her pretty. A feeling of disloyalty to his wife's memory descended on him. Hadn't he been widowed only a few months now? The thought sent a thread of grief weaving its way into his heart again. *I didn't even know Helen two years ago,* he thought. Yet his entire life had changed since they met, twice over.

He pushed the papers across the counter. "Could you print these, please?" His voice was husky.

"I'm sure we can," she said, her face warming with a smile as she took the notes and read them over. She quickly scanned Brother Carlisle's note, murmuring, "That's right. He told me he'd be doing this . . ." But as she read Jeremiah's words, her eyes narrowed slightly.

"Is something wrong?" Samuel asked.

"A wild horse for sale, is it?" Her mouth went tight. "I believe I've seen that horse—a chestnut in the field north and west of here?" She pointed in the direction of the Hancock farm.

"That's right," Samuel said.

"I assume you work for Jeremiah Hancock?" The woman smoothed out the paper and raised an eyebrow at him. Her tone sounded as taut as the rope he'd tried pulling the filly with.

"Oh, no," he said hurriedly. "I work for Brother Carlisle up at the Church stables. I'm just acting as messenger for Mr. Hancock. I—uh—I saw the horse and . . ." Should he say more? By the look on her face, he could tell that she knew how the horse had been treated. Even so, he figured he'd better tread lightly. In a small town, offhanded words could spread like a wildfire. "I convinced the owner to sell her. I thought perhaps she'd do better under someone else's care."

Her mouth softened into a smile as if she understood and was relieved. "That was very good of you." Her fingers tapped Jeremiah's note several times as if in thought. "Such a beautiful horse," she said as if to herself.

"Yes, it is, Miss . . . ?"

She shook her head as if returning to the present. "It's . . . Chadwick. Tabitha Chadwick." She held out her hand. He shook it, wondering why she had paused before her own surname.

"Samuel Barnett."

Their hands didn't release right away, and Samuel felt a lump in his throat. Tabitha's hand was soft and delicate, so much like Helen's. He didn't want to let go. She gently pulled away, however, and turned back to the notes. "Thank you, Mr. Barnett. I'll be sure that both are in the next edition, which will be out Monday evening." She scribbled something on a ledger.

"*You* will?" he asked suddenly. "I thought the paper belonged to Theodore Christensen."

"It . . . it does," Tabitha said, stammering. "I—well, I work here."

Samuel pulled out the money. "How much?" He counted out several coins and slid them across the counter. "Is this enough? I'm still not sure about American money."

She nodded, pushing one coin back toward him, then scooping the rest into her palm. "This will cover them both. And thank you for coming in . . . Mr. Barnett."

"Miss Chadwick," he said with a nod as he headed for the door. He stepped out, put on his hat, and looked back before the door closed. Tabitha Chadwick was still watching him, and he found himself suddenly glad of that. It was nice to know he hadn't become completely repulsive since working in the stables.

CHAPTER 10

THAT AFTERNOON, TABITHA TOLD VICTOR and Joseph, the two men who ran the press, to set the type for Brother Carlisle's advertisement, but she put off doing the same for Jeremiah Hancock's. She kept his notice tacked to the wall next to the type cases.

Every time she entered the printing room, she'd see the notice. Several times she opened her mouth to tell one or the other of the young men to please set it, but then she'd remember something else she needed to do—check the books or edit the story her employee Natalie had turned in—and leave it for another time.

Tabitha never did run Jeremiah Hancock's advertisement. After seeing it looming from the wall beside the boxes of type for days on end, she just couldn't get herself to run it. Monday morning her fourth edition of the paper was printed by her staff—without Hancock's notice—and sent off in bundles on the wagon that delivered it to the surrounding cities. She watched the wagon until it turned onto Main and she couldn't see it anymore. Had she done the right thing?

She went into the printing room, where Victor and Joseph were cleaning up from the job of printing the paper for the day. She walked past them, drawn once more to the scribbled note on the wall. She pulled out the tack and held the note, reading it for what had to be at least the hundredth time.

That poor horse. She couldn't get the images out of her mind of the animal whinnying from pain, bucking away from her master, ears flat against her head, eyes wild.

The idea of the animal being sold to someone else—someone who might also wield a whip without remorse or starve the poor animal—was unthinkable. Of course, the mare might go to a kind and gentle person, but there was no guarantee of that.

Tabitha couldn't allow another cruel master to be an option. She *couldn't*. With a gulp, she headed through the printing room to the front desk. After digging in her pocket for the key, she unlocked a desk drawer and withdrew the money box. She quickly counted the amount the Hancock man had paid for his notice—he would need his money refunded—then replaced the box in the drawer and locked it.

What am I doing? I can't break a horse by myself, she thought, fingering the coins. *This is absolute madness.*

All the same, she couldn't do anything else.

She poked her head into the printing room and spoke to Joseph, who was four years her junior and had attended school with her long ago. Back then he had seemed so young, but what had felt like a generational gap back then had shrunk to almost nothing now that they were adults.

"I'm running an errand, Joseph. Will you take care of things here while I'm gone?"

"Sure thing, Sister Chadwick," Joseph said with a nod as he wiped down the press. "We'll be done here in about an hour. Do you want me to lock up?"

"Thanks, but I'll be back before then." She pulled her head out of the room and paused, wondering whether she should remind him that her married name was Hall, not Chadwick. But everyone in Manti remembered her as a Chadwick.

She had been Tabitha Hall for years in Logan. But why should she go by a name that had really only belonged to her for a few weeks? Hearing her maiden name felt good. Besides, she reminded herself, hadn't she introduced herself that way to the man who had brought in the advertisements? And she had considered doing the same with Jeremiah Hancock.

As she walked out of the office, she thought back to the man who had come in last week. He sounded British. Judging by his callused hands, he was of the working class, not from some rich aristocratic family in England. She smoothed her hair, trying to get a flyaway piece to go back into her bun, then headed down the walkway to the street, Hancock's note still clenched in her fist.

She remembered the Englishman's name without trying. It was easy to recall because she had always liked the name Samuel and had considered it for Will. Somehow this Samuel Barnett wouldn't leave her mind. Had Jeremiah Hancock paid him to bring the notice? Did Samuel know about the horse's mistreatment, and if so, what did he think of it?

Those details didn't matter right now, she reminded herself; she had a job to do. She marched along the road, but as she turned the corner that would bring her to the farm, her pace slowed, and she rethought her position.

It's not wise to rush headlong into something this big, she told herself. Realistically she had no idea how she could expect to care for a horse in the way it needed to be. Sure, she had learned a few things from Brother Merrill, but certainly not enough. She didn't know if she could afford to keep a horse, and between moving and buying the paper—and now buying the horse—her reserves would be depleted.

But then Tabitha remembered the sound of the whip as it snapped through the air—the pained whinnies as it struck. The rotting hooves and emaciated frame. The memories spurred her along the road until at last she found herself standing before Jeremiah Hancock's property. She had never seen the front of it before—only the back of his small, seedy cabin and the corral where she had witnessed the abuse.

The property was unkempt, with tall weeds growing everywhere. The front windows must have once held glass, as a few shards still clung to the one on the left. Threadbare, faded curtains hung behind the window frames, moving limply in the breeze. The door barely clung to its hinges as it drooped to one side, and the yard was piled with rubbish and old, rusting tools. No bushes, trees, or flowers grew anywhere except for whatever nature had managed to spring up on its own, which consisted mostly of sagebrush and rough grasses.

A drop of pity entered in Tabitha's heart. What a miserable place to live. Was Mr. Hancock a widower or a bachelor? Surely no self-respecting woman would live in such a place. But just as quickly, she quashed any sympathy, reminding herself that this man had been cruel to his horse. She allowed her fury to bubble up, making her want to storm inside, but somehow the formality of the log-hewn door made her take pause. She knocked briskly a few times and hoped that he was inside instead of out back. Mind spinning, she tried to think of what she'd say when facing the man and steeled herself to be strong.

After a few moments, the door was pulled open to reveal a sunburnt man with leathery skin and a scowl. "You again. What do you want?" When he spoke, it sounded as if he had pebbles rolling around in his chest. "Here to pester me about how to break a horse again?"

"No, I—"

"Then you're surely raising money for something. I'm tired of women coming by, begging an old bachelor to pledge a subscription for this cause or that one. No, thank you. So if you don't mind . . ." He moved to close the door, and Tabitha surprised herself by putting her foot out to block the way. Hancock looked at her boot then back to her face. His bushy eyebrows lifted, challenging—and possibly impressed at her pluck.

"Mr. Hancock—sir," she began. She breathed in deeply to compose herself. "I'm interested in buying your horse."

"Saw the notice, eh?" He leaned back and folded his arms.

"Well . . . yes." She reached into her pocket to return his money, but he wagged a finger at her and interrupted.

"I won't take a penny less than I asked for, ya know."

"I'm happy to pay your asking price," she assured him, even though she knew full well that the horse wasn't worth as much as he was demanding, not in her condition. But Tabitha wasn't about to argue the matter. She'd pay whatever it took to save the poor, tortured thing.

Jeremiah stabbed one finger in the air. "And you'll have to catch her to take her away. I won't be bothered with the beast any longer. Once she's yours, she's yours."

At this, Tabitha's eyes widened. How in the world would she capture and move the animal? She had assumed that he'd do that much, seeing as it was wild. For that matter, she had yet to arrange a place to keep the horse; her parents' tiny stable didn't have room. But something drove her to press on. Everything would work out—eventually.

"That will be just fine," she said, managing to sound calm but having no idea how she'd finagle such an arrangement.

"Good," Jeremiah said, almost looking surprised. "Then I want the money in cash, and the beast gone—both by Friday of next week. I'm not going to spend another penny on feeding her after that."

"Oh," Tabitha said, taking a step back, her mind reeling. She could produce the money in that time, but figuring out a solution for transportation and housing that soon would be tricky at best. She calculated the date. The next week Friday was Independence Day. Rather fitting for the horse.

"All right," she said. "I'll have her gone by then."

He closed the door so suddenly and with such force that she jumped. The money from his notice still rested in her hand, but she hadn't been given a moment to give it back or explain that she hadn't run the advertisement.

She turned away with a pit in her stomach, hoping he wouldn't be angry when he found out. *But why would he be,* she thought. *He's getting rid of her at the price he asked.*

Tabitha walked around the back of the cabin to see the horse—*her* horse. The stable was much larger and better built than the cabin. She couldn't help but wonder if it were just newer or whether someone else had done the work for him. She unlatched a door and entered, squinting at the sudden dimness of the interior.

Sun filtered through some cracks in the walls, showing bits of straw floating in the air. The scent of animals came over her, bringing with it sweeping memories of Chester—assisting his birth, watching him grow, helping to train him, sitting in his saddle as his first rider—all the times she had gone to his stall for comfort, a refuge. Her throat constricted; she hadn't expected such emotion to well up the first time she entered a stable since leaving Chester's.

Swallowing away the tightness, she ventured further inside until she found a stall that opened up to the corral beyond. The door was open in the back, and the horse wasn't inside. *No wonder he keeps her in this one,* she thought. *Most likely, Hancock can't get her into a stall without a fight.*

The horse stood on the other side of the pen, tail flicking nervously. Tabitha pursed her lips and whistled, holding out her hand, trying to lure the mare toward her. She tapped the wooden boards, whistled louder, rubbed her fingers together. Every so often the horse whinnied, trotting around the corral, but when Tabitha called out, she suddenly drew to the far end of the enclosure and went silent.

She's scared of me, too, Tabitha thought glumly. She bit her lips together. *This horse will learn to not be afraid.* She brushed dirt from her hands and headed out into the bright afternoon sun. Latching the door behind her, she nodded to herself.

She needs someone to help her overcome her fears. And I'll be the one.

* * *

After her visit to Jeremiah, Tabitha went back to the office. She finished up a few loose ends and sent her staff home for the day. Then she locked up. The sun was setting already, but before heading home, she took a copy of the newspaper and walked with it to the stable in the Little Fort. She wanted to be sure Brother Carlisle saw that she had published his notice about getting another hand. She entered the Little Fort from the east, tapping the newspaper against her hand as she looked around for . . .

Until that moment she had thought she was looking for Brother Carlisle, but she realized she'd rather hoped to see Samuel Barnett instead. Ever since seeing him at the cemetery, she had wanted to meet him properly—not the hurried, brief meeting they had experienced at the newspaper office—and talk to him.

She also wanted to ask what he was doing at the cemetery and what he had seen. What had he thought of her staring blankly at Fred's grave? What had Samuel's life been like before immigrating to Manti? Not that she would ever pry in that way, but she was curious. She could guess that he was a recent convert who came to Zion like so many dozens of others who arrived all the time. But something seemed different about him.

Why his opinion mattered, she had no idea, but somehow it did, because he had watched her at her husband's headstone; he had intruded upon her private moment. She wanted to know what he thought he had seen.

Stepping toward the stable's side door, she reached for the handle, hoping that she wouldn't come across Brother Carlisle after all. Then again, if she saw Samuel, what would she say? "Hello. I caught you staring at me the other day. I'd like to know why"?

Before she could open the door, it swung out on its hinges, and a tall man sauntered out. Tabitha yelped, stepping out of the way of the swinging door. She looked up and caught her breath when she realized who stood before her—none other than Samuel Barnett.

His step halted abruptly, and he stared at her for a second before saying, "Good afternoon, Miss—Chadwick, wasn't it?"

Unable to find her voice for a moment, Tabitha merely nodded. She cleared her throat and held out her hand. "Yes, and you were . . . Mr. Barnett?" She had paused before his name as if she hadn't remembered it offhand, which wasn't even almost true. She had kept her eyes open for any Barnett children at Will's school, and last Sunday at church she couldn't help looking around in case she spotted him. Yet she hadn't heard of any Sister Barnett in town. Why? Surely a man of his age was married.

She gestured to the newspaper. "I came by to give this to Brother Carlisle so he could see his notice." She held it out, hoping Samuel would just take it and not fetch his employer.

Samuel tucked the paper under his arm. "He's not here right now, but I'll bring it to work with me when I come back in the morning. I'm leaving for the day."

"You're going . . . *home*—now?"

"Day's work is done, thank the heavens," Samuel said. "I even managed to milk Dolores without getting kicked more than twice." He worked his right shoulder and grimaced. "But thank you for bringing this by. I'm sure he'll appreciate it." Touching the brim of his hat, he made to move on when Tabitha suddenly spoke up. She had to know.

"And where exactly do you live?"

Samuel turned back, an eyebrow arched. "At Sister Mirkins's, a few blocks east of here, just south of the hill," he said, hooking a thumb over his shoulder. "I'm letting a room with her—for now."

"I didn't realize she had room for a whole family in her home," Tabitha said, trying to sound innocent in her query, but she inadvertently added emphasis on *family*. A simple band circled a finger on Samuel's left hand.

He must have noted her eyes stray to the ring, because he folded his arms as if to hide it, making the newspaper crease. "I don't have any family here. I'm alone. My wife . . . she passed not long ago."

"Oh, I'm so sorry," Tabitha said, feeling a wave of guilt for prying. The sensitive details of his life were none of her business. She had experienced plenty of prying over the years when well-meaning—or sometimes plain-old-curious—people had tried to delve into her past during her years in Logan. Sometimes she didn't mind, but other times, she'd grit her teeth and try not to imply with her tone just how rude these people were, digging about in the private recesses of her heart. Now she had done the very same thing.

Yet now she understood those nosy people. Even though she wouldn't dream of asking another question, she had an itch to find out more. Did he have any children? How long ago did his wife die? How?

Instead, she waved a hand. "I'm sorry. I shouldn't have pried. I've been gone from Manti for some time, and I'm still trying to learn all the new faces." It was the best she could come up with—without spilling her own sad story, that is.

"It's all right," he said with a wan smile. "It's no secret that I'm on my own." He laughed sadly. "You know, I didn't remember how miserable bachelor life was. At least I'm not trying to cook for myself, or I don't know that I'd see next week for starving."

Tabitha laughed lightly at that, after which they lapsed into an awkward silence. "Well, it was good chatting with you, Mr. Barnett, I—"

"Call me Samuel," he interjected. "And if you don't mind the smell . . ." He lifted his arms to the sides, indicating himself. "I wouldn't mind a bit of company on my way."

Tabitha took a tiny step back at the sudden invitation. Then she stunned herself by saying, "It would be a pleasure."

They headed out of the Little Fort by the east entrance, Samuel leading the way and Tabitha not having any idea why she was walking with a strange man or why she had accepted the proposition. He didn't give her his arm, saying that he'd spare her the filth and smell of such an offer.

"You're recently returned to Manti, then?" he asked after they had walked a block in silence.

"That's right," Tabitha said without elaborating. Yet she wanted to speak of her past to someone who might understand, someone who didn't know the Tabitha Chadwick of her youth, who had no preconceived notions about who she was and what she had done by leaving. "I've been away from Manti for six years. I was up in Logan."

"Where's Logan?"

Tabitha pressed her lips together and thought quickly. "It's quite a distance from here, in a valley some eighty miles or so north of Salt Lake City. I went to school there and did some teaching as well."

She glanced up at him, then over to a grove of trees so he wouldn't notice her attention. He had lost a spouse. She could tell him the entire story; surely he'd understand why she had to leave. Then again, maybe not. Their stories might not be similar enough for true empathy.

How long had he been married? Did he miss her terribly? At least on one count, they were similar; they had both lost a spouse. So she added, "You see, I left Manti shortly after my husband passed."

She wasn't sure, but she thought she detected a slight trip at her words, a pause with the toe of Samuel's boot. He glanced at her. "I'm sorry to hear that."

"Thank you," she said, then sighed. "But it was a long time ago. It must be harder when it's still fresh." Their eyes caught for a moment, and Samuel smiled his appreciation for her understanding that he hadn't yet experienced the blessing of time healing over some of the ache.

He looked to their left, where Temple Hill presided over the valley—it was hard to go anywhere in the city where the rising white oolite walls and the scaffolding around it didn't look down on you. Right now the stone seemed to shimmer as the sun lowered in the west. He pointed at the hill. "Was the temple under construction when you were here last?"

Stopping at a crossroad where the temple was more visible, Tabitha also paused and looked at the building. With a shake of her head, she said, "I just missed it. It was quite a sight to see when I first came back. Back when I left, the hill was nothing but dirt, rocks, and sagebrush."

"It's hard to imagine that now," Samuel said.

"It is," Tabitha agreed. "I was here when the site was dedicated in 1877, just a few months before I married, but there was a lot of work to do to prepare the hill, so the cornerstones weren't laid for almost two years, not until after . . . well, after I left."

Samuel seemed to sense that she didn't want to talk more about the past. He thrust his hands into his pockets, and together they continued their stroll. He brought the conversation into the present. "So what brought you back, if I may ask?"

"Working with the newspaper. And a chance for . . ." Her voice drifted off, and she wondered whether telling him about so much of her life—things that included Will—would be too much for such a new male acquaintance.

"A chance for what?" Samuel asked absently, staring at the road and avoiding a pothole.

"A chance for my son to know his grandparents." Tabitha said the words quickly before she could change her mind about sharing her personal life.

"You have a son?" He paused, and she held her breath, hating the fact that she cared about his reaction to that part of her life. She nodded, and Samuel smiled. "I'll bet he loves horses too." With a chuckle, he headed down the road again.

Confused, Tabitha, picked up her skirts and followed. "What do you mean, 'loves horses too'?"

A smile twitched the corners of Samuel's mouth. He seemed to study the tops of some trees as he tried to come up with an answer. He shrugged. "Hancock's notice."

"What about it?" Tabitha stopped walking and folded her arms in challenge. She still didn't want to admit to herself that wanting to know Samuel's role in that was the real reason she had gone to the stable.

Smiling wryly, Samuel turned to her. "You nearly snapped the head off my neck like a green bean when you thought I approved of his behavior toward his horse."

"Well, I . . ." Tabitha swiped at a pile of dirt with her toe, frantically searching for something to say. She *had* jumped to conclusions there. "You said you convinced him to sell."

"That's right. But I didn't meet Hancock until that day. I don't work for him."

She raised her head, eyes narrowed in thought. "Were you trying to save her? The horse, I mean?"

"You could say that." Samuel shifted uncomfortably. "But if Hancock gets wind of that, I'll deny it."

"Thank you, Samuel," she said, touching his arm in gratitude. "Thank you so much. She needs a new home. I don't know how I'm going to do it, but . . ."

Had she been completely rash earlier that day? Of course she had. She didn't have the means or the skill to break a wild horse.

"What?" Samuel asked, his curiosity apparently piqued.

"I'm buying her from Jeremiah," Tabitha said in a rush. She began walking again, with swift strides. "I want to break her myself. Is there room in the stable for another horse? Do you think Brother Carlisle would let me keep her there?" Her brow furrowed. "But where would I train her?"

"There are a couple of empty stalls," Samuel ventured. "I don't know how much they charge for boarding. And Brother McCleve lets us use his round pen for training. I imagine he'd let you keep her there for a spell until you can get her broken enough to stay in a stall."

"Really?" Tabitha hopped a step in her excitement. "Then perhaps it might just work. Oh, I hope they both agree." It would be one more problem she could remove from her worry list. Then, of course, she would have to worry about breaking the horse and training her. But she could probably find help with that, too—someone who had more experience with such things than she did—someone like a stable hand who spent his days with horses. She turned to Samuel abruptly, making him stop with a puff of dust around his boots. "Would *you* help me train her? I'm not so sure that a woman has the strength, and I'm sure I could use someone with your experience."

Samuel hesitated for just a moment before saying, "I'll help any way I can."

"Thank you so much," Tabitha said. "This is such a load off my mind."

They walked a few yards in companionable silence until Samuel paused. "I must have a stone in my boot." He went to the side of the road and leaned against a fence, where he pulled off his boot and shook out the offending pebble.

An oddity about his boot struck Tabitha. Streaks of what looked like red paint marked the heel. She glanced down to his other boot and noted the same streak on it. "Red heels?" she asked, curious. "I don't think I've ever seen any boots quite like that."

"It's something my wife did to them," Samuel said, putting his boot back on. He pulled at the top then stamped his foot on the ground to get his toes inside. "Better."

He returned to the road, where he lifted his foot, turned heel up so they could both see the marks better. "It might look silly, but it was her way of spotting me in the factory we worked at. She couldn't look up from her work without risking her fingers getting caught in the machinery, so all she could see of the men was their boots."

"How thoughtful," Tabitha said, seeing the boots in a very different light. "She sounds like a lovely woman to think of such a thing."

Samuel got a far-off look in his eyes. "She was certainly that."

CHAPTER 11

LATE INTO THE NIGHT ON Thursday, a banging on the side door woke Tabitha from her sleep. She sat up with a start and hurried out of bed, grabbing a robe and putting it on as she ran to the door. Who in the world was making such a racket at this hour?

She unlocked the door and pulled it open just enough to see who it was—Victor, from the paper. "Goodness, is something the matter?" she asked, glancing in the direction of the paper to make sure there wasn't smoke rising into the sky from a fire.

The young man nodded but didn't seem overly upset. He jabbed a thumb over his shoulder. "There's a ruckus a couple of blocks that way," he said. "The constable is arresting someone. Thought you'd want to get over there and see what's going on. You know, for the paper."

"Absolutely," Tabitha said, eyes flitting to the south. What was going on down there? She tried to remember who lived in that general direction but drew a blank, possibly from the hour, possibly because she was still relatively new to the area. "Let me get dressed properly. I'll be right out."

She scurried inside, got dressed, and twisted her hair into a bun. Pulling back the comforter, she gave Will a quick kiss, then threw a shawl around her shoulders. Before hurrying out the door, she snagged a notebook and pencil. Victor waited at the end of the walkway, and together they half walked, half ran toward the commotion.

They rounded a corner to find a handful of men gathered in front of a house. On the front yard a man—presumably the home owner—held another man pinned to the ground with his arm hiked painfully behind his back.

"I wasn't stealing your stinkin' money!" the restrained man yelled. "Let me go!"

"Not until the constable gets here, I don't," the other said, ramming the arm a bit higher and evoking a scream. "Sure, you weren't thieving me. What exactly *were* you doin' in my study, then?"

"Not stealing from ya, that's what!" He fought against his captor but didn't appear to be as strong. The two rolled to the side, revealing the suspect's face. Tabitha stared into the eyes of Jeremiah Hancock. He had a bright red spot on his forehead that trickled blood.

"You," she said under her breath.

Victor leaned in. "Not a huge surprise, if you ask me. He barely ekes out a living. Crotchety old coot would probably do almost anything for money."

Tabitha approached a man beside her. "When did all this start?" She whipped out her notebook and began jotting information down.

"I got here ten or fifteen minutes ago, maybe," he said. "Heard the noise from my house across the street there. Couldn't have been much happening before that."

"Victor, what time is it now?" she asked as she furiously wrote.

"Ten after one," he said, then tucked his pocket watch back into his coat. He looked about. "There's the constable now."

A carriage rumbled down the street, and the small crowd parted to make way. It rolled to a stop right before the house. At seeing the constable alight from the carriage, Jeremiah struggled even harder. "I didn't do nothing wrong," he demanded. "Let me go."

"We'll let a trial decide that," the constable said, slapping on handcuffs and tightening them. With a bit of stubble shading his face, the constable looked tired and disheveled and didn't have on his uniform. He pulled the scowling Jeremiah to his feet. "You'll be coming with me."

Under the constable's rough hand, Jeremiah stumbled toward the carriage. He reluctantly climbed inside, still proclaiming his innocence, and was locked inside with the clang of a sliding bolt. The constable lifted himself back onto the bench and flicked the reins. The horses moved on, and the crowd watched as it went down the road and into the night. Tabitha finally got her bearings and looked around.

"Whose house is this?" she asked of the man standing beside her.

"Mortimer Daggett's," he said. "Businessman. Came over from England with his wife about a year ago."

Tabitha's brow furrowed. "What would Jeremiah Hancock want here?"

The man shrugged. "Money, I suppose. Hancock's not exactly well off, and rumor has it that Daggett had quite a fortune back in England." He yawned. "Well, if there's nothing else going on here, I'm going to catch a few winks before dawn." The man tipped his hat and strolled away.

Tabitha watched him leave, debating what to do next. Spying what she assumed were the man and woman of the house, she headed for the front door, where they were standing. He was the same person who had restrained Jeremiah earlier. Now he seemed intent on comforting his wife. Both of her hands clutched his shirt, and he had both arms around her. Face pale and drawn, she wore a nightcap and flannel gown and seemed to wish she could melt into the safety of her husband's arms.

"Mr. and Mrs. Daggett, I presume?" she asked.

"That's right," Mr. Daggett said, in his lilting English accent. He eyed her suspiciously. "And you are?"

"I'm Tabitha Chadwick of the *Sanpitch Sentinel*. Would you mind talking with me for a few minutes?"

"That rotten man is a thief!" Mrs. Daggett said suddenly. "He is. Could have murdered us in our beds, that one!"

Her husband held her closer. "Now, Dorothy, let's not get carried away. He was just after some money. Neither of us got hurt. Things could be much worse."

"So he *was* trying to steal from you?" Tabitha asked.

"Appears that way," Mr. Daggett said. "I heard something while upstairs in my room and decided to investigate. Came upon him in my den, fiddling with a desk drawer where I keep important documents and some cash. He already had a bag filled with money in one hand when I found him. He tried to make an escape, but I caught and held him while Dorothy went for help. We made quite a ruckus, didn't we?" He indicated the people milling about, who were now thinning. Then he glanced askance at the ground, where an abandoned fire poker rested. Tabitha wondered if Daggett had used it on

Jeremiah and shuddered at the thought. It would explain the bleeding from his forehead.

"Is the money still here, then?" Tabitha asked.

"I think he dropped the bag in the study," Mr. Daggett said.

His wife suddenly perked up, eyes wide. "We'd better find and hide it so no one else tries any mischief."

Tabitha allowed herself to follow them inside, where they indeed found the bag on the floor beside a writing desk. Mr. Daggett dug through the burlap sack and withdrew two stacks of paper bills and a smaller cloth sack containing coins. He nodded. "These are most definitely mine."

"And I *made* that coin sack!" Dorothy said, as if having a thief take her handiwork was even a bigger insult than taking the coins it carried.

"I believe it's all here," Mr. Daggett said after counting the bills. "Which is a relief. My business partner wouldn't be too keen if I had lost my promised investment."

Dorothy collapsed into a chair with relief. "I'm so glad. Brother Tidwell was already reluctant to start the business. Losing the money would have done us in."

"We're starting a freighting company," Mr. Daggett explained to Tabitha. "Brother Tidwell's already struggling financially, and I had to do a lot of dancing around to convince him that the risk wouldn't be too great and that we'd get a handsome profit within a year. If Hancock had managed to do away with the money . . ." He shook his head. "Both of our families would be sunk." He put the money back into the bag. "I'll be hiding this somewhere else from now on. Too bad we don't have a bank in town."

"I plan to tell the story in the paper so other folks can be warned," Tabitha said, knowing she'd do so with or without their blessing. A burglary in the middle of Manti was definitely something the citizens would want—would need—to read about.

"That would be a wonderful thing to do," Dorothy said. "Thank you."

"Is there anything in particular you'd like me to mention?"

"Not really," Dorothy said, smoothing back her hair. "Just so long as you make it clear to everyone what a scoundrel that Jeremiah Hancock is."

I couldn't agree more, Tabitha thought, scribbling on her pad.

She hoped to be able to speak with Jeremiah before running the piece, letting him have his say if he wanted it. *But what will he have to say for himself?* she wondered. *And why did he try to steal the money? I'll be paying him for the horse soon, so it's not like he doesn't have any means. Greedy old coot.*

* * *

Tabitha stood outside the constable's office, gripping her notebook between her hands. She had gotten up early that morning—without having slept well after the burglary anyway—to plan the questions she'd want to ask Jeremiah later that day.

I wish this were over, she thought. *Or that the thief had been anyone besides Jeremiah Hancock.*

She took a deep breath and went up to the door. The constable answered her knock and quickly led her inside to the small cell in the back of the building where Jeremiah lay on a cot. When he saw her, he scowled and sat up.

"What do *you* want?" he snarled. "Don't you go thinking you can just have my horse now without paying because I can't do anything about it. Think again."

"I have no intentions of taking your horse without payment, Mr. Hancock." Tabitha gulped. "I'm here to get your side of the story before I print an article about . . . the events of last night."

Jeremiah clasped his hands, leaning his arms on his legs, and licked his lips. He avoided her eyes. "What do you want to know?"

The constable brought a chair over for Tabitha. "Thank you," she said with a smile, then sat down and cleared her throat. Jeremiah was behind bars. Why was she so nervous? "What were you doing in the Daggetts' home last night?" She held her pencil poised over the page, awaiting his answer.

He stared at her for a few seconds before responding. She wondered if he was thinking through his options, wondering how much truth to tell, how much to fabricate. "I was returning some stolen money."

Tabitha's head snapped up; she hadn't expected that. "*Returning* the money?"

"That's what I said."

"Money that you had stolen before? Were you returning it out of remorse?"

"I didn't take it," Jeremiah snapped.

Tabitha wrote the information down furiously. His answers drove her planned questions out of her head. She hadn't expected the conversation would go in this direction. "If you didn't take it originally, then who, may I ask, did?"

Jeremiah pursed his lips in thought. "Can't tell ya that. But it wasn't me."

"Really?" Tabitha leaned back in the chair, feeling more confident and relaxed now that he seemed to be putting forth a baseless defense. "So you just *happened* upon a bag of money, knew it belonged to Mr. Daggett, and decided to sneak into his house to return it?"

"Didn't say I don't know who it was. It just wasn't me." Jeremiah turned to face her full-on. This time when he spoke, his voice was quiet, intense. "It wasn't me."

For some inexplicable reason, Tabitha believed him. She fought the feeling. This was a man who had practically tortured his horse, who was known for being ornery and mean and stingy. Who made no bones about his opinion of those who still attended church meetings and paid tithing. Who yelled at anyone who came near him. Who was poor. And yet, something in his eyes told her that he really *didn't* steal the money.

But how could she print *that*? Last night's circumstances painted a very different picture, one that her logical mind still wanted to believe. She asked the only question she felt that she could. "Why didn't you just bring the money to Daggett during the day? Why break into his home?"

He turned his gaze away and didn't answer.

He must be protecting the person who really took it, Tabitha thought. *But who? And why?*

"Is there anything you want me to include in the article, anything you want to say?"

"Just one thing," Jeremiah said, his eyes intent on the wooden floor. He paused, then raised his gaze to Tabitha's. "It wasn't me."

CHAPTER 12

TUESDAY AFTERNOON TABITHA ONCE AGAIN met with Brother Christensen. In past weeks, they'd met the morning after the paper came out, but due to his wife's illness, this week's appointment was postponed until midday. The staff had left for their lunch, and Tabitha stayed in the office alone, waiting for the former owner.

She'd put out five papers now, and she felt more confident in her abilities all the time. Each week brought up new questions and issues, and at their weekly meetings, she had the chance to pose them. Brother Christensen offered suggestions and solutions. Week by week, the operations of the business were getting smoothed out.

With satisfaction, she read over yesterday's four-page paper. Thanks to the telegraph wire, she was privy to nearly all of the major events taking place in the United States and Utah, so her little paper kept the people informed as well as any bigger paper in the territory. Advertising revenue was up since she'd taken over, as evidenced by the columns taken up with notices for everything from cleaning fluids to the latest hair products and medicinal cures.

She reread several of the pieces, most written by herself, a few by Natalie, and one by Joseph. She paused and looked over the piece she had put at the bottom of the first page: "Unclear Circumstances Surround So-Called Burglary."

Tabitha bit her lip, wondering what had really happened that night. She reread her brief report, recounting what she had witnessed at the scene, quoting Mr. Daggett, the constable, and, of course, Jeremiah, who stated his innocence. She had concluded the piece with, "Hancock will stand trial on charges of burglary at a date yet to be determined. As the only evidence thus far is circumstantial, the law may have a difficult time proving him guilty."

The bell on the door chimed, and Tabitha looked up to see Brother Christensen. His face looked tired as he closed the door, the latest edition of the paper under his arm.

"Is Sister Christensen feeling better?" Tabitha asked, standing.

"She's doing well, thank you." He took the paper from under his arm and tapped the counter with it. He seemed disturbed by something, hesitant to speak.

Tabitha raised her eyebrows. "Are you well? Shall we meet tomorrow instead? I don't think I have any pressing questions. Everything seemed to go off this week without a hitch." There was only one major issue at hand, as far as she was concerned, something urgent she wanted to discuss.

"No, no, I'm fine," he said, looking up and putting on a smile. He pulled up a chair and said, "There is just one item I wanted to bring up; but first, is there anything *you* wanted to talk about?"

Tabitha folded her copy of the paper and set it aside. "Actually, there is. I was wondering . . . do you think it's almost time?"

They both knew what the question meant: when would they announce her ownership of the paper and stop the charade of signing *T.C.* to mean Theodore Christensen instead of Tabitha Chadwick?

"Not yet," Brother Christensen said. He rubbed a hand over his balding head as if trying to rub away a worry.

Tabitha persisted. "When? People are noticing that I'm the one managing the place and that you're not here much anymore. I don't know what difference it would make to officially state the sale in the paper. We could draw something up right now . . ." She searched for some paper and a pencil on her desk.

"Not yet," he repeated, this time raising a hand. He sighed and admitted somewhat reluctantly, "I was thinking it would be in the next week or so, but now . . ."

She stilled in her search for something to write on and looked at him. "Now . . . what?"

He looked at the newspaper. "Do you really think it wise to stir up contention in the city?"

Tabitha sat back down, confused. "I don't understand. I'm not trying to stir up anything."

"Then what is this?" He held out his copy of the *Sentinel* to the article about Jeremiah.

"It's a report on what happened last week at the Daggetts' . . ."

"You're taking the side of the guilty," Brother Christensen said.

"Excuse me?" Tabitha said. She was doing no such thing. "I'm simply trying to tell all sides of the story, to be objective."

"Objectivity doesn't always have a place," Brother Christensen said. "You must understand—the *Sentinel* has always been a Christian business. We shun evil and uphold the good."

Tabitha narrowed her eyes, finally understanding. "But I'm not making a judgment or upholding evil, I'm merely—"

Brother Christensen interrupted. "It sure sounds like you think this Hancock fellow is innocent of any wrongdoing . . . yet he was *caught* in the act."

"I reported the facts," Tabitha said evenly. "I didn't take sides. Hancock says he's innocent, so I included his statement. I don't know whether he's really innocent, but it's his right to make the claim."

Brother Christensen rubbed his chin, shaking his head. "That's not what it sounds like. Looks like you approve of the man."

Tabitha stifled a groan. "Isn't it my duty to report facts? It's not my job to be the jury. What happened to 'innocent until proven guilty'?"

"A technicality," Brother Christensen said with a disdainful shake of his head. "The man *is* guilty. I know it. The entire town knows it. You're asking for trouble by implying anything else." He sighed. "Look, I think that until this whole Hancock case blows over, it would be best not to announce that you're at the helm. I'll take enough flak for this one story as it is—but if I can blame it on an *employee,* it'll be better for the paper than if you try to bear the brunt as the owner and publisher."

"I'm not afraid of public opinion," Tabitha said.

"You ought to be." He shook his head and sighed. "I understand where you're coming from, Tabby. I do. But this is a business, and you must keep in mind who your readers are if you want to *stay* in business."

What about keeping in mind my integrity? Tabitha thought. But she didn't say it. Instead, she nodded. "I see where you're coming from."

"Good. So let's just wait a few more weeks to see how this whole thing turns out. Let people simmer down about the Hancock story.

Let it disappear. Avoid running anything else about it, and it should pass quickly. Then, when people have regained their confidence in you, we make the announcement."

"I'll take that under consideration," Tabitha said stiffly. "Is there anything else?"

"No. No, I don't think so. Aside from this Hancock scandal, you're doing fine."

Tabitha bit her tongue and counted to ten to calm down. "So you're aware, Brother Christensen, I receive at least half a dozen queries every week as to when your retirement will take place—and what will happen to the *Sentinel* after that."

"You do?" The gentleman sat up a bit straighter. His eyebrows drew together in concern.

"I do. Regardless of what happens with Mr. Hancock, I'll need to come forward with the full truth sooner than later."

"What have you said to such questions thus far?"

"Oh, you needn't worry," Tabitha said, anger bubbling beneath the surface. She almost wished the statement weren't true—that she hadn't kept the truth to herself and instead had spilled the beans to *someone* in town. "I deflect the questions as best as I can. But it's hard, and quite frankly, it won't work for much longer."

"The final decision is up to you, of course," he finally said, standing. "But I've run this business for many years. You can trust me when I say that it would be best for the paper—and for you—to hold back for a spell and let the Hancock story die." He picked up his hat from the table and muttered something about needing to get back to check on his wife then went out the door.

Tabitha wished him good day. She leaned against the doorjamb as he walked down the street. She crossed her arms. "Soon I'll simply *tell* him that it's time," she muttered under her breath. "And as for the Hancock and Daggett story, let them heap on the coals. I can handle it."

* * *

Brother Carlisle walked through the stable, inspecting Samuel's and Horace's work and making notes about items he needed to fix or order. Samuel felt relatively good about his skills; he was getting better at mucking out stalls and otherwise caring for the animals they housed. He didn't like it any better, but he was learning to endure it. Since he'd arrived in Manti, the blisters on his hands had healed, and he had managed to avoid making any more. That was progress.

Samuel spread chicken feed in the coop when Brother Carlisle tromped to the end of the corridor and peered into the cow's stall, then grunted as he added an item to his paper. "Dolores keeps kicking a hole into that wall. It's almost enough to drive a dry man to drink. I've repaired holes in that wall probably a dozen times now, and she's done made another one again—only this time in a new spot." He looked up and chuckled. "She must be getting tired of how easy it is to kick through that one board, eh?"

Samuel flushed slightly and turned his attention back to the chicken feed. He knew how that hole had gotten there; it wasn't Dolores this time. This morning, after a particularly difficult milking—during which Dolores knocked over the milk pail a record *four* times—it was Samuel's own boot that kicked the hole into the wall.

Brother Carlisle walked back and tsked. "There are days I wonder if that cow's worth the trouble."

Feeling like he needed to confess his role in the latest broken board, Samuel tied off the bag of feed, set it on the ground, and said, "Sir, I—"

"But then I see that she more than pays for her keep from the milk we sell." Brother Carlisle went on as if he hadn't heard Samuel at all. "Some ladies in the city won't have anyone's milk but Dolores's for their cheese, and they're willing to pay a pretty penny for it. Good for the temple fund. Suppose I couldn't get rid of her without official approval anyway."

At long last he stopped talking, and Samuel opened his mouth again to admit to kicking out the board, when Brother Carlisle went on. "So Sam, can I trust you to fix the hole? Why don't you reinforce the old spot, too. Let's use some bigger, thicker board for it—the ones out back—and double them up so she won't be able to kick through anywhere near a thirteenth time."

"Certainly," Samuel said. If he was the one who would be repairing the hole, then he supposed it didn't really matter how it got there. Besides, this was the type of job that Samuel welcomed—the kind with plain old tools—just a hammer, nails, and pieces of wood. No animal with a half-baked brain to cause him any grief. But when Samuel made a move to head for the wall that held the tools, Brother Carlisle stopped him.

"Not now," Brother Carlisle said, putting a hand on Samuel's arm. "Fixing the hole can wait 'til morning. I've got another job I'd like you to do today."

As he slowly turned around, dread filled Samuel. What were the chances that this job *wouldn't* involve a contrary creature with a brain and four legs? He should have known that the relief of work with simple tools wouldn't come without a hitch.

"What is it?" he asked lightly.

Scratching his head, Brother Carlisle said, "I promised a lady I'd send a hand to help her transport a horse to McCleve's place. We'll be boarding it soon."

The sinking feeling was confirmed. Tabitha Chadwick. She had to be the woman with the horse. Samuel had already said he'd try to help her out, which was pure lunacy on his part. Now this. How was he supposed to help get a horse to McCleve's pen when he couldn't even manage to get a young filly to obey him?

He shifted his feet. "You know, Brother Carlisle, I don't think that's—"

But once again, the stable manager didn't seem to be paying attention. He chewed on a piece of straw and read over his notes as he talked. "Apparently she just bought the animal but doesn't have a place to board it. I think she said it still needs to be broken." Clenching the straw between his teeth and pointing westward, he said, "Do you know the Hancock place?"

Samuel warred with the leaden ball in his stomach. Just as surely as he hated manure, he'd be useless trying to get any horse back to the stable, let alone an unbroken one like Jeremiah Hancock's. On the other hand, since the lady was Tabitha Chadwick, he wouldn't mind doing the chore just so he could see her again.

Brother Carlisle pulled a watch from his pocket and consulted it. "She'll be at Hancock's at four o'clock, and it's a quarter to four now, so you'd better get a move on." Brother Carlisle patted Samuel's upper arm, adding, "I sure appreciate all your hard work," then walked off before Samuel managed to form a coherent sentence.

"But I—" he called out as the wooden door slammed shut. He ran his hand over his stubble and sighed. This wouldn't be pretty.

What else could he do but go to Tabitha and admit defeat?

Carlisle told me to go. And I did tell her I'd help, Samuel thought as he walked out to the stable and trudged to the Hancock place. *At least, I told her I'd help as much as I could—which isn't much.*

He blew the air out of his mouth, puffing out his cheeks. Then, fisting his hands, he steeled himself. He'd help Tabitha Chadwick move that horse if it killed him.

And it just might, at that.

As he walked, he lifted his hat and scrubbed a hand through his hair. Why couldn't she need help repairing something—like a power loom? He laughed under his breath at the ridiculous thought. In his former life as a repairman in a textile factory in London, he knew everything there was to know about the machines and how they worked, how to fix them. He knew the quirks of the carding machines and how to temper the power looms. And how *not* to mess with the dyeing machine.

Not much good any of that has done me here in farm country, he thought grimly. *And I've got a feeling things are only going to get worse.*

Curiously, he felt as eager to reach the Hancock place as he did to prolong his arrival. Tabitha would be there waiting for him. He couldn't help but admit that seeing her again would be a bright spot in his day. He just hoped that whatever came next wouldn't ruin *her* day.

All too soon—and at the same time, not nearly soon enough—he reached the fence post where he had first seen the horse. There across the field was Tabitha at the corral, where the horse shook its head then cantered back and forth inside the enclosure as if looking for a way to escape. Samuel climbed over and trod through the long grasses.

Toward the horse, he told himself. But really toward Tabitha.

Now he could see Tabitha reaching her hand out to the horse, and he could imagine her speaking softly, trying to coax it near. The mare watched her closely, nostrils quivering, catching her scent. Then the animal whinnied and ran away. Tabitha's arm dropped to the top board of the pen, and her shoulders fell.

"Afternoon," he said when he was in earshot.

She turned her head. Instead of wearing a smile, her expression looked forlorn, her voice near desperation. "Samuel! I'm so glad you're here. I'll need your help, especially after the day I've had." She blew some hair out of her face and sighed. "I don't suppose you read the latest issue of the paper?"

"No, actually," he said, wishing he had and deciding right then to order up a subscription.

"Then never mind." She waved a hand and smiled.

"What was in the paper?"

"Oh, something that ruffled a few feathers." She shrugged. "But you can't please everyone, and isn't it my job to report events? It's not to make judgments, especially before a man has had his day in court, right?" She stopped speaking abruptly, as if realizing that she was getting a bit too heated about something he knew nothing about.

"Right," he said, hoping that was the correct answer.

She smoothed her bodice and chuckled. "Sorry. Like I said, it's been a difficult day. But thank you for coming. I wanted to get this matter taken care of as soon as possible."

Samuel brought a fist to his mouth and cleared his throat uneasily. "Happy to oblige. What do we do?"

Heading toward the stable adjoining the corral, she said, "I figure the best thing to do is lasso her." She spoke over her shoulder as she walked, glancing back to be sure that Samuel followed. "With her temperament, she'll never let us get close enough to put on a halter."

"A lasso . . . of course." The jig was nearly up; he couldn't pretend much longer that he knew anything. A few weeks ago he hadn't known the difference between a halter and a bridle. "And then we'll . . . do what?" He already had nightmarish images in mind of what lassoing involved—mostly falling down in a tangle of rope around his arms and legs while the horse felt free to mutilate him.

Tabitha paused at the stable door and looked back, her brows raised. "Tie the rope to the back of Jeremiah's wagon, of course. I'm assuming since he wants to get rid of her that he'll let us use the wagon and his two other horses to pull it."

She opened the door and went inside, where she went to a wall with tack and other supplies. Samuel ducked into the dim enclosure as well. It smelled dank and rotten—far worse than Brother Carlisle's stables. One hand rose to his nose to block the stench.

Tabitha seemed to hardly notice, although her nose scrunched up a bit. With hands on hips, she surveyed the shelves, hooks, and stacks until she found what she was looking for. "Ah," she said, reaching for a coiled rope hanging from a wooden peg.

"I don't understand," Samuel said as she hefted the coil over her shoulder.

"Don't understand what?" she asked as they headed back out into the blessedly fresh—if hot—afternoon air.

"Well, if the horse isn't halter-broken, how will we get it to follow the wagon?"

"How will we get it to—" Tabitha's step paused, and she turned to look up at Samuel, a quizzical expression on her face. She walked back to his side and looked up at him. "Have you . . . How much time have you spent . . . ?" She seemed to be searching for the right words.

To save her the embarrassment of asking the full question—and knowing it was well past time to confess—Samuel jumped in. "To be honest, I don't know the first thing about animals. I lived my entire life in the city until I left London. I've been here only a few weeks." He lifted his arms helplessly. "I said I'd help you as best I can, but the truth is that I shouldn't have made such a promise. The best help I can give you is still a useless proposition."

A smile flirted with the corners of Tabitha's mouth, making Samuel wish he could find a different way to help her that didn't involve a horse. Her chestnut eyes mocked him. He gestured toward the road and took a step backward. "I suppose I'll just—"

"Don't go." Tabitha suddenly said, right as Samuel was about to leave. He paused and looked over. She smiled warmly. "Thank you for being willing to help me. Only a true gentleman would offer such a thing when he didn't know how he'd do it."

Her eyes bored into him; his ears felt ready to burn. If he remained flushed much longer, his ears would turn into ash and fall right off. He shifted his feet and kicked a dirt clod. "Well, uh, you're welcome," he said, avoiding her eyes.

"She'll have to come along when we've got a team of horses pulling her."

Samuel looked side to side, confused. "What's that?"

Gesturing toward the corral, Tabitha said, "That's how we'll get her to move. Horses are smart; they figure out what to do quick enough. Oh, she'll fight it at first, but after a spell, her neck will get tired of pulling against the rope, and she'll realize it's simpler—and less painful—to follow."

"That makes sense," he said, returning to her. She *wasn't* mocking him. The realization made him smile in return—made him willing to stick this out and try to help. "So how exactly do we lasso the thing?"

"Well," Tabitha said, adjusting the rope in her hands. "First we have to tie the lasso, like this." She wrapped the rope, threw one end over the top, worked a knot, then pulled. The result was a tangled mess. With a laugh, she said, "It's been a few years since I did this."

She untied the knot, then with her tongue showing between her teeth, she narrowed her eyes and slowly retied the lasso. This time it worked perfectly. "Got it!" she declared triumphantly, holding up her success.

"Very good," Samuel said.

"Now comes the hard part," Tabitha said, looking at the horse as she pulled rope between her fingers, opening the lasso wider. She sighed. "I was never very good at this." She climbed through the fence crosspieces into the corral, snagging her skirt on the wood as she did so. Samuel leaned down to free the fabric just as she, too, reached for the hem. Their hands touched and froze. She raised her gaze to his, and it held. He tugged the hem loose.

"Thank you," she said.

"You're welcome." He thought he saw a hint of color in her cheeks as she turned and slipped through. A swarm of moths erupted inside his middle.

"Coming?" Tabitha asked over her shoulder.

"Into *there* with the *horse?*" He pointed to the corral.

"Naturally. How else are we going to lasso her? She won't bite . . . I don't think."

In spite of Tabitha's grin, Samuel wasn't sure if she was kidding. He stared at the horse, feeling a dread in his chest that even the old dyeing machine at the factory had been incapable of generating. The rusty old machine, for all the grief it gave him, hadn't been able to *trample* him.

"She's more afraid of you than you could possibly be of her," Tabitha assured him.

He wasn't nearly so sure of that. "She must weigh half a ton. She could kill me without a second thought," Samuel countered, eyeing the thick muscles, the powerful legs. Even though the animal was clearly ill, she had plenty more power in one leg than Samuel did in his entire body.

"But she *won't* kill you," Tabitha said.

Was such a statement supposed to make him feel better? He looked at the mare twitching her tail and shaking her head nervously. For all her anxiety, she was a gorgeous creature. And he was not about to be outdone by an animal—least of all in front of a woman. If the last breath he took was in this corral, at least he wouldn't die looking like a coward.

He ducked under the fence railing and walked forward, stopping at Tabitha's side—or a few inches behind her. "Now what?"

"You go to that side to block her from trying to go to the other side of the pen," she said, gesturing to her right as she kept her eyes trained on the mare. "She's so scared of people that you'll easily be able to scare her away from that side." She took a deep breath. "Meanwhile, I'll see if my aim is any good after all these years."

With a nod, Samuel retreated several feet. How he was supposed to stop a galloping horse if it came at him he had no idea. He used to take a hammer to the dye machine to stop its ticking, but that wasn't quite an option here—although that's essentially what Hancock had tried to do, he remembered, and shuddered.

"Ready?" she called.

Samuel suddenly realized he was standing in a pile of horse droppings. Grimacing, he lifted his boots one at a time. The mess stuck to them in clumps. "Ready," he said after making a face and stomping hard to clean the soles as best he could.

Tabitha raised the rope and swung it over her head in slow, easy circles. Just as she released the lasso, the horse spooked and ran to the right. A jolt went through Samuel, and without knowing what else to do, he yelled, "Hiyah!" like his wagon driver had done, then waved his arms wildly, his heart pounding in his ears.

Not ten feet from where he stood, the horse neighed, reared up, and ran the other way. A surge of victory coursed through Samuel's veins. "Yes! I did it!" He clapped and punched his fist into the opposite palm.

"Now if only I can . . ." Tabitha said, her voice low as she drew in the rope. The horse stopped and shook her mane. Tabitha adjusted the size of the loop and once again raised her arm then began the swooping motions of the lasso.

As the horse saw the flying rope, she ran, this time right at Samuel. He abandoned his fear in favor of a blank void with one thought—stop the horse. Without time to think through his actions, he lunged forward and grabbed her neck in a terrifically vain attempt to slow it. The horse rose onto her hind legs, taking Samuel upward. A glance up brought into his vision the wildest eyes he had ever seen rolling back in the horse's head. Panicking, he let go and fell to the ground. The horse pawed the air and came down, just missing Samuel, who had fallen directly into the manure he had stepped in before.

He sat up gingerly, knowing by the moisture already seeping into his shirt that his back was covered in the nasty substance. He raised one hand and shook the green stuff from his fingers, disgust curdling his stomach. The horse whinnied loudly, startling him. The mare ran forward, and before Samuel could scramble out of the way, the horse thundered past, planting one hoof square on his thigh. A yell burst out at the shock of pain.

"Is everything all right?" Tabitha asked in a panic. "Is she hurt?"

Samuel's leg throbbed as he tried sitting up. He shook manure off his hand, wiped it on a clump of grass, and glared. "Oh, *she's* just dandy."

He rolled onto his knees and carefully put one foot and then the other under him. His left leg burned with pain as if—well, *since* a horse had stepped on it. Being able to walk to the edge of the corral showed that he had no broken bones, as far as he could tell, but he could only imagine the array of colors his thigh would exhibit in another few days—and the pain he'd be experiencing from now until then.

"Are—are you all right?" Tabitha asked, coming to his side as he clung to the corral fence, his right leg supporting all his weight.

Now she asks.

"I'll be fine," Samuel said, smiling through gritted teeth.

"I'm sorry," Tabitha said, covering her mouth. Her eyes crinkled at the corners with sympathy and a bit of humor. "My aim isn't all that good anymore. I was hoping before that whomever Brother Carlisle sent would be a good hand at this type of thing."

Samuel put weight on his leg and sucked in his breath at the sharp jolt shooting up it. "Sorry. I should have left."

"No, no. I'm glad you stayed," Tabitha said, coming over to him. Her voice registered sincerity. "I'm so sorry you got hurt on my account."

The cabin door opened, and Jeremiah Hancock lumbered out. Tabitha started with surprise. "Mr. Hancock. What are you doing here? I thought you were . . ."

"A convict? In jail? Yeah, well, I got out on bail. Planning on using the time to prove my innocence."

Tabitha swallowed hard; she seemed unnerved. Apparently *this* was the reason she had been so eager to get the horse removed today—Mr. Hancock's supposed absence. She shifted her feet and said, "I wasn't expecting you."

"Obviously." He snorted. "Your little article didn't help me much, so thanks for nothing."

"Funny you'd say that," Tabitha said, seeming to regain her spunk.

"Oh?" Jeremiah retorted.

"Apparently some people are upset that instead of condemning you outright, I left the question of your guilt unanswered."

Jeremiah's mouth quirked into what might have been a smile. "Interesting, that." He ambled over to the far side of the corral, where he rested his arms across the top and growled, "So, it doesn't look like you're having any luck, are ya?"

"No, not yet," Tabitha said as cheerfully as if she had informed him that the mail hadn't arrived. Samuel noted a fire in her eyes as she turned around and retied the rope.

Jeremiah spat on the ground. "Well, you'd better get it done. You're running outta time. If that beast isn't off my property by Thursday, I'm selling it to a man out in Ephraim."

"Just one minute," Tabitha said. "You said I had until *Friday*."

"Now I'm sayin' Thursday," he said, his voice gravelly. "The man over in Ephraim is willing to pay eight dollars for her. That's three more than you paid, remember."

"But—"

"Mr. Hancock, I'm surprised at you," Samuel said, stepping forward with a slight limp. "I took you to be a man of your word. If you said she had until Friday, she should have until Friday. And after all, the lady *did* defend you in the paper."

"*Defend* is a bit of a strong word," Jeremiah said. His eyes narrowed, and he grunted. "Fine. Friday then. But not a minute longer." He returned to his side door and pulled it open with stubby, grime-coated fingers. "But I expect payment today, then. Used any money I had—and my pig—making bail."

"That's no problem," Tabitha said. She dropped the rope and hurried to the side of the corral where she had left a bag. "Here it is," she said, walking around to meet him. He closed the door of the house, clearly surprised that she already had the funds with her. "Five dollars, plus the two bits you paid for the newspaper ad."

The wrinkles in Hancock's deeply lined brow deepened into furrows. "Why are you giving me these extra two bits?" he asked suspiciously. He opened the bag and fished inside, pulling out a twenty-five cent piece. "I don't want to be beholden to nobody."

"Oh, no—it's yours," Tabitha said, waving the coin away. "See, I work at the *Sentinel* now, which is how I found out about your intentions to sell. I decided I wanted the horse, so there was no use in running the advertisement in the paper." As soon as the words left her mouth, she regretted them. They sounded so hollow, her justification empty.

"You never ran the notice?" Hancock said sullenly.

"I tried to tell you earlier," Tabitha rushed on. "Do you remember when I came over and offered to buy her? I had the two bits with me then, but I didn't get a chance to return it. I tried a couple of times, but—"

"What kind of shoddy, shady kind of business are you purportin' to run?" Hancock snarled.

"I'm sorry. I really am. I didn't mean anything like that. I figured since you already had a buyer—at your own asking price—there wouldn't be a need for the notice, and you'd get your money back anyway."

At that, Hancock just glared at her, seemingly unable to argue with the logic—he hadn't lost anything after all. "Fine," he said, pulling the tie closed on the bag. "Just get 'er off my land."

He turned to leave, but Tabitha walked after him, interjecting, "Please, Mr. Hancock, could you help us? It would be a quick and easy matter if we could just get her lassoed and tied to a wagon—"

"I'm not in the mood to be all that helpful," Hancock shot back. "Not when I've spent time in the city jail and am accused of something I didn't do. The horse is *your* problem, not mine. I'll have nothing to do with her anymore." Hancock stabbed the air with a finger. "And you'd better not be thinking about using my wagon or my animals." His eyes caught at something lying in the corral. "Is that my rope?"

Tabitha glanced at it and coughed, feeling suddenly sheepish—and shady. "It—it is. I didn't think you'd mind if we used it."

"And you didn't think I'd be around to see you taking it, neither. Use your own." He gave her a look of disdain—and Samuel a look of derision—then shook his head and walked back to his house, banging the door shut behind him.

Tabitha jumped at the noise, then turned to Samuel. Tears filled her eyes. "Thank you for convincing him to keep his end of the agreement. I don't know what I would have done if he hadn't relented. At least she's really mine—until Friday." She rubbed her fingertips against her forehead, as if she could smooth out her worry. She threw her arms open into the air. "But now what are we going to do?" She asked the air as much as Samuel, since they both knew he didn't have any answers.

She climbed back into the corral and picked up the rope. Her thumbs rubbed up and down the ends as she eyed the beautiful horse on the other side. "I can't lasso worth beans. Jeremiah won't help. Father's health isn't what it used to be—he can't run his own land anymore, and he uses a cane—so I'm sure he can't wield a lasso . . ."

And I'm useless, Samuel added mentally.

She gestured toward the horse, which now stood pressed against the far side. Tabitha's tongue curled around her front teeth, and her eyes squinted in thought. "We need a wagon, because even if we get her lassoed, we certainly can't control her enough to walk her to Brother McCleve's place."

"No, not without being halter-broken first," Samuel agreed, as if he knew much of anything about horses. He did know this much, however—Hancock's horse wouldn't behave for anyone, including the young boy who had taken Samuel down a few notches with the filly. "Tricky situation," he added.

"It truly is," Tabitha agreed, studying the corral. She stretched out her arms and motioned as she spoke. "What we need is a chute built onto the corral, where it narrows toward the end, so she can't turn around. We could scare her into the chute, drive her down the end, and block her from behind so she can't get out."

"Won't being scared and trapped get her more upset?" Samuel asked warily.

"At first," Tabitha agreed. "But we can talk to her, calm her down, and eventually get a lead rope on her. Then we attach it to the wagon, and a team of two horses can do the job of leading her along. It would work. I'm sure of it." The more she spoke, the faster her words came out, the more confident she looked. But then she sighed. "That is, it would work if we could build a chute onto the corral in the first place."

Samuel's mind caught onto one phrase. *Build a chute? I* can *build things. Tools* belong *in these hands,* he thought.

"You're smiling," Tabitha said with eyebrows raised. "Do you have an idea?"

"If you can figure out how to get her into it, I can build the chute. There's some old wood behind the stables I can use."

Tabitha's eyes shot wide open. "Are you in earnest? You'd do that for me? Goodness, that is so generous. I don't know how to repay you. I . . ." She broke off her effusion, then quietly finished with, "Thank you, Samuel."

"I'm glad I can be useful," he said, meaning every syllable of it. He'd finally work at something he was good at and feel as if he could contribute to the welfare of someone here in Zion.

CHAPTER 13

"GET UP, SLEEPY HEAD," TABITHA said gently the next day. She opened the muslin curtains, and Will grimaced as bright light streamed in.

"That hurts," he said, his voice sounding strained as he pulled the bedclothes over his head and burrowed under them like a mole.

"Now, now, let me see you," Tabitha said, sitting on the edge of his bed. Smiling, she drew back the quilt, then furrowed her brow when Will's face came into view. It was covered in bright red dots. She put her hand against his forehead and found it blazing hot, then leaned back and breathed out with worry. "I think you have the chicken pox."

"What are those?" Will asked then put a hand to his throat, wincing with pain.

"It means you're sick, that's what." Tabitha eased him back against his pillow. "I'll steep some chamomile in hot water. That'll soothe your throat and help you feel better."

"Thanks, Mama," Will said with a wan smile.

Poor boy looks like a speckled toad, Tabitha thought, standing and moving to the door. She pulled the bedroom door closed behind her. *I hope it's not a serious case.* She had heard of children with chicken pox who ranged from being mildly uncomfortable for a week to a child dying from the disease—and hoped Will would be out of bed in short order.

"Mother," Tabitha called as she entered the kitchen. "Will and I will be staying home today. It appears he has the chicken pox."

"Oh goodness," her mother said, throwing a dishcloth onto the table. She looked ready to bolt into the bedroom. "Poor boy."

"I'm sure he'll be fine," Tabitha said, then rummaged through a cupboard. "Just a bit feverish and the like. Enough that I'd better stay with him if possible. I don't have the heart to leave him," she added, knowing that her mother would offer to stay with Will.

"Can your father or I help with your work at the newspaper?" her mother asked. "That is, if you need anything done today so you can stay here with an easy mind."

"There's certainly work to do, but I don't know how I can give it to you," Tabitha said as she measured chamomile leaves into a kettle. "Perhaps I'd better go to the office a little later for an hour or two just to make sure things are moving smoothly." Printing day was several days away, so there wasn't as much work waiting as there would be later in the week.

"Do," her mother said, taking the kettle from her and filling it with water. "I'll sit with Will while you go."

Tabitha smiled as her mother put the water onto the stove. It felt good to have her mother do such a small act of kindness. To have someone care for *her,* even in this slight way, to have family to turn to when she needed help. "Thank you, Mother," she said, and knew she meant it more sincerely than she ever had before.

Her mother looked up, curious. "For what?"

"For helping with that," Tabitha said, nodding toward the stove.

Her mother put a hand to Tabitha's cheek. "It's a pleasure to finally be *able* to do something for you besides pray and write letters. I'm so glad you're home."

Tabitha covered her mother's hand with her own. For so long Tabitha had been the mother. She pressed her mother's hand to her cheek, relishing the sensation of being a daughter. The side door opened, and her father came in, struggling beneath an armload of firewood. Tabitha hurried to his side and took half the load.

"Thank you, dear," he said, depositing his load in the woodbin. The pieces knocked against one another until they settled in a heap. Tabitha did the same with her load then wiped her palms together.

"Father, you shouldn't be doing that," she scolded. He used a cane to get about; what was he thinking trying to lug in firewood?

He ignored her, instead smiling and saying, "Morning, dear." He spoke a bit breathlessly. He gave his wife a kiss on the cheek then looked about the room as if something weren't quite right. "Where's Will? Isn't he usually up with the rooster?"

"Usually, yes," Tabitha said. "But not when he comes down with the chicken pox."

"Chicken pox?" Her father was to the bedroom door before Tabitha could say anything. He opened it and peered inside. Through the gap, he made a silly face, got a tired giggle out of Will for his efforts, then closed the door and returned to the kitchen. With a shake of his head, he said, "Poor little tyke looks like he was bit by a swarm of mosquitoes."

"Father," Tabitha said in attempted reproach, but she couldn't help laughing.

Instead of answering, her father walked to the door and grabbed his jacket.

"Where are you going?" Tabitha asked, noting that her mother had gone back to stirring a pot of mush and didn't seem at all surprised that he was leaving.

"Goin' to fetch another elder," he said, shrugging into the coat. "Gotta get that boy a priesthood blessing."

Of course. Why hadn't she thought of that? Having a priesthood holder in her home was almost a forgotten concept to Tabitha. How sad that seeking a blessing didn't occur to her even when it was for her son's sake.

She crossed to her father, rose up, and kissed his bewhiskered cheek. "Thanks, Papa."

He waved away the sentiment. "It's what grandfathers are for, I figure," he said, giving her a bone-crushing hug anyway.

Before he could leave, a knock sounded. Her father's brow knitted together. "Who could that be at this hour? It's a bit early for a social call," he said, moving to the front door with Tabitha following behind.

He opened it to reveal Samuel Barnett on the other side, holding his hat in one hand and a couple of crinkled papers in the other. "Good morning," he said with a slight bow. He seemed a bit uneasy, as if his eyes didn't know where to look. They drifted to the ground, to his greeter's face, to his hands. "You're Brother Chadwick?"

"That's right," her father said. "Can I help you with something?"

Samuel held out the papers in his hand. "Actually, yes. I wanted to show your daughter . . . Is Miss Chadwick here?"

Tabitha hurried forward. "Mr. Barnett is a friend of mine," she explained, then said to their visitor, "Good morning, Samuel. What brings you here?"

Samuel looked from her father to Tabitha. The moment felt uncharacteristically like a courtship situation—as if she and Samuel were young things in need of a chaperone. Tabitha glanced at her father. "I'll be fine," she said as a gentle hint.

He nodded. "Of course." But as he moved away, he paused, turned back, and shot at Samuel, "Are you an elder?"

"Uh, yes," Samuel said. "Why?"

Tabitha suddenly understood and felt grateful to her father for thinking of it. "Because my grandson is sick. He needs a blessing."

Samuel blanched. "I've never—I don't know how—"

"That doesn't matter," Tabitha's father said, returning to the door. He urged Samuel along by the shoulder. "I'll teach you; it's simple. All we need really is someone with worthiness and faith. You got those, I presume?"

"Well, yes . . ." Samuel said as he folded the papers and tucked them into his waistband

"Terrific. He's in here."

The two men went into the bedroom, and Tabitha followed behind. Will burrowed deeper under the quilt, either shy or embarrassed at having a spotted face. She watched as her father explained how to anoint the oil on Will's head and what words to say. The two of them placed their hands on Will's head and pronounced first the anointing and then the blessing. Will kept his face covered the entire time, revealing only a shock of tawny hair, which was practically hidden by two sets of large hands. As the men spoke in turn, a warmth and peace filled the room. Suddenly Tabitha realized just how much she had lacked over the years she had lived without a spouse, one more thing she had lost with Fred's death—the peace of having the priesthood nearby, ready to call upon in times of need.

Truly, a priceless gift.

When they finished, Will gave his grandfather a big hug, and Samuel discretely left, perhaps aware that Will didn't want to be seen by a stranger. After he left the room, Samuel walked to the front door.

"May I speak with you for a moment?" he asked Tabitha.

"Of course," she said, following him out to the porch. "Let me just check on Will first." She peeked into his room, where Will was sitting with his grandfather, learning how to fold a piece of paper into a glider.

Smiling, she pulled the door closed then led Samuel outside to the porch and closed the door behind them. She stepped to his side by the railing. "Thank you," she said, folding her arms against the morning cold. "I'm so grateful you were here to help Will."

"You're welcome," Samuel said. "I'm glad I could. I was ordained a day before we boarded the ship. I didn't know why they had decided to make me an elder already, but I'm glad they did."

"So am I," Tabitha said, looking up at him admiringly. Samuel was truly a remarkable man—and didn't seem to have any understanding about that fact. He had no ego, no self-important air, no off-putting pride—simply a quiet strength, humility, and a desire to be good.

He pulled out the folded papers from his waistband. "Here. I sketched out my ideas for how to build the chute we talked about yesterday," he said, smoothing them on the top of the railing. "But I wanted to make sure what I had in mind would work. I wanted to get a good start on it today . . . I hope it's all right that I came so early."

"It's no problem," Tabitha said. She stepped closer and looked over the sketches showing the edge of the corral and a chute coming off one end. Samuel had made the drawing in detail, showing places he'd reinforce and where pieces were attached to one another. "I don't know anything about carpentry, but this looks simply wonderful."

"It'll work, then?" Samuel pressed. "Is there anything I should change?"

"Let's see . . ." Tabitha pointed to the page and traced the lines. "Perhaps the opening could be wider here where it attaches to the corral. And maybe have it curve a little more like the corral does. That way as she runs forward, she'll think she's just following the edge of the pen and won't realize she's running into a dead end."

"Good idea," Samuel said. He penciled in a curve. "Like this?"

"Exactly."

"What about keeping her in the chute at the narrow end? Should I build a gate right here?"

"No. We'll probably have to block her in gradually as she moves forward," Tabitha said. "So a gate would be tricky. Sliding thick poles through the sides would probably work better. They'd prevent her from backing out, and we can move them forward as needed along the posts."

Samuel drew in some vertical slats between which the poles could be placed. "Anything else?"

"I don't think so."

He folded up the papers and tucked them back into his waistband. "Glad I could be of use to someone," he said with a self-deprecating smile. "I'll let you know how it goes. Are you . . . going to the newspaper office already? I could walk you there."

"No, not yet," Tabitha said, feeling disappointment at the fact. "I'll go a bit later on, but I'll stay here with Will for a spell first."

"Of course," Samuel said. "Maybe another time."

"Yes, another time. Definitely."

"Good day, then." Samuel nodded, and their eyes held for a second. Tabitha's stomach flipped over itself, and she put a hand to her middle.

As she watched him turn and saunter down the pathway, Will's voice carried through from the back room. "Mama?"

"Oh, Will, you poor thing," Tabitha said, returning to the present with a jolt. She picked up her skirts and hurried back into the house. When she reached Will, he wore a pathetic expression on his face, even though his grandfather stood beside the bed. "What's wrong?" Tabitha asked, feeling a clenching in her heart.

"I needed you." His glider was abandoned beside him.

"A grandfather just isn't the same as a mother," her father said, stepping to the side.

"Well, I'm here now," Tabitha said. She picked up Will's lanky six-year-old body from the bed, tucked a blanket around him, and carried him to the rocking chair. "Would you like to rock with me for awhile?"

He nestled close to her and nodded. "That's so much better, Mama." He took a deep, easy breath and closed his eyes. Tabitha rocked back and forth, her cheek on the top of his head. Her father quietly excused himself. Periodically Tabitha kissed Will's hair or stroked his face, then held him a little closer. After a time, her mother brought in the chamomile in a ceramic mug, but Will was sleeping soundly in Tabitha's arms.

Her mother quietly placed the drink on the end table by the bed, smoothed Will's hair from his face, then leaned in and pressed her cheek against her daughter's. Tabitha closed her eyes and smiled. "Thank you," she whispered.

With a smile that said, "You're welcome," her mother left, and Tabitha closed her eyes again, leaning her head against the back of the rocking chair.

Mother, daughter.

Mother, son.

This was how it was meant to be. This felt right.

* * *

Tabitha made only a brief appearance at the *Sentinel* office that day; she couldn't bear to leave Will for more than the few minutes it took to meet with her staff and delegate assignments so she could race back home. She assigned Natalie the job of manning the telegraph line and managing the incoming advertisements, most of which would probably arrive with the post that afternoon. She needed to investigate further on the Hancock–Daggett situation, but that would simply have to wait. Since it wasn't yet time for typesetting or the press run, if there was a day for Will to be home sick, this was it.

When she returned to the bedroom, he reached an arm toward her. "Mama! I need you!"

Tabitha sat on the rocking chair and pulled him onto her lap again. "I'm here now, baby," she said as he snuggled close. His fever seemed to have ebbed, and he didn't seem to feel too itchy, either.

Thank you, she thought, sending a prayer heavenward. The priesthood blessing seemed to have had an effect already.

"Here," her mother said softly. "Use this." She handed Tabitha a cool, damp cloth and set a bowl with more water on the end table. A second, smaller bowl held soda to dab onto the spots and ease the itching. "He sure missed you. Even a grandmother won't do when a mother's love is in order."

"I need my mama," Will said in a groggy voice as he snuggled close.

Tabitha kissed Will's head and rocked gently. "And I need my Will."

CHAPTER 14

SAMUEL LOADED UP THE OLD wood and all the tools he'd need and had Stephen drive the lot over to Jeremiah's place. Any extra time Samuel could find over the next couple of days was spent behind the barn at the Hancock place, building the chute that would help capture the mare. With few nails to spare, he used each one judiciously and made do otherwise—fitting joints together, using rope, and holding sections together with glue. No point in using labor-intensive wooden biscuits to hold anything together, he figured, when they wouldn't be using the chute again. Any nails could be taken out and reused later.

Sawing another length of a board, his arm went back and forth as the blade cut, sending sawdust flitting into the air and floating downward. When the chunk dropped off the end to the ground, Samuel wiped his brow with his sleeve and reached down to retrieve the piece. An evening breeze kicked up, wafting through Hancock's stable before it reached his nose—and with it, the stench of the animals he so loathed.

He walked to the end of the chute, where he was building a sturdy gate, and eyed the fit of the crosspiece he had just cut. Satisfied that it had the correct dimensions, he slathered it with glue, held it in place, then attached a clamp to hold it together until the section dried.

Hands on hips, he surveyed his work. The next day was Friday, Hancock's deadline for getting the horse off his property. The chute would be ready by morning, so assuming he and Tabitha didn't run into much trouble getting the horse into it . . .

But his thoughts stopped there. What were the chances of *that?* Samuel had worked tirelessly on the contraption so it would be done in time. Whenever he thought there wasn't enough time to finish, he'd first remember the haunted look in Tabitha's eyes when Hancock had given his ultimatum. Then he'd remember what he told her— that he could get it done in time, no problem. He'd help Tabitha get the miserable horse out of harm's way.

Another brush of wind brought the odor of animal waste over him, and he grimaced. *This had better be a success,* he told himself.

He picked up a stick and began figuring the next length of wood, thinking about how he would define "success."

Making her happy would fall under that category, he decided.

But he purposely didn't allow himself to think too far, such as defining whether the "her" in his thoughts referred to Tabitha or the horse.

* * *

When Friday arrived, the chute was complete, if rather awkward-looking. It curved to the right, just as Tabitha had suggested, and got narrower at the end. The gate would open to let the horse out once it was tied securely with two ropes—again, per Tabitha's suggestion. Several feet from the opening, he created points where the poles could be inserted every six inches or so as the horse moved forward, preventing it from backing out. The thing wasn't all that pretty, but it was sturdy and would do the job. When it was time to round up the horse, they'd still need to dismantle part of the corral and attach the chute to that.

Samuel put the final touches on the chute that morning, tightening a section here, adjusting the fit there, experimenting with pushing the poles in and out, until he was satisfied that the whole thing would work. It was strong enough to withstand even a healthy, vibrant—spooked—horse. He went back to the stables to wait for Tabitha. They'd hook up a team of Brother Carlisle's horse and head over to Jeremiah's together.

Moments after he arrived, Brother Carlisle approached, holding out a letter. "This is for you," he said. "From Sister Chadwick. My wife said she dropped it off a couple of hours ago. Hope it's not too late, whatever the message is."

Samuel unfolded the note, hoping it didn't contain any bad news about Tabitha's son. If the boy were worse off, she wouldn't be able to come to transfer the horse—and then it would revert back to Jeremiah's ownership. He couldn't let that happen. To his relief, the note confirmed that Tabitha would be along soon. Her son's fever had broken, and he was on the mend. He had spent a couple of days resting, but today he was up and about. Samuel looked at his watch and noted that she would be arriving any minute.

"Good news?" Brother Carlisle asked.

"Yes, it is," Samuel said, folding the note. "Everything is on schedule. Now, which horses did you say we could use?"

"Take Blossom and Hank," he said, waving Samuel into the building. "They're the two calmest horses we've got. Use the wagon out back."

They stopped before Blossom's stall. Temperament aside, she was also the second-largest horse, so Samuel had doubts about her. Just because she *intended* to be gentle didn't mean she couldn't accidentally flatten a man. He knew a large dog that had once bowled him over in its attempts to play in the streets of London.

Brother Carlisle stuck a piece of straw between his teeth and nodded to Blossom, who ate her morning meal of oats. "She'll be less likely to get spooked if that wild mare acts up. Same with Hank," he added, jabbing his thumb over his shoulder at the other horse—the biggest one of the lot.

"Will you help me hook them up?" Samuel asked casually.

"Nah," Brother Carlisle said. "I wasn't planning on being here much at all today. Just came by to bring you that note. I've got grandchildren visiting from Price, and I've got to get back to them. You'll find the collars, hames, traces, and everything else you'll need on the shelves over there."

How Brother Carlisle continued to be oblivious to how uneasy and unskilled Samuel still was with the stable animals, he'd never know. The man somehow never noticed how Samuel avoided contact with anything on four legs by volunteering for jobs like shoveling muck—as much as he detested doing it.

Brother Carlisle took the straw from between his teeth and said, "Be sure to rub them down and get 'em some oats when you're done."

Then he walked off down the corridor and out the door. If it hadn't been for the grandchildren visiting, Samuel might have called him back. Instead he hung back with a lurching stomach. Directly behind him, Dolores kicked and bellowed as if in warning.

"Don't you be worrying, you old cow," he shot over his shoulder. "I'll have nothing to do with *you* today." Then, thinking of transporting the wild mare, he added under his breath, "I'm afraid that I'll have something even worse than you to contend with."

He reached up to a hook on the wall and grabbed Blossom's bridle, figuring that it was the first item he'd need to get the horses ready to go. He hated putting on bridles; he was so bad at it. The only way he could get the horse to take the bit was to smear a little honey on the metal pieces. On tasting the sweet treat, the horse would practically gobble up the bit—and Samuel always hoped it didn't take off a finger in the process. He had no honey with him today.

As he opened the stall door, the hinges whined, making Blossom's ears perk up and her head turn toward the noise. She shifted her feet, rotating her heft in his direction. Holding the bridle, Samuel froze, both arms raised warily. He tracked every hoof movement to make sure he wouldn't end up with a broken foot.

His heart began thumping in his chest. *I can do this,* he thought. *Thousands of men do this every day and live to tell about it. Come on. Do it already, you ninny.*

Slowly, he lowered his arms and held out a hand to Blossom so the horse could get accustomed to his scent. She nuzzled his palm as if searching for a treat. *So far so good.* He stepped forward gingerly, first one foot and then the other. He shifted the bridle in his hands, the metal pieces clinking against one another.

"Very good," he said aloud—commending both himself and the horse—as he raised his right arm, keeping the bit low in the left. "You're going out today with Hank."

When he put the bit close to her, she shied away, pulling her head to one side. Gritting his teeth, he tried again. "Come on, girl," he said, mimicking the quiet, even voice he had heard other stable hands use. "Easy does it now." He prepared himself again, ready to smooth the bridle over the horse's face and behind the ears—if only she'd let him get near.

Blossom neighed irritably and swayed, shifting her feet. Suddenly the bulk of her abdomen pushed against Samuel. He stepped back, raising his arms out of the way, and found himself pinned between the side of the stall and the horse.

Gentle, my eye, he thought irritably. *This beast is deliberately holding me hostage.* With the bridle dangling from his fingers, he placed both hands against the side of the horse and pushed. She didn't even seem to notice. Her enormous ribcage rose and fell with her breath, alternately squeezing and releasing Samuel's middle. When she shifted slightly, he tried to get a better foothold. His feet couldn't find purchase on the wet straw, and instead he slipped, catching himself from falling to the ground by grabbing the top of the wall. But before he could stand, Blossom shifted closer. Now he was pinned against the wooden partition by his chest and couldn't even get his boots underneath him for support.

This is ridiculous, he thought, fear for the horse being drained away in the wake of rising anger. He pushed against the horse again without any effect. His boot soles scrambled beneath him but found no traction. "Get out of my way, you stupid creature. Get off!"

The squeaking of hinges sounded. Samuel snapped his head around; so did the horse, which not only looked to the sound but moved toward it. Blossom released him so suddenly that he dropped straight onto a patch of fresh manure, landing clumsily on his backside with an "Oomph!"

"Oh!" came a surprised and amused voice.

Samuel grimaced at the muck he had landed in, certain that no other stable hand fell into manure this often, and looked toward the voice. *Tabitha.* His ears grew instantly hot. "Morning," he managed in what he hoped was a cool, even tone instead of the heated frustration he felt.

Tabitha stood at the stall opening, biting her lips until they were white. Humor toyed at the corners of her eyes, and he could tell that it took effort for her not to laugh. "Can I help you?" she asked, then cleared her throat, stifling a chuckle.

Samuel debated. Telling her *no* would be an out-and-out lie. On one hand, as a stableman he needed to learn to harness a horse to a wagon by himself, so perhaps he should send her away and figure it out alone. Telling her *yes* would be true and would certainly expedite the matter. But it would also strip him of any shred of manhood he might still possess in her eyes.

Then again, he didn't know what in tarnation to do with hames or collars or . . . what was the other thing Brother Carlisle had listed? Traces?

Before he could answer, Tabitha stepped into the enclosure and leaned down for the bridle, which had fallen into the straw.

"She's a moody one," Samuel warned, holding the sides of the stall to keep his footing as he stood. Once vertical again, he grabbed a handful of dry straw and used it to clean off his pants and hands. By the time he looked up, the horse was on its way out of the stall. The bridle hung on its hook, where Tabitha must have returned it. Apparently a bridle wasn't what was needed to hook up the horses. Tabitha instead held the lead rope and clicked her tongue. Blossom obediently followed.

As she and the horse disappeared down the corridor, Samuel searched for something to say and called, "Glad to hear your son's doing better."

"I'm sure a lot of that has to do with the blessing. So thank *you*," Tabitha called over her shoulder. She paused, and miraculously, the horse did the same. Had Samuel been leading it, he was sure it would have walked right over him. She gestured toward the back door. "Is the wagon out back?"

"Yes . . . yes, that's right." Samuel stood there, dumbfounded at how well she handled the horse—and how breezily she seemed to stand there, as if she hadn't done anything more significant than put on her own boots. "Here, let me open the doors for you."

I can do that much without landing on my face, he thought, scooting past her and hurrying down the passage to the large back doors. He removed the wooden crosspiece and pushed the doors open, after which Tabitha followed behind with the horse. To her credit, as she passed by, she didn't laugh or say anything about what had happened in the stall, not the least of which was that apparently Blossom didn't need the bridle, at least not yet.

She walked outside to a ring in the barn wall, where she secured Blossom. She returned inside for Hank, and when he too was tied to the ring, she began decking the horses out, beginning with slipping the large leather collars over their heads. Samuel watched her hands moving deftly and without hesitation, knowing exactly what to do next and where each piece belonged. Soon she led horses to the wagon and hitched them up. The golden afternoon sun struck her hair, creating a halo. She paused long enough to tuck a stray lock behind her ear then stepped to the other side of the horse, drawing the reins along what he now knew were the traces, since that's what Tabitha had just called them. She turned to him.

"All done," she said, wiping her hands and putting them on her hips. Her smile triggered something in Samuel's chest, something that seemed to waken his heart and make it thump. It took a moment for him to recover before being able to speak.

"Thank you," he managed. "I . . . well, you know me." He shrugged and laughed at himself as he remembered the open door, which he had stood beside mutely as he watched her. He pushed one side closed and then the other, wondering wildly if Tabitha were watching his back. If he looked and she wasn't watching, his ego would be trampled. On the other hand, if she was looking his way, he'd be caught wondering about that very thing. He couldn't bear either, so he stifled the urge to look over his shoulder and see—and intensely hoped that regardless, she wouldn't notice the heat creeping up his neck.

With the doors safely shut, he returned to the borrowed wagon and the horses. "Ready?" he asked, and mentally answered his own question. *Hardly. But here goes nothing, as they say.*

He handed Tabitha into the wagon and climbed in after her. She held out the reins in one hand as if offering them. "Would you like to, or shall I?"

Unable to be a complete infant about such matters, he determined to at least attempt to behave like a man on the frontier was supposed to. "Oh, I'll do it," he said, cavalierly taking the leather pieces and holding them in each hand as he had seen others do it. "You can have a turn on the way back."

When we're hauling a wild horse.

To his amazement, he managed to drive without much trouble, although navigating the corners became interesting when Samuel realized that the extent of his driving knowledge consisted of starting and stopping the wagon. For the first two corners, when it was painfully clear that he had no concept of how to get the horses to veer right or left, Tabitha leaned over without a word and pulled on the correct rein, then placed her hands back in her lap, apparently enjoying the scenery.

"Thank you," Samuel said both times, grateful for her help—and for the fact that she did it without show. He knew many women who would never have such consideration for a man's feelings, instead laughing at him for his ineptness. Admiration for this remarkable woman flowed over him. If only he had the courage to say such things outright—although he wasn't sure what exactly he would say if he had the gumption. Regardless, doing so might send the wrong message.

Or would it? That depended on what message he wanted to send to Tabitha Chadwick. He already felt drawn to her. They had both lost a spouse. Yet they were both relatively young, with lives ahead of them . . . alone.

A matter of weeks ago, he would have said he couldn't have imagined spending the rest of his life in this forsaken desert without Helen. But he was gradually—oh so gradually—coming to accept the grim reality of her death, that he'd never have her with him again, not in this world. Yet he couldn't imagine spending years and years as he had spent the last few weeks—as a boarder, working only for himself, spending his nights in solitary, uneasy slumber. All alone, without someone to care for and experience it all with.

How did Tabitha view her future? Without turning his head, he eyed her from under his hat. The wagon hit a bump, and she gripped the side of the bench, then, as if sensing his gaze, looked over and smiled.

His heart repeated the acrobatics it had started in the stable yard.

"Turn," she said.

"What?" The world seemed to have faded, leaving little besides Tabitha's creamy skin and hazel eyes.

"Turn!" She reached for the reins and yanked them as the wagon was about to pass the cross street. Blossom and Hank made the sharp curve, whinnying in protest. Samuel jerked back to reality and took a firmer hold on the reins as the wagon lurched to the side, straining against the force of the turn.

As they straightened out, the horses shook their manes and continued in a more relaxed trot. Samuel let out an embarrassed chuckle then looked down and realized that his hands were entwined with Tabitha's. Hers were slender and warm to the touch, so much smoother than his callused, dry ones.

Her gaze followed his, tracking from the horse to their hands, then up to his face. She lowered her eyes shyly and slipped her hands from his. "Sorry," she said, a sudden patch of rosy color appearing on each cheek. Samuel had a sudden image in his mind of leaning over and kissing each spot. He shook his head lightly to clear the thought. Getting distracted by a pretty woman was proving costly to his masculine pride. If he kept this up, he'd wreck the wagon and lose the horses.

Not that he regretted a moment of it if it meant holding her hands and seeing her blush.

CHAPTER 15

SAMUEL AND TABITHA SPENT THE next hour or more working at Hancock's corral, dismantling a section of the fence so the squeeze chute could be put into place. The horse stayed on the far side, eyeing them warily. Then they'd put the wagon on the other end and hope for the best in their efforts at getting the mare into the chute.

"You're sure about this part?" Samuel asked as they approached the fence. He could see no other way to use the chute than to take apart the fence, but having Jeremiah fly off the handle at them wouldn't be pleasant.

"I already spoke with Jeremiah about it," Tabitha said as she studied a knot in a section of weathered leather lashings on a post. "He certainly didn't like the idea—balked quite a bit, in fact—but when I explained that it was either this or lasso the horse himself, he gave in. I think he's glad to be rid of her in spite of all his bluster about selling her elsewhere."

Samuel eyed the horse as he ducked under the fence and went inside, unwilling to put his back to the animal but knowing he'd have to as they undid the leather lashings. He worked faster at untying the pieces than Tabitha did, likely because his fingers were stronger and he often used his hands for such work. But also because he wanted *out* of the pen.

"Horses are funny things," Tabitha said as she struggled with a knot.

"How so?" Samuel asked, tossing aside a lashing and moving to one on the other side, which held the crosspiece he worked on. *"Funny things" are they?* He could think of several other descriptive words that applied better than *funny.*

"I've always found it amazing that as big and strong as they are, horses don't usually attack. They prefer to run away if they feel threatened."

"Really?" Samuel surreptitiously looked over at the skittish mare. He had been secretly waiting for her to run over and kick him until he saw stars.

"Really," Tabitha said, glancing up. She scowled at the knot then leaned down and tried biting the leather.

Samuel laughed. "That won't work; it's too weathered. Here." He pulled out a pocket knife and wiggled it under the sections of the knot, slowly releasing the tangle a tiny bit at a time.

"Thanks," Tabitha said when it was looser and she could undo the rest with her fingers. "Anyway, seems to me the only way horses can be truly tamed is when they respect the confidence of their masters, put their trust in the trainer or the rider." Her knot released, and she unwrapped the lashing, then went on. "Naturally, since a horse is so much more powerful than any man, it wouldn't have to obey. Yet a firm but kind hand can make the horse not only trust a rider, but also obey him . . . or her."

"Then Hancock's way of breaking doesn't work, does it?" Samuel asked.

Tabitha leaned against the nearest post and sighed, gazing at the mare. "No, it doesn't, which is why it's so sad when someone thinks they have to try forcing their will onto a horse. It's more than being cruel; it's a plain foolish way to break a horse if you want it to be of any use to you later."

"But it must work on some level," Samuel said. "Or no one would break a horse that way."

Tabitha's head tilted to one side and then the other. "Well, it works to a point," she said, going back to untying the pole from the post. "But in the long run, it ruins a good horse. Since a horse's first nature is to flee, not fight, if it's broken using fear and pain, it learns to be frightened of any person trying to control it. That can ruin a horse forever. But I don't think she's ruined. Not yet."

Samuel didn't follow. "If it's frightened and abused into submission, the horse is still in submission, isn't it? Not that I think whipping a living thing is right, but if it works, then it's understandable why some people would try it."

"How can I explain?" Tabitha wrinkled her forehead in thought, then said, "A good, solid horse will have confidence in its master and do what the master says." When Samuel nodded his agreement, she continued. "Even if it's scared or nervous, the animal can *feel* the calm confidence of the rider and be reassured by it. The horse will trust that whatever its master is ordering will be the best thing to do."

Comprehension slowly came over Samuel. "But a horse that is beaten into submission won't trust its rider. If it's in a threatening situation, it'll still try to flee."

"Exactly. It will panic and flee no matter what its master commands," Tabitha said with a nod, recognizing that he understood.

Samuel was feeling more comfortable all the time. Most likely, the mare behind him wouldn't attack him unless he gave it a good reason to.

Tabitha shrugged. "Training by fear is most unfortunate when it comes to injuries, because when a person gets hurt riding, it's quite often when the horse is frightened."

Samuel stiffened. Hancock's animal was definitely fearful right now. That didn't bode well.

Tabitha didn't seem to notice his unease. "Can we separate these two sections now?"

They hefted the top crosspiece to the ground, then worked quietly on the other two. With the area between two poles now open, they dragged the squeeze chute into place so it followed the curve of the corral. At last they were ready.

Tabitha's idea was to startle the horse and make it run toward the opening. If that worked, then Jeremiah's horse would run straight down the chute, thinking it could escape them through the end, only to pull up short at the dead end in the chute and not be able to turn around. They'd slide the poles in right after she passed so she couldn't back out into the corral.

"One of us will have to shoo her that direction, and the other will have to be near the wagon, ready to slide the poles into place," she said, moving toward the pen.

"You stay here; I'll go inside," Samuel said, raising a hand to prevent her approach. He couldn't let her go in there with a wild horse, no how. Not after learning that a scared horse is the most dangerous kind.

"Are you sure?" Tabitha asked, eyebrows raised.

"I'm sure," he said with a quick nod he hoped would convince her of his confidence. "You wait ready to slide the poles into place when she gets into the chute."

She smiled with pleasure—and possibly admiration. "All right," she said, then walked next to the chute, where she turned around. She lifted a pole, which she rested the end of on the chute, ready to slip into place. "Ready," she said.

Samuel had a feeling of swelling pride in his chest. Aside from demanding Jeremiah stay true to his agreement, this was the first time he had done something to appear, well, *masculine* for Tabitha. And she had noticed. He turned and faced the mare. She seemed to sense a change in the air, so she turned to face him. Pawing the ground, her ears folded back. A puff of air escaped her nose.

This feels like something from a bull fighting ring, Samuel thought. *But horses rarely attack,* he reminded himself. *They are afraid. They flee.* Gaining courage, he raised his arms wide, strode toward the horse, and yelled at it. "Har! Git! Hah!"

The mare pulled back, leaning against the pen. Encouraged, Samuel pressed forward with more of the same. Still yelling random noises, he moved left to force the horse the other direction. It whinnied and backed up. He risked a glance toward the wagon, where Tabitha stood, blocking the area between the end of the fence and the chute. She nodded encouragement.

Samuel made a sudden movement toward the mare; she turned and headed away from him, clearly unnerved. "Hah!" he yelled again, waving his arms. At first man and beast made progress by inches, but when they reached the gap in the fence, Samuel put all his effort into the job. He wanted the horse to run straight into the chute, not walk or hesitate—or worse, spook, hurting Tabitha in the process.

He took a deep breath, glanced down to ensure he wouldn't slip and fall, then let out a bellow and charged. When he was an arm's length from the animal, she neighed loudly and reared up on her back feet. For a moment, Samuel panicked. Would her powerful hooves come crashing down on his head?

But at the last second, the horse threw her bulk to one side, landing to Samuel's right. Before he could react, she turned about and ran. His stomach flipped over itself. The horse was heading straight for the chute. Would it turn and miss the opening? Samuel ran to the side, cutting off the horse in case it tried to turn back to the center of the pen. The horse saw him and shook her mane. Samuel yelled again, this time moving forward and smacking the horse on the rump. The impact jolted her forward, and she ran straight ahead, along the curve of the chute and toward the closed gate at the end. Tabitha gleefully slid the poles into place, making a secure section where the horse was trapped. Samuel stood there, stunned, staring at his hand.

I just swatted a horse.

Tabitha worked quickly, tying the poles with rope even as the mare tried backing out. Samuel joined her, securing each pole tightly.

"We did it!" Tabitha cried. She turned to him and threw her arms around Samuel's neck. "*You* did it!"

He wrapped his arms around her and breathed in her rosewater scent—then as the thrill of the moment cleared from their minds, they quickly released one another.

Tabitha took a step back and wrapped her arms about herself, holding her elbows. "Sorry," she said, shifting her weight and flushing, a crooked smile on her face. "I suppose the excitement went to my head."

"Me too," he said, but he wished she hadn't apologized—or that either of them had pulled away quite so quickly. "It was pretty exciting."

Especially for me, he thought, still unable to believe that he had faced a horse, charged at one. *Swatted* one. How had he managed it? He found the answer surprisingly simple—because he could not allow Tabitha to face the danger of a spooked animal.

"Come here," Tabitha said, beckoning. "I'll show you how to treat a horse."

They approached the chute, where the mare tried moving forward and backward, getting nowhere, of course. She began to quiver and shake.

"It's all right, girl. We're here to help," Tabitha said in a soft voice. "No one's going to hurt you anymore." She reached through the wood pieces and let her hands glide along the coat. The horse flinched under her touch and continued to tremble.

Samuel whispered to avoid upsetting the mare. "What do we do now? She's obviously terrified." He remembered all too well what *that* meant.

"We'll rub her down and talk to her for a spell until she realizes that we aren't going to hurt her. Horses are smart like that."

"And then?"

"Then we'll gradually put on a halter. And we'll need that big cotton rope around her neck too," Tabitha said, pointing to the wagon bed, where it was coiled. "If she pulls too hard—which is likely—she might break the halter altogether. Then we'll need the extra rope to restrain her. Without it, we'd be right back where we started from."

"Except that she wouldn't be in the corral anymore."

Tabitha smiled grimly. "Exactly. And she'd run away." She continued stroking the mare for some time, speaking softly, and the horse gradually calmed down. It seemed to take forever.

After some time, Tabitha spoke to Samuel, using the same easy voice she had been speaking in for the horse's sake. "Let's try the halter." It took several tries—plus going back to stroking and talking quietly to calm the mare yet again—but eventually she got the halter onto the horse, then tied the cotton rope around the neck as well. The horse no longer shook with fear; she seemed nervous but not nearly as skittish. Tabitha handed the ends of the two ropes to Samuel. "Will you tie both the halter rope and the cotton one to the wagon?" she asked. "Nice and tight so they'll stay."

He followed her instructions, and when they were both secured, Tabitha let out a deep breath. "I guess we're ready. I'll go take the reins. Do you mind opening the gate?"

"Not at all," Samuel said, a brazen lie. But he didn't want Tabitha in the way if the horse decided to bolt out of the chute. He unlocked the gate and slowly opened it. Instead of running forward, the horse pulled against the ropes, pulling her head back. Samuel watched for a moment before scurrying to the front of the wagon and climbing up. To his relief, Blossom and Hank didn't seem the least perturbed over the snorts and other noises the mare made behind them as she fought the ropes.

"How long do you suppose she'll resist?" Samuel asked.

"Shouldn't be too long," Tabitha said, shifting to look back at the horse, which was still tugging and pulling. "Her neck muscles will tire out pretty soon, and when she sees two other horses here, happy as clams, she'll figure out that we mean her no harm."

Tabitha turned back and eased the team forward at a slow pace, just enough to urge the mare forward. The horse took a couple of reluctant steps, still trying to rear back. Samuel looked over his shoulder, grateful they had a heavy wagon and two horses doing this job. Clearly, even a weak and emaciated horse had amazing strength when it felt vulnerable.

They made their way to the road, one slow revolution of the wheels at a time, the horse resisting every step. Tabitha glanced over from the reins. "Thank you," she said. "I don't know how I would have done this without your help. You've done so much."

"You're welcome," he said, wishing he could embrace her again, have another whiff of rosewater.

She flicked the reins to encourage the team to move a little faster. "Let's see if she's ready to follow. I want her away from this place."

"What about the fence?" Samuel asked. "If you need me to, I can come back and fix it later."

"That would be wonderful," Tabitha said. "I was planning on doing it tomorrow with my father, but he's not as strong as he used to be." As they rode, Tabitha's shoulders seemed to pull back, her head held higher. A light seemed to fill her eyes as happiness seeped out of every part of her at what they had accomplished.

And I got to be part of it, Samuel thought. *With her. What a lucky man am I.*

After they navigated the first corner, Tabitha smiled. "She's going to be all right now, isn't she?"

"You've done a good thing," he said, resting his palms on his thighs.

"*We've* done a good thing," she corrected, touching her hand to his for a second.

Her hand moved away, but he still felt the pressure of her fingers. He flexed his hand and made a fist, as if doing so might keep the feeling longer. Their arms touched slightly, and he couldn't help but be pleased that she didn't scoot over to make room between them. He breathed in deeply and looked to the side of the road, wonderment in his heart. He thought he'd never feel these kinds of things again. He had thought that the part of him capable of such emotion was buried at sea with Helen.

Helen.

The same kernel of guilt sat in the back of his mind, but this time he challenged it. What would Helen think of the stirrings of emotion he was feeling for Tabitha? Not that anything would ever result of them, he reminded himself. But thinking in purely theoretical terms . . .

He couldn't allow himself to think about such things if doing so were unfaithful to Helen's memory.

As they bumped along the road, the horse made anxious noises and dug her hooves into the dirt. Her neck muscles continued to strain against the ropes. The halter finally snapped, making Samuel look back; fortunately, the extra rope still held firm. As he turned forward, his gaze passed over Tabitha—her sweet face and determined eyes. She too looked at the horse, then returned to face front, relieved to see the cotton rope holding fast.

Samuel sighed and sat forward again, analyzing his guilt regarding Helen. If *he* had been the one to die, what would he have wanted for her? He pictured her in a boarding house like Mrs. Mirkins's. What would Helen have done to earn her keep? Perhaps weaving cloth, selling vegetables, or making soaps. She'd have gone to bed in a dark room with a narrow bed, lying in the cold emptiness, just as he did every night.

No, Samuel thought. *I wouldn't want that life for her. I'd want her to have companionship, someone to care for her, someone to love her.*

By the time they reached McCleve's round pen, which stood open, the horse was no longer straining against the rope. "Must be tired," Samuel said, gesturing toward the horse.

"Probably," Tabitha said. "She gave herself quite a run trying to fight for so long. I think she might have learned a thing or two, though. She might not be quite so scared now." She pulled the team to a stop. "Here we are."

"Here we are," Samuel repeated huskily. He looked at Tabitha, thinking now of what Helen would want for him.

She wouldn't want me *to live like this, either. She would want me to find someone else.*

"Samuel, are you . . . well?" Tabitha asked, tilting her head.

A slow smile spread across his face, and he nodded. "I'm quite well. Let's get her untied."

CHAPTER 16

"I CAN HARDLY BELIEVE WE managed it," Tabitha said, admiring the skittish horse walking about Brother McCleve's round pen. Samuel could hardly believe it, either. Not only that they'd gotten the mare there safely, but that Tabitha was able to lead it to the side and tie it up so they could get the wagon out of the pen. Now the mare rubbed against the posts, raced along the fence line, and whinnied, seemingly pleased to be unrestrained, her lead rope released from the side of the fencing.

Samuel and Tabitha had returned the wagon to the stable yard and rubbed down the horses, then went back to check on the mare and leave her some feed.

"We make quite a team," Samuel said with a nod. Tabitha smiled, still gazing at the horse as if she couldn't yet believe the beautiful creature was safely hers. She reached into the pen and grabbed some hay, then stood on a crosspiece and held it out, calling to the horse.

"Come here, girl," she said in a soothing voice. "Come here."

Not surprisingly, the horse did nothing more than warily eye Tabitha, who dropped the hay back into the pile and wiped her palms together, removing small bits that clung to her skin. With a sigh, she turned and leaned against the corral. "I'm glad we managed to get here before the Independence Day celebration started. I don't think she would have reacted well to that. There's always such a crowd gathered to watch the Maypole dance."

"Maypole?" Samuel echoed. "I haven't seen a Maypole in a crow's age. Why a Maypole for Independence Day?"

"Because they're fun," Tabitha said with a laugh. "This was always one of my favorite times of the year. I always made sure to be one of the Maypole dancers."

"*Was* one of your favorites?" Samuel asked. "You don't enjoy it anymore?"

Tabitha considered. "It's different now that I'm grown up. When I was younger, I loved doing the braiding, dancing with the other girls—it was fun to be the focus like that." Samuel didn't interrupt Tabitha. Instead he tried to picture her ten years younger and dancing around a pole with a streamer in her hand. She went on, her voice interrupting his thoughts. "Now that I'm older, I'd rather not have people staring at me."

She stopped talking and seemed pensive as she walked. It made Samuel take pause as he suddenly realized that Tabitha had experienced a lot of unwanted stares since coming back to Manti. In some ways he had thought of her as being as new to the place as he was.

She waved a hand as if shooing an annoying fly. "But that won't be something I need to worry about this year. The Maypole dance is for the younger set. I'll enjoy watching it this time."

As they walked, moving aimlessly down a street, Tabitha lapsed into a quiet thoughtfulness that seemed to border on worry or sadness. Eyeing her, Samuel continued to think on the idea of how much extra notice she was attracting lately and if that was what troubled her now. Perhaps she wished to simply fade into the scenery of dusty roads and scrub oak.

Unfortunately for her, Tabitha wasn't capable of evading notice in a place where so many people must have known her since before she could walk. Samuel had overheard a few conversations in town and in the Little Fort where townsfolk told stories dating to her childhood or discussed her late husband and his death. She had likely heard and seen the same things or was aware that people talked about her. If she cringed from the attention, Samuel certainly couldn't blame her. In her shoes, he probably wouldn't have come back home after leaving in the first place.

"My son has never seen a Maypole dance," Tabitha said, kicking up dust with her boots. "I think he'll enjoy it."

"He's well enough already?"

"Surprising, isn't it?" Tabitha said, gladness in her voice. "It's only been a couple of days. Sure amazing what a priesthood blessing can do."

"So where is the Maypole?" Samuel asked. "I don't recall seeing anything like that around here. Back in England, some cities keep their poles up year round."

Tabitha halted her step and pointed northward to an open area where a crowd was gathering. A tall, wooden beam well down the road rose into the air. "See? It has red, white, and blue streamers. They always keep it up after May Day so it can be used again for Independence Day. After the dance, there's lots of food, dancing, and games."

"So are you going?" he asked.

"For a bit," she said.

"Just for a bit?" He tilted his head and studied her, then added teasingly, "Why, is there something sinister I should know about the holiday? Is the food something terrible?"

"No," Tabitha said, a smile tugging at her mouth. "It's been a long day. I don't think I'll stay for all the festivities."

"You need to stick around and have some fun," Samuel insisted. "Besides, I could use some diversion and good food after all that work."

"You do deserve it," Tabitha agreed. "And Mrs. Mirkins might not be home tonight to cook for you, expecting you to eat in the square with everyone else, so it's good that you're going. You should go."

He looked over, wondering what exactly that meant. Did she *want* him with her or not? Was his coming a good thing because it was simply practical, as her words implied? Samuel decided to take a bold risk. "Do you mind if I join you and your family?"

Tabitha didn't flinch at the suggestion. "Not at all. My parents are bringing my son to meet me over by the fairgrounds." She nodded to the block ahead, where they were approaching the crowd gathered across the street west of Temple Hill. "I'm sure there's plenty of food. Mother always overcooks. She can't seem to adjust to preparing food without a house full of children, even though Charles, the baby, got married almost five years ago."

"I should probably clean up a bit first," Samuel said, gesturing to his trousers, which were covered in dirt and manure.

"I should too," Tabitha said, holding out her messy skirts. "Meet you back here in twenty minutes?"

"I'll be here," Samuel said.

* * *

Eighteen minutes later, Samuel returned to the street corner in clean clothes and combed hair, hoping that he didn't smell. Tabitha arrived a couple of minutes later, looking fresh and excited in a pale green calico.

"We clean up rather handsomely, don't we?" Tabitha asked with a smile, looking him up and down. It made the hairs on the back of his neck stand up. "Ready?" she asked.

"Very much so," Samuel said. They walked side by side down the street. Looking at their arms nearly brushing against one another, he suddenly felt the need to swallow a lump forming in his throat. While he had proceeded with every intention of enjoying the celebration with Tabitha, he suddenly felt pulled two ways.

First was the fact that he liked the idea of spending time with her—time that didn't involve an animal with enough strength to flatten him. The bruise on his thigh from earlier that week was plenty reminder of that. It had already turned a kaleidoscope of colors, and walking on it still caused minor discomfort. But at the same time, was it really wise to venture into such a public event with a woman—so soon?

It's not the idea of being with Tabitha that's bothering me so much as the idea of betraying Helen.

The thought struck him with force, and he had to admit it carried significant weight, even after his mental conversation earlier about how Helen would approve, that she'd want his happiness with another woman. But Samuel hadn't really noticed any woman besides Helen in nearly three years, when he had first laid eyes on the beautiful being who he was determined would become his wife.

Not until Tabitha, at least. Now, anytime he thought of her, he felt warm inside—but that sensation was quickly followed by an icy guilt that seemed to course through his veins. Inevitably, thoughts of Helen came on the heels of the ones about Tabitha. But he couldn't stop thinking about Helen watching his every move from above. She couldn't miss him; the boots still bore their red streaks.

It's all right, he tried to assure himself. *Helen won't mind.*

"I think I'll stay long enough to eat with my parents," Tabitha said, interrupting his thoughts. "And of course to take my son to see the Maypole. Then I'll turn in for the evening. I'm afraid I don't have the energy I did as a youth for long nights of dancing."

"You aren't calling yourself old, are you?" Samuel asked with a chuckle. "Because if you're old, I'm ancient."

"I highly doubt that," Tabitha countered. "You don't look a day older than I am."

Samuel paused just long enough to think through what she said and laugh. "So basically, we're both old?"

Tabitha's fingertips flew to her mouth. "Oh, no. That's not what I meant—"

"Truthfully, Sister Chadwick," Samuel interrupted, deliberately using her maiden name, "if you didn't have a son, I would swear you were a slip of a girl, no more than eighteen." He glanced over, thrilled to see a flush of pink creep up her neck.

"Mr. Barnett," she said, looking embarrassed, unsure where to train her eyes.

"It's *Samuel.*"

"Of course. Samuel." Tabitha glanced over shyly as she fiddled with her gloves in one hand.

In spite of the battle between warm honey and icy water inside him, Samuel hoped she'd be willing to stay longer than just for the meal and the Maypole, that she wouldn't mind his company for the duration. But the familiar tug-of-war wouldn't go away. He was thrilled to be walking beside Tabitha. Yet he felt guilty for doing so—especially when townspeople noticed the two of them. And they *did* notice.

He knew that more than likely it was Tabitha they were staring at and muttering about rather than him, but it still made a knot twist in his gut. It didn't matter that these people knew nothing about Helen; he still felt a stifling need to explain. Then there was the matter of whether his presence made Tabitha uncomfortable as an object of curiosity because she walked with a man who wasn't the Fred that settlers here had known and loved. Samuel nodded greetings to several people, knowing beyond doubt that his cheeks were turning bright pink.

From the exertion of a hard work day, he wanted to say to passersby. *Not because I'm self-conscious about walking with a beautiful woman whom I can't stop thinking about.*

Surely not that.

Out of the bustling crowd came a high-pitched squeal of joy. "Mama! Over here," followed by hurried footsteps. Tabitha was nearly bowled over by a boy wrapping his arms about her waist. Samuel recognized the tawny hair of the boy he had helped bless. Maybe this time the boy wouldn't be so shy, and Samuel would get a good look at his face.

Tabitha's son popped his head up and said, "Mama, Grandpa says you were gone getting the horse. Well, did you get her? When can I see her? Can I help train her? Can I?"

His mother laughed and hugged him hard, then kissed his forehead. "Yes, you can see her. And we'll talk about whether you can help, but all of that can wait." She pulled her son back. "Will, I'd like to introduce you to Mr. Samuel Barnett. You met before, in a manner of speaking. He was the one who helped Grandpa Chadwick give you a blessing earlier this week."

The boy looked quite healthy. Samuel was amazed and had to remind himself that the priesthood was real and could heal people from real illnesses—especially when the faith of a child was involved. Samuel was about to extend his hand but stopped short when he recognized the boy. He still had scabs where some of the pox had been, but there was no mistaking the features as he turned to face Samuel, grinning and showing gaps amid a hodgepodge of baby and adult teeth. His disheveled blond hair needed cutting as it hung almost into his eyes. Will pushed his bangs out of the way and pointed.

"Hey, you're the man I had to help lead the filly!" He slapped his thigh with delight and laughed as if the realization—or perhaps Samuel himself—were the funniest thing in this world or the next.

If Samuel's cheeks had been pink before, he was certain they turned fiery red now.

"You *know* each other?" Tabitha asked, sounding somewhat dumbfounded.

"We've met before . . . in a manner of speaking," Samuel said.

Will rushed on. "Mama, remember when I told you about the little filly I saw on my first day of school? The one I had to help with?"

"I remember," Tabitha said.

"That was *him!*"

Samuel felt the urge to point out that he was the *man* involved, not the *filly.* "As you know now, I'm not very . . . experienced with horses."

"The filly was just a little thing!" Will said with a bounce and a giggle. "You should have seen him, Mama. He couldn't get it to walk a single step. I think he was scared—"

"I'm glad you've met," Tabitha said, interrupting her son, for which Samuel was intensely grateful. He didn't know how much more of the humiliation he could endure.

So much for not being embarrassed again in front of a woman, he thought. That determination had given him the courage to get into the corral in the first place. Too bad this boy had to bring up a debasing situation.

No one said anything else for a moment, but Tabitha's eyes caught his, and suddenly the two of them burst out laughing. Will did too, and this time Samuel didn't mind so much. The boy was young, full of life, and awful proud of being able to outdo a man nearly thirty years his senior. As a boy, Samuel himself would have been just as cocky, given the same circumstances.

At least Tabitha knew about my horse "skills" before this.

Desperate to change the topic—and to shift the focus of the conversation from himself—Samuel said, "You have a very intelligent son."

"Yes, I do," Tabitha said, hugging her boy from the side.

Obviously proud of the compliment, Will stuck out his chest and tucked his thumbs under his suspenders. "I'm the best speller in my grade." Then he turned and strutted toward the crowd, calling over his shoulder, "Grandma and Grandpa are over here. I told them I'd come get you." With that, Will snapped his suspenders and ran off.

Samuel cleared his throat and looked at Tabitha. "So much for avoiding further humiliation . . ."

Tabitha seemed lost in thought, making him squirm as he waited for her to speak. Her gaze finally left the spot where Will had gone into the crowd and turned to his. Her eyes softened with a smile. "Thank you, Samuel. I'm still grasping what a sacrifice it must have been for you to do all that you've done for me. And frankly, I couldn't have done it if you hadn't built the chute and helped me get her into it. Not to mention that Jeremiah would have just sold her out from under me if you hadn't intervened."

He ran a hand awkwardly through his hair. "My pleasure." The story of the filly seemed to make her see that his plea of ignorance was genuine and just how lacking his experience was.

"It means so much that you would help me with Mantia." With a smile, she tucked her arm through his, and together they followed Will to his grandparents.

"Mantia, is it?" Samuel asked as they walked.

"I thought it a fitting name."

They soon reached Tabitha's parents, Will panting heavily beside them. "He's the one I told you about!" he said between breaths.

Wonderful, Samuel thought with a wry smile. *My manhood gets denigrated before I arrive.*

Tabitha ignored Will's comment and turned to look at Samuel. "Mother, Father, do you remember Mr. Samuel Barnett, who arrived from England not two months ago? He works for Brother Carlisle at the Little Fort stable. He's the one who helped me with the horse."

"Yes. I'm so grateful for your help blessing my grandson the other day. So you did move the horse, then?" her father asked.

"Just now," Tabitha said, her eyes showing a glint of pleasure. "She'll be there until we can break her, and then she'll be boarding in the Little Fort stable after that."

"Glad to hear it," her father said, giving her a hug from the side.

The elder Sister Chadwick stepped forward. "Welcome, welcome," she said, shaking Samuel's hand. "It's so good to see you again, Mr. Barnett."

"How do you do," Samuel answered, tipping his head slightly. Tabitha's mother had the same wide, brown eyes and slender nose as her daughter. She might be very much how Tabitha would look in thirty years, with wrinkles clustered around her eyes and mouth—fine lines representing the threads of life experience. She was a handsome woman.

Brother Chadwick extended a hand. "Thank you for helping her with that horse, Brother. My daughter here didn't even tell us about the harebrained idea until this morning, when there wasn't a lick I could do about it."

"That's only because I didn't want to burden you with my problem," Tabitha interjected.

"Burdening? That's what family is *for,*" her father said, somewhat exasperated but also with a teasing tone. Then to Samuel, he said, "She's always been the headstrong one of the family. You'd have better luck getting a rattle off a rattlesnake than shaking off an idea she's attached to."

"Father, please," Tabitha said with a slight roll of her eyes. She glanced awkwardly toward Samuel as if gauging his reaction to her father treating her like a young girl. "If I had mentioned the horse, you would have offered to pay for her or board her yourself—which we both know you can't do." She rushed on when her father opened his mouth to protest. "You know it's true."

"I could have at least helped with the moving," her father said, wagging a finger.

"You have a bad back. Lassoing a wild horse isn't something a man of your age should be attempting."

Samuel noticed that she didn't mention the fact that her father walked using a cane. He wouldn't have been able to help even if she had asked.

Brother Chadwick's mouth hung open for a moment as if he were trying to invent a retort, but he finally closed it and laughed. He cocked his head to Samuel. "Told ya there was no use arguing with her. She wins every time."

A loud voice boomed over the crowd, and a hush gradually rolled over the people as they turned to the source—John Hougard, the mayor and master of ceremonies, standing on a platform at the end of the open area. Red, white, and blue bunting decorated the front of the podium, with bouquets of daisies on the corners. Samuel and the Chadwicks turned to face the podium. Will jumped up and down, saying, "I can't see! I can't see!" so Samuel picked him up and put him on his shoulders.

"Neat!" Will called from his perch. "I'm taller than everyone!"

"Welcome to our annual Independence Day celebration," Mayor Hougard called over the crowd, who cheered and clapped. Will whooped. The mayor went on. "Please welcome a surprise guest, President Joseph F. Smith from the First Presidency, who arrived just moments ago. He'll be joining us in the festivities."

The mayor put his arm out, gesturing toward the road, where a carriage entered the area, passing under a floral arch certainly made for just this occasion. President Smith leaned out the window and waved at the crowd, who clapped and cheered. The driver brought the carriage right up to the front of the podium and stopped it there. He hopped down and opened the door to the carriage. Samuel watched carefully, eager to see one of the Lord's anointed. He had hoped to see a Church leader when he arrived in Salt Lake City but had been put on the wagon bound for Manti before he had the chance.

The Apostle, who looked to be about sixty, took the extended hand of the driver and climbed out, then spoke what looked like his thanks to his driver. He had a long, narrow face, round glasses, and a thin beard that separated into two points at the bottom. He took his driver's arm and used the support as the two of them walked onto the platform, where he placed both hands on the podium. "Thank you, Ben," he said to the driver, a man in his early forties.

"You're welcome, President Smith," the driver said. "It was an honor to drive you. I hope I did all right."

President Smith patted Ben's cheek and turned to the crowd, saying loudly, "See this man? He's an excellent example of a willing servant. My regular driver is ill right now, and Ben Adams here agreed to step in and fill the need. We should all be so willing to lend a hand. But I understand the people of Manti do just that—and if a willing heart can be judged by the progress you've made on the temple here, I believe the Lord is pleased with your offering."

He spoke a few more words, particularly about the great land that was the United States, all with a voice loud and strong. It almost looked as if the man had more strength when he was acting as a leader and speaking to the people under the influence of the Spirit than when he had gotten out of the buggy. President Smith finished and turned away from the podium. Ben found him a seat and took a seat behind the mayor, who stood to continue the services.

"What a treat it is to have one of our dear leaders with us," Mayor Hougard said. "We hope you'll share more wisdom with us soon." He consulted a piece of paper and went on. "We'll begin with an opening song sung by a choir organized for the occasion, conducted by Brother Moody. Following that we'll have a prayer from Brother Jim Crawford. Then we'll get to watch the Maypole dance before we all enjoy our dinners." He gestured to his right, where the Maypole stood in its red, white, and blue glory in an open area.

The choir filed onto the platform and began their hymn, a lively rendition of "Onward, Christian Soldiers." In the middle of the second verse, someone pushed their way past Samuel. He turned to see who it was—a plump, middle-aged woman who tapped Tabitha's shoulder.

"Tabby, dear," the woman whispered.

"Why hello, Sister Sorensen," Tabitha whispered in hopes of not disturbing those around her from enjoying the musical number.

"I'm in a bind," Sister Sorensen said, lowering her voice to match Tabitha's. "Could you do me a quick favor?"

"I'd be happy to," Tabitha said, her brow furrowing in concern. "What is it?"

"It's Berta Reid. She managed to fall and twist her ankle. She can't walk on it."

"Oh dear," Tabitha said. "Is she all right?"

"Yes. Her mother is with her now, and I'm sure she'll be fine," Sister Sorensen said, waving a hand as if that weren't the issue. "But now I don't have enough girls for the Maypole dance, and it's about to *start.*"

Tabitha took a small step back. "Surely you don't expect *me* . . ." The woman's face showed that she did indeed expect just that. "It's been almost a decade since I've done the Maypole dance. I don't remember it."

"Sure you do," Sister Sorensen said, tugging on Tabitha's hand. "It's a simple combination. I'm sure it'll come back as soon as the music begins."

Tabitha hadn't *wanted* to get noticed, and here she was being thrust with a vengeance into the center of attention. Samuel could tell she struggled inside with what to do. To him, she seemed like the kind of person who frequently came in and solved problems—as evidenced by her determination to save Mantia. But that part of her seemed to war with the side that wanted anonymity.

Without giving an actual answer, Tabitha let Sister Sorensen drag her away. She called up to Will, "I'll be back soon. You stay with Brother Barnett until I get back."

Will waved happily as she disappeared through the crowd. The choir finished their number, and after the invocation, Samuel turned to Will's grandparents. "Do you mind if I take him closer?"

"Not at all," Sister Chadwick said. "I think that's a wonderful idea. We'll get the picnic ready over by that tall pine tree there."

Samuel looked up at Will. "From up there, tell me where you think we can see the Maypole best."

The boy raised a hand to his eyes and scouted across the crowd like a sailor searching for land. He pointed. "There!"

"All right, Will, show me the way." Samuel followed the boy's outstretched arm until they reached a spot to the side of the podium where, sure enough, the crowd was thinner and Samuel could see the Maypole well. They settled into position just as the music began. A circle of dancers surrounded the pole, each holding a colored streamer. Samuel searched for Tabitha, finding her on the right side of the circle, with a red streamer in her right hand and a look of anxiety on her face.

"I see her!" Will called, smacking Samuel's hat with both hands and effectively pushing it down over Samuel's eyes. "Look! Over there!"

"Yes, I see, I see," Samuel said with a chuckle, lifting his hat so he actually could. Then he covered his head in an effort to protect it from further assault. He settled into watching the dance—Tabitha and the younger girls weaving in and out in a pattern, Tabitha searching the circle for cues on what to do. Within a minute or so, however, she seemed to relax. Her movements became more fluid, and the tension in her face ebbed. A smile made its way across her face as if she had finally remembered the pattern and no longer had to worry or concentrate quite so intensely. Her feet began to move lightly as she wove under and over streamers.

Holding Will's legs steady over his shoulders, Samuel leaned against a wooden pole and enjoyed watching the dance. Wisps of hair escaped Tabitha's loose bun and framed her face, swaying with her movement. The exercise made the color in her cheeks deepen.

In no time the streamers were fully braided down the pole and the circle of dancers was so small that the women touched arms. By that point, Tabitha was laughing with the other girls as she pranced under an arm then held up her shortened streamer for a girl to dance beneath.

Tabitha *looked* like one of them, too. Carefree and young. For the moment she had abandoned the look of maturity that she usually wore, the one that said she had plenty to do and that she knew no one would do it for her. Responsibility. That's what that look was, the one she usually wore. And duty.

Must be a tiresome burden to carry all the time, Samuel thought, *if abandoning it for just a few moments transforms her so.*

The music wound down, and the audience clapped and roared their approval. The dancers curtsyed in response. Tabitha appeared to be breathing heavily, but she still smiled as she smoothed back her hair and hugged a couple of the other, much younger, dancers.

From above Samuel, a shrill whistle sounded, making him cringe. "Heavens, Will! Not so close to my ear!" he cried, putting his hands to the sides of his head.

At this, Will removed his fingers from his mouth and laughed uproariously. Instead of apologizing, he cupped his mouth with both hands and cried, "Yeah, Mama! You were amazing!"

Samuel laughed and patted Will's knee, then searched for Tabitha, whom he saw approaching across the open circle. He lifted Will off his shoulders, and the boy raced off, smacking his head into Tabitha's middle and wrapping his arms around her with all the force in his small arms.

"That was terrific, Mama! I didn't know you could do that."

Tabitha hugged him tight. "Why, thank you, Will," she said as they walked toward Samuel. "I didn't know I still could either."

"Impressive," Samuel said sincerely.

"Why, thank you, sir," she answered with a slight curtsy and an air of mock formality. Then she shook her head, putting a hand to her chest. "I thought for sure I would stumble all over my feet and mess up the braid, but somehow it worked out." She looked back at the Maypole and with a shake of her head, added, "I forgot how fun that is."

Samuel nodded, about to compliment her dancing, when he caught the eyes of a woman standing about ten feet off. She appeared to be in her sixties, with hair more gray than brown. Deep lines tugged the corners of her mouth downward. Her jaw was firmly set, and she stared at him with eyes of cold steel. When she saw him looking back, she stepped forward, clearly coming toward them.

He swallowed and shifted his feet, then reached across his body to rub a shoulder muscle, which was tight after carrying Will. "Should—should I know her?" he asked Tabitha quietly, indicating the woman who was approaching.

"Hmm?" Tabitha wiped her damp forehead with the back of her hand as she turned to see whom he meant. Her smile vanished. "No, but *I* do," she said without further explanation.

The woman stopped in front of them and waited to be greeted.

"Good evening, Mother Hall," Tabitha said, her voice suddenly stilted and overly polite.

Mother Hall. Samuel's mind whirled, trying to figure out what that meant.

"Evening, Tabitha," Mother Hall said shortly. Then she waited, looking from Tabitha to Samuel and back again, the silence stretching longer with each second, like pulled taffy on a winter day. One of her eyebrows rose, whether in question or challenge, Samuel couldn't say, but it clearly made Tabitha uncomfortable.

She gestured toward Samuel and opened her mouth to speak, but before a word came out, Will hopped forward and exclaimed, "Hi, Grandma. Grandma Chadwick made some cake and bread pudding. Are you going to eat supper with us?"

Grandma? Ah, Samuel realized. *This is her late husband's mother. And here I am with Tabitha . . .* He grimaced, understanding how this woman must suddenly feel at seeing him with her daughter-in-law.

When Will's grandmother didn't seem intent on answering her grandson's query, instead staring at Tabitha, he stuck out his hand. "I'm Samuel Barnett," he said quickly before the moment became any more unbearable. He noted Tabitha's grateful look. "I arrived from England not long ago." In response, she continued her fixed gaze in silence, a look he couldn't read. "I . . . work in the stables with Brother Carlisle. Do you know him?"

She blinked once. "Quite."

"Very good. Well, then . . ." Samuel wasn't sure what to say or how to act around this woman. He decided to explain his relationship with Tabitha—such as it was. "Yes, well, at the stables, we'll be boarding Tabitha's—that is, Sister Chadwick's—new horse, you see."

The woman seemed to flinch at the name. "Chadwick?"

Tabitha gulped. "A lot of people in town remember me that way; they forget to use my married name," she said, meek in voice. But Samuel noticed a trace of defiance in her eyes. He remembered all too well how she had hesitated on her surname when introducing herself. This was why.

The tension in the air was palpable. He hurried on. "At any rate, *Tabitha* and I just came from getting the horse settled—"

"Samuel was most helpful in transporting the horse," Tabitha interjected, putting a hand on his arm. "She's nearly wild, you see. I simply couldn't have done it without him. So, naturally, to show my gratitude, I invited him to supper with us. Like a true *Christian* would." She smiled broadly at her mother-in-law, but it didn't reach her eyes. Samuel knew it was meant as much to placate the woman as to challenge her in return—what would *she* have done in a similar instance—not shown gratitude to the man? As such, it didn't bother him that she had supposedly invited him to be polite. Something told him her motives were different.

He felt a bit deceitful leaving this woman with the impression that he had been so indispensable to Tabitha. All he had really contributed was a saw, hammer, and muscle. But he feared the alternative—that by admitting he knew nothing about animals, she would suspect he had other reasons for helping Tabitha. Which, he was just starting to admit to himself, he did. But this Mother Hall didn't need to know that and become envious or possessive for her son's sake—making life that much more awkward for Tabitha.

Did Sister Hall have any reason to be envious of how Tabitha felt toward him? As Tabitha's cheeks grew even redder with apparent nerves, Samuel wished he knew what Tabitha was thinking. Did she feel the same pull he did? Or was he ridiculous in thinking that this beautiful, capable, strong woman would see anything in him but a useless, bumbling fool?

At least I'm well-intentioned as I bumble.

Sister Hall cocked her head to the side. "My, my. You've gotten yourself settled quickly, Tabitha," she said in a sickly sweet voice. "Making *male* friends already. That's something indeed."

Tabitha's eyes darted to Samuel and back. "I'm getting to know all kinds of people. Manti sure has changed in the *six years* since I left." She gently emphasized the length of her absence as if needing to point out that she wasn't newly widowed.

But I am *newly widowed.* As before, thoughts of Tabitha continued to lead to thoughts of Helen. Should it be any other way? Maybe he should let himself feel guilty for thinking about Tabitha, even if Helen might approve of him finding another person to fill his life.

"I'll be going now," he said to Tabitha. Then with a slight bow to her mother-in-law, he added, "It was a pleasure meeting you, Sister Hall."

"But what about your supper?" Tabitha asked.

"I'll make do," Samuel said, suddenly eager to escape—for both his sake and Tabitha's. By leaving, he'd perhaps be able to both appease Sister Hall's jealousy about him as well as his own guilt over spending time with her daughter-in-law—and enjoying it. Missing a meal didn't particularly matter to him. Perhaps Sister Mirkins had left him something after all; since they hadn't discussed the day's events, he doubted she would just assume he'd be at the celebration during supper. And if she hadn't made a meal, he could probably find a slice of bread in the kitchen. He nodded to the women again. "Good evening."

As he stepped away, Will grabbed his arm, pulling him back. "Don't go, Mr. Barnett. You hafta stay for supper. Grandma Chadwick also made raspberry cobbler. *Raspberry.*" Will emphasized the last word so intensely that his little neck looked like a turtle's, stretched out as far as it would go.

Will's eyes pleaded, making Samuel hesitate and reconsider—until he caught Sister Hall's expression. While he couldn't quite read it, she no longer wore the bitter look of before. It had softened into a saddened, grieving one. The pitiable woman was still mourning her son, no doubt. He didn't have the heart to rub salt into the wound. "I'm sorry, Will, but I have to go. How about you eat enough cobbler for the both of us?"

"Well, all right," Will said with a stomp of disappointment. He brightened slightly and looked at his mother. "I can eat more than you, Mama."

"I'm sure you can," Tabitha said, looking at Samuel as she spoke. She gave a wan smile that seemed to say, *I wish you could stay, but thank you for understanding.*

"Evening, Sister Hall, Tabitha," he said, nodding to each woman. He strode off, careful this time not to let Will snag his sleeve. As he withdrew, he could almost feel Sister Hall's eyes boring into the back of his neck.

I'm sorry for the loss of your son, he wanted to say to the woman as he left, not allowing himself look back. *I know how it hurts to lose one you love.*

CHAPTER 17

"COME ON, GRANDMA HALL," WILL said, tugging on her arm. The woman remained immovable, her eyes fixed on Tabitha's. Will tried again. "Grandma, let's go. You're eating supper with us, right? That's what Grandma Chadwick said." He pointed into the distance. "We're by that tall pine tree over there. Did you bring your apricot preserves?" His excited effusion paused, waiting for her response.

When Mother Hall didn't answer him, he looked at the two women eyeing one another, concern etched around his eyes as if he didn't dare speak again. He took a small step back.

Tabitha wanted to do the same. Feeling ready to cower under her mother-in-law's gaze, she shot a furtive glance in the direction Samuel had gone, grateful he had been thoughtful in the face of the awkward circumstance but wishing nonetheless that he'd come back so she wouldn't feel so alone. Mother Hall noticed and broke her stare just long enough to track where Tabitha had looked.

I'm not being disloyal to your son's memory by being friends with Samuel Barnett, Tabitha wanted to say. *Besides, I hardly know the man.* Not that she didn't have a budding desire to get to know him better. But no number of wild horses could drag that fact from her, not under the circumstances.

"It was sure kind of Mr. Barnett to help me," Tabitha ventured. They were both thinking about him; there was no use pretending otherwise by discussing the weather.

"Yes, I suppose," Mother Hall said stiffly. She sniffed. "But if I were you, I would be cautious of bachelors. They rarely do good deeds for single women just for the sake of being good Christians."

Tabitha balled her fists. Was Mother Hall testing her loyalty or simply making assumptions about it? And should Tabitha correct her? She could either deny that Samuel might have other intentions—*did he?* she wondered—or point out that a widow of six years had every right to walk through the streets of town with a man. No. Such statements would only rile the woman further.

Instead, Tabitha took a deep breath, put on a smile, and tried to change the subject altogether. "So are you joining us for our picnic, then?"

Will clapped and did a little hop. "Yes, are you coming, Grandma? Are you?"

"I am," she said.

"Then I suppose we can go find my parents," Tabitha said, turning away eagerly and taking Will's hand. They walked briskly through the crowds, heading for the tree. She didn't need to look back to make sure her mother-in-law had followed; she could feel the woman's presence all too well. Tabitha closed her eyes briefly, wishing that this Independence Day celebration did *not* include her mother-in-law.

They reached the shady pine tree to see Tabitha's mother organizing a picnic meal of cold chicken, potato salad, and dried fruit. The food was spread over a tattered quilt her mother had made years ago. The sight made Tabitha take an easing breath. That quilt held memories of more joyful events than she could count. The faded blue background and the red- and green-pieced design brought a sense of childhood happiness over her. No single memory stood out, just a feeling of family, of belonging. All things she needed right now.

She sat beside the picnic basket, tucking her skirt folds under her legs. "Can I help with anything, Mother?"

Will reached into the basket and with a look of triumph in his eye, withdrew a piece of molasses candy. His Grandmother Chadwick placed a fist on her hip as if in reprimand, but Will grinned innocently, his gapped teeth showing clearly.

"Can I have it, Grandma? Please?"

"You little ragamuffin," she said, ruffling his hair. "Fine. You can have that one piece, but no more until after your supper."

"Thanks, Grandma!" With that, Will plopped himself down against the trunk of the tree and took a bite out of the chewy, sweet delight. "Mmm, mmm," he murmured with pleasure, shaking his head from side to side.

Mother Hall settled herself on the edge of the quilt, looking every inch a rigid statue. Tabitha reached into the basket to help her mother with the feast. Just as she pulled out a paper parcel holding cheese, two men strolled slowly behind her, talking.

"I don't know what Theodore's thinking," the first said. "First he threatens to retire, and then he runs headlong into foolishness by printing something so outrageous. Hancock's obviously guilty. Why didn't Theodore just say so?"

Tabitha's fingers tightened around the block of cheese.

The other man grunted his agreement. "You know how he gets when he makes a decision. He'd beat a mule at a stubbornness contest for sure."

"But it's not the wisest business move he's doin'. The whole town's talking about it. They want Hancock behind bars. My Louise has started locking the doors to the house, she's so afraid that someone will come in and terrorize us during the night. Who ever thought we'd need to lock doors here?"

The two paused in their step as if searching for their families. Tabitha turned her back to them, heat creeping up her neck as they continued chatting. The second man—Tabitha recalled him as Jones or Johnson or something similar—sniffed and said, "Worse, Pete down at the cooper's shop was wondering if Theodore's going to sell the place to that woman who's working for him now."

"A *woman*." The other man snorted. *Albert Hansen,* Tabitha thought, eyeing him through lowered lashes—although he looked much older than the last time she'd seen him. She lifted her left hand slightly to shield her face, hoping they didn't recognize her. The way he'd said *woman* made it clear what he thought of her gender in general.

Her mother gave her a furtive look of sympathy but, to Tabitha's relief, said nothing. While the sale was final, she was still keeping her end of the deal by not discussing it outside of her family until Brother Christensen felt the time was right. Besides, when she finally did tell someone about it, Wilhelmina Hall was certainly not on her list of people to share the news with, so Tabitha had not a sliver of desire to discuss it in her mother-in-law's presence.

"Do you think that *woman* is responsible for the piece on Hancock?" the one named Jones or Johnson said.

"If she is, it should wake Theodore up right fast. Show 'im that a woman *can't* handle the job. I'd hate to see the newspaper crumble apart. It's such a pillar of the community." He spoke as if the paper's crumble were the inevitable result of a woman—and Tabitha in particular, apparently—at the helm. She unfolded the paper around the cheese, trying hard not to register the disturbing sense of unease in her middle. She couldn't help but clench her jaw.

Immediately she began planning out her speech for the next time she met with Brother Christensen. She *would* write up an announcement about the sale and publish it. Not wanting to broadside him, she'd give him a week of knowing her plan to prepare for the idea. This time he wouldn't stop her. How could he? The *Sentinel* wasn't his any longer.

But there was still the matter of Jeremiah's guilt or innocence. Had she made a mistake in suggesting that his guilt wasn't necessarily a definite thing? A piece of cheese crumbled off, and she absently put it into her mouth. Was Brother Christensen right that if he didn't take full responsibility for the paper now, it would only tarnish her chances of success?

I have to publish what I believe in, what I believe is right, she thought. She took a knife from the basket and began cutting slices of cheese, wishing she knew what had really happened that night in Mr. Daggett's den.

Jeremiah hadn't been convicted of anything. Mentally she couldn't help adding, *At least not yet.*

* * *

Tabitha spent part of the next day at Constable Reeves's home with her pencil and notebook. She sat in his parlor, eager to hear his side of the story. Normally, she didn't spend her Saturdays chasing down stories, but this was different. With Monday as press day, this was her last opportunity to talk with those involved with the Daggett case if she wanted to print anything about it. And she did want to run another story.

At least, she *thought* she did.

"Have you found any clear evidence that Mr. Hancock committed a crime?" she asked.

Constable Reeves chuckled. "You mean aside from being caught inside Daggett's home with a bag of money clenched in his fist?"

"What if . . ." Tabitha's voice trailed off as she organized her thoughts. She shook her head and tried again. "Technically, we don't know what Hancock was doing in that study. What if he was *returning* stolen goods, not taking them?"

Reeves cocked his head in disbelief. "Why would a man like Jeremiah Hancock be returning stolen property?"

Leaning forward, Tabitha said, "Now, see, you're getting ahead of yourself. You're assuming what kind of man he is."

Why am I defending Jeremiah? she thought. *I know firsthand that he's mean and ornery. Why* would *he return stolen money instead of keeping it for himself?*

But aloud, she pressed on. "What about the presumption of innocence? As the accused, he has that right, doesn't he?"

"What, are you studying to be a lawyer, then?" Reeves said with a disdainful lilt to his voice. He leaned forward as well, clasping his hands. "Look, Miss Chadwick, I understand how you want to write up something really exciting and inflammatory. That must sell papers."

If you only knew, Tabitha thought. Brother Christensen was right in that people weren't taking well to her calling Jeremiah a "suspect" rather than a "thief" and saying that his crime was "alleged." She'd already received several subscription cancellations, and the columns she normally reserved for advertisements weren't as full as last week's. She was hoping more would come in today and on Monday morning before the paper went to press.

"This has nothing to do with selling papers," Tabitha said shortly. "It's a matter of objective reporting. Can you or can you not tell me of any evidence you have in the case?"

Reeves leaned back in the high-backed chair and regarded her. "Wouldn't telling you be a breach of ethics, up there with, I don't know . . . *presumption of innocence?*" He grinned and raised one eyebrow.

He's maddening! Tabitha slapped her notebook closed. "Very well, Mr. Reeves. If you don't want to speak to me, that's your prerogative. Thank you for your time. Good day." She gave a slight nod of her head. "I can see myself out."

She left him behind and went out the front door, feeling as if steam were rising from her ears. *Accusing me of trying to stir up trouble just to sell papers, indeed.* If she were, she certainly wouldn't be tracking down this story. Doing so was something she needed to do; it gnawed at her, but she didn't know why. She headed down the road, trying to decide what to do next. She needed more than Constable Reeves gave her if she was to pull together a follow-up story for Monday.

Why do I care? I should be happy Jeremiah was caught, she thought. *Even if he's innocent of burglary, he deserves jail time for what he did to Mantia.* Yet the gnawing feeling returned. She tapped her pencil against the notebook as she walked, trying to decide what to do. She could talk with the Daggetts again, but that hadn't yielded much the last time. Jeremiah might talk, but after fighting about her deadline to take Mantia, she was in no mood to face the man, and he likely wouldn't be amenable to talking with her anyway. The constable had been useless. Who else was there?

Maybe I should talk with Mr. Tidwell, she thought, figuring that Mr. Daggett's business partner probably had something to say about the matter, considering how close they both came to ruin that night.

She had the Tidwells' address from Mr. Daggett; their home wasn't more than a few blocks away. She headed south until she reached their street then headed east until she reached the Tidwell home. It was small and unassuming but neat and tidy, with a planter hanging beside the door trailing flowers and greenery. Her knock was answered in short order by a woman a few years older than herself—a woman with sleek, dark hair and a heart-shaped face. Betty Hunsaker. Now Betty Tidwell.

"Well, hello," Tabitha said, hoping her surprise didn't show. She wondered why she hadn't realized that Betty still lived in town. A brief taste of the old envy flared up, and Tabitha stamped it down. *Fred picked me,* she reminded herself, even though she knew that her mother-in-law still wished Fred had chosen this brunette beauty.

"Goodness gracious. Tabitha Chadwick, is that you? What a surprise," Betty said, clasping her hands. "Please, do come in."

Tabitha entered a bit uneasily. Betty closed the door then led the way to the parlor, which was tiny but elegantly decorated with silver candlesticks on the mantel, pretty red curtains, and a pianoforte in the corner. When they were settled on soft chairs, one of Betty's daughters came in and whispered something. "I'll be there in a few minutes," she told her. "I can't come now; I have a visitor." After gently shooing the girl out of the room, she turned to Tabitha. "Now, to what do I owe this visit? I don't think I've seen you since you left town all those years ago."

"It has been awhile, but it's good to be back," Tabitha said. Then, not wanting to pussyfoot around the subject, she came right to the point. "I don't know if you've heard, but I'm working with the *Sentinel.*"

"The newspaper? How delightful." The woman seemed as false as a glass figurine.

"Yes, that's right," Tabitha said. "I'm currently following up about the Daggett robbery. Since your husband is Mr. Daggett's business partner, I was hoping to talk with him about it."

Betty tilted her head in surprise and looked suddenly stiff. "Arthur's not home right now," she said, her eyes narrowing. "But I'm curious as to why you would want to talk with him about it. It's not as if Arthur would have stolen the money."

"Well, of course not." Tabitha was taken aback. Why would Betty have jumped to such an odd conclusion? Of course Tabitha didn't think Arthur Tidwell had committed the crime; doing so would make no sense. It would be like robbing himself. But Betty looked tense and nervous. Tabitha tried again, this time sounding more casual. "I thought perhaps Mr. Tidwell would have some insight into the situation, something he'd like to tell the thief, perhaps. Maybe he'd like to make a statement of some kind. You know, as someone with a vested interest in the matter?" Tabitha held up her notebook. "I've spoken to nearly everyone involved, but I'm lacking a statement from him."

"Well, I suppose he wouldn't mind giving you a *statement,*" Betty said, her face cracking into a painfully polite smile. "But I don't know that it will be very interesting or useful." She sighed a bit dramatically. "You see, we're just an average, hard-working family trying to get by. Mr. Daggett is sure generous to be sharing the business with us; he's got so much more money than we do, although it's our animals and wagons that will be doing the bulk of the work. *If* the company becomes successful, of course."

"You don't think it will be profitable?" Tabitha asked. Betty didn't seem like a very supportive spouse, and she seemed to resent their property being used as capital.

"Oh, I do hope it is a roaring success. Don't get me wrong," Betty said in a rush. Her smile looked carved out of wood. "But I worry. That's what we women are best at, right?" She chuckled.

"Yes, I suppose we women tend to be worriers," Tabitha said vaguely. If Arthur Tidwell wasn't around, Betty would have to do. Tabitha could get a statement from him another time. "Do you have any idea who all knew about Daggett's money and where it was stashed? It's odd that . . . the *thief* . . . would know where to look."

"Heavens, I have no idea who knew about the hiding place," Betty said. "Of course, it's no mystery that Daggett comes from a family with loads of money—everyone around here knows he's rich. But as to where exactly it was hidden?" She shrugged. "I imagine only my husband and Mr. Daggett himself knew that."

Someone else must have known for Jeremiah to find out. Unless he learned of the hiding place from Tidwell or Daggett, Tabitha thought as she scribbled notes. She looked up. "Was Mrs. Daggett aware of the hiding place, perhaps?"

Betty waved away the thought. "No, no. In fact, I overhead our husbands talking business the other day, and the hiding place came up. Mr. Daggett implied that he daren't tell his wife that it was hidden in the false drawer of his desk, because she might up and spend it on the blue silk—" Her voice cut off abruptly. She looked away from Tabitha and cleared her throat. "Might spend it on the blue silk she's been eyeing. Buying pretty fabric for pretty clothes is another thing we women are good at." She chuckled nervously and finished. "I'm sure Mrs. Daggett has no idea. Would you like some tea?"

"No, but thank you," Tabitha said, standing. "I should probably be going anyway. I hope to see your husband another day."

"Well, thank you for dropping by," Betty said. "It's sure been good to catch up with you, Tabby."

Tabitha paused in her step to the front door. *I am* not *a cat.* She turned back to face Betty. "It's been a pleasure. Thank you again for taking the time to talk with me."

With a wave, she headed out the door and back to the *Sentinel* office. In spite of Betty's insistence that she hadn't known where the money was, she obviously *had* known—she had just told Tabitha. So at least three people knew about it: Mr. Daggett, Arthur Tidwell, and Betty. One of them must have spilled the information to Jeremiah. But who? And how?

It wouldn't surprise me if Betty told half the city about the hiding place "in confidence," Tabitha thought. As a youth, Betty had been known to be a sieve when it came to keeping secrets.

Regardless, somehow Jeremiah had found out about it. He was discovered in the drawing room right beside the writing desk with the money—with nothing else in the room disturbed. He could have heard about the hiding place from any number of people if Betty had let the secret loose. Or he could have overheard the conversation between Daggett and Tidwell.

Unless Betty had intentionally told Jeremiah about it . . .

Tabitha shrugged off *that* idea. It was too ludicrous. Why would she tell a virtual stranger about the hiding place? At least Tabitha now had enough information to write a follow-up piece. She wished she had found out more about the actual robbery.

Did Jeremiah do it? The question burned inside her. She had to know.

CHAPTER 18

TABITHA GOT THE NEXT ISSUE of the paper printed and sent out on Monday as usual. Tuesday morning, as she awaited Brother Christensen's arrival for their weekly meeting, she reread portions of her update on the Daggett situation. She liked how it had turned out.

> *According to Mrs. Tidwell, very few people knew of the money's location prior to the events of June 26: Mr. Daggett, Mr. Tidwell, and herself. Whether Hancock had overheard the secret or was told it by another party remains unknown. Hancock continues to deny any wrongdoing, saying that he was only returning monies that were stolen by an unnamed individual. Constable Reeves has not disclosed any evidence in the case. Hancock's trial will be held August 27.*

She wondered what evidence—if any—Reeves had actually found. Was there enough to put Jeremiah into prison? And why wouldn't Jeremiah name the real thief?

I'm still assuming he's innocent, she thought.

She didn't know why. The one thing she did know was that she couldn't try him in the court of public opinion the way so many people seemed to be insisting she do. Presumption of innocence was a core value of the country's legal system, one she wasn't about to destroy, even if doing so protected the man who had abused poor Mantia.

Even ornery coots have rights, she thought.

The front door opened quickly and slammed shut. Tabitha looked up from the paper, expecting to see Brother Christensen. She hadn't anticipated his beet-red face.

"What were you thinking?" he said, stomping forward and smacking the paper onto the counter.

"What do you mean?" Tabitha asked, taken aback.

"Mrs. Tidwell visited me last night. She was all in a dither."

"Why?" Tabitha asked, looking back at the paper as if it would provide an answer.

"Why?" Brother Christensen said. "Why? Because you all but accused Mrs. Tidwell of blabbing her husband's secret. Her husband was unaware that she knew anything about where Daggett hid his funds, but now the entire city knows she knew."

Tabitha's ire was rising. "She *told* me that information—to a newspaper reporter. What did she *think* I would do with it? She never asked me not to print it, and as it was relevant information, I ran it."

"No, *I* ran it," Brother Christensen snapped. "At least that's what your readership thinks. It's still *my* initials you're signing. It's still *my* name listed as publisher."

Slapping her hands on the desk in front of her, Tabitha stood up and leaned forward. "Then why don't I finally let everyone know who's really running this place?"

"Fine by me," Brother Christensen said, pushing away from the counter. "Leave me out of the situation altogether. Just don't come complaining to me when your ship sinks." He twisted the doorknob so hard it nearly broke off in his hand as he pulled the door open and stormed out.

Tabitha sat down again, shaking. She was free to tell the world that the *Sentinel* was her paper. That's what she wanted, wasn't it? To have total control, to no longer hide behind Brother Christensen's name, to have full ownership and full responsibility?

But what if he's right? she thought, bemoaning the events to herself. She eyed the paper he'd left on the counter and grimaced. What if she had messed everything up? Perhaps she should have been more discreet in the facts she reported. Maybe the situation was exactly what everyone else purported it to be—a simple break-in and burglary by an old man of few means.

She opened a drawer in her desk and pulled out the announcement she had written up weeks ago about the ownership. She read over it for probably the thirtieth time—the text was simple and straightforward, showing respect and appreciation to Brother Christensen and his years of work, while making it clear that she was now the one responsible for the news in the area. She had thought it was the perfect way to make the switch and had planned to inform Brother Christensen that the next issue would be running it.

But now . . .

She sighed, knowing that a new announcement might be needed to explain that the last two articles about the Daggett matter were all her doing, that Brother Christensen was not involved in any way with them. The idea of publishing such a statement felt like an admission of wrongdoing.

I'm writing what I feel is right, she thought indignantly.

She pulled her round watch out of her skirt pocket and checked it. The staff would be arriving in less than thirty minutes, and they needed to be the first to know of the official change. Victor already suspected, she thought. But she wondered how Joseph and Natalie would take it.

Unable to keep her mind still, she stood and paced the room, rethinking all the criticisms she had heard recently, from Brother Christensen's words a moment ago to the men at the Independence Day celebration, to a few other nasty comments she'd heard at church. She'd even gotten a few complaint letters shoved beneath the *Sentinel* door, all about the Daggett scandal and Jeremiah's supposedly obvious guilt. A few of the letters had come by post, showing that some people in the outlying areas who received her paper—in Moroni, Ephraim, Nephi, and other areas—also disagreed with her. Those folks hadn't seen her at the office and gotten used to even the idea of a lady editor. A lady owner and publisher would come as quite a shock.

The switch wouldn't be nearly as smooth as she had hoped. *Should I let the story die as Brother Christensen suggested?* she wondered, gazing out the front windows. After all, there were plenty of other things she could fill the paper with—stories about calamities in Chicago, criminals in New York, politics in Washington. She could ignore the story—if it weren't for the memory of Jeremiah's voice insisting, "It wasn't me."

She still held the paper in one hand. There on the bottom of the front page was her weekly editorial, signed yet again, *T.C.*

Theodore Christensen.

Tabitha Chadwick.

She dropped the paper onto a bench beneath the window and rubbed her forehead, two factions warring within herself. The part of her that had charged forward, attended college, and bought the paper in the first place insisted that she make the announcement *and* continue to follow Jeremiah's situation in the paper. Let the people bluster all they wanted.

The other part hesitated—and she loathed that part. It was the fearful young girl of years past that whispered, "What if it all back-fires? Your nest egg is gone. What will you do when the paper fails?"

What was it about coming back to Manti that dredged up such emotions?

She sank to the bench and closed her eyes. Hands clasped, she silently prayed. *Help me know what to do. Am I on the right path? If so, give me strength for whatever the consequences may be. Help me do what is right.*

Opening her eyes, she stared at the floor in front of her. Immediately she knew that she'd continue on the same course. Her conscience wouldn't allow her to stop telling the stories—or to hide behind "T.C." as she did it. Her hands trembled, so she sat on them to still them. She hadn't expected that making her announcement would also bring a panic to her chest.

She sat on the bench for several minutes, trying to calm herself. The door creaked open, and she expected to see one of her staff members. Instead, Samuel stepped inside and closed the door behind him.

"Well, hello, Samuel," Tabitha said, standing and shedding her professional demeanor. "What a pleasant surprise."

"You look a bit flushed," Samuel said, considering her. "Are you well?"

Tabitha glanced at the announcement sitting on the bench, then back at Samuel. "I'm quite well, thank you. It's just some business matters with the paper are getting tricky. You see . . ." She gulped and said the words she had ached to say for so long. "I bought the paper when I came to Manti. It's mine."

"That's plain wonderful!" Samuel said, slapping his hand on the counter.

"Yes, it is," Tabitha said, grateful that someone thought it newsworthy. "I hope others see it in the same light. That's actually why I came back to Manti. It's been mine this entire time, but I'm only now making it public."

"That's fantastic news," Samuel said. "I say you need to celebrate."

"Celebrate now? But it happened weeks ago," Tabitha said with a laugh—which felt good after the worry from before.

"Did you celebrate when you first bought it?" Samuel probed.

"No . . ." Tabitha admitted.

"Then a celebration is far overdue, and I know just the thing. See, I read about some folks putting on one of Sister Sidwell's plays as a benefit for the temple fund." He chuckled with a sudden realization. "Then again, I suppose you know all that, considering that I read about it in the *Sentinel.*"

Tabitha nodded with a smile. "It's Friday night, isn't it?" She picked up the paper from the bench and turned it over to the back page. "Yes, right here. Friday, July 11, eight o'clock at the South Ward Assembly Hall. 'Proceeds to benefit the temple fund.'"

"That's right," Samuel said. Then he coughed nervously. "Your owning the paper is reason enough to celebrate, but the reason I came over is in hopes that perchance . . . I mean, would you consider accompanying me, Tab . . ." At shortening her name, his eyes grew round, and he flustered. "I'm sorry. I shouldn't—I shouldn't have presumed . . ."

But Tabitha curled her toes with pleasure. He hadn't called her *Tabby.* She felt like the ten-year-old on Temple Hill when Fred had first called her that. "Oh, I don't mind," she said—one of the greatest understatements ever uttered. "I like *Tab.*"

"Good," Samuel said with obvious relief. "Well then, Tab, would you do me the honor of going to the benefit with me tomorrow night?"

"And consider it a celebration for the purchase?"

He nodded, and her stomach seemed to tumble over itself as if a swarm of butterflies were trying to escape. "I'd love to."

A slow smile spread across his face, making his eyes come alive. "I'll pick you up around seven-thirty." He nodded politely then opened the door and headed out. Before closing it behind him, he looked back into the room and caught her eye. She couldn't help but grin at him.

"See you then, Samuel."

"Good day to you, Tab."

The newspaper crinkled as her hand tightened around it with excitement. When the door clicked shut, all thoughts of her discussion with Brother Christensen fled. Stale topics such as business ownership or burglary scandals flew out of her head for the moment. She was too preoccupied trying to decide how to style her hair for Friday.

Joseph arrived a minute later. He gave her a brief greeting before going back to the printing room to get to work.

"I'll call you when we're ready for the staff meeting," Tabitha told him.

She sat down at her desk and tried to clear her mind by transcribing some of the latest telegraph communications, but she remained a bit distracted until the door opened with a bang. Startled, Tabitha looked up. *What now?*

With a lowering glare, Jeremiah Hancock stomped inside and slammed the door shut with his boot. He walked to the reception counter and planted both palms on top. Under one was yet another copy of the *Sentinel.* Tabitha was getting tired of seeing that edition.

She raised her eyes to Jeremiah's steely stare and managed, "May I . . . help you, Mr. Hancock?" Considering how much she had done with his case, she would have expected him to look happy instead of irritated and angry. She stood and folded her arms in challenge.

"What do you think yer doin'?" he growled.

Tabitha almost retorted by asking what in tarnation the man was talking about, but she wouldn't have been able to get the words out anyway; Jeremiah went on as if he were plowing through a field.

"How I come to find out about where Daggett's money was hid—that's my affair. Don't go dragging anyone else into it."

"Mr. Hancock," Tabitha said, finally getting a word in edgewise. "I'm not trying to 'drag' anyone into anything. I'm simply trying to uncover the facts—facts, I might add, that might help keep you out of jail." Her voice was rising to match the intensity of his. The last thing she needed was another outburst by someone who disagreed with the way she ran the paper—especially the man she was struggling to defend in spite of her misgivings.

"If I go to jail, then I go to jail," Jeremiah said. "You ain't dragging others with me."

Narrowing her eyes, Tabitha tried to get the man to see reason. "Why shouldn't I try to find the truth? I've tried to defend you. It's been a very unpopular position to take, I might add. Would you rather I stand idly by and let the public do what they will with you?"

Jeremiah's mouth worked as he thought. "It's not your matter," he said, his gruff voice sounding a little shaky.

He was handing her the perfect opportunity to stop reporting on the story. If most of the community was against it—and the defendant himself didn't want it in the paper—then why should she bother? As tempting as the idea was, she couldn't do it. "You said you're innocent," she said, leveling an intense gaze at him. "Is that the truth?"

They held each other's eyes for several seconds before he answered, "It's the truth." He pushed away from the counter and shook his head. "You don't understand. I just can't have anyone else getting hurt, that's all. Now, I want to talk with the publisher of this here paper and make sure he agrees—no more stories about me and that Daggett thing."

Tabitha stood a bit taller. "I'm sorry, but the publisher won't be agreeing to any such demand."

"You can't speak for him," Jeremiah snapped. He jabbed a finger at the paper. "I've been reading this here paper for the last five years, and I happen to know that the owner is Theodore Christensen. Now where is he?"

"T.C.?" Tabitha said. She folded her arms, a wry smile on her face. "You're speaking to T.C. *I* own the *Sanpitch Sentinel.*"

"No, no, no," Jeremiah said, waving her answer away. "You just moved here. You *can't* be T.C."

"Theodore Christensen was the previous owner," Tabitha said. "But the paper is mine now, and my initials are also T.C."

Just then the printing room door opened, and Joseph poked his head through the crack. "Did that box of leading ever arrive, Sister Hall?"

"It's under the counter next to the tool box," she said.

"I'll look there. Thanks."

When the door closed, Jeremiah chuckled. "So, your initials are T.C., are they? Then why'd he call you *Hall?*"

"Hall is my married name," Tabitha said irritably. "But most people hereabouts still know me by my maiden name—Chadwick. Tabitha Chadwick. T.C."

Jeremiah ground his teeth. "So you're really the owner?" he asked with a bit of a snarl in his voice.

"I am." She couldn't help but feel a tad triumphant.

He snorted. "Perfect," he said, rolling his eyes. "Difficult, meddling women . . ." He turned and yanked the door open.

As he stomped out, Tabitha stared after him. *He's protecting someone,* she thought, not for the first time. It was the only thing that explained why Jeremiah wouldn't want her to continue to dig into the story.

Only this time, she had an inkling of who it might be—Betty Tidwell. She was the only new person Tabitha had mentioned in the story. How the two of them were connected and why Jeremiah would want to protect her, she had no idea, but it was the only explanation that could make sense of Jeremiah's outburst.

CHAPTER 19

SINCE MANTIA'S TRANSFER TO HIS round pen, Brother McCleve had done the bulk of feeding and caring for the horse as she recuperated from her time with Jeremiah. He provided extra grain during the day in hopes of fattening her up, and he kept the area clean so Mantia wouldn't end up standing in rotten muck like she had before. One hoof was split, but even it was healing up nicely.

It was Thursday, so this was Mantia's seventh day away from Jeremiah. Each day after work, Tabitha spent time at the corral in hopes that the horse would gradually get used to her scent and eventually learn to trust her. The horse had already plumped since arriving here, and the sores from the whip were starting to heal. It wouldn't be long before Tabitha could try her hand at horse training.

In the evenings, she and Will sat on a railing and watched Mantia, sitting against the wind so their scents would blow to her. Their hours at the pen proved to be a good chance for mother and son to spend time together, but Tabitha enjoyed it equally because it provided a way to sit and think, to breathe in the fresh air and try to sort through things like business issues, and more recently, what it would mean for her when she announced to the county that she was the one in charge—and was running the articles about Jeremiah.

Tabitha sat on the corral fence and watched Mantia eating oats. Will sat beside her, poring over his reader. School had dismissed for the summer a month ago, but he was intent on being head of the class when it began again in the fall. Not wanting to interrupt his studies, Tabitha merely smiled at him and looked back to the corral. Knowing him, he'd read all during the break until his eyes turned red.

A particularly nasty cut on one of Mantia's legs worried Tabitha. It seemed to fester just as much as before, but they couldn't do much about it until she was tame enough to let them wash and bandage the wound. Mantia still stayed away from Tabitha—and all people—but the look of anxiety in the horse's eyes, and the constant flattening of her ears, had eased considerably since the mare had been brought there. She no longer got so startled at the sound of people approaching, and while she wouldn't let anyone near her, she didn't shy away to the far side of her pen just because someone was nearby.

It's not fair what he did to you, Tabitha thought angrily. *Jeremiah Hancock, the curmudgeonly old coot.*

Somehow it all rankled that much more that she was defending the man who had done this to her horse—a man who didn't seem to want defending. If Brother Christensen's dire predictions came about, if she kept along these lines with the paper, it would be her undoing. She gripped the wood, her fingertips white with pressure. After all she had done to be self-sufficient and get an education, after all she had worked for, could something like this take it all away?

Her heart said no. She was standing up for what was right by not passing judgment until a court did so, and especially with no evidence.

But if people stopped placing their trust in her publication, if advertisements didn't come in, if subscriptions fell too low, what then? Then all those people who didn't want a *woman* at the helm would cluck their tongues and say they'd been right all along.

"Will, you stay here," Tabitha said, hopping off the fence.

"Yes, Mama." Will glanced at her for just a second, going back to his book. Then he snapped his head up and stared. "Whoa. Are you going to train her now?"

"Shhh," she said, but smiled her positive response to him. He closed the primer and watched her every movement.

Tabitha held out her hand so Mantia could see and smell her better then slowly walked forward, taking care not to make any sudden movements. The horse looked over and snorted hard, tossing her head, seemingly nervous as she assessed the situation. Tabitha stopped and waited for the horse to shy away. She didn't. Encouraged, Tabitha spoke softly while taking another hesitant step forward. Then another and another.

"There's a good girl. Easy does it, there we go . . ."

From the fence, Will called, "Mama, look how close you are!"

Tabitha put a finger to her lips and widened her eyes at him. He clapped his hand over his mouth and nodded, getting the message.

Inches at a time, she continued, finally closing in on Mantia, who sniffed Tabitha's hand a few times, then shook her mane. With an uneven breath, Tabitha reached out and touched the side of the chestnut neck. The mare's hooves shifted, but that was all. She actually allowed herself to be petted for a few seconds before turning her head and walking away.

Tabitha didn't follow; she just watched her mare canter to the other side of the pen, her insides warming. She wanted to jump and shout in celebration but contented herself with a grin.

I did a good thing for her.

* * *

"Annoying cowlick," Samuel said, looking into the dim, warped reflection the mirror on the wall cast. He licked his fingers again and tried to smooth back the offending lock, but instead of lying flat as it was supposed to, it stood up again the moment his hand left his head. He grunted in frustration and pressed his palm against it yet again.

She has seen me looking foul and smelling of manure, he reminded himself. Tonight she would probably be glad to walk next to a man who didn't reek. She certainly wouldn't notice or care about a bit of hair out of place.

Yet that misbehaving piece of hair bothered him terribly. A starched shirt with pressed trousers weren't enough. He wanted this night to be special. He and Tab had spent a lot of time together, but never in a way that could be construed as courting. Not until tonight.

He took a step back and looked over his shirt, straightened the brown cravat around his neck, and put on his Sunday-best jacket. "Big step you're taking, boy," he murmured under his breath.

After he pocketed enough money to pay for the performance, he headed out the door, half wondering if she would have agreed to go with him had they not been attending an event that had such a beneficial cause.

That's ridiculous, he chided himself as he grabbed his hat from the bed and headed down the stairs. He bid good-night to Mrs. Mirkins, who looked up from her knitting and said, "Mmm-mmm, Mr. Barnett. You're looking all polished and shiny tonight. Going somewhere special?"

His neck grew hot, and his overly casual voice cracked when he said, "Yes, actually. I thought I'd attend the benefit play. For the temple." He added that last bit in a rush, as if defending his actions. He turned away, hoping as he grasped the door knob that she wouldn't ask whether he were escorting a young lady.

She did. "Certainly you aren't going alone? I mean, I've never known a man to get so cleaned up and dressed to the nines unless a lady would be on his arm."

"A lady will be attending with me," Samuel admitted. "Good evening, Mrs. Mirkins." He quickly ducked out of the house before she could pry further.

The walk to the Chadwick home wasn't long, for which Samuel was grateful. He paused at the base of the corner pathway that led to the front door and took a deep breath. He took a step forward then noticed a figure silhouetted at the window of the round tower room on the left.

Tab.

From the outline, he couldn't tell if she faced him or the inside of the room. A shorter figure bounded to her side and raised an arm— pointing at Samuel.

Will. A tender smile curved Samuel's mouth. A soft spot in his heart was beginning to form for the young boy, who had never known a father. Samuel wondered if he could fill that void. Will tugged at his mother's arm, dragging her toward the door.

Samuel moved down the path and rapped lightly, waiting for the door to open. Will yanked the handle backward and grinned with his mishmash of large and small teeth.

"Mr. Barnett!" Will cried. "Doesn't Mama look pretty?"

Tab blushed and looked down at her hands, clasped together around a handkerchief. Ringlets framed the front of her hair. The back was swept up into a pompadour, with a pretty black comb on one side and a bit of red ribbon wound throughout. Her gown shone with the candlelight behind her—possibly silk, he thought—a deep red that matched the ribbon in her hair and made her soft brown eyes look warmer than ever.

His pulse sped up, and he took a deep breath to rein in his response. "Yes, Will," he said, gazing at Tabitha. "Your mama looks very beautiful."

"Good night, Will," Tabitha said, leaning over and giving her son a kiss and a hug. "Mind Grandma while I'm away."

Will smiled broadly with a mischievous glint in his eye. "Grandma says she made special tarts from wild currants for when you're gone. I'll *try* not to eat too many and get a tummy ache."

"If you can manage it, maybe you can save one for me," Tabitha said as she extricated herself from Will's embrace.

"Should I save one for Samuel, too?" Will asked.

"I'd like that," Samuel said. Then to Tab, he held out his arm and said, "Shall we?"

Tabitha gently placed a hand on his arm. With a final wave at Will, she closed the door and walked down the pathway with Samuel.

For the first time in their acquaintance, they both remained frightfully silent. Samuel couldn't think of a single thing to say, and Tabitha wasn't speaking either. Was that because she felt uncomfortable with him or because she, too, recognized the difference between this stroll and all the others they had gone on together?

"So how is Mantia?" he finally asked.

"Much better," Tabitha said. A little color appeared in her cheeks as she went on. "She let me touch her yesterday. I think she knows I rescued her. You'll have to come see her soon."

"I'd like that," Samuel said, and almost laughed when he realized he genuinely meant that he'd enjoy seeing a *horse*.

They turned a corner toward the South Ward Assembly Hall, Tabitha holding her skirts up with one hand as she stepped over a small puddle. "It's sure good of you to take me to the benefit tonight," she said. "The temple fund really needs more donations in money rather than in kind."

Samuel glanced at her and tilted his head to side. "I suppose. But if I'm being completely honest, I'm not doing this out of purely altruistic motives."

Tabitha's eyes shot up to his face. She seemed surprised—but pleasantly so, if the shy smile was any indication.

A man from their ward came along the road, walking toward them. When the gap was only a few yards, he stared at them and scowled. Tabitha's hand tightened against his arm, and Samuel instinctively put his hand over hers.

"Aren't you the gal who married Fred?" the man said gruffly, blocking their way.

"Yes," Tabitha said uneasily as they slowed their step. "Uncle Ezra, I'd like you meet Samuel Barnett."

The man took in Samuel's appearance head to toe. "Evenin'," he said. Nothing in his words or tone was accusatory, but Tabitha seemed to stiffen at the attention anyway.

She cleared her throat and lifted her face slightly. "We're going to the benefit at the Assembly Hall to support the temple fund."

"I invited her to come with me," Samuel added, not knowing why he felt the need to explain anything to this stranger—this relative, however he was related to Tabitha. Somehow this man was upsetting to Tabitha, and Samuel figured it had to be that she was seen in such an obvious courting situation on the very stomping grounds where she had courted and married her first husband. That *could* be awkward, he realized, feeling responsible for her discomfort.

"Good evening," Samuel said pointedly, gently walking around him so they could continue down the street. He steered her around a corner toward a stand of trees. Tabitha pointed toward the Assembly Hall, which they were heading *away* from.

"But—" Tabitha began, pointing toward the hall.

When they reached the seclusion of the small grove, Samuel released her arm and turned to face her. He let out a deep breath.

Furrowing her brow, Tabitha said, "Is something the matter?"

"Are you sure you want to do this?" Samuel asked. "I hadn't thought about what going out in public with me—like this—would mean for you. The benefit will be attended by a lot of people, and—"

"We're going," Tabitha said. When he opened his mouth in surprise, she went on before he could get out another word. "Uncle Ezra took me off-guard, plain and simple. I shouldn't have let him upset me. You see, he's Mother Hall's brother, so I didn't know what he'd think of . . ."

"Ah," Samuel said with understanding. *Family loyalties.* "I don't want to put you in an uncomfortable position—" Samuel started, but Tabitha cut him off.

"I'm putting myself in the position," she said. "And it's high time I face the past. When I moved back to Manti, I knew I'd have to." She looked to her right, where the windows of the Assembly Hall glowed with candlelight. "Since I have to face these lions at some point, I'd rather do it with an ally at my side—as long as it's not too uncomfortable for *you.*"

Samuel let out a breath, his mouth curling on one side. Tabitha never ceased to amaze him. "I think I can handle it. Shall we beard the lions, miss?" he asked, holding out his arm.

"It would be a pleasure, kind sir," she said with a grin and a mock-formal nod.

They walked back to the hall, where Samuel paid for their tickets. They found seats halfway back on the right. After they settled onto a bench, Samuel looked around, increasingly aware of people noticing Tabitha and her companion. Some pointed and whispered to their neighbors while others smiled and waved. As far as he could tell, they were nearly all cordial and warm, which made him relax. Tabitha, too, seemed to be enjoying herself until a woman stood in front to announce the beginning of the play—Tabitha's mother-in-law.

Samuel gulped. Tabitha's only outward reaction was a sudden tense clasping of her hands.

"Welcome to this evening's performance," Sister Hall said sweetly. "As you know, tonight's proceeds will benefit the temple fund, so we thank you for your generosity and support." Her gaze swept back and forth across the audience. When she reached Tabitha, she stopped. Her eyes seemed to flicker between Tabitha and Samuel, and her smile faltered. She cleared her throat and went on. "Following the play, we'll have some poetry recitations. Until then, enjoy tonight's performance."

Samuel leaned over. "Tab, do you want to leave?"

She sniffed and shook her head valiantly. "No. I'm going to stay. The lioness will not defeat me." She glanced over and gave him a wan smile. "But thank you for the offer."

The audience clapped as Sister Hall exited the stage area. Tabitha noticeably relaxed, and Samuel did too. They watched the play in companionable silence without any further disturbance. After the play and four poetry recitations, Sister Hall came out again. That's when the color seemed to drain from Tabitha's face. Samuel had an urge to take her hand for support but felt that would be too forward. Instead he shot her a sympathetic glance.

Sister Hall took her place once more at the front platform. Her eyes scanned the assembly briefly then found Tabitha again. As she spoke, she stared at her daughter-in-law as if directing the words to her. "For our final performance of the evening, I will be reciting 'To My Dear and Loving Husband,' by Anne Bradstreet."

Tabitha swallowed. Samuel felt a wave of anger rising up in him. He had hoped that the evening would continue without any trouble. But if one person could cause Tabitha grief, it would be this woman, and here she was, reciting a poem about a wife's devotion. Samuel couldn't quite believe her subject choice was a coincidence.

Sister Hall took a deep breath, closing her eyes in preparation. Then she opened her eyes and began. "'If ever two were one, then surely we. If ever man were loved by wife, then thee.'"

Tabitha's jaw clenched. She looked down and picked at her gloves, clearly avoiding her mother-in-law's stare. The poem—blessedly—was a short one. But even to Samuel, the ending felt like a dagger to the heart.

"'Then while we live, in love let's so persevere that when we live no more, we may live ever.'" Applause erupted at the emotional performance, and Sister Hall curtsyed. Tabitha pressed her eyes closed.

Samuel clapped less than enthusiastically, noting that as Tabitha opened her eyes, they were full of unshed tears. With a grim line of determination on her mouth, she lifted her chin and clapped.

Sister Hall nodded elegantly and thanked the attendees for coming, after which the audience stood and slowly dispersed. Only too happy to leave, Samuel stood to lead her into the aisle. But Tabitha didn't stand right away. She waited until the room was nearly empty before she stood. She walked to the front of the room, Samuel right at her side. When she caught Mother Hall's eye, she said with severe politeness, "What a wonderful performance, Mother Hall. You've always had such a . . . *theatrical* flair."

Before the woman could respond, Tabitha turned, swishing her skirts on the floor. At the back door, she paused and turned inside for a moment. Mother Hall stared at her, open-mouthed. Tabitha deliberately placed a hand through Samuel's arm and nodded to her across the room's expanse. With that, she turned on her heel and left, Samuel leading her out the door and into the crisp night air. He had to force the twitching in his mouth not to turn into a smile. Tabitha's walking out on his arm was an act of defeating Sister Hall at her own game.

They were several yards away—well beyond earshot of the Assembly Hall—when Tabitha burst out with, "The nerve of that woman. The *nerve!*" She covered her face with both hands and took a deep breath. "I'm sorry, Samuel. I shouldn't be reacting this way. I was purely monstrous in there. It's just that . . ."

"You have no need to apologize," Samuel said, gently pulling her hands away from her face so he could peer at her. "I understand. I do."

She sniffed, her tears having finally fallen. "But I used you to get back at her. That wasn't right. It was childish and . . ."

The twitch returned to Samuel's mouth. "But it served her right," he said with a laugh. "It was beautiful what you did in there."

Tabitha chuckled, making Samuel laugh harder. He took her hand and put it through his arm. "Come, let's get you away from this place."

They walked in the cool night, brilliant stars sparkling above them. Every so often Tabitha wiped her cheek with her fingertips, but she seemed to be feeling better with every step. When they reached her home, she paused at the walkway and turned to him.

"Thank you for a wonderful evening, Samuel."

"And thank you for coming with me."

She smiled, turned toward the door, but paused and looked back. "Truly, thank you . . . for everything." With a sudden movement, she stepped close and rose on tiptoe, giving his cheek a quick peck. Then she spun on her heel and quickly pattered up the walkway and into the house.

Samuel stood there in mild shock. His fingertips touched his cheek in wonder. He remained immovable for several minutes until, slowly, he turned around and headed back down the footpath, thinking that if there were ever a time he didn't want to bathe, it would be now. He wouldn't wash that cheek until he absolutely needed to.

CHAPTER 20

ON MONDAY, TABITHA COULD HARDLY focus on her work. As she sat at her desk, a barrage of thoughts from the weekend played out in her mind—Mother Hall's less-than-subtle hint with her recitation, Samuel's sincere support, and the kiss she had given him. She rubbed her forehead.

What had she been thinking? Samuel must surely see her behavior as brazenly forward.

Today was not a good time to be distracted; the issue being printed was the one with the big announcement. So she tried to put off the thoughts about how Samuel must view her, but in their place came worries over the announcement and whether the paper would survive it. She had prayed about the decision all weekend, and she felt that running the announcement and following Jeremiah's story were the right thing to do. What she *hadn't* felt was a reassurance that doing so wouldn't destroy her little press.

As Joseph and Victor tied off the bundles and loaded them into the wagon, she tried to calm her mind but suddenly felt nervous over what the public response would be to the change of ownership. When the wagons took the printed and tied stacks and hauled them away, she left the office, desperately needing to distract herself.

She retrieved Will from home and headed to see Mantia, knowing that Will loved to spend time with the horse. As they passed the Little Fort, she wondered if Samuel was still at work. She hadn't seen him since the benefit except for a brief glimpse during sacrament meeting yesterday. The thought of seeing him again was both a bit exciting and frightening. She had been *so* forward.

When she and Will reached the pen, they climbed onto the fence around the corral. Side by side, they sat on the top beam and watched the horse walk around the area as they had on many other days.

"So how soon before we can ride her?" Will asked.

"Not for a while," Tabitha said. "She still has a lot to learn."

"But she'll learn real quick, because she knows you're nice," Will said as if it were a statement of fact that Mantia's training would be complete in short order.

"I hope you're right," Tabitha said with a smile.

"What are you going to do with her first?" Will asked. "I mean, does she know how to wear a bridle?"

"Unfortunately, we're nowhere near that," Tabitha said with a shake of her head. "She's scarcely halter-broken, and that's only if you count the trip over here. And her hoof hasn't healed all the way, either."

"Hooey," Will said solemnly with a shake of his head. "Mama, you've sure got your work cut out for ya."

Tabitha looked over at him and bit her lips together to avoid laughing aloud. Will had surely just echoed some adult he had heard say the same thing, down to the same intonation and gesture of adjusting his hat. Now Will leaned one elbow on his knee and rested his chin on his hand, putting the other on his hip—just like so many of the grown men did.

"Yes, Will, we sure do have our work cut out for us," Tabitha said, glad her voice didn't betray her with a chuckle.

A moment later, Samuel walked up behind them. "So how is she today?"

Will whipped around and nearly jumped off the railing and into Samuel's arms. "Hey! You're here! We're going to try a bit of trainin' today."

"You are, are you?" Samuel leaned his arms against the fence railing and nodded toward Mantia. "Looks like she's gained some weight."

"You think?" Tabitha asked hopefully. Samuel appeared casual and friendly as usual, with no trace of awkwardness. She wasn't sure if that was a good thing or not. "I thought she looked better, but I wasn't sure if it was just wishful thinking on my part."

"I'm sure of it," Samuel said with a nod. "Don't you agree, Will?"

Will, pressing both hands on his thighs, pursed his lips tightly and examined the horse with squinting eyes. With a slow nod filled with six years' expertise, he said, "Yep. I think you're right."

"Wish me luck," Tabitha said. "I'm going to try getting a halter on her again. See if she'll trust me after the trip over here. She's had over a week to get used to me." She lifted a halter from the fence post beside her and hopped down into the pen. She took a deep breath and walked slowly, easy step by easy step, toward the horse.

"Mantia," she said in an even, soothing voice. She held out her hand and the halter for the mare to sniff at. "Come here, girl."

The horse snorted, turned, and trotted a few feet away, shaking her head. *But she's not afraid of me,* Tabitha thought happily. *She's just avoiding me. We've made progress.*

Undeterred—but very aware of Samuel watching—Tabitha tried again. Mantia looked distrusting, suspicious, but there were no signs of fear. Walking slowly again, Tabitha reached the mare's side and put out a hand. Mantia didn't pull away but instead smelled Tabitha's palm then snorted and turned away. Tabitha continued speaking. She was hardly aware of what she said; she just wanted to keep her voice in the air, to continue to calm and reassure the mare. Tabitha moved extra slowly, finally making contact. With her fingers splayed, she held her hand in one place and felt the ribcage go up and down. Still Mantia didn't move away. Encouraged, Tabitha let out an uneasy breath. She drew her hand slowly up to the horse's neck, and suddenly the horse whinnied and pawed at the ground. Her ears twitched.

Tabitha stopped moving. "Easy, girl," she said, reaching out her left hand, the one holding the halter. Mantia leaned in and sniffed it but again didn't pull away. Tabitha glanced over her shoulder at Will and Samuel, who grinned their encouragement. Will bounced up and down on the fence, looking fit to burst with excitement, but fortunately, he kept quiet.

Swallowing, Tabitha gripped the halter with both hands and slid it over Mantia's nose. The horse started at first but didn't seem too upset, so Tabitha quickly buckled the strap behind her ears. The horse whinnied and shook her head from side to side and then up and down, trying to get rid of the foreign object. But she didn't have a wild look in her eyes. She didn't rear up, and her ears didn't lie flat—

all hopeful signs. Tabitha took a step backward to be out of the way, biting her lip, her hands clasped beneath her chin as she watched.

I did it, she thought. *One more step toward success.*

She glanced back at Samuel and realized that he didn't look tense or nervous—and that if he were feeling anxious, Mantia would have sensed it by now. *Everyone's making progress,* Tabitha thought happily. Getting up her courage, she reached for the lead rope and took a step back. When the rope grew taught, Mantia resisted it, but Tabitha kept the tension, pulling at an angle to the horse's body, which made her smoothly move to the side to relieve the pressure. Soon they were walking—slowly but surely—in a circle.

Unwilling though the steps might have been, Mantia was learning to follow Tabitha's lead, who, with each step, grew more secure in her belief that this horse would do great things, that with a little love and encouragement, she would rise above her past.

And I'll make it happen, she thought. *As long as it takes.*

She continued working with Mantia, circling the pen over and over again. The first lap around took a painfully long time, with Tabitha demanding every step and Mantia reluctantly giving in. But an hour later, they had made many rounds, each one a bit quicker than the last and a bit less forced.

To her surprise, Samuel quietly walked into the pen and stood beside her. "I'm betting your arms are tired," he said. "Shall I spell you?"

Grateful—and somewhat surprised by the offer coming from Samuel of all people—she agreed. "Of course."

He stepped closer, and Tabitha handed off the rope into his warm, strong hands. The touch sent a thrill up her arm and down her back. She stepped out of his way, and rubbed the sudden gooseflesh from her arms. She hopped back onto the corral fence beside Will and watched Samuel guide the horse around and around as if his muscles would never tire and as if he had broken a horse hundreds of times.

At one point he looked at her and grinned. "Not too shabby for a London boy."

"Not shabby at all," Tabitha agreed.

Eventually it was clear that Mantia had had enough for the day. Tabitha hopped back to the ground and walked to Samuel's side. "Let's get her some food as a reward," she said, reaching for the rope.

But Samuel merely drew in more of the length and led Mantia to the feeding and watering trough himself. After her exercise, the mare happily drank her fill. Tabitha turned to see Samuel tying the rope to a post.

"We did it," she said, reaching into her pocket and withdrawing a couple of carrots taken from her father's garden. Her arm extended, she held out a carrot in an open palm. Curious, Mantia left her water and sniffed it. She began to turn away but returned to sniff again, then quickly snatched the orange stick.

"Yes, we did it," Samuel said. He nodded thoughtfully. "And not once did I land in manure."

"That's definitely progress," Tabitha said with a laugh. "Mantia, I'll see you again soon." The horse pulled away, but Tabitha didn't worry about it. "Someday we'll be great friends. You'll see." Mantia cocked her ears forward—almost as if she had heard and maybe understood.

They laughed, and together they headed back to where Will sat. As they walked, Tabitha watched Samuel. He seemed perfectly at ease around her after the other night.

At least we're still friends, she thought. *I haven't chased him away.*

* * *

Jeremiah sat at his small wooden table and reread the letter. It was written in a delicate hand on a small sheet of off-white paper. It gave off a hint of lavender, foreign to his rugged and dank cabin. He'd already gone over the words several times, and although each reading seemed to pierce his heart and threaten to make an old man cry, he found himself beginning again as soon as he finished the final line.

Dear Father,

I've never called you that before. Indeed, I've never felt that you were really my father. That is, not until the events of the last several weeks. Words cannot express my gratitude at your willingness to sacrifice yourself on behalf of my family.

Contemplating jail and being away from my husband and children for any amount of time makes me shudder and weep. I

dearly hope you will not pay for my crime, that somehow you will
be acquitted. If the court finds you guilty and you must be
confined, however, know that your daughter is praying for you
and thinking of you every day.
Now I can say with all honesty that I love you, Father.

Your loving daughter,

Betty

Jeremiah lowered the letter to the table and closed it at the fold. His
callused fingers smoothed it flat. Over the course of his life, he hadn't ever
lived up to many standards. He despised himself for that as much—or
more than—most people hated him, and could come up with plenty of
appropriate monikers if the townspeople ever ran out of ideas on what to
call him. Lately they seemed to have an unlimited supply. He didn't
mind; he could put up with it for her sake. He was a rapscallion, after all.

And I got a temper, he thought, ticking off his weaknesses. It's that
temper that made him lose control when trying to get that fool horse
to cooperate, plus a sense of wanting to have some power or control
over something. *I'm pathetic,* he thought. *Only a coward feels powerful*
by hurting a creature. But I've always been rash.

He unfolded the letter yet again, smoothed it out on the table,
and looked at the signature at the bottom. She'd written her name in
a pretty script. His finger traced the curling letters. Betty was the
result of what was arguably the most rash and foolish act he'd ever
done, one that eventually led him to the life he now had. Had he
handled things differently, been a better man, maybe Patricia would
have stayed with him instead of marrying that Donald Hunsaker.
Then he would have been able to raise Betty as his own rather than
watching her from afar and having nothing to do with her. But it was
too late for "what ifs."

At least Donald accepted her as his own, he thought, wanting to
give the man his due. Donald was a much better man than Jeremiah
had ever been.

Protecting Betty now might be the best thing he'd ever tried to
do. At first it had started out as nothing more than that—trying to fix

her foolish actions so she wouldn't get into trouble. But now? Now he'd go to jail happily for her. She'd called him *Father*.

A knock sounded on the door. With a start, Jeremiah stood up and looked at the letter. He hurriedly shoved it into his pocket then crossed the small room. His visitor knocked again before he pulled the door open.

"What is it?" he called grumpily, then laid eyes on Tabitha Chadwick. "Oh, it's you. What do you want now?"

Tabitha held out a newspaper. "I brought a copy of yesterday's edition, just in case you hadn't seen it. It states that I am in fact the owner of the paper. I thought you might like to know that it's official."

He took the paper, which was folded so the announcement was on top, going down in one of four thin columns, but he hardly bothered with more than a glance. "I already know you're the owner. You told me, remember? Why are you really here?"

She didn't answer at first. "Honestly?" she asked. "Very well. I want to know why you refuse to defend yourself. You said at first that you didn't steal the money. Now you're upset that I'm upholding that statement." The woman eyed him directly as she spoke; it was disconcerting. He was used to people avoiding his gaze.

"Just let the matter be, woman," Jeremiah said, holding the paper out for her to take. "I'll serve some time, and no one else need be bothered with it."

"But that's wrong," Tabitha said. "If you didn't commit a crime, then someone else is going scot-free. I've been defending you in the paper for weeks now, and a lot of people are upset about it. I'd like to think I wasn't doing it for naught. I think you know who did it, and you're covering for them."

Her face was flushed with emotion. The color made her prettier, Jeremiah thought. "I'm sorry I've caused you trouble. But please—leave it be."

He moved to close the door, but Tabitha stepped forward and held it open with her hand. "Don't, Mr. Hancock."

"My life is mine to live, Miss Chadwick. Good day." He jolted the door a bit to make her let go. Her eyes went to the ground, and she stooped to pick something up. He took the opportunity to close the door in her face. Once back inside, he went to the fireplace and moved the wood about, checking whether he had enough coals to make himself a meal yet. He set the poker to the side then instinctively put his hand into his pocket to retrieve the letter.

It wasn't there. His eyes went wide, and he whipped around—searching the table, the floor, and the fireplace for the precious paper.

"Mr. Hancock?" The voice came from the other side of the door. It was the blasted newspaper woman again. He didn't want to answer the door, so he waited, hoping against hope, when she called again. "You dropped something out here, Mr. Hancock."

His temper flared. He bolted to the door and ripped it open, making Tabitha jump in surprise. When she recovered, she held out the letter. "Here. I believe this is yours."

He snatched the paper and studied her face. Had she read it? Did she know? He muttered a thank-you but hesitated in closing the door. If she knew . . . He opened his mouth to speak, but she beat him to it.

"I understand now," she said.

His heart about leapt out of his chest. "You—you read it."

"It fell open. I didn't read the whole thing, but it was hard *not* to see how you were addressed . . . and who sent it."

His teeth worked against his lips as he tried to formulate a thought and words, but all that came out was, "Please . . ."

"Mr. Hancock, you can't go to jail for this. It's not right."

"What if I *want* to?" he demanded. "It's my life."

She smiled wanly. "But it's not your crime." She paused, thinking. "Look, I don't think Daggett would necessarily want to press charges if he were to find out it was Betty who did it. And the courts would probably be more lenient on a woman anyway."

"I've never been able to do anything for her before," Jeremiah said helplessly. "Now I can."

"I'm a parent, too, Jeremiah," she said—the first time he recalled her using his given name. "As a mother, I have to let my son stumble at times. The only way he'll learn from his mistakes is to be accountable for them. It's hard, but it's what a parent must do."

"No. For once I can give her—"

"Saving her from the truth isn't a gift," Tabitha said firmly. "Love her enough to let her face what she's done."

The woman was right. Jeremiah wished with his entire heart that she wasn't, but he knew otherwise. *Foolish, meddling woman.*

"I don't think she'll understand," he said. "She may hate me if I reveal her."

"You might be underestimating your daughter," Tabitha said, touching his arm. "Give her credit for having a bit of the Hancock spirit. It's a force to be reckoned with." She smiled a bit at that, and Jeremiah had to chuckle even as his vision grew blurred with moisture.

"*Spirit,* ya call it?" he said gruffly, refusing to let the tears fall. He pointed at the newspaper which she still held in one hand. "You goin' to print this, then, in your paper? About who's really responsible for the thievin'?"

"I don't want to, but I think I have to," Tabitha said, but by the look on her face, the idea didn't give her any satisfaction.

Good woman, that, Jeremiah thought, amazed. She really meant what she said, that she had to stand up for what was right.

"You go talk to her," Tabitha said. "It's only Tuesday. Nothing will be public until Monday afternoon."

Jeremiah pictured Betty's horrified face when he told her that he wouldn't be protecting her any longer. His little girl. His baby. No longer able to hold back tears, Jeremiah felt them tumble down his cheeks. His body shook with emotion. Tabitha stepped forward, and to his surprise, she put her arms around his neck. He embraced her in return and cried into her hair.

"You're doing a good thing, Jeremiah Hancock," she whispered.

"I hope she sees it that way," he murmured.

CHAPTER 21

ANOTHER BLAST SOUNDED FROM THE quarry in the distance. Sitting at her desk, Tabitha gritted her teeth. It seemed as if there had been more black powder used today than in weeks—she jumped every few minutes, it seemed, at another one. But perhaps it was just because her nerves were already on edge. The noise hadn't bothered her much for weeks. The strain she was under was surely making her nerves raw.

She rubbed her forehead and groaned, then balled up her latest attempt at writing an article about Betty Tidwell's guilt and confession and threw it into the trash can. The last several days had been difficult. Tabitha had already made four other attempts to write out the story. Each time, the end result was the same. She questioned whether reporting the discovery was the right thing to do. She *thought* it was. She had ensured that Jeremiah had plenty of time to tell Betty, so it wouldn't come as a shock to her.

But what if the community hated Tabitha for doing it? They'd already convicted Jeremiah in their hearts; having him revealed as innocent and a supposedly upstanding woman of the town blamed instead . . . That would certainly make for some angry people.

And possibly the end of the Sentinel *to boot,* she thought grimly. She set her pen down, wiped the nib clean with a cloth, and corked the ink bottle. She'd give it another try tomorrow, Saturday. She'd *have* to find a way to say it by then. Her staff had already left for the day. She'd lock up the office and visit her horse. On Tuesday—before she'd gone to talk with Jeremiah—she'd tried putting a saddle on Mantia, who'd worn it with apparent ease. Tabitha had repeated the effort every day since. Today she'd try mounting her.

With school out, Will often came to work with Tabitha and helped with odds and ends or sat beside her, scribbling his own stories or reading books. Today she deliberately left him home with his grandmother, knowing that with all the pressure she felt, she needed some quiet at the office. She also didn't want Will around when she first mounted Mantia.

She locked up and headed down the street, feeling uneasy. Every time she passed someone and wished them good day, she wondered how this person or that one felt about the announcement—and how they'd feel about her upcoming article.

The thoughts weren't unfounded. Ever since that week's announcement, she'd been feeling a quiet withdrawal of support from her readership. It wasn't overt; no one stopped her on the street to express their dismay. But eight regular advertisers had pulled their spots, and fifteen people had canceled their subscriptions—so far. Not to mention the nine letters of complaint that arrived by post. As things stood, her next issue would be two pages long instead of four.

And that issue would include something far more upsetting to a lot of people than her ownership. She grimaced at the thought of what next week would bring. More cancellations? More angry letters?

She went to the Little Fort stable to retrieve Mantia, where the horse now boarded when she wasn't training at the round pen. It was quite an accomplishment that she was able to be led through the city streets without any ruckus. She met Samuel at the stable as he finished his work.

"May I join you?" he asked. At her pleased nod, he took the lead rope and clucked to Mantia. The threesome walked out of the stables and down the street toward McCleve's place. Tabitha wanted to share her frustrations and worries with Samuel but resisted. He didn't need to be burdened by her cares. She tried to wear a happy face so he wouldn't know that anything was amiss. After a minute of silence, Samuel asked, "So what is on the agenda for her today?"

Grateful for a topic unrelated to the paper, Tabitha latched on to it. "She wore the saddle well all week, so I'm thinking about seeing if she'll let me mount." She looked up at him with a worried expression. "But I'm a bit nervous; I don't know if either of us is truly ready for it. No, that's not entirely true. I am very ready for it. It's just . . . *here* already."

"I can imagine," Samuel said.

It was one thing to buckle up a saddle; it was something else entirely to climb onto a horse and sit in the saddle. This was why Tabitha had purposely not gone to fetch Will from home to join her today. While she didn't *think* the horse would spook or even throw her, there was no way to know for certain, and she refused to risk Will's peace of mind over something of that nature. Not to mention that if there was talk of someone sitting on the horse, Will would plead on his knees to be Mantia's first rider. Such a plan would never gain her approval in this life or the next.

"I'm sure she'll be fine. You'll *both* be fine," Samuel said as they reached the pen.

Tabitha unlocked the gate, and Samuel led the way inside. After securing the latch, Tabitha went up to where Samuel had tied the horse to a post. She stroked Mantia's neck. "You're such an amazing girl, you know that?" she said. "Look at how far you've come. Today is going to be special."

Despite her nerves, Tabitha was all too ready for this moment—the one where she would sit on her formerly wild horse for the first time. Now that she was with Mantia, it was easy to put away her worries about the paper for the time being. They'd be waiting for her when she finished here anyway.

"You said yourself that you're both ready," Samuel said, smiling as he looked at the horse instead of her. He nodded. "Go on. You know it's time."

He was right; it was time. Mantia was ready. After trying to win her trust, often finding only a snippet of success there—at times no more than a glimmer of the victory that might lie ahead—Mantia was ready to take the next big step.

In silent cooperation, Tabitha and Samuel fetched the tack. He retrieved the saddle while Tabitha carried the saddle blanket and bridle.

"Hello, girl," Tabitha said to Mantia, putting her hand out. The horse nuzzled her palm as if looking for a carrot. Not finding one, the mare turned away calmly. Tabitha still found even that simple act thrilling—the fact that Mantia trusted so implicitly, was so calm in their presence, made Tabitha want to laugh out loud in victory.

She petted the side of the horse's face and neck then put the bridle on. Mantia shook her head as if the leather around her face and the metal bit in her mouth still felt unnatural and distracting.

"It's all right, girl," Tabitha soothed, patting her again. With a final snort and a shake of her head, Mantia calmed and took a few small steps from side to side. "It's all right. Good girl," Tabitha continued in the reassuring voice she always used at the stable. She nodded to Samuel, who came closer.

Putting one hand on Mantia's neck, she walked into position, all the while keeping her hand tracing her movement along the coat so the mare would know where she was at all times and have no surprises.

"Here's the blanket," Tabitha said. "You remember it, right? Nice and easy, now." Tabitha smoothed the thick cloth onto Mantia's slightly swaying back and ribs, which had rounded out properly. Her coat shone in the sun thanks to Tabitha and Will's regular grooming. Even the worst of the sores had nearly healed, now that the horse let them close enough to wash and bandage the wound. She now looked almost like a normal, healthy, beautiful horse. In a few more weeks, after the last crack in her hoof healed completely, even someone who sold horses for a living would have to look closely to see any effects of her past life.

At Tabitha's nod, Samuel picked up the saddle with a heave and gently placed it on Mantia's back. Tabitha kept talking to and touching the horse the entire time. "Good girl," she said. She adjusted the position of the saddle then cinched it tight. She let Mantia wear the saddle for several minutes before taking the next step.

"Here we go," she said, breathing out unsteadily, nervous about how Mantia would react when Tabitha put her foot into the stirrup and sat on top.

Samuel stood by Mantia's head, letting the horse sniff him and recognize his now-familiar scent. He smiled at the horse, and Tabitha watched the exchange with pleasure. She remembered Mantia getting frightened and running over Samuel's leg. Who would have thought that the two of them would ever be friends?

"Are you ready then?" Samuel asked, holding the top of the lead rope next to the mare's face.

With a firm nod, she said yes. She grasped the reins in her left hand and slipped her left foot into a stirrup, then reached up to the saddle horn. *Here goes nothing.*

After a couple of hops on her right foot, she gripped the saddle horn hard and pulled herself up to the saddle. She had worn a split skirt for this very reason, knowing that training side saddle would be difficult. The leather creaked under her weight as she settled into place and held her breath for Mantia's reaction. The horse turned to look at Tabitha sitting in the saddle, and for a moment her body quivered. Then she snorted and stood still.

"What a good girl," Tabitha said, leaning forward and stroking her neck in a gesture of comfort. Mantia held her position, head erect, as if waiting for her mistress to tell her where to go and what to do. Tears pricked Tabitha's eyes, and she looked to Samuel in triumph.

He folded his arms and nodded with pleasure. "You did it."

Tabitha covered her mouth with one hand as emotion filled her. Looking from Samuel to the horse and back, she said, "I did, didn't I?" She patted the horse again. "We did it together, didn't we, girl?"

She sat atop the horse for several minutes to give the horse a good sense of what a rider felt like. When the horse began shifting her feet with impatience, Tabitha decided it was time to get down. Once she was back on solid ground, Samuel removed the bridle and left the halter then removed the saddle and the blanket, which Tabitha took from him and returned to Brother McCleve's stable. Samuel gave the mare some carrots as a treat, then returned to Tabitha's side. He had done all of it as if each step were as natural as putting on his boots in the morning.

Tabitha untied the lead rope, and together she and Samuel led the horse out of the pen and up the street toward her new home at the Little Fort. "You're good with her," Tabitha said, her voice filled with admiration.

"It helps to have had a good teacher," Samuel said, following at her side. He paused in the road. "You look tired."

"I am," Tabitha admitted. "It's been a trying week at the paper." She shook her head. "Some very difficult issues to sort out."

"I heard," Samuel said with a nod. "Can I help in some way?"

Tabitha simply shook her head.

He squeezed her shoulder gently. "Please let me know if I can do anything. Anything at all."

She lifted her chin proudly, trying desperately to stay strong. "I'll manage, but thank you. This is my problem to sort out."

A flicker of hurt crossed Samuel's face but left as quickly as it appeared. *It's not his problem,* she thought. *It's mine, and I must handle it. I cannot rely on someone else to be my strength.*

"All right," he said, but his eyes held hers for a moment, his gaze steady and pleading. It made her want to melt into his arms and weep, but a woman of strength—a woman who could fight the lions—wouldn't do that. "Tabitha, at least let me take care of Mantia for you."

She could surrender this much; Samuel was a dear. "That would be a great help," Tabitha said hoarsely, handing over the lead rope. "Thank you. Good night, Samuel."

Samuel waved at her and moved on with Mantia. "Go get some rest," he said as he withdrew.

"Good night," she called, then turned and walked toward home. Before long her thoughts turned to Will, who was probably watching for her through the window by now. He'd surely bound out of the house and ask when they'd be going to visit Mantia this evening. She'd have to tell him that they weren't going. But when she reached the house, she saw no sign of Will and instead saw an unfamiliar wagon out front.

Curious, she crossed to the wagon to figure out whose it was. At the edge of the bed, she lifted her heels and peered inside. All at once, she felt sharp pains on both sides of her torso. She yelped loudly, her heart racing as she whipped around.

Her older brother Nathaniel stood there, laughing. "You're so easy to sneak up on," he said, catching his breath.

"You know I hate being tickled," Tabitha said, rubbing her sides.

"And *you* know I can't resist." He opened his arms. "Hug? I promise to be good. It's been a lot of years since I've seen my little sister, after all."

Tabitha laughed and went into his embrace. "It's good to see you, Nathaniel," she said, hugging him tight. "Just don't tickle me again."

With his arm around her, they were heading up the footpath to the front door when footsteps sounded behind them. Tabitha looked over. It was Mother Hall, not a stone's throw away and heading straight for the house.

Tabitha stiffened and turned toward her. "Good evening. To what pleasure can we attribute your visit this evening?"

Without preamble, Mother Hall folded her arms and spoke. "I am duly shocked that someone who bears my family name would willfully deceive the community." Tabitha opened her mouth to speak, but her mother-in-law bowled right over her. "Furthermore, I am dismayed that you would support a scoundrel such as Jeremiah Hancock." She slapped an envelope into Tabitha's hands. "This cancels my subscription to *your* paper. I hope you think hard about what you're doing, my dear. I don't think Fred would have approved."

She spun on her heels and marched away. Tabitha bit her lips, wanting to tear the envelope into tiny pieces and stomp on them. Instead she closed her eyes and sighed. "On that delightful note, let's go inside."

Nathaniel pointed toward Mother Hall then at the envelope. "I think we have a lot to catch up on."

"A lot has happened," she said vaguely, not sure if she wanted to relive her problems by telling them to her brother. She put her arm through his, and together they walked up to the house, her head resting on his arm. As much of a tease as Nathaniel always had been, he'd also been fiercely loyal.

I need that right now, she thought.

* * *

After supper, Will got on his uncle's back and rode on pretend horseback through the sitting room, the young boy shrieking with joy whenever his uncle bucked and reared. Hearing Will laugh and romp with an uncle he had never known made Tabitha smile.

She questioned whether coming back to Manti was the correct choice after all.

She disdainfully tossed Mother Hall's envelope into the fire without opening it then sat on a chair and watched the flames curl the paper and turn it black. Her newspaper was falling apart. She wanted to hide in a cave until everyone forgot about her position there, to stop printing for a few weeks until people had forgotten about the ruckus, then begin again with a fresh slate. Maybe tell only the news people wanted to hear—the only negative things being the ones taking place far, far away. But at the same time, she couldn't do that, and she knew it. She had to tell the truth about what was happening there in Manti. Right there, right then. Even if it meant she'd have to still her printing press.

Watching Will and Nathaniel, she wished she could freeze the moment and never reach press day again. *Will wouldn't be playing with his uncle if we'd stayed in Logan,* she thought. There had been many good consequences from her returning home. She had to keep reminding herself of that.

Nathaniel rounded the crackling fireplace again. This time he sat up, kneeling, and effectively slipping Will off his "saddle." The boy clung to his uncle's neck. Nathaniel pretended to choke then dragged Will around to the front and tickled him until the boy gasped for air.

"Hey, Mama," Will finally said, sitting up and breathing heavily. He jumped to his feet and ran to her. "Uncle Nathaniel says you used to put toads in his dinner pail for school. Is that true?"

"That's not quite how I remember it," Tabitha said with a laugh. "Don't let him fool you; Uncle Nathaniel is the real trickster in the family. *He* put them in *my* pail." She gave him a big hug and tousled his hair. "Go get ready for bed now, Will."

As he opened his mouth to protest, Tabitha's mother came in, took his hand, and led him off. "Off we go, Will," she said cheerfully.

"Thank you, Mother," Tabitha said, giving her a peck on the cheek as the two of them passed.

"Go catch up with your brother," her mother said with a smile. "I want to be Grandma."

Nathaniel took a seat opposite her and wiped a sleeve across his forehead, damp from the exertion of playing horse.

"So what's bothering my little sister?" he asked, sitting back into the cushions. "I imagine it has something to do with that letter you tossed in there."

Tabitha shrugged. "It's nothing."

"It's hardly nothing," Nathaniel said. "I can tell by the look in your eyes and the way you're holding your mouth. It's the same look you wore after you forgot the lyrics at the school Christmas concert when we were kids. *Something* is bothering you."

Dear Nathaniel. He always could read her face. She sighed heavily. "It's just business problems. Nothing worth discussing."

He leaned forward, a mischievous look on his face and the fingers of both hands extended. "Are you going to tell me what the trouble is, or am I going to have to tickle it out of you?"

"Very funny," Tabitha said, looking back to the fire.

With sudden movement, he sprang from his chair. Tabitha shrieked and wrapped her arms about her protectively. Nathaniel, now standing by her side, burst out laughing. "I told you I'd do it."

She shook her head. "I should always believe a threat coming from you, shouldn't I?"

Nathaniel settled back into his chair. "Seriously. What's wrong?"

Tabitha studied her fingernails for a few seconds, trying to decide how much to tell him. When she lifted her face to speak, every detail came out: her first letter from Brother Christensen, the robbery, Brother Christensen's ire at her handling of the situation, the community's reaction to her ownership, and finally, her discovering who had really perpetrated the crime at the Daggett home.

When she finished her story, she held out her hands helplessly. "I wish I could just hide and wait for the storm to blow over."

"Maybe it will blow over," Nathaniel said. "Why don't you and Will come up to Ephraim for a spell?" He grabbed an iron poker and prodded the fire with it. "Mary and I would love to have you over, and the little ones would have their eyes glaze over with excitement if they got to play with a new cousin. Stay away for a week or so. Let it blow over."

"And run away again?" Tabitha stared at the flames as they leapt to life with new fuel to consume. She shook her head adamantly. "I can't do that." As much as she desperately wanted to. She shrugged. "Maybe Will could go up for a few days while I fix things. I'm sure he'd enjoy that."

"Consider it done." Nathaniel replaced the poker in the iron stand beside the fireplace and pulled his chair closer so their knees nearly touched when he sat down. "But Tabitha, there would be no shame in *you* going away for a few days too. No one would blame you for it."

"I know, but I *can't*." She leaned forward, touching his hand, and tried to make him understand. "Don't you see? I can't just run away from home whenever life gets difficult. I'm not that person anymore."

Nathaniel searched her face, his forehead wrinkling. "What do you mean, 'anymore'?"

In her brother's eyes, Tabitha saw love and concern—and confusion. Her eyes teared up, making him appear blurry, but she didn't look away. "I'm not that weak thing who broke into a thousand pieces when Fred died. I left that girl behind and grew up . . . I can't let myself run away again. I have to face my problems head-on."

Her brother cupped her hands between his own. "You hear me now, Tab, and hear me good. As young as you were when you became a widow, you handled yourself with amazing grace and fortitude."

"No, I didn't," Tabitha said, shaking her head. "I let myself fall into utter despair."

"Something perfectly natural to do after experiencing a shock and enduring such grief—during a pregnancy, no less."

He still didn't understand. She tried to explain. "But I *ran away.*"

Nathaniel would have none of it. "No, you didn't. You bettered your life. Look what you've done since leaving—not running away from, but *leaving* Manti—you've gone to school, become a teacher, taken care of your son single-handedly, written for a newspaper—and now you *own* one . . ."

She pulled her hands away and covered her mouth with them, standing. She walked to the fireplace mantel, where she gripped it, wishing for strength. The heat of the fire felt scorching this close. When she spoke, it was to the pinewood mantel, in almost a whisper. "I only did those things *after* I left, after I ran away." She turned to face her brother, who now stood behind her. "If I run again, I'm becoming that weak little girl again. And if I become her again . . ." A lump rose in her throat. "If I do that, I might lose everything I've gained."

"You don't really believe that, do you?" But after searching her eyes, he nodded. "I *think* I understand—at least a little." He sighed. "Well, can Mary and I at least help with something—anything? You know our home and hearts are open to you. We'll do anything we can—just ask."

"I appreciate the offer, but this is something I have to face myself," Tabitha said.

He nodded, his eyes narrowing. "But you'll let me know if you think of anything I can do, right? Even if it's something like, oh, breaking someone's nose." His mouth cracked into a slight smile, and Tabitha laughed aloud. She had no doubt of his willingness—or ability—to do exactly that in her defense.

"It's funny . . ." she said, her voice trailing off as she studied him, a bit of wonder in her voice.

"What?"

She shrugged. "That you've grown into such a sweet, dear man, willing to do anything for his annoying little sister."

"I'm shocked," Nathaniel said, pretending to be offended. "How else would I behave?"

"Like the mischievous boy who used to torment me."

He leaned an elbow against the mantel. "What, do you still think that I, as a mature adult, am still capable of throwing you onto the manure heap?"

"I have no doubt you are fully capable—and *willing*," Tabitha said, trying to keep her face straight but not *quite* succeeding. "Or worse."

Nathaniel made a sudden move as if to grab her, and Tabitha yelped as she dodged him, running behind a chair for protection. Her heart beat crazily from the jolt, but when she paused, she laughed, panting. "The rascal will always be somewhere inside of you."

"I hope to never lose him completely," Nathaniel said with a grin. His face softened, and he added, "But I'm on your side of the battle, sis. Remember that. You don't have to fight this alone."

With her throat getting tight and eyes watering again, Tabitha nodded, but the words she wanted to say only echoed in her mind.

Yes, I do.

CHAPTER 22

MONDAY MORNING, NATHANIEL PACKED UP his wagon after a weekend of helping their father with some work. He hefted a small sack into the bed for Will, who stood by his mother. Tabitha gave him a crushing hug. "Be good for Aunt Mary and Uncle Nathaniel," she said. "And be safe. Remember to say your prayers every night."

"I will, Mama." He kissed her cheek then bounded over to Nathaniel, who hoisted him up to the bench. Tabitha wrapped her arms about herself, feeling wistful. Her son would be fine. He'd be safe and happy. He'd have a delightful time getting acquainted with his cousins. But she had never been apart from him more than a few hours. Her motherly heart ached.

Nathaniel lifted his hat and waved. Will looked over and mimicked his uncle, lifting up his own cap and waving it back and forth as his uncle snapped the reins and moved forward. Tabitha laughed and raised a hand too.

"Have a good time," she called.

"Oh, I will, Mama!" Will called over his shoulder. "Uncle Nathaniel says he'll teach me how to hunt for frogs!"

Oh, lovely, Tabitha thought with a laugh. Then again, her son had been without the regular influence of a man for most of his life. Learning a few things from his uncle would be good—even if it meant some schoolgirl in Manti finding a frog in her dinner pail this fall.

Tabitha watched him go, grateful for how happy he seemed. Will had good friends in Manti. He had a wonderful relationship with his grandparents. This week would bring him closer to his cousins. While he'd never seemed unhappy in Logan, Will had certainly bloomed into a fuller version of himself since coming to Manti. The move had been good for him. This trip would be good for them both while his mother sorted through things.

Tabitha sighed and glanced down the street in the direction of the *Sentinel* building, wondering whether coming to Manti would end up to be as good a choice for her. She hadn't seen any blossoming for herself as yet, at least that she could see—only more demons of the past to face all the time.

With the wagon out of sight, Tabitha wrapped her shawl about her shoulders against the morning chill and headed west for Jeremiah's place. Today was the day. She wanted to be sure he'd done what they'd agreed to before she ran the article, which she'd finally written late Saturday night.

The walk to his front door went even faster than the time she'd gone there offering to buy Mantia. Dread made every step feel as if it took her much too quickly to her destination; the road seemed to fly beneath her feet. When she reached his place, she could hear Jeremiah out back, chopping firewood. She rounded the cabin. Jeremiah swung the axe, which *thunked* into a piece of wood.

"Good morning," she called.

Jeremiah looked over. He wiped a sleeve across his brow, which shone with perspiration. "Oh, it's you." He worked the axe head out of the wood and swung again. He grunted with exertion as it landed in the wood. "What do you want?"

"The paper will be printed today."

"I know. You told me already." The axe swung down again, this time breaking the piece in half. He put one of the halves on end and swung again, splitting the wood in two.

Tabitha watched him split another piece before continuing. "Did you talk to Betty? Is she aware of what the paper will say?"

Jeremiah's arm dropped to his side, and his shoulders seem to droop. He didn't look at her as he spoke. "She knows."

Wanting to say something but not knowing what, Tabitha opened her mouth, but nothing came out.

"Now please, just go," Jeremiah said, still facing away from her. "It's bad enough that I have to turn against my own blood. You don't need to rub salt into the wound."

"I don't mean to—"

"Go," Jeremiah interrupted gruffly.

Tabitha nodded to herself. "Very well. Good day, Mr. Hancock. For what it's worth, I'm sorry." She turned and headed for the *Sentinel,* feeling the sheet of paper in her pocket that bore the article.

She arrived and unlocked the office door and went inside. This time she went into the printing room, a place she didn't spend much time in. But today . . . today was different. She knew how to typeset now. And this was an article she felt she needed to typeset herself. Somehow she felt an obligation to place the letters, side by side, and own even this bit of the responsibility that would come with changing Betty's life. And Jeremiah's. And quite possibly her own.

* * *

Joseph and Victor walked into the printing room as she finished typesetting the article. It wasn't long, but it was the first article at the top of the first page.

"Sister Chadwick, what are you doing in here?" Victor asked.

"Getting some work done, that's all," Tabitha said. She grabbed a rag from the counter and wiped some grease from her fingers. "I believe I'll leave the rest of that to your more capable hands. The rest of today's stories and advertisements are on the counter." She headed toward her desk but paused in the doorway. "I think I'll go visit Mantia for a spell," she said. "I'll either be at the Little Fort or McCleve's place if you need me."

"I think we'll be fine," Joseph said. "But we'll be sure to let you know if we run into trouble."

Tabitha nodded, knowing that the men could put out the paper quickly today without her help. Normally, on Mondays she stayed in the office, where she went over the books and planned out some of the next week's edition. Today her nerves felt unraveled. She wouldn't be able to sit in that chair all day, knowing what was being printed just a few yards from her. "Could you please leave a copy on my desk? You two can close up after the wagon leaves."

"Will do, Sister Chadwick," Victor said with a nod.

"Thank you." Tabitha's voice was a bit breathless. She left the office and walked to the Little Fort, feeling much as she had in Logan when going to comfort herself near Chester. She was suddenly grateful for her purchase of the horse.

Inside the stables, she went straight to Mantia's stall, where she brushed the horse down and cleaned her hooves—which were now beautifully groomed and healing well. The mare nuzzled around as if looking for a treat. Tabitha had to smile. This wasn't the same animal she'd first seen cowering and bleeding. She put the brush onto a shelf and took the lead rope.

"Come here, girl," she said. "Let's go get some exercise." She led the horse down the center of the stable and out the door, where she nearly bumped into Samuel.

"Well, hello there," he said with a tilt of his head.

Tabitha's insides warmed. "Good morning."

"Are things looking up today?" Samuel asked. He looked up at the rafters as if avoiding a sensitive topic. "Better, I mean, than the last time I saw you?"

When I turned you away, Tabitha thought. "That remains to be seen," she said. "Today is my day of reckoning. I'm printing something rather . . . *big* . . . today. If it goes over poorly . . ." Her voice trailed off, and she suddenly had to swallow to keep the emotions at bay. "Thank you for asking."

"It's the least I can do," Samuel said with a smile.

And the only thing I'll let him do, Tabitha thought again. Why wouldn't she allow Samuel to get close to her? He was a good man, a helpful man. A man who made her insides go weak. *A man I kissed on the cheek,* she reminded herself. She pitied Samuel—he surely had no idea what went through her female mind. *She* hardly knew herself.

Fred's body being carried from the mine popped into her head. *That's why I can't get close,* she realized. *I don't want to lose someone else—and myself—again.*

"I'm going to work with her at the pen," she said. Samuel nodded. With uncharacteristic spontaneity, she blurted, "If you have some time later, perhaps you can join me."

What am I doing? she thought. Inviting Samuel to come would only confuse her emotions more. Yet, at the same time, she *wanted* him to accept the offer.

"I'll see what I can do," he said. "Maybe I can come along in a couple of hours."

"I'd like that," Tabitha said, surprising herself yet again. "I hope you will."

Samuel bid her good-bye with a smile, which sent Tabitha's heart rate up. She turned and clucked her tongue at Mantia then headed to Brother McCleve's pen. When she got there, Tabitha walked the horse in circles, giving them both some easy exercise as well as giving herself some time to think and to breathe some fresh air. Mantia followed along calmly, her hooves clopping rhythmically on the hard-packed dirt as if she'd done the same thing for years instead of weeks. Tabitha brought her to the edge of the corral and tied her up so the horse could get a drink of water. They'd been at the pen for a good hour by this point, and Tabitha figured the horse could use a rest.

She sat on a stool and took a rest herself, trying to keep her mind there with Mantia rather than back at the press where Victor and Joseph were probably getting the paper printed by now. She got back up and fetched the tack and began saddling the horse, who seemed to hardly notice as the saddle landed on her back or as Tabitha cinched the buckles. The two of them had come so far in trusting one another.

"She's sure looking well," came a voice. Tabitha looked over to see Samuel leaning against the corral.

"I think so," Tabitha said, feeling a swelling of excitement. He'd come, just as he said he would. Her nerves about the paper could use his friendly face. "I'm going to ride her for a spell. Want to come inside?"

Samuel climbed to the top of the fence and sat. "I like the view from here," he said with a grin.

She had to look away to hide the pleased flush on her face. With Mantia done drinking, Tabitha added the bridle and then mounted. She gently pushed her heels into the horse's sides, sending her into a slow walk. Tabitha was teaching commands at a snail's pace, so trotting and galloping would wait. Right now she was content that the mare had learned to go right, left, and stop, all in the course of a week.

"Sister Chadwick?"

She squinted against the sun to see who was speaking; it certainly wasn't Samuel. "Hello, Victor." She pulled Mantia to a stop, her hands tensing around the reins. "Is something wrong?"

"Sorry to bother you, but the press is busted. Joseph and I have been trying to fix it, but we can't figure it out."

With a sigh, Tabitha dismounted and crossed over to Victor, leading Mantia behind her. "What's wrong with it?"

"When I pull the lever, it doesn't do anything."

The lever normally acted on another set of levers, which then turned the screw and pushed the press onto the paper. Not having the lever do anything at all was definitely a problem.

"Maybe something's lodged in the press," Victor went on. "Or, I don't know, maybe something's loose. I'm not all that handy with tools and machines, and Joseph's worse."

For a moment Tabitha thought that having the press broken might be a sign that she wasn't supposed to run the article. If nothing else, it would certainly be a good excuse to wait until next week.

But no. She needed to keep the paper alive every week, especially if it were to pay for itself. By this hour, the press should be going full steam if it were to get off on the wagon in time to be shipped out to the outlying cities that afternoon.

She rubbed her eyes and sighed. "I don't know what to do," she said. After her last encounter with Brother Christensen, she didn't exactly want to approach him for help. "I'll be right over to see if I can figure it out."

Samuel cleared his throat, and Tabitha looked over to where he sat on the fence. "You know, I happen to be pretty handy with tools." He shrugged. "I'm sure a press is a mite different than a loom, but if you don't mind, I'll see what I can do with it."

Why hadn't she thought of that? "Thank you, Samuel. That would be wonderful. I'll be right there." Samuel waited as she led Mantia to some shade and a bucket of oats, where she tied her up and unsaddled her. As she worked, she berated herself. Of course Samuel could help. He'd been asking to for days now. Why was she so all-fired insistent on trying to do everything herself? She knew the answer as quickly as the question popped into her head—because if she let herself become dependent on another person, she risked becoming the scared little girl she had once been.

She left the pen and walked back to the office with Samuel and Victor. Once inside, Samuel headed straight to the printing room.

The toolbox lay beside the press—a mess of screwdrivers, hammers, and other assorted tools dumped haphazardly inside, the result of Victor and Joseph trying to fix the machine.

Samuel crossed to the press and examined it. He fiddled with the main lever, examined the screw mechanism and how it worked on the wooden platen that held the type. He tried to move some other pieces then nodded to himself and turned to the tool box.

"Looks like some of the screws are missing in the lever sequence here. They're not attached to one another anymore."

"Screws are missing?" Tabitha asked, hardly able to believe the problem was that simple. The press in Logan had broken down regularly, but that was reportedly because it had several parts made of wood that couldn't bear the pressure. Suddenly she felt appreciation for Brother Christensen investing in one made almost entirely of iron.

Samuel dug around for a moment and selected a couple of tools. He got down on his knees and searched the floor, where he found three screws. Then he pulled a stool over, sat down, and got to work. What felt like just a few moments later, Samuel dropped the tools back into the box and wiped his hands, declaring, "Done. I noticed a few other loose pieces, so I took care of those, too. Then I oiled a few joints; it seemed to be squeaking a lot. She's in better shape now than she has been in awhile probably."

"Wow," Victor said with a shake of his head. "You're good."

Tabitha walked over and pulled the lever. The press moved smoothly and silently, the screw mechanism pushing the platen down firmly and lifting it open again. "Thank you so much. You're very good with machines," she said with admiration.

"You're very welcome. This is the kind of thing I *do* know how to do." He folded his arms with satisfaction as they shared the mutual joke, neither mentioning his blue-and-black thigh or how he had landed in muck too many times to count.

CHAPTER 23

Tabitha hardly slept Monday night. She imagined every literate person in the county reading her article and hating her for it. She pictured the Tidwell children without a mother. The *Sentinel* closing its doors. Jeremiah's angry face. Every bit of it was her fault.

Having Will away didn't help; she couldn't distract herself by singing him lullabies or stroking his back to help him sleep.

By morning she was more tired than when she had retired the night before. She got out of bed and went to her toilet table, where she washed her face and did her hair mechanically. She went through the motions of fixing up the bed and eating breakfast but couldn't swallow more than a few bites of hash browns.

Daggett. She had to visit Daggett this morning before he took any action against Betty.

"Thank you for breakfast, Mother," she said, taking her dishes to the counter.

"Are you well, child?" her mother asked. "You hardly ate a thing, and you look rather peaked. Is that Daggett case still bothering you?"

"Oh, I'm fine," Tabitha said, smiling. Her mother hadn't yet read yesterday's edition, so she was unaware of the latest developments. And in her typical independent fashion, Tabitha had wanted to handle the situation herself instead of asking her parents to shoulder some of the burden. She'd tell them about it later—when she knew how it was resolved. "I'm going out to talk with some people. Newspaper business."

"Of course, dear," her mother said, gathering more dirty dishes from the table. "I'll see you later. Let me know if I can do anything for you."

Tabitha smiled. "Thanks, Mama," she said, but she knew that her mother couldn't help with what faced her. "Have a good day."

With that, Tabitha walked out, forcing each foot to continue moving toward the Daggett home. It seemed that many of her walks lately were ones she didn't want to take. When she reached the front door, she remembered the last time she was there, talking with both Mr. and Mrs. Daggett about the robbery. How certain she had been back then that Jeremiah was at fault. It had made perfect sense.

She rapped and waited nervously for an answer. Mrs. Daggett looked surprised when she opened the door. "Why, it's Miss Chadwick, isn't it? Can I help you with something?"

"I'm hoping I can speak with Mr. Daggett. Is he in?" Tabitha asked. Her heart drummed in her throat as she spoke.

"Yes, he is," Mrs. Daggett said. "Go sit down in the parlor, and I'll fetch him for you." Smiling widely, she stepped to the side to let her guest in.

"Thank you," Tabitha said, somewhat confused at the overly friendly tone. She entered the parlor and found a seat on a stiff-backed chair. It seemed fitting for the circumstances; she could hardly sit in the soft, stuffed chair in the corner and be comfortable at a moment like this.

Only a minute or two passed before Mr. Daggett entered the room. "Hello, Miss Chadwick, hello," he said, smiling.

Perhaps he hasn't been reading the paper of late, Tabitha thought.

He pulled out the chair from his writing table, put it down across from her, and sat on it. "Now," he said, clasping his hands. "What can I do for you today?"

"I came today because . . . because, Mr. Daggett . . . have you read yesterday's paper?"

"I most certainly have." He inclined his head toward the writing desk, where the paper was indeed sitting. "Quite an investigator you are, Miss Chadwick. I'm most grateful to you."

"You're . . . excuse me?" Tabitha leaned against the hard chair back, trying to digest what he'd just said.

"My dear wife hasn't slept well since the night Jeremiah Hancock was arrested. She's been terrified of someone killing her as she sleeps. To discover that there is no such criminal in our midst is certainly a relief to us all."

"I . . . see," Tabitha said. But she didn't, not at all. "But you do know what really happened to the money, then?"

"Oh, yes. It appears that we've underestimated Mr. Hancock over the years, haven't we? To think that he was simply trying to right a wrong. Well, I think it's wonderful."

"But what about Mrs. Tidwell?" Tabitha insisted. "Are you going to press charges against her?"

"No, no, no," he said with several shakes of his head. He rested one arm on the back of the chair and seemed to consider Tabitha. "It's a bit upsetting, of course, to learn that the wife of my business partner was so distraught over the venture that she would resort to something like this."

"I imagine it would be," Tabitha said, her head reeling.

"But you see, she's young. She was worried and afraid. Last night my wife and I paid a visit to Mrs. Tidwell, and she begged for our forgiveness."

Here Tabitha had come to do the same on Betty's behalf, and Mr. Daggett already seemed to have moved on from the incident. Tabitha almost smiled. Had she lain awake all last night for nothing?

Mr. Daggett went on. "Said she regretted the action the moment she'd done it but was too frightened to set things right."

"Until Mr. Hancock stepped in," Tabitha finished.

"He's a better man than many," Mr. Daggett said. Tabitha had to agree. The man had his faults—*many* of them—but deep down, he had a good heart. He didn't show that heart all that often and sometimes went about doing things a bit backward, but in this case, his intentions were honorable.

"I'm going to visit the constable today to be sure he drops the entire issue." He paused thoughtfully then added, "You know, Miss Chadwick, this whole experience has been a good lesson for us. Mr. Tidwell and I will be reviewing our plans and making sure that both of our wives feel comfortable with any decisions *before* we move forward with them."

"That sounds wise," Tabitha said. She seemed to be at a loss for words during the entire conversation. The only thing she could do was smile—and breathe.

He stood and held out a hand. "Now I have some business to get to, but I must again express my gratitude and appreciation. Thank you so much for your work." They shook hands, and then he walked her to the door to see her out. She stepped through, but before she left, he leaned in conspiratorially and added, "I heard some rumblings about town against you over the last little bit, but I must say, you did right by standing beside your principles. Just you wait and see. This will turn the tide of opinion."

"Thank you, Mr. Daggett. I hope you're right."

The door closed, and Tabitha walked into the road, feeling as light as a sparrow. Daggett wouldn't be pressing charges. Betty wouldn't be going to jail. And maybe . . . maybe her paper wouldn't be sunk after all.

She nearly sailed as she walked to the *Sentinel* building, but when she rounded the corner and the front door came into view, her step came up short. The door was littered with notes. Tabitha put a hand to her middle to calm the jumpiness that erupted. She walked forward slowly now, praying that the letters weren't complaints, protests, or more canceled subscriptions.

When she reached the door, she pulled off the first of the notes, attached to the door with a tack.

Dear Editor,

I judged you wrong. I applaud you for sticking to your guns and your beliefs. Consider me a lifetime supporter. No one can say any longer that a female can't run a business.

Isaiah Murdock

Tabitha let out a weak breath of relief. *One good response among many.* She pulled another off the door, bracing herself for what it might contain.

To whom it may concern,

Please disregard the cancellation notice that was sent last week and renew my subscription to the Sanpitch Sentinel *for another year.*

Cordially,

Regina Walsh

One by one, Tabitha read each of the many notes. Each one was in support of the paper. Some were vocal, some were more subtle, but none of them held the diatribes and ridicule she had expected. She read another and then another, stunned. Her hands began to tremble. Many of the notes were detractions from previous complaints and cancellations. Others expressed admiration for her work and forthrightness. She could hardly fathom it: the very thing that could have ruined the paper was the one thing that cemented the community's support of it.

Weeks of pressure and worry finally got the better of her. Holding a stack of notes against her chest, Tabitha leaned against the door. Tears streamed down her face, and she began sobbing with relief.

I did it, she thought. *Thank you, Father, for guiding me.*

Someone approached along the street, and Tabitha wiped her cheeks dry. Mother Hall stood not a stone's throw away, her back rail straight and her hands clasped before her.

"Good morning, Mother Hall," Tabitha managed. Why did she have to come now of all times, when Tabitha had such reason to celebrate?

"I came to . . . to apologize." Mother Hall nodded slightly.

Hardly believing that she'd heard correctly, Tabitha said, "I'm sorry?"

"I believe I was a bit hasty in canceling my subscription. Of course, somehow I received another paper this week anyway."

Tabitha flushed; she had burned the request and never logged it. "I'm sorry."

"No, that's quite all right," Mother Hall said. "It appears that I misjudged both you and Betty Tidwell. I believe that you are doing good work with the *Sentinel*."

"Why, thank you, Mother Hall," Tabitha said. She could think of no higher praise than that coming from this woman.

"That's not to say I approve of everything you do," the woman added hastily.

Of course not, Tabitha thought glumly.

Mother Hall held her chin up. "But I suppose . . . that Fred chose a suitable wife."

"Thank you, Mother Hall," Tabitha said. "That means so much to me."

The woman gave her a nod and then walked on, quickly disappearing around the corner. Wilhelmina Hall still had reservations about her daughter-in-law and obviously still disliked her. But Tabitha had to give the woman her due; it couldn't have been easy to admit that she'd been wrong, about anything.

Victory. She'd had it on yet one more front. Tabitha picked up her skirts so she could run. Samuel. For some reason, she wanted to let him know what had happened. She hurried toward the Little Fort, her feet kicking up dust as she ran. The east entrance was open, and she raced inside, nearly bowling over a man carrying a feed sack over his shoulder.

"Oh, excuse me!" she cried, backing up and laughing. Now that the stress of the last month was in the past, she felt like cheering and laughing all day.

"Well, good morning," Samuel said, turning around with a chuckle. "I didn't expect to be knocked over at this hour."

"I'm so sorry," Tabitha said, grinning so widely her cheeks hurt. "Just . . . look at these!"

"What is it?" Samuel set the feed sack onto the ground and took the papers she had thrust at him. He glanced at one then flipped to the next and the next. His face lit up. "Are they all like this?"

Tabitha nodded. "Isn't it wonderful?"

On impulse, she threw her arms around his neck. Samuel picked her up and swung her in a circle in celebration. When he put her down, he held onto her for a moment longer. Tabitha breathed in his scent and had to restrain herself from kissing his cheek again.

"That's wonderful," Samuel said. "I'm so happy for you."

* * *

Tabitha spent the rest of the day working with a light heart. The only thing that could make it better would have been Will being home to celebrate with. After a full day's work, she bid good-night to her staff and closed up the office, then headed for the stables. A brief ride on Mantia would be a great ending to a great day.

As she entered the Little Fort, she blushed slightly, remembering her actions of that morning. She had wanted to celebrate with Samuel but once again had been rather forward. What must he think of her? And what if he felt similar things, but she pushed him away? It wouldn't be fair to him to act as if she wanted a romantic relationship, only to push him away when she couldn't allow a man into her heart. She shook off such thoughts in favor of her plans for Mantia. Maybe she'd try trotting today.

Tabitha opened the side door of the stable and furrowed her brow. Loud bangs and shuffling noises came from the interior, followed by a man yelling, "Get back; she's thrashin'!"

She? Picking up her skirts, Tabitha hurried inside, trying to convince herself that the sounds had nothing to do with Mantia. *Probably Dolores making a ruckus again,* she thought, but her breathing sped up, and she rushed down the corridor, unable to feel at ease until she knew.

"Barnett, can you reach her lead rope?"

Samuel grunted. "Trying. Can't . . . quite . . . reach . . . got it!"

"Careful now," Brother Carlisle cautioned, lugging a heavy bucket and coming up from behind. "Try to get her to stand up, but don't get yourself kicked in the process."

They were at Mantia's stall. Tabitha stopped beside it and peered over the top, holding her breath and trying to take in what was going on. Her horse lay on the stall floor, rolling back and forth with quick, jerky motions—not at all like her normal playful rolls to scratch her back. Her hooves punched the air, and her eyes rolled wildly. With Samuel and Brother Carlisle both straining on the rope—and trying to stay out of the horse's way—Mantia finally stood, but kicked at her belly with her back hooves and tried to bite it. She shifted back and forth uneasily, then reared up. For a heart-stopping moment, Tabitha feared the horse would come down on Samuel, but she twisted to the side and continued to paw nervously.

"What's wrong with her?" Tabitha called out. Everything she had witnessed had lasted only a few seconds, but it felt like an eternity. Something was desperately wrong. Mantia hadn't behaved this wild since leaving Jeremiah's place.

Brother Carlisle, who set down the bucket and hefted a rubber tube with a funnel on one end, explained, "She's got a bad case of colic."

"Colic?" Tabitha repeated. A thought flashed across her mind that the situation might not be anything serious; colicky babies weren't in any danger, just uncomfortable. She didn't know what colic meant for horses, but the tone in Brother Carlisle's voice left no mistaking that he didn't think the situation was good. "What does that mean?"

"Keep her standing, Barnett," Carlisle said, ignoring her question and waving at Samuel. "Even if we can't get her to walk, I don't want her making things worse by rolling around if she's got twisted innards."

Twisted innards? Tabitha's eyes flew open. That didn't sound good. *Her belly hurts.* Having twisted insides would make sense. But what did that mean for a horse? How could they fix it? Tabitha refused to entertain the fleeting thought that such a condition might be untreatable.

"She's calming down a bit," Samuel said, sounding a tad relieved but still speaking warily as he held onto the rope while Mantia tried again to shy away. The horse breathed out hard and shook her head uneasily.

They watched for a few minutes, Brother Carlisle trying to speak calmly to her so the mare would relax. More than once she threatened to pull against the rope and lie down, but Samuel managed to prevent that by keeping the rope taut and wrapping it around a pillar of the stable. The horse stopped fighting, and a few minutes later when she still seemed calm, Brother Carlisle nodded.

"Let's see if we can try this now," he said, bringing the bucket and the rubber tube over. He glanced at Tabitha's questioning face. "Castor oil. To help lubricate her insides. With a little luck, it'll clear a blockage. Stephen's making up some bran mush. That might help."

As Brother Carlisle stepped past Tabitha, she put her hand out and touched his arm, making him pause and look back. "What about the twisting? Will it help with that, too?"

Brother Carlisle avoided her eyes and kept his attention fixed on his work. "I don't even know if she's twisted; I'm just guessing she might be."

He pushed past and handed the bucket to Samuel. It didn't escape Tabitha's notice that the stable manager hadn't answered her question. Brother Carlisle took Mantia's face in his hands and tried to get the tube down her throat. Tabitha cringed at the battle between them—the horse not knowing why he was shoving a foreign object into her or that it might help her feel better.

"Why the tube?" Tabitha asked, wanting to snatch it away from the stable manager. Mantia's head flailed from side to side. She was obviously under distress, and having a tube down her throat wasn't helping. "Can't she just drink the oil?"

"Would *you* drink oil? Besides, in her state, she might inhale it. Oil-coated lungs would do her in for sure." Brother Carlisle held the tube and the funnel as Samuel ladled oil into the top. "It's okay, girl," he said with obvious effort at sounding calm. "Just a little longer now. There's a good horse."

Tabitha tried the same. "It's all right, girl," she said, hoping Mantia would recognize her voice and be comforted. "You can do this, Mantia. That's it. Easy now."

The men managed to get in only a couple of ladlefuls. Brother Carlisle insisted she'd need a gallon or more, but Mantia fought too hard, kicking the ground, tossing her head and making irritated noises.

"Let's take a bit of a break," Brother Carlisle said, pulling out the tube. "If we let her rest, she might be willing to take more in a spell." Brother Carlisle patted her neck, speaking smoothly to the horse. "There you go, girl. That's right," he said, then paused, keeping his hand on one spot. He concentrated for a moment, narrowing his eyes as he stared at the floor. "Hmm," he said, looking worried. "Pulse doesn't feel good."

He pulled out a pocket watch and tried feeling her heartbeat again. With a shake of his head, he said, "Way too high—already at fifty. She feels feverish, too." His voice sounded grave.

"Come out of there, Barnett," he said, wiping a sleeve across his forehead and motioning for Samuel to follow him out of the stall. With both men and Tabitha in the corridor, Brother Carlisle closed the wooden door on its creaky hinges and sighed wearily. "Barnett, let's get working on some of the other evening chores, then come back in an hour and see if we can't get more oil into her. Will you see to cleaning out Dolores's stall? I'm sure James already finished the evening milking."

"No problem," Samuel said, really seeming to mean it. Maybe wrestling with Mantia made facing the ornery cow pale in comparison. Just in the last few minutes, Tabitha could hardly believe how naturally he had seemed to work with the mare; no one coming into the stables right then would suspect that Samuel hadn't grown up in one.

His employer headed off, and Samuel wiped his sweaty face with a bandana. Mantia snorted in pain again and raised a hoof as if she were about to stomp but paused and let it fall to the ground again. The movement was obviously painful. Tabitha's eyes pinched with worry, and as Samuel tucked the square of cloth back into his pocket, he caught her worried expression.

"She'll be all right," he said.

"Will she?" She wanted Samuel to say it again and mean it. To know it.

"Listen, have you had supper yet?" Samuel asked. The question was out of the blue, as if he was trying to distract her from the horse. Nothing would keep her from thinking about Mantia right now. "Tab, why don't you go get a bite? You look pale."

"I'm not hungry." She hadn't eaten since breakfast, she realized. Her mother would have supper on the table soon. But right now she didn't care. She turned to the stall and unlatched it. "You go to work. I'm staying."

Samuel stepped in front of her. "You need to go somewhere else for a spell."

Tabitha tried to open the door anyway.

"Don't go in there," Samuel said, taking her hand away from the latch and refastening it. "She's in so much pain that she got close to seriously hurting Carlisle—and me."

"That's because she doesn't know and trust the two of you. She won't hurt *me*," Tabitha insisted. "Of all the people in the world, I'm the only one who could go in there and give her some measure of comfort."

Samuel arched an eyebrow. "And you of all people know better than to try that. She won't know what she's doing."

He doesn't know diddly about horses, Tabitha thought, trying hard to justify why she wanted to go in and comfort Mantia, who was nipping at her stomach and neighing with pain. Tabitha shrugged. "I can't leave her. She needs me."

"I know," Samuel said gently. "But for right now, stay out here. Going in won't help anyone."

From the other end of the stable, Brother Carlisle called, "You coming, Barnett? That stall won't clean itself."

"I'll be right back," Samuel said, then turned back to Tabitha.

Her eyes drifted to the latch and back. "Please hurry."

"Of course." Samuel threw her what was probably meant to be an encouraging smile before he jogged down the corridor toward Brother Carlisle, where he fetched a shovel and wheelbarrow. He rolled them back and past Tabitha, stopping at the end of the corridor. As he opened the gate, he paused again. "She'll be fine."

Tabitha merely nodded, and Samuel went to work. He moved Dolores out of her stall and locked her inside one across the way so hers could be cleaned out. When Tabitha heard the sound of the shovel scraping against the ground, she glanced the other way. No sign of Brother Carlisle or anyone else. She slowly opened the stall door and eyed the oil bucket and tube, but decided trying to use them alone would be pressing her luck.

Mantia shifted about restlessly. Tabitha didn't dare speak too loudly for fear she'd be heard by the men, so she whispered, "It's all right, girl. It's me. You'll be just fine." She reached out to stroke her cheek and neck. The horse whipped her head about, nearly knocking Tabitha over. "Whoa, girl," she said, backing up and nearly stepping in the oil bucket. Her pulse quickened.

Maybe I shouldn't be in here.

She dismissed the thought; she *had* to be there. No one else could handle Mantia like she could. No one *cared* like she did. Mantia needed comfort—not unlike Will had needed a caring hand when he was ill.

"It's all right, girl," Tabitha said, reaching out. She clicked her tongue in a way that usually had a calming effect, but the horse didn't seem to even hear it; she kept throwing her head about.

Tabitha held out her hand and took a tiny step, easing closer, still speaking in the same calming tone she had used when they'd first gotten to know one another. "Everything will be fine, girl. You'll see. There you go. Easy now." She reached out and touched the dull coat. Mantia shuddered at the contact but allowed it, making Tabitha let out a breath she hadn't realized she'd been holding.

"Good girl. There you go," she said, stroking Mantia's face. "Everything will be all right."

Mantia jerked suddenly with a cramp, making her snort and kick, throwing her weight around. She shoved Tabitha. A hoof landed right on the tip of her boot, just missing her toes.

"Whoa," she said, backing out of the way. As she pressed her back against the stall wall, her heart stuttered in her chest. Something about Mantia being out of control sent stabs of fear through her that she'd never felt before. When the two of them had been in the training ring, every action the mare took was explicable. Tabitha had tools to use, things to try with each reaction—a way to explain everything. Now, nothing the mare did was predictable. She was no longer ruled by logic—only by pain.

Tabitha leaned against the stall and gazed at her poor horse. *I can still try to comfort her.*

Down the corridor, Tabitha heard Samuel talking to Brother Carlisle, punctuated by the sounds of a shovel scraping earth. "Almost done here," Samuel was saying, when Tabitha realized he was talking to *her.* "I'll be back in jiffy."

Unwilling to be caught in the stall against Samuel's wisdom, Tabitha inched to the door and peered out. She stepped into the opening and was about to pull the door closed, but first she turned back to Mantia. "It'll be all right, girl," she said, glancing quickly down the corridor and then back.

Another spasm must have hit; without warning, Mantia neighed loudly, then bucked, kicking her feet backward. The door slammed into Tabitha's face.

The next thing she knew, she was opening her eyes after lying on the ground for who knew how long. A bang sounded—through the fog in her brain, she figured it had to be a stall door closing—and Samuel's voice called her name. "Tab? Tab, are you all right?"

Disoriented and weak, she lifted her head, revealing a puddle of blood. She furrowed her brow and touched her face. Her hand came away red. She couldn't think clearly. Every attempt felt muddled. *What just happened?* she thought, trying to reorient herself. She looked around.

Stable floor. Samuel. Stall door.

Mantia kicked against the wall, and Tabitha jumped, making her remember with vivid clarity what had happened. "Is she all right?"

Samuel squatted down and looked at Tabitha's nose, which dripped red. "Are *you* all right?" Without waiting for an answer, he held a cloth to her face and helped her sit up. She scooted to the side of the corridor so she could lean against a wooden partition. The world seemed to wobble; she closed her eyes and put her hands down to feel the firm ground beneath her.

"Mantia!" She opened her eyes suddenly at the thought, but the name sounded mumbled to her ears.

"Don't worry about her right now. *You're* hurt."

Loud noises came from inside the stall—Mantia throwing herself onto the ground and frantically rolling again. A sudden high-pitched neigh reverberated off the gables as she thrashed about. Tabitha scrambled, trying to get her feet beneath her. "Something's wrong."

Samuel eased her back down. In her faint condition, she was no match for his strength. "Don't worry. Everything will be fine."

"But—"

"I'll check on her. You stay here and hold this to your face to stop the bleeding."

Tabitha nodded meekly and leaned her head back again, pressing the cloth against her nose. She was becoming more coherent by the second—the world no longer pitched to and fro. She trained her ear toward Mantia. That sudden high-pitched whinny wasn't right, and Tabitha wouldn't be easy until she knew what had happened.

Samuel poked his head over the stall wall, and his eyes grew wide at whatever he saw. He didn't look at Tabitha as he rushed past—for that matter, he seemed to be avoiding her face as he called, "Carlisle! Come quick! She's hurt herself."

Tabitha's heart leapt into her throat as Samuel hurried past her and down the corridor.

She eased herself to her feet and walked to the stall. A wave of dizziness overtook her, so she held on to the wall for a few seconds until her vision stopped swimming and she could view Mantia clearly. At first all she saw was the horse's jerking movements, the kicking hooves as she tried to ease her discomfort. But then the horse rolled toward Tabitha and stood, revealing a four-inch gash in her hindquarters. The cut was bleeding, the skin hanging down and revealing tissue and bone. Tabitha sucked in her breath and almost passed out again. She gripped the side of the wall.

Within seconds, Carlisle and Samuel had returned, the former taking in the scene with a set jaw and lips pressed together. "How the devil did that happen?" Carlisle asked, scratching his beard. He reached a shovel handle under the stall door and fished about, then withdrew a bloodied, rusty nail sticking out of a piece of wood. He shook his head wearily. "Where'd this come from?" he asked of no one in particular.

"What should we do?" Samuel asked, studying the gash.

"Somehow we'll have to get the wound cleaned and bound, but I'm afraid the colic is a bigger danger than that cut right now. Besides, I don't see how we'd get close enough to clean and bind it without hurting her or ourselves." He turned slightly and started when he laid eyes on Tabitha. "What happened to you?"

She looked sheepish as she pulled the cloth away. The bleeding had nearly stopped now, but the rag was covered in scarlet splotches. "I was trying to comfort her," she confessed with a one-shouldered shrug. "She kicked the door into my face."

Instead of the lecture she expected, Carlisle just came over, brow furrowed, and took her face in his hands. He examined her nose closely. "I'm betting it's broken," he said. "But she couldn't have hit you too hard, and if it was head-on, you might be lucky and have it heal straight. Then you won't end up with a crooked snout like Jack Wilson's."

Trying not to think about the less-than-cheerful prospect, Tabitha put the rag back up to her face and spoke through it. "Is she going to be all right, then? Is there a veterinarian in town who can help?"

"Dr. Porter is way up in Price," Carlisle said. "I've already sent word to him about the colic. I'm hoping he'll be here in the next day or so."

"But couldn't that be too late?" Tabitha asked.

Carlisle cleared his throat and didn't answer. He ran his hand over the back of his hair and said, "Barnett, why don't you take her home? Tell her mother to keep a cool, wet cloth on that nose. Might help keep the swelling and bruising down a tad."

"I want to stay," Tabitha said.

"And do what?" Samuel said with exasperation. "Get hurt again? No one can help Mantia right now. And you need to lie down. You're coming with me." Samuel guided her down the corridor. "Either you'll walk or I'll carry you home over my shoulder like a sack of potatoes. Your choice."

"You wouldn't dare . . ." Tabitha began.

Samuel shrugged. "Very well," he said, then stepped forward and leaned down with his arms out, as if he were about to pick her up.

"I'll walk! I'll walk! Goodness, you're as bad as my brother," Tabitha said, backing up, her hands flying into the air. The sudden movement sent a wave of nausea over her. She pressed one hand to her middle and the other to her forehead. "Actually, I'd thank you for accompanying me. I don't know that I'd make it alone."

"Of course." Samuel put his arm around her shoulders and turned her toward the door.

Carlisle called after them. "I'll let you know about the horse, Sister Chadwick. And I'll do everything I can for her, mark my word."

Tabitha paused in her step and looked back at him. "Thank you, Brother Carlisle. Truly."

CHAPTER 24

TABITHA SPENT THE REST OF the evening lying in bed on her mother's orders. No amount of assurance from Tabitha that she felt just fine and could certainly get up dissuaded her mother.

"It's good Nathaniel has Will for the week," her mother said. "I'd hate to have him here where he could see you hurt like this."

Tabitha had to agree on that point. After the happiness she felt over the community's response to the paper, she had wished Will could come home early. Now she prayed there would be no evidence of her injury by the time he came home on Saturday. It was in his nature to worry over his mother as much as she worried over him. Would her mother let her out of the prison of a bed by the time Will came back? She'd better. With Will's tender heart, he would fret unduly upon seeing his mother lying in bed.

Within a matter of hours, her nose swelled up, making it necessary to breathe through her mouth. She felt weak and shaky at first—and nauseated due to the blood dripping into her stomach from her nose, making her vomit several times. But most of the discomfort lasted only a few hours, and soon she felt herself again, and instead of recuperating, she lay there worrying about Mantia and holding a damp cloth to her nose to help with the swelling.

That night, before extinguishing the bedside lamp, Tabitha's mother came into the room. "Let's get you a new compress," she said, taking the old cloth from Tabitha and handing her a clean, freshly wetted one. Before putting it to her face, Tabitha picked at the cloth. "I worry about Mantia. I wish I could go to her—do something for her."

"I know, dear," her mother said, sitting at the edge of the bed and brushing some of Tabitha's hair back. "It'll all work out in the end. You'll see."

"I hope you're right," Tabitha said. "Having a blockage is bad enough, but her insides might be twisted, and now she's got a horrible cut on her hindquarters. What if the wound gets infected? What if—?"

"Shhh . . ." her mother said gently.

Tabitha tried to take a deep breath. Her mother's touch had always calmed her as a little girl, and it had the same effect now. She closed her eyes and tried to still her worries, but tears leaked out and ran down the sides of her face anyway. "If only we had some kind of medicine that could help."

"Hmm."

Tabitha opened her eyes to see her mother deep in thought. "What is it?"

"Well, I do know of someone who makes a salve that heals cuts right well."

"Oh, who?" Tabitha asked, sitting up suddenly.

Her mother hesitated but finally came out with, "Wilhelmina Hall's bear tallow salve."

"Oh. Of course," Tabitha said, leaning back against her pillows again. She had forgotten that Mother Hall was known for her home-grown treatments. But wasn't there someone else? Probably not with her experience and supplies. Tabitha knew that. She stared at the crossbeams in the ceiling. Mother Hall had only just reached out an olive branch—and a small one at that. It was probably too early to ask for favors. "How can I ask her to help me? She's still angry with me, Mother."

"Angry? Why?" Her mother looked genuinely confused. "I mean, I know you two haven't ever been bosom friends, but I didn't think there was any real animosity between you."

A pained laugh escaped Tabitha. "Oh, Mother. There has *always* been animosity between us. I must have hid it well during the time Fred courted me. But ever since he passed . . ." She shook her head miserably. "She blames me for his death, you know."

"That's preposterous!" Tabitha's mother huffed, a mother-bear intensity on her face. Her lips pursed. "That woman—blaming you for an accident. An *accident!*"

"At one time she was quite vocal about wishing Fred had married Betty Hunsaker." Her mother laughed at that, and Tabitha smiled a bit too. "Not anymore. She's changed her tune about that. But there's more now. She's seen me with Samuel. Oh, she's mighty jealous, Mother. You should have seen her face at the benefit." Seeing how upset her mother was becoming, Tabitha purposely neglected to mention the poem Mother Hall had recited. That would only make her more irritated. "With all of that, I doubt she'd give me something to help Mantia."

Her mother took her hand and patted it. "Can't hurt to ask. The worst that can happen is she'll say no."

"I suppose," Tabitha said thoughtfully. She smoothed the quilt across her lap. "Will you deliver a note if I write one?"

"Of course. Just be sure you don't apologize for anything. You've done nothing wrong."

She smiled at her mother. "Thank you," she said, but knew better. She had deliberately exacerbated the situation at the benefit. *Not exactly charitable or Christian,* Tabitha thought glumly.

But oh, I hope she'll help me—if not for me, then for Mantia's sake.

* * *

Tabitha spent most of Wednesday in bed. She wrote up a note about the salve, which her mother delivered to the Hall residence. No word came in response. She got up later that afternoon for a spell to manage affairs at the paper—against her mother's vehement protestations—but left early because she felt weak.

Thursday morning she got out of bed and announced that she had to work today. But first she visited Mantia. The horse looked worse. She still nipped and kicked at her belly, but not with the same energy as before. Her ears and eyes seemed wilted. Even her tail hung listlessly. It was as if, although she was still in pain, she no longer had the energy to fight it.

She walked to the *Sentinel* downhearted, but when she walked in the door, Joseph met her with a stack of papers in his arms.

"Look at this," he said, grinning. "There's more over there." He nodded toward her desk.

"What?" Tabitha asked, moving that direction. "What is all this?"

"All kinds of things," Victor said, coming through the door from the printing room. "New subscriptions. Letters to the editor—singing your praises, I might add. And a slew of new advertisers."

Tabitha had forgotten that she hadn't seen this week's post yet. Apparently a lot of people in the county—not just Manti—had appreciated what she'd published this week. She flipped through page after page, hardly able to believe it.

"Looks like this week's edition is going to have to be six pages," Joseph said.

"I hope that's not too burdensome," Tabitha said with a laugh. She couldn't help but grin. "How many more subscriptions do we have this week?"

"So far we're up fifty," Joseph said.

On impulse, Tabitha dropped the papers onto the counter and threw her arms around both Joseph's and Victor's necks. "Thank you for being loyal to me," she said. "You two have been wonderful."

Their arms stuck out awkwardly at their sides for a moment before they closed around her slight frame. The men patted her back. "You're welcome, I suppose," Joseph said.

"Yes, you're welcome," Victor echoed. "You've been a great employer. Always fair."

They pulled back, and Joseph lifted a shoulder in a shrug. "Can I be honest? I had my doubts about a woman running the place. But you know what? You do a better job than Brother Christensen did. Although I won't admit to saying that." He laughed.

Victor pointed at her. "Sister Chadwick, if you don't mind my asking . . . what's wrong with your face?"

She covered her nose and chuckled. "Broke it. The bruises are showing up now. Pretty, aren't they?" She lowered her hand and showed off her black eyes.

"You're pretty no matter what," Victor said, then flushed. "I mean, you look just fine."

"Thank you, Victor," Tabitha said with a wan smile. "Now, let's get busy. We have a lot to do."

* * *

Tabitha worked doubly hard all day, trying to make up for the time she'd missed the day before. After going home for a midday meal, she decided to make a quick check on Mantia before getting back to the office. She'd gotten more done that day than she had expected to, so she could spare a few minutes.

As she pulled the stable door open and went inside, she called out, "Samuel? Stephen? Brother Carlisle?"

No one answered. She went to Mantia's stall, where the horse lay on the straw, her breathing rapid and shallow, her eyes watery and staring blankly ahead.

"Oh, Mantia," Tabitha said over the stall door. She knew better than to go inside without Brother Carlisle's approval now. Had she still been inside the stall when the horse kicked the other day, a broken nose wouldn't have been her only problem. She might have lost her life or been seriously disfigured. At the sound of her voice, the horse's ears twitched, and Tabitha smiled to herself.

"That's right. Tab's here now." She looked around again for Brother Carlisle and found him as he walked into the stables. He went to the wall of tack and selected the bridle belonging to one of the camping groups in the Little Fort. Before he could leave, Tabitha called to him. "Brother Carlisle!"

He paused and looked over. "Oh, hello, Sister Chadwick."

"She looks tired, but is she better?" Tabitha asked hopefully. "She's not rolling around in pain anymore. Does that mean the colic is gone?"

Brother Carlisle sighed and looked at the ground before answering. "She's feverish, Sister Chadwick. I think she busted open some of her insides. And that gash on her flank isn't looking good, either."

"But did Dr. Porter arrive yet? What did he . . . ?" Tabitha couldn't—wouldn't—let herself comprehend the implications of what Brother Carlisle was telling her.

"He got the wound cleaned and stitched up last night."

"Oh, good," Tabitha said, turning back to the stall, a tiny bit of the weight lifting.

Brother Carlisle replaced the bridle on a hook in the wall and closed the distance between them, his boots clomping on the ground with a steady rhythm. When he reached her, he put a hand on her shoulder. "It doesn't look good, Tabitha."

"But she's not thrashing anymore." She kept holding onto that idea like a lifeline.

"That's 'cause she's too weak. If the insides broke open and aren't twisted anymore, that would mean she's not in as much pain, but it also means she has a serious infection." He quietly opened the stall door.

"I can go in to see her?" she asked, surprised.

He nodded and gestured toward the stall. Tabitha stepped inside. Brother Carlisle followed. He knelt down and pressed his hand to the throbbing vein on the horse's neck. "Feel here," he said, resting his fingertips on the correct spot. "The pulse is well over sixty." He removed his hand, and Tabitha knelt down and put her hand where his had been.

"Sixty is bad?" she asked after a moment.

He didn't say a word, waiting for his face to tell her the truth. She nodded mutely then stroked her horse's face and neck, trying to give comfort in the only way she knew how. After a few moments, Brother Carlisle stood and quietly left her alone, for which she was grateful.

She spent the next couple of hours with Mantia, trying to comfort her. Wiping her fevered face with a clean, cool cloth. Brushing her mane and forelock. The tear in Mantia's rump looked red and inflamed, and Tabitha grimaced. At least she had eaten humble pie and sent word to her mother-in-law for the bear tallow salve. Being humbled to the dust like that would be worth it if it meant helping Mantia get better. Of course, Mother Hall had yet to respond to the note, but Tabitha kept her hope alive that the woman would be unable to say no to helping another living creature—even if it meant helping the daughter-in-law she resented. The salve could help, Tabitha thought—prayed. It might make Mantia well again.

"I'll be getting something for your cut soon," Tabitha said in a soothing tone. "Everything will work out. You'll see." The last bit was as much for Tabitha's sake as Mantia's.

CHAPTER 25

TABITHA SAID GOOD-BYE TO HER staff and finished up a bit of the books before closing up shop, grateful that her work week was mostly done. She might have to come in tomorrow and Saturday to finish up a few details before the Sabbath, but otherwise she could rest—and do so knowing that her livelihood was safe. She debated going to the Little Fort to see Samuel. When she'd left at midday, she'd seen him over at the camping area helping some visitors and hadn't been able to talk with him.

Normally she spent this hour training Mantia. To go straight home would feel empty, incomplete. She closed a register and pushed herself to standing, stretching her stiff back. She grabbed her shawl from the coat rack and wrapped it around her shoulders, then went out the door. Before locking it, however, she heard a voice.

"Done for the day?"

Tabitha whipped around, startled but then pleased to see Samuel strolling up the walk. "I am," she said. "You?"

"I am too. Carlisle let me off a little early."

She pulled the door shut and locked it. "Oh? Why?"

Samuel hedged. "It might be because in the morning I'll be heading over to Temple Hill for a couple days of tithing labor for the temple. Tomorrow and Saturday."

"Might be?" Tabitha asked, sensing he was holding something back. "Is there another reason?"

"I think he wanted me to come talk to you."

"Talk to me? About what?" The reason dawned on her with a heavy weight. "He doesn't want me to go to the stable tonight, does he?"

Hands in his pockets, Samuel nodded grimly. "I think not."

She sighed deeply and walked beside him to the road. "It's that bad?"

"It doesn't look good," Samuel said. "But you know I'm not an expert in these matters."

Nodding, she bit her lips and tried to change the topic. "So what will you be doing on the temple?"

Samuel took the hint and went along with the conversation. "Stonework, I believe, seeing as how I'm supposed to check in with Brother Parry. He's the master mason, and word has it that he's worked on several temples."

She nodded absently and turned east. "Care to walk me home?"

"I'd love to have such a beautiful woman on my arm," he said, his warm eyes meeting hers. He put out his arm, and she took it, flushing and looking down, ridiculously pleased and flattered. Her heartbeat quickened, and she wished that she had an excuse to walk around the city or otherwise stay with him longer—maybe find another problem with the press for him to fix. She suddenly found herself saying as much.

Pointing to the *Sentinel* front door, she said, "So can I call on you if the press breaks down again?'

"Absolutely," Samuel said. "Of course, I could always teach you how to tighten the screws and lubricate the joints."

"Now why would I want to do that? I wouldn't have an excuse to call for you to come and help me." Tabitha could hardly believe she'd said that. Her stomach flip-flopped. Something about the way Samuel looked at her after the remark made her weak in the middle. He suddenly acted a bit embarrassed, shuffling his feet in the dirt, and she thought she caught a slight pinkish hue in his cheeks.

It really would be so nice to have a man around to care for things like the press, she mused. *And take care of me.*

Someone strode up the street right then, and they both looked over to see Wilhelmina Hall, her face looking pinched as she glared at them.

"Mother Hall," Tabitha said, surprised and a bit flustered at being seen with Samuel again when Fred's mother was there—and looking as if she had just eaten a rotten gooseberry. "Good afternoon."

The woman raised an eyebrow into a high arch. Lips pursed into a tight pucker, she put a fist on one plump hip and looked from Tabitha to Samuel, a challenge in her eyes. Apparently Tabitha wasn't entirely in the woman's good graces. Samuel and Tabitha exchanged uneasy glances. Mother Hall held out a small, earthenware crock. "Here you go. It's the tallow ointment you asked for. I don't know that it'll do much good on a horse, but you never know, I suppose. There's not a lot in there, but a little goes a long way."

"Thank you," Tabitha said sincerely, taking the container and slipping it into her pocket. "I appreciate this so much."

"Takes a lot of work to make that ointment. Don't waste it."

"I won't," Tabitha promised.

Mother Hall sniffed and eyed Samuel from tip to toe. "And what are *you* doing here?"

"Mr. Barnett has been kind enough to help me recently," Tabitha interjected. "He fixed the press, and today he came by to update me on the condition of my horse." Which wasn't the entire truth, but it was close enough.

"He . . . *helps* you a lot, doesn't he?" Mother Hall said, as if accusing them of something terrible. She sniffed again. When she spoke again, her voice was snippy. "If *I'd* lost my husband young, I would *never* have so much as looked at another man."

Stunned at the woman's rudeness, Tabitha choked on a response. She was tempted to say that no other man would *have* her. What had happened to Fred picking a "suitable" wife?

Fortunately, Samuel stepped forward and saved her from speaking. "To say such a thing makes you a fool."

"Excuse me?" Mother Hall's voice went up nearly an octave. "How dare you speak to me in such a tone? And who are *you* to be poking your nose into other people's private affairs?"

To his credit, Samuel didn't let her outburst bother him, at least outwardly. He didn't even accuse her of poking *her* nose into someone else's private affair. "Sister Hall, you cannot expect a young woman— a young *mother*—to make it alone in this world. Your daughter-in-law has done marvels in caring for herself and her son, a feat that's almost impossible for many other women in her shoes."

Tabitha threw Samuel a grateful look.

"She's managed . . . quite . . . well," Mother Hall admitted, some- what reluctantly. "But that just goes to show that she doesn't need to dishonor the memory of her husband by philandering."

Philandering? Tabitha gritted her teeth.

Mother Hall lifted her chin obstinately as if challenging them.

Tabitha felt such rage that she couldn't keep quiet any longer. "Was it dishonorable for Sister Cooley to remarry after her husband died, leaving her with five small children and one on the way? Was it disgraceful for Brother Cooley to marry her, when he, too, had just lost his Eleanor, not five months previous—and had *seven* little ones to care for?" She stepped forward, but Samuel put a hand out calmly and held her back. He remained amazingly dispassionate as he opened his mouth to speak. Tabitha hoped the woman would listen to a level-headed man's side—even if that man were threatening to take Fred's place in only a small way.

"Sister Hall," Samuel said in a voice that held no defensiveness. "I know many men and women who have remarried after losing a spouse. Don't you?" He paused, but she didn't answer right away. Of course she knew plenty of couples in the same situation, but she wouldn't say so, not when doing so would hamper her argument.

"I haven't."

Samuel tried to make her see reason. "Sometimes remarrying is a matter of survival, of caring for children, of managing a farm, of doing so many things a man or a woman cannot do alone."

"Yes," Mother Hall finally conceded. "Marriages for *practical* reasons abound."

"Then why are so you against my friendship with Mr. Barnett?" Tabitha asked, bewildered. "He helps me with practical things. And we're just *friends.*"

Mother Hall clenched her jaw. Samuel eased closer and put a protective arm around Tabitha's shoulders. They weren't "just friends," and Tabitha knew it. So did Mother Hall, if her flared nostrils were any indication.

"She's against it, Tab, because our friendship isn't *practical.*" He turned to Mother Hall. "That's it, isn't it?"

Her gaze went to his hand, wrapped around Tabitha's form, then slid to Samuel's face. The fire in her eyes said what her mouth did not. "You don't know what I've been through. You don't know what it's like to lose your only son. If she hadn't taken Fred away from his home, he'd still be here." Her voice was sharp, accusing. Tabitha flinched. The edges of her lips trembled.

"I don't know what it's like to lose a son," Samuel said, "but I do know what it's like to lose a spouse. And it's not Tabitha's fault that Fred died." How he could still keep his voice so calm and even was beyond Tabitha. But she could tell he was no longer *feeling* calm; his eyes burned, and his face was turning red.

"What happened was an accident," Samuel continued, "an unfortunate event that took place while Fred was trying to build a life for his bride."

Mother Hall huffed at the word *bride.*

Burning tears welled up behind Tabitha's eyes. She took a slight step forward and defended herself. "Mother Hall, I know that you never wanted me to be part of your family. I understand that. I'm sorry that part of your loss included a portion of your livelihood, but that money has helped me raise your grandson. Regardless, in some ways, you can consider me as being out of your family now, out of your life. I'm as sorry as anyone about what happened. But next month makes that event *seven years* ago. I have a son who will never know his father, yet I've striven to make a good life for him." She glanced up briefly at Samuel, her courage wavering at what she wanted to say. "Being a young widow is a very lonely way to live. So if someone can be part of that life and offer me some friendship—some companionship—I'll welcome it gladly. And nothing you say will change that."

She didn't quite dare say she'd welcome someone offering more than companionship—such as *love.* Not in front of Mother Hall. Not in front of Samuel, either.

"Now if you'll excuse us," Samuel said, taking a step backward—and Tabitha with him, since he still had his arm about her shoulders—"we'll be going now." He nodded politely, steering her back toward the *Sentinel* office door. Tabitha unlocked the door, and they went inside. Samuel closed the door behind them soundly.

Tabitha peered through the sheers on the window, praying Mother Hall wouldn't follow them inside, then pulled back. She could almost feel Mother Hall's eyes burning through the glass. *I'm sorry. So sorry,* she wanted to say. But talking to the woman never did do any good, and it certainly wouldn't help today. Tabitha forced herself to step away from the door and not look back.

A moment later, Mother Hall turned about and walked away. Samuel let out a deep breath. He took Tabitha's hand and drew her further into the room, where no one outside could see them. Tabitha looked up at the planed boards in the ceiling and closed her eyes, willing her tears at bay. It didn't work; a couple from each eye dripped onto her temples and rolled into her hairline. She wiped them away.

"Are you all right?" Samuel asked quietly.

She nodded briskly and sniffed. "I'm fine. I'm just . . ." How could she explain? She hardly understood her own emotions. So many feelings swirled inside—anger at Mother Hall, gratitude toward Samuel—*more* than gratitude toward Samuel, if she were being perfectly honest with herself. And even a sliver of guilt about Fred. For even though she denied it openly, his mother's words had cut her to the quick. "I'm . . ."

"Confused?" Samuel ventured.

"Yes, exactly," Tabitha said helplessly. Samuel's feet shifted, his boots scraping against the wood, and he took both of her hands in his. She opened her mouth to speak, but nothing came out. When Fred died, she hadn't spent much time grieving him for his own sake. She grieved for herself and for the upside-down world she found herself in. She had mourned for her personal loss, her personal devastation, hopelessness, confusion. Fear.

Didn't Fred deserve to be mourned by a wife who adored him above all else? But she had been too young for such a thing. Certainly she had cared for Fred. Loved him—as deeply as she could have loved a man at that age. But they hadn't built a life together; she had barely left her girlhood years. When he died, and she fell apart, her grief had been as much about feeling lost and unsure of the future as it was about losing her new husband, the one man she had ever loved.

But she had loved him in a young way, a different way than she felt her innermost desires moving toward Samuel. This was something that felt deeper, something that reached a part of her that she hadn't known was there—a part of the woman who hadn't existed seven years ago. She almost felt as if she owed it to Fred to have felt this way about him.

"Come here," Samuel said quietly, pulling her close. Though she had never been this near him, the action felt natural and familiar. She rested her head on his chest, reveling in the security and warmth of his arms and the even beating of his heart.

"I'm confused sometimes, too," he said, stroking his cheek across her hair.

"You are?" she murmured, lifting her face and searching his. Suddenly she understood. Of course he would feel confusion too. Why hadn't she seen it before? Her widowhood went back years; his went back only a few months. How would she have responded to meeting Samuel if Fred had died only a short time ago? He laid her head back down again and felt Samuel nodding.

"I suppose a little confusion is natural," he said. "I still miss Helen desperately. I will always love her. And yet . . ."

And yet . . .

The two words summed up how Tabitha felt as well. She waited breathlessly for how his trailing voice would finish the thought.

Samuel brushed back a wisp of her hair. "My confusion hasn't muddled me entirely. I'm quite clear about wanting one thing." He lifted his head off hers, and she looked up, eager to know what he was thinking.

"What?"

His warm eyes seemed to penetrate hers, and for a timeless moment, nothing but the two of them existed. A smile pulled on the corners of his mouth, and he leaned closer. Tabitha held her breath as a flurry erupted in her middle. With her hands resting on his chest, she lifted her heels, rising nearer. They both paused, hesitating, before Samuel closed the distance and touched his lips to hers. His arms went around her frame and drew her in. Tabitha leaned against him, a warm energy filling her as he kissed her and she kissed him back, first softly, and then with more intensity. When Samuel pulled away a moment later, he rested his cheek against hers, his budding stubble scratching gently against her face. Her hand reached up and stroked his other cheek, feeling the rough growth of his beard as she stayed on her toes, unwilling for the magic to end.

After a moment, Samuel kissed her forehead and drew back slightly. Tabitha lowered her heels to the ground. Her face felt flushed, and her heart pounded crazily. She hadn't felt this alive—this *happy*—possibly ever.

"Now . . . seeing as we're not properly chaperoned, I suppose I'd better be a proper gentleman." He tilted his head to the door. "I should go."

"Good day, Samuel." She hoped he could hear everything else she wanted to say but couldn't yet verbalize.

"Good day, Tab." He lifted her hand and pressed the top with his lips, then leaned forward and quickly pecked her cheek, too, before hurrying to the door and walking out.

CHAPTER 26

THROUGH THE SHEERS ON THE window, Tabitha watched Samuel walk away. At one point he paused and looked back over his shoulder. Though he probably couldn't see her at that distance through the window, she could tell he was smiling. Tabitha hugged herself and felt as if her entire body were smiling. He continued on his way, and when she could see him no longer, her fingertips brushed her lips. She remembered his kiss, the tenderness behind it, the undeniable emotion, feelings that had sprung up inside her as well.

Samuel had started out as a dear friend, but he was turning into something so much more. The thought excited and terrified her. After a spell, she moseyed home, feeling as if everything in her world might finally turn out right.

As she ate supper with her parents, the air outside darkened with an oncoming thunderstorm. Wind whipped the trees out front and tossed a tumbleweed across the road.

"It's been a dry summer," her father said, noting the change. "We could use a little water."

Her mother's brow furrowed. "But it's so dry out. I sure hope there aren't any lightning fires."

It's a mother's job to worry, Tabitha thought with a smile. *That's what we do.* She hadn't thought about fires caused by lightning, but the wind and rolling clouds made her worried for Will, who tended to be frightened of thunder. Surely Nathaniel and Mary would ease his fears, she thought. He could curl up in warm quilts with his cousins and play games to wile away the time.

What about Mantia?

With concerns over Will abated, the new thought intruded. Tabitha's fork paused midway to her mouth. She hadn't been to the stables yet today. Samuel's visit had more than distracted her from going.

After the meal, Tabitha helped her mother with the dishes. She felt tired and was tempted to collapse onto her straw tick but couldn't get Mantia out of her mind. Her parents settled beside the fire, her father reading a book and her mother knitting a sweater for Will.

Tabitha glanced at the clock. She hadn't seen her horse since yesterday evening—and now she had the tallow ointment that might help the gash. She grabbed the small crock from her bedroom, wrapped a shawl around her shoulders, and headed toward the door.

"I'm going to visit Mantia," she told her parents. "Don't wait up for me."

"But it's so cold," her mother protested.

Her father lowered his glasses. "And it's raining now. Sure you want to go out in that? The roads are probably nothing but mud."

"I'll be fine," Tabitha said with an encouraging smile. "I need to try Mother Hall's salve." She held up the crock.

Her mother lowered her knitting needles. "She *did* bring it to you. How wonderful. I hope it works."

Tabitha glanced at the crock and nodded. "I do too. I won't be too long."

Gripping her shawl around her neck with one hand, she hurried into the ebony night. A sharp rain pelted down, making Tabitha pull her shawl above her head and scurry through the street, which was getting slicker by the minute. When she arrived at the stable, she went inside and lowered the shawl to her shoulders, shaking the rain from her dress.

Wind whipped through the rafters, making it difficult to light the kerosene lamp she found hanging from a nail. The flame finally took but shuddered in the wind. Feeling uneasy, Tabitha quickly made her way to Mantia's stall, where she went inside and found her horse lying in the straw, weak and listless.

A lightning flash illuminated the stall and the pained expression on the horse's face. Tabitha put a hand to her own heart. She hung the lamp on a nail then sat down, stroking the horse's face as tears poured down her cheeks, the damp shawl clutched around her shoulders in a pathetic attempt to keep the chill at bay.

How long she stayed there, she wasn't sure. At first she counted lightning strikes, wondering if the storm were passing yet, but lost count after thirty. She hardly noticed her teeth chattering or that her fingers were starting to grow numb. What did any of that matter when Mantia burned with fever and her eyes showed such agony, when there was nothing Tabitha could do but sit beside her and try in some small way to comfort her?

In the darkness, the barn door banged open and then shut. A moment later, Brother Carlisle sidled up to the stall and sighed. "Thought I saw a light in here. Sister Chadwick, she's a lost cause. There's no point anymore."

"I'm sorry, but I can't believe that," Tabitha said defiantly. She angrily wiped at traitorous tears.

He sighed. "Please. Go home." He pushed off the stall edge and walked away. The sound of his boots echoing off the walls made the barn seem hollow, empty. The outer door shut with a bang, and they were alone once again.

She tried to get Mantia to drink or eat or swallow more oil. She took out the crock and carefully dabbed the precious ointment onto the cut. She wrapped a halter around Mantia's face and tried to urge her to stand but wasn't nearly strong enough to lift the horse's dead weight.

Water might help cool her fever, Tabitha thought, jumping up and racing to the other end of the barn to find a bucket. She found one, filled it with water from the barrel just outside the stable, then lugged it back to the stall. After dipping a cloth in the cold water, she swabbed Mantia's face, neck, and side. Then she sat back on her heels.

What else? What else might help? She remembered a poultice her mother used to make. Even if Tabitha had the heart to wake her mother, there was little chance such a poultice would work any better than the salve. She wondered if steeped peppermint leaves, a family remedy for soothing stomach trouble, would help. Even if it were to soothe the discomfort, it wouldn't solve the real problems, she knew.

Tabitha continued to wipe down the feverish coat and speak softly to Mantia, refusing to raise the white flag of surrender the way Brother Carlisle had.

And of course she prayed. She constantly prayed.

She pressed her hand against Mantia's neck, feeling for her pulse. It was thready and fast, worse than before. Panic swelled in Tabitha's chest. What more was there to do? She had exhausted everything she had ever known about caring for horses and people. She collapsed against the horse's body, exhaustion and emotion flooding out.

"Mantia, no. Please. You can't do this to me!"

She sat there, crying, until anger overpowered her. So she stood, feeling an insane urge to kick the walls of the stall, to rage and scream into the night. She had felt that surely if she would just carry on, a solution would present itself and she would come out on the winning end. Fighting for success had always worked before; it was the only thing she knew with unwavering confidence that she *could* do. Carrying on was the only solution to an overwhelming problem. It had worked—eventually—with the paper. It had worked after Fred died.

Pressing forward kept the fear and pain at bay.

"You have to get well, Mantia. You *must*," she pled, kneeling again. She ran her fingers through the horse's mane. "Mantia, please."

A creak behind Tabitha startled her, and she stumbled to her feet and saw Samuel at the stall door. She wiped her freezing fingers across her cheek, daring him to tell her to leave, that it was hopeless, like Brother Carlisle had said. She put up her wall of strength once more, hoping he hadn't seen or heard her being weak a moment before, but knowing he probably had.

As Samuel stepped into the stall, he didn't say anything about giving up. Instead, he quietly closed the door behind him until it latched. He crossed to the other side of the stall and knelt down beside Mantia, where he stroked the horse's nose. "Poor thing," he said, looking at Tabitha. She had a feeling that he didn't mean just the mare.

She knelt beside him and stroked the horse's flank. A fresh flood of tears erupted, and she sniffed, trying to squelch the uprising. *Strong. I must be strong.* Why had she let her reserves come down? Mantia needed her. Crying wouldn't help anything, and Samuel certainly didn't need to see her being weak like this. She wiped her hands on her skirt then leaned forward to take Mantia's pulse.

After several seconds, Tabitha sat back on her heels and shook her head to clear it. She put on a schoolmarm air and said in her best matter-of-fact tone, "She's getting weaker now. I don't know what else I can do."

Samuel looked at her with sad eyes. "Tab, don't do this again."

"Don't . . . do what?" She knew what he meant—don't take on the burden alone, as she had when the Daggett case seemed to threaten the paper. But it wasn't in her to ask for aid. She had always relied on herself—that's how it needed to be. The one time she had turned her life over to someone else, he'd died.

For a moment, she almost broke, but instead, she stood and walked to the lantern to check the wick. "It probably won't be long now. I doubt she'll last through the night. Of course, I'll have to find a way to tell Will." She gave the slightest glance at Samuel over her shoulder. "He'll be heartbroken, I'm sure."

She felt Samuel's hand on her shoulder, warm and strong, and closed her eyes, pressing her lips together as he spoke. "Tab. You don't have to be strong all the time."

Emotion bubbled so close to the surface that she couldn't say much. "Yes, I do." She wished to say more but couldn't, not until she could rein in her feelings and be sure to speak without blubbering. After several steadying breaths, she turned her head enough to look down at his boots instead of his face. She focused on the weathered black tops, wishing she could see the familiar red streaks on the heels. Looking into his eyes would be too hard. She daren't see that dear, kind face that could read her heart. The future was never certain, so she couldn't ever let down her guard.

"I've *had* to be strong, Samuel, don't you see?" Tabitha gripped the edge of the stall, needing to feel something solid beneath her hands. "I was a weak little girl when Fred died, and it nearly killed me. The only way Will and I have made a life for ourselves is by my being strong and capable and never allowing myself to crumble or waver or . . ."

There was the emotion again, threatening to wash over her like a tidal wave and beat down the defenses she had built. She forced it back down, digging her fingernails into the wood beam.

"I know," Samuel said. This time he moved closer. He put both hands on her shoulders and turned her around to face her full-on. She stared at the straw littering the ground as he spoke. "Tab, there was a time for you to be like a fortress." He paused for several seconds, making her raise her head. Samuel's eyes were soft, sad, penetrating. He sighed, shaking his head with a look of incomprehension on his face. "I don't understand. Doesn't being strong all the time get tiring? Don't you ever wish you could just rest? Don't you worry that you'll collapse beneath the load?"

"Always." Slowly, Tabitha nodded, then felt her face crumple. Wanting to hide the weakness, she raised her hands as sobs came out, sobs she couldn't order behind the wall. They came out unbidden, and more tumbled out on top of the others, her exhaustion and grief releasing. Samuel pulled her close and wrapped his arms around her.

"I'm so weary all the time," she said, crying into his chest as she spoke.

"At the very least, turn some of the burden over to the Lord. That's what He's there for. 'My yoke is easy and my burden is light,' remember?"

Tabitha nodded. "He's the only person I *can* rely on."

God was the only one who wouldn't ever abandon her.

Samuel sighed. "You can put your trust in people, too, Tab. You don't have to keep living this way."

"Yes, I do." Tabitha's tears turned from forlorn to angry ones. She made fists and pressed them against his chest, demanding, "What other option do I have? No one else is going to be strong for me or for Will . . . I have no choice. I've done everything I could to take care of us, just like I've done everything I could for Mantia, but I'm still losing her. I shouldn't have let myself care for her. It hurts too much . . ." Her rant gave way to a fresh bout of tears.

Samuel pulled her closer and gently stroked her hair as she cried. He didn't try to ease away the tears, undo the past, or make promises for an untarnished future. He just let her cry. When her sobs lessened and she stood trembling in his arms, he said, "Tab, could—could you let *me* be the strong one sometimes?"

Not responding right away, Tabitha sniffed and wiped her face. She lifted her head, unsure, and stared at him.

Samuel leaned in and kissed the top of her head. "Men and women aren't supposed to be alone. We're supposed to help bear one another's burdens, take turns, and let the other one rest so neither has to bear the weight all the time."

She smoothed the area of his shirt that her tears had wetted and tried to even out her breath. "What are you saying?"

"That you and I could both use someone else to help bear the load." He scowled at his own words, then tried again. "That sounds too . . . practical. What I mean is, you're the woman I'd like to be with, whether that means I'm being crushed under life's burdens or hoping to carry a part of yours."

A tiny smile threatened to curl Tabitha's mouth. "I suppose you mean more than fixing a printing press?"

"Oh, yes," Samuel said, leaning in. She could feel his breath on her cheek as he added, "Much more. Will you let me carry some of the load?"

Tabitha closed her eyes and took a deep breath. It took an enormous amount of will to say, "I'll try." When his eyebrows went up in question, she added, "I promise."

"Then that's the best I can hope for." Samuel leaned in, closed the gap, and kissed her.

CHAPTER 27

THE FOLLOWING MORNING, SAMUEL LEFT Mrs. Mirkins's house with a lighter step—and a toolbox in his hand. For the next two days, he'd be doing tithing work on the temple. Forty-eight hours in the open air and sun rather than inside a dank, musty barn that reeked of animal waste. As he approached Temple Hill, he breathed in deeply, relishing the crisp morning air, still gray but starting to grow pink and golden as the sun crested the hills to the east.

A man approached Samuel, walking with a determined step and a look of consternation on his face. Arms swinging, he nearly passed by, then suddenly came up short and pointed at Samuel. "You. Don't you work at Carlisle's stable?"

"I do," Samuel said. "The name's Barnett."

"Larsen," the man said gruffly by way of introduction. He scratched his short, ruddy beard, looking about distractedly.

"But today I'm not at the stables," Samuel said. "I'm at the hill." He nodded northward in the direction of the construction. "Is something wrong?"

Larsen grunted. "You could say that. The mules aren't at the stable. Hard to haul stone without them, you know. One of Brother Parry's men went to get them ready for the day's work, and they were just *gone*. We're all in a dither trying to sort out the mess, and I wondered if maybe the brutes ended up at the Little Fort stable somehow."

"I haven't been there today," Samuel said, "but we didn't have them when I left last night." Of course, he hadn't been aware of much besides Tabitha and Mantia last night, but he was quite sure that there were no stray mules around.

"Well, the way I figure, they probably got loose in the night sometime. I'm hoping someone brought them to the Little Fort stable, not knowing where they belonged. So I think I'll go check just to rule it out." Larsen sighed. "They could get themselves killed or captured by Indians, and then we'd be in a fine how-do-you-do. Sure hope they didn't get stolen or wander out of town." He spoke as though he had little hope for a successful outcome.

"I'll see if I can help with the search after I check in with President Peterson," Samuel said. He wasn't sure what the stake president and superintendent looked like, but plenty of others did, so they shouldn't be hard to find.

"Thanks, Barnett. Sure appreciate it." Larsen headed off almost before the words were out of his mouth.

Samuel continued to Temple Hill, keeping an eye out for the stray mules. Chances were that someone had forgotten to secure them last night and they had wandered out. With any luck, they'd turn up soon. He reached the base of the hill and saw several men standing around discussing something in heated voices. One man had a set of architectural plans unrolled and pointed to the towers in the drawings. Not wanting to interrupt and knowing that one of these men was likely the superintendent, Samuel held back and waited to introduce himself.

"The addition of a lightning rod would destroy the artistic lines," the man holding the drawings said. "It would look dreadful, regardless of whether it has a sharp or blunt end."

"What if we added a decorative ball on top?" asked the tallest of the three, whom Samuel thought might be President Peterson. "I've seen some buildings do that, and it's mighty pretty, Folsom."

The architect—Folsom—shook his head. "I'd rather not, but of course, it's your decision."

Samuel had half a mind to tell them that of course they should add a lightning rod; they should protect the House of the Lord with any means possible. He put down his toolbox and took a step forward, hoping to catch someone's eye so he could introduce himself or at least add his opinion—not that he had any authority over the matter.

But then the third man, a portly, bald fellow, hitched his pants higher on his abundant waist and said, "Brethren, do you think the

Lord would really allow lightning to strike His house? I for one don't think He would, so a lightning rod is completely unnecessary."

Folsom and Peterson looked at one another and considered this. Peterson nodded slowly. "Perhaps you're right. I'll give it some thought. For now, proceed as if there will not be a lightning rod. We'll make a formal decision about it later."

As Folsom rolled up the plans, Samuel stepped forward. "President Peterson? I'm Samuel Barnett, reporting for my tithing labor."

"Good to have you," Peterson said, extending a hand, which Samuel shook. "We're grateful for your willingness to work. I believe that Brother Parry had plans to use you for blasting stone over on the southeast side there, but before that, I'm afraid we need some help rounding up a few mules."

"I heard about that on my way here," Samuel said. "Still have no idea what happened to them?"

"None whatsoever," Peterson said. "Quite the mystery."

A sudden commotion of men's voices came from the north side of the hill, making the group turn to look. A man ran, wending his way down the path that ran down the west side of the hill between the terraces, waving his hat and whooping for all he was worth.

"Burton, is that you?" President Peterson called. "What is it?"

"We found 'em," Burton called with his hands to the sides of his mouth. "We found the mules!"

"All of them? Are they hurt?" Peterson demanded.

When the man came closer, it was clear by the jolly look on his face that he'd been laughing. He leaned his hand on his thighs to catch his breath then shook his head with a chuckle as he stood to relate the story. "Apparently, those mules are more eager than the men to get this temple built. A few of us decided to go ahead and try to get some work done without the mules, but when we got there, turned out they've been waiting on *us* all morning—they're over on the north side, standing ready to be hitched!" He threw back his head and guffawed, and the other men burst into laughter as well.

"Praise the Lord for that," the portly gentleman said. He wiped his shiny scalp and said, "Someone better tell Parry and Larsen. The two of them are about fit to kill over losing those mules." He gestured to Samuel and added, "I'm Willardsen. Nice to meet you, Barnett.

You come with me, and I'll get you set up with the quarry stone now that we don't need your help finding those eager-beaver mules."

He'd be working with stone. Plain old stone. Not even with the mules. Just cutting, blasting, hefting. With *tools*. After his trial by manure, this was the nearest thing to heaven that work could possibly be.

He picked up his toolbox and followed Willardsen, nodding to Peterson and Folsom as he left.

This is going to be a great day.

* * *

On Friday, Tabitha worked like one in a dream. She kept watching the clock, waiting for midday, when she could flee to the stable to check on Mantia.

An hour before Tabitha planned to leave, Natalie put a hand on her shoulder. "Sister Chadwick? Can I do some of your work? I'm afraid those circles under your eyes aren't just bruises anymore. They're from worry and fatigue, aren't they?"

"I suppose they are." Tabitha said with a sigh. She leaned back in her chair and rubbed her forehead.

"Go take an early dinner. I can handle things here for a couple of hours," Natalie said, urging Tabitha to her feet.

She stood and looked over her desk. The paper was running smoothly now. There was a lot to do, but perhaps she could let Natalie do some of the work for a spell. "All right," she said. She wanted to be sure to finish up as much as she could today so that she wouldn't have to come into the office the next day, on Saturday. Will was coming home. "I won't be too long. Thank you, Natalie."

She hurried to the stables, where she found that Mantia's condition hadn't changed at all. She was no better, but then, she was no worse, either. After spending several minutes with her horse, Tabitha felt the need to escape. With Brother Carlisle's permission, she saddled Blossom and rode toward the winding paths of the eastern foothills.

The chilly morning air bit her nose and cheeks and blew through her hair, which she had left down that day. Her brown locks flowed behind her, waving in the wind as the horse loped in a light gallop. She and the horse were one as Blossom jumped shrubs and rocks, and

Tabitha leaned into the movement and sailed through the air. She gave Blossom free rein, allowing the horse to go wherever she wanted to—and as fast as she liked.

This is how flying must feel, Tabitha thought. She'd hoped to have this kind of experience with Mantia someday.

After some time, Blossom slowed to a trot and then to a walk, her breathing quickened. Tabitha closed her eyes and relaxed in the saddle, enjoying the slow rocking motion of the horse's gait, the breeze licking her face. She thought back to the night before—first to the agony of being with Mantia, ill and suffering, then to her tears when trying so hard to shore up her emotional barriers. Then of Samuel's arrival—Samuel holding her close and encouraging her to cry, to let it out, to allow herself to lean on him.

She thought of the sweet kiss that sealed her promise of trying to give up on being the solitary strong one, of letting Samuel into her heart and inside her walls of defense. At the memory, she leaned her head back. With her eyes closed, she relived the feeling of his lips on hers, of his arms wrapped around her, and of leaning against his chest and hearing the powerful drum of his heart. She had never felt so safe, so secure before.

I never felt so safe . . . not even with Fred, she thought sadly. The realization bothered her for a moment, but then she realized that when they had married, she had no *need* to feel such things, at least not in the same way. *I didn't yet have experience with the frightening things life could bring.* Such trials stripped a person of her sense that all was well in life, in the world. So when safety and peace did arrive, she was all the more grateful for it.

That feeling of security had flitted at the edges of her conscious-ness a few times with Samuel, but she had always commanded it to leave. She couldn't flirt with such dangers. Life wasn't safe. It wasn't peaceful or predictable or any such nonsense. She had had to be on guard, ready to withstand whatever blows the world had to offer. Allowing herself to feel secure would only erode those walls she had built up to protect herself.

But now . . . now she *wanted* those walls to crumble. Not entirely—just a chink here and there. Enough so Samuel could enter and slip inside with her. After letting her walls come down last night, she realized how good it felt, and she wanted to be able to feel that way again—that everything would turn out all right, that she didn't have to be so strong. Samuel really could carry part of the load, leaving her shoulders lighter.

She leaned closer to Blossom's neck and stroked her mane. "I'm lucky, aren't I?" she whispered as if speaking any louder would tarnish the moment. Sitting straight again, she gathered the reins and sighed. "Ready to go home?" After feeling Tabitha's heels gently nudge her flanks, the horse moved forward, guided by her rider as they turned and headed back toward town.

They hadn't gone more than a few dozen feet when the ground trembled. Pebbles skittered down the hillside in rivulets. Tabitha slowed slightly, unsure what it meant. An enormous boom thundered through the air with an almost physical force. With a sudden intake of air, Tabitha instinctively froze in her seat. Her lungs sucked for breath but seemed paralyzed.

This was far more than the sound of blasting stone. She had managed to get used to *that*. She knew how loud the quarry noises were, and they no longer bothered her.

This—this was different. And she knew what this was; she had heard it seven years ago in Coalville.

An explosion.

The two words rang in her mind with brutal clarity. The shock of hearing it—several times louder and more powerful than any of the quarry detonations she had heard over the last several weeks—sent her entire body trembling. Emotions buried deep in her memory reared their heads, gripping her insides like claws. She looked down to see her hands going white and knew her face must be pale too. A gasp finally brought air into her chest, and she struggled to regain control of her emotions. Blossom fought for her head, her ears lying back, and for a moment Tabitha couldn't think clearly enough to know what to do. She finally reined the horse in.

I'm not near a coal mine, she reminded herself. *Whatever the sound was, it was* not *a mine collapse. It's nothing to worry about.* She took several deep breaths, and she chided herself for overreacting. She looked over the valley, trying to see where the sound had come from. A cloud of dust drifted somewhere in the north, but she couldn't tell if it had anything to do with the noise.

She took a deep breath, then urged Blossom onward. "I'm ready, girl. Let's go."

The horse must have sensed Tabitha's unease, because she didn't want to obey at first.

"It's all right," Tabitha said, surprised at the weakness—and barely restrained emotion—in her voice. "It's all right. Let's go."

Blossom shook her head and whinnied her displeasure but moved forward, her hooves clopping on the sun-baked earth of the foothills. Tabitha searched the landscape for more of a sign of what had happened in town.

The sound was so much louder than the quarry . . .

Her heart continued to hammer against her ribcage, refusing to still. *This is ridiculous,* she thought, annoyed at her tremors—at the fear bubbling just beneath the surface. *It's not as if I'm married and could lose a husband to a collapsing mine again . . .*

But the fact remained that the only thing she could think of that might use enough gun powder to cause such a terrible sound was what she had already thought of—the stone blasting at Temple Hill. But not once since her return to Manti had she heard anything *that* loud coming from that area. *Something must have gone wrong with a blast.*

Panic gripped her chest, and her eyes snapped northward.

Samuel!

Tabitha gathered the reins tightly and kicked her heels into Blossom's sides, pressing the horse into a gallop. *Faster, faster!* she thought, her mind in a frenzy. *Lord, I cannot do this again. Don't take him from me!*

She pressed her heels deeper into the horse's flanks, but Blossom was already galloping across the uneven terrain as fast as she could. Tears streamed down Tabitha's cheeks; the trail blurred into indistinct shapes of brown and gray, interspersed with the blue-green blurs of shrubs.

With the back of her hand, she wiped at her nose, no longer swollen but still tender from the break. A sensation of light-headedness swept over her, making her grip the reins tighter to keep from flying off the saddle. Yet as the thought of falling crossed her mind, she glanced at the swiftly moving ground beneath her. For the briefest flash, the idea of flying headfirst into scrub oak didn't sound so terrible. Not if leaving this world meant an escape from her problems. Not if Samuel were injured and might also die . . .

No. I can't think like that, she chastised herself, narrowing her focus on the landscape ahead. *I have Will to think about.*

The image of her son made a sob creep up her throat. He gave her an enormous reason to keep living, no matter what. She pressed her eyes closed, refusing to contemplate the *no matter what.* The thought made her grip the reins harder.

For Will's sake.

Until this moment she thought she had managed to grieve and put away that young girl, leaving her in the past to become a new, mature—strong—woman. Surely nothing from that time could faze her in the same way ever again.

But her reaction to just the sound of the explosion told her otherwise.

When she reached the city streets, Blossom was still at a gallop. It didn't take much to keep the horse at a breakneck pace; it seemed to sense her urgency. They raced northward through the city blocks and quickly came to the base of Temple Hill. A moderate crowd had gathered, making it impossible to see anything. She slowed unwillingly, coming to an abrupt stop behind several people at the back of the throng. Tabitha hurriedly slid off and nearly ran Blossom to a hitching post, where her hands fumbled with the reins, taking twice as long to secure the knot as it normally did. She finished and whirled around to race to the crowd. She pushed her way through, her heartbeat in her throat.

Samuel. Where is Samuel?

"Excuse me," she said, not-so-gently squeezing between people. "Excuse me. *Please.*" The begging tone that came out surprised even her, bringing to mind the last time she shoved her way through a crowd.

Coalville.

A shudder went through her, and she moved faster. *I must get through.*

"Pardon me. *Excuse* me!"

Finally she reached the front of the gathering at the base of the terraces, just in time to see a man being carried on a litter down the zigzag path between the huge walls. Some men in charge prevented anyone from venturing onto the hill itself. Tabitha stood behind one of them to the left of the path, clasping her hands together as she waited, trying to make out the face of the person being carried. As the litter came near, she still couldn't identify the face. It was turned away and covered in blood.

The man carrying the front end rotated slightly in his path, revealing the victim's boots. Black . . . with red-streaked heels. A cry escaped Tabitha's throat. A shaking hand covered her mouth as her knees buckled, and she dropped to the ground.

Samuel! Samuel, no!

The crowd parted as the stretcher was carried past. She whimpered and scrambled to her feet, hurrying after them. "Stop! Please, stop!" The men paused, and they looked over at her in question. She stared at Samuel's bloodied face. She couldn't help but glance at his legs. He still had both—but one was covered in red and looked distorted. His left arm lay across his torso at an awkward angle.

"What happened?" she demanded, still staring at him.

"Dunno," the man said, shrugging her off as he continued picking his way down the hill toward the street.

She hurried forward to catch up, making them pause again. She took Samuel's hand in hers. His usually warm skin was cold as stone. Tabitha's chest constricted, and she squeezed his fingers. "Samuel, it's Tab. Can you hear me?"

He didn't open his eyes or acknowledge her, but he did moan slightly.

He's alive, she thought, crying with relief. The men kept walking, and the crowd parted just enough for them to pass then closed into a human river again, preventing her from continuing at his side. For the moment, her feet felt planted to the ground anyway.

What a fool she had been to think it was wise to let herself feel safe, at peace. How could Samuel share her burdens when he might not live to see the morning?

He's hurt, but he's alive, an inner voice reminded her. *And he'd better stay that way,* she added, trying to muster some anger to shove out the other, weaker, emotions threatening to overwhelm her.

Anger would make her strong enough to keep standing. Slowly, she worked her way through the stifling crowd, through what felt like layer upon layer of people. Did Manti *have* this many people in it?

Finally free of the suffocating throng, she picked up her skirts and ran. Not seeing the stretcher anywhere, she stumbled to a stop and caught her breath at a house just south of the temple on a street corner. She looked up and down both streets it bordered, searching, but found no trace of Samuel. As she wiped beading perspiration from her upper lip, she noticed Bishop James half running, half walking down the hill almost in her direction.

"Bishop! Bishop, please can you tell me what's happened?"

He paused unwillingly, scarcely slowing his step before hurrying on. Tabitha ran forward to meet him. "What happened?" she demanded, walking beside him.

"There's been an accident," he said, agitation in his voice. "Heard tell one of the workers used twice as much powder as he was supposed to because it was taking too long to blow. Knocked another worker out cold."

The bishop appeared ready to hurry on and dismiss the conversation, but Tabitha continued to press her cause, not knowing if the bishop would know it was Samuel. "Please. I need to know about the injuries."

"Praise the Lord, there weren't many, which is nothing short of a miracle. Arlin Morris broke his foot when a stone landed on it, and a few others have cuts and scrapes. Only one man was seriously hurt."

"How seriously?" Tabitha asked, touching his sleeve.

The intensity of her voice must have finally caught his attention, because the bishop's step came up short. He looked at Tabitha. "That's right. I had forgotten about you and Barnett." His face softened, and then his eyes flickered to the small corner house Tabitha had left. Her eyes followed.

"Is he in there?" she asked, already picking up her hem and making her way toward the building. The house had a second story, and a balcony extended over one corner that acted as a roof to the porch below. A dark brown railing went around the balcony, and a small window on the second level seemed to be the only access. It was an odd little house, but for the moment all Tabitha cared about was getting inside it. She prepared to knock, but the bishop put up a hand to block hers.

"Sister." He gently took her by the elbow and turned her to face him. Tabitha gave him a challenging look as she waited for him to speak. "I'm not letting you in there. Such things aren't for women's eyes."

Tabitha wanted to rail about how she had already seen him covered in blood, that she was plenty tough to handle such sights. That she just needed to know for herself whether Samuel was well.

"I have to go in," she said simply.

"And I'm not letting you." The bishop moved between her and the door and folded his arms. Tabitha gulped, knowing that he meant exactly what he said. She couldn't force her way past a man with arms as thick as logs.

She peered inside a slender window beside the door, hoping to see any evidence of Samuel—perhaps the heel of one of his boots—but could make out nothing behind the curtains that hung in the way. She swallowed against what felt like a pebble in her throat.

"Will you let me know how he is?" she pled. "I'll—I'll wait out here." The promise stuttered on its way out.

"Very well," Bishop James said after a moment of consideration. "I'm going to administer to him. When I come back, I'll let you know."

"Thank you," Tabitha said.

The bishop knocked and was shortly let inside the house. The door banged shut behind him. Tabitha began pacing back and forth along the street, wringing her hands. She noted a short barrel beside the house and went to sit on it. She nearly collapsed. Her face in her hands, she fought with images that plagued her mind.

Samuel's red heels.

The matching scarlet blood streaking his face.

Paired with those images were ones of Fred being carried on a stretcher. She could still see his lone boot lying there, the other one missing, blown off somewhere inside the mine. His head had been covered in blood just like Samuel's was. Both men's hands had been smudged with black.

As it was, she felt as if her emotions balanced on a knife point. She had fallen to the ground when she first saw him. Since then, she had reinforced that wall with brute force. But she knew her inner fortress was on the verge of collapse; if she allowed herself to waver, she just might fall into madness and lose all control. She'd end up lying in bed again, crying during the night and staring at the ceiling by the day.

The last time she felt this fragile, she'd had a child growing within her that tied her to the man she had lost. This time she would have nothing from Samuel but a few choice memories and a crumpled program from their evening together at the benefit. A sob threatened to escape her throat, and she clamped her lips tight to hold it back.

I cannot do it again.

The thought repeated itself in her mind. As far as she could see, her choices lay in two directions—either suffer a thousand deaths of the heart if Samuel were to be taken to his grave, or cut off her heart so that no matter what happened, she wouldn't collapse under the weight.

Life was uncertain. Eventually she would lose Samuel one way or another. Of that she was sure. If not today, then on another day. She could not bear it.

And I have Will to think about.

Her son needed a strong mother, not a weak, sniveling thing that spent her days whimpering under an afghan. The only way she could be sure of avoiding such a fate was pulling her feelings away from Samuel. Of course that would hurt too, but not nearly as much as allowing herself to fall deeper in love with him, only to lose him later.

The only way to find peace is by clinging to what I have and can do. I am a mother. That is all.

Emotionally, she took a pair of shears and broke the strings connecting her heart to his—one fast, clean cut. She would put him behind her. She wiped her eyes, sniffed, and forcibly stood, her back as ramrod straight as her determination to follow her chosen course. With her head held high, she walked, intending to retrieve Blossom and bring her back to the stables. Behind her, the door of the house opened, and she heard Bishop James step out. Tabitha battled with herself—should she keep walking or turn to hear his report?

"Sister Chadwick?"

Tabitha stopped and closed her eyes tightly. She didn't turn around. Could she keep her resolve if she saw bad news reflected in the bishop's face? Instead she stared at a stone in the ground a few feet off. She wanted desperately to shower the bishop with questions— *How does Samuel look? Where are his wounds? Is he awake?*

Will he live?

Instead she took a deep breath and said a single word. "Yes?"

"He . . ."

Her ears strained to hear his voice. Why didn't he just spit it out?

Her heart sped up with anxious anticipation. *I cannot do it again,* she reminded herself, then took out the emotional shears again.

I cannot care about Samuel Barnett as anything more than a friend, an acquaintance. I cannot.

Snip.

The bishop sighed but finally said what he came for. "He lost an ear, broke an arm, and he may still lose a leg. He's lost a lot of blood as well."

Tabitha turned her cheek slightly toward him and struggled to ask one question. "Will he . . . live?"

"I don't know."

She felt tears spring to her eyes then forced her emotions into a compartment and locked them up. "Thank you, Bishop," she said in a deliberate, even voice. "Good day."

CHAPTER 28

BLASTING POWDER IS JUST AS *unpredictable as a bloomin' cow*, Samuel thought as he shifted positions on the bed. Burning pain shot through his leg and arm, making him suck air between his teeth. As the pain subsided, he let out a shaky breath and leaned against the pillow. He delicately probed the bandage where his right ear used to be. His fingers came away dry; the bleeding had stopped. But he still felt weak, and his head throbbed. How long had it been since the accident?

Footsteps sounded on the stairs, and Dr. Baker came into the room, smiling. "So, Brother Barnett, how are you feeling this fine morning?"

"A bit like I was caught in an explosion and hit with flying debris," Samuel said with a wry smile.

"Hmm, also as if your leg was pinned under a rock, perhaps?" Dr. Baker grinned. "Glad to see your spirits are up." He took Samuel's pulse on his wrist and nodded with approval, then pulled up a chair and sat down.

If only my spirits were *up,* Samuel thought dismally, but he refused to show his melancholy state of mind to others. Dr. Baker asked various questions: When did he last eat and what did the meal consist of? When was his head bandage last changed? Had he felt feverish? Samuel answered each one with short, clipped answers. His mind roamed outside the four walls of the room, and he gazed through the small window at the other end of the room, from which he could see a few feet of the rising temple walls and a pale blue sky with streaks of dismal gray clouds. They looked remarkably similar to how he felt.

What about Tabitha? Did she know what had happened? Was she worried about him? Why hadn't she come? Perhaps he had deluded himself into thinking that she really cared. Perhaps he would be alone in this world, after all.

"You'll still need to stay here for a spell," Dr. Baker said, putting his supplies back into his black bag and snapping it shut. "At least until we know how that leg is shaping up. No going home for now."

Home? Samuel turned away and stared at a knothole on the wall. *It's Mrs. Mirkins's home, not mine. I have no home.*

Where is Tab?

For a moment, he forced the thought away so he could wear a jovial face for the doctor, who was trying to help him. "Thank you," Samuel said. "I appreciate all your help."

"My pleasure." Dr. Baker took a step away and raised a hand in a wave. "Just be sure you don't try using that arm before it's ready. You get some rest now."

"I will," Samuel said, then watched the doctor descend the stairs, hating that there was little but resting he could do while lying in bed.

He let his mind wander to avoid the pain—but it always seemed to wander into other, more hurtful areas. Eventually someone else came up the stairs. Brother Stephenson stepped in. "I brought up a bite for you," he said, holding out a tray.

"Thank you," Samuel said, but he wasn't hungry.

Brother Stephenson, an elderly widower with a ring of gray hair, pulled a chair closer to the bed and rested the tray on top. "It's not much—just biscuits and gravy—but it's nice and hot," he said as he helped Samuel get to more of a sitting position. The movement was painful, and Samuel gritted his teeth.

As the elderly gentleman retrieved the tray and rested it on Samuel's lap, an envelope caught his eye. It was tucked next to the plate. "What's this?" Samuel asked, picking it up in his good hand.

"That? Oh, yes," the man said. "I almost forgot. Came about an hour ago for you. It's from a pretty slip of a girl. Here, let me help you open it." Samuel waited with growing anticipation as the man slipped his finger under the seal and then pulled out a single, folded paper and handed it over. "Here you go. I'll be downstairs if you need anything. Just holler."

"I will, thank you," Samuel said. Tabitha had sent a letter. His pulse spiked thinking about it. He waited impatiently until he was alone to unfold the page and read her lightly angled script.

Dear Samuel,

I was so sad to hear of your accident, although I am grateful you are receiving good care. The situation is such that I doubt whether I can be true to the promise I made you the other night. I cannot share a yoke again without it destroying me. I'm so afraid. I must protect my son's mother. I hope you understand.

I have and will continue to pray for your recovery, and will always remain

Your dear friend,

Tab

Samuel wanted to throw the tray at the wall, to get out of bed and run to Tabitha, to insist that she reconsider.

On the other hand, what did it matter how well *he* felt? His eyes moved from the window to his throbbing leg, which might still be taken off. No one had told him as much directly, but he had heard Dr. Baker whispering in hushed, dark tones to Brother Stephenson when they thought he was sleeping.

With an ear blown off, he was already maimed. Losing a leg would compound the problem. How would he work now? What would he do besides become an object of charity for the Saints to care for as he sat alone in some room, unable to earn his keep for the rest of his miserable life? He wouldn't blame Tabitha for not wanting half a man. She would have to be the caretaker *and* the breadwinner. It wouldn't be fair to her.

He breathed in deeply, trying to settle his emotions. *It's better this way,* he thought. *She's right to leave me alone.*

* * *

On Saturday, instead of staying at home and waiting for Will to return, Tabitha had gone into the office in an attempt to distract herself. She'd hoped that sending a letter to Samuel would be enough to let her stop dwelling on him. Instead, she looked up from her desk, her gaze landing on the spot where Samuel had first kissed her.

Unable to stand being at the office any longer, she left for the stable, where she found Mantia holding onto life with the thinnest of threads. No matter where she looked in the barn, memories of Samuel assaulted her. Every few minutes she'd hear footsteps and think that it was Samuel walking by on his way to clean the chicken coop or feed the cow. The thought would make her mood lift—until the reality of where he really was crashed back down on her.

What she wouldn't give to weep with him over Mantia, to share this one burden.

I can't share it. I have no one, not even Samuel. And I will not let myself break again.

The red-streaked heels on the stretcher flashed in her mind. She banished the image with a sharp shake of her head and stood to retrieve a brush. She stroked Mantia's fur, trying to do something for her poor horse. Against her will, the memory of Samuel coming to her the other night sneaked into her mind. They'd stood here in the stall, and she'd told him she'd try to share her burdens.

She began brushing with increased vigor, gritting her teeth. *No. I can't think like this. I cannot think about . . . him.* She deliberately avoided thinking of his name. *I cannot let myself break again.*

Mantia would yet pull through, she told herself, banishing all other thoughts. Brother Carlisle hadn't believed she'd last this long; surely that meant she had a chance, that she was over the worst.

Reluctantly, Tabitha forced herself to go home. Will would be returning anytime, and she wanted to be there when he arrived. During the short walk home, she determined to keep a pleasant, unruffled demeanor around Will. His tender heart would be wounded by the things that had happened while he was away. She'd have to avoid questions about Mantia and Samuel.

She wandered through the trees in the family yard, waiting. She hadn't been there more than a few minutes when the sounds of wagon wheels and horses' hooves drew near, signaling Will's arrival. Her heart leapt, and she hurried to the corner to see her dear boy's face. And there he was, standing up and waving his hat in the air.

"I'm home, Mama!" Will cried joyfully. He jumped up and down. Nathaniel laughed and encouraged him to sit so he wouldn't topple off the wagon. When they pulled to a stop, Will nearly dove off the wagon as he threw himself into his mother's arms. She held on tight, relishing the feel of him in her arms, smelling his hair, never wanting to let go.

"I missed you so much," she said, only now realizing how empty her days had been without him there to brighten them.

"I missed you too, Mama," Will said, pulling back. "But I had *so much* fun!"

"I'm so glad," Tabitha said, trying not to show her emotion. He didn't need to see her crying.

Nathaniel hopped down, tied up the horses, and came over to her. "How are you doing, Tab? Really?"

She smiled wanly. Had he asked that question on Tuesday, she wouldn't have been able to express how great her joy was—everything had been wonderful then. "The newspaper is doing very well," she said. "All of that mess is cleared up."

"Glad to hear it," Nathaniel said with a nod. But then his eyes clouded. "So why do you look so sad? And what happened to you? Did you get into a fight with that Tidwell woman?" He gave a crooked smile and gestured to her face.

"Broke my nose," she said with a shrug. "Long story. My . . ." She glanced at Will, who seemed preoccupied by some bugs on the ground. "My horse isn't doing so well."

"Mantia? What's wrong with her?" Will demanded, standing up. She'd thought he hadn't been listening.

"She's . . . she's a little sick, Will," Tabitha said, bracing herself.

"Like I was sick a little while ago?" Will had asked.

"In a way." She hoped he wouldn't prod further.

"I'm sure she'll get better soon," Will said, apparently not too concerned. "Where is Samuel? When can we see him? I need to show him a stick Uncle Nathaniel helped me carve. It's so neat. Have you and Samuel been training Mantia more? What can she do now? When can I ride her? Oh, I can't wait for Samuel to see me riding her."

Somehow the boy had a knack for posing questions that pierced Tabitha to the core. Fortunately, he continued chatting, not stopping long enough to get answers. He took his mother's hand on one side and his uncle's on the other then led them into the house where he could tell them more about his bully of a week.

They went inside, where Tabitha's mother provided a simple, cold meal. While they ate, Tabitha didn't speak, instead allowing Will to chatter on about the adventures he'd had with his cousins. He told of Uncle Nathaniel's silliness and constant jokes. "He acts like a boy *my* age," Will insisted. Tabitha smiled at her brother, who shrugged, acknowledging the simple fact.

"Oh, and the other day, I caught a garden snake," Will announced, peach syrup dripping from his chin. "Uncle Nathaniel thought I should leave him at his house, so I can visit him every time I go back."

"Very good idea," Tabitha said, grateful her brother hadn't brought a pet snake home.

"Guess what I named him?" Will said. "Samuel."

At this, Tabitha nearly choked on a piece of cold chicken.

The family sat around and chatted for hours. Nathaniel went out to put up the horses out back. He'd be staying over the Sabbath and would go home on Monday. The family enjoyed one another's company. Tabitha held Will on her lap, not wanting to put him down. Even so, part of her mind was distracted. Mantia had been doing very poorly earlier. Tabitha wanted to check on her. Maybe later.

After the evening meal, they gathered around the fireplace. The sun had almost set, dimming the light and sending a cascade of colors across the sky. Will hopped off her lap and tackled his Uncle Nathaniel, saying, "Let's play horse again!"

Tabitha bit her lip. Perhaps she could sneak out to see Mantia briefly while Will played with her brother. She'd be back before he needed to get to bed. She stood and stepped quietly to the door. Her secretiveness didn't work. As soon as she was out of his line of vision, Will hopped off his uncle's back and appeared at her elbow.

"Where are you going? Can I come?" Will asked, shoving his feet into his boots as he spoke. "Are we going to see Mantia?"

How does he know? Tabitha thought helplessly. She couldn't lie to her son, but she didn't want to take him with her, either. She looked to her parents for help, but her mother said, "I think you should tell him, dear."

"Can I come, Mama, can I?" Will practically hung on the door as he begged, his puppy eyes pleading as much as his voice did.

Tabitha sighed. "Yes, I'm going to see Mantia. Remember how I said she's been sick?" Will nodded and waited for more. "Well, she's . . . *very* ill. I don't think you want to see her this way."

With a frustrated roll of his eyes, Will insisted, "That's why I want to come—to help her feel better. I won't get in your way or anything, I promise."

A lump formed in Tabitha's throat. Something inside her decided to yield. She nodded mutely and put out her hand for Will to take.

He virtually threw himself at her. "Oh, thank you, thank you, Mama! Mantia will be so happy to see me, I just know it. I've missed her. I bet she's missed me, too."

She took his hand—it felt tiny, warm, and soft inside hers—and waved at her parents and brother. "We won't be too long." She closed the door behind them and went on their way. Will hopped as much as skipped as they made their way to the twilit road, then up the street toward the stables.

"It'll be just like when I was sick with the chicken pox," Will said cheerfully, as if getting such an illness were a pleasant matter. Tabitha still couldn't get herself to speak. A feeling of dread weighed down her stomach as if lead balls were stacked inside. No matter, Will continued talking as they passed houses lit up with candles.

"Remember how when I was sick I felt so rotten? Remember, Mama? Remember?" He tugged at her arm insistently until she responded.

"I remember." She recalled that rocking Will to sleep, giving him some measure of comfort, had brought her a sense of well-being that nothing else could. "Of course I remember."

"Well, *I* remember one big thing about it," Will went on. "Anytime you were in the room, I felt worlds better than whenever you had to leave. And if you held me on your lap, I felt even better, like that first morning when we were in the rocking chair. I felt almost *all* better then. It was like you were the best medicine ever."

A slight chuckle escaped Tabitha, and she squeezed her son's hand. "I'm glad."

"That's what I'll be like for Mantia," Will said, his voice quickening with excitement. "If she knows I'm there, she'll feel better. I just know it. And I'll sit by her and pet her, so it's kind of like when you held me in your lap." His lips twisted to one side. "Maybe I should sing, too . . ."

"Maybe," Tabitha said, feeling a queer mix of heavy but optimistic feelings inside. She hoped Mantia would be able to know that Will was there, perhaps even feel his love, easing her pain for a spell.

When they reached the stables, the darkness was deepening, softening the last strips of pink sunset into a dark blue. Tabitha paused at the door. "Are you ready?" she asked, aiming the question partly at herself.

Will threw her one of his gap-toothed grins. "Ready!"

With a short nod, Tabitha pulled open the door, and they went inside, where the dimming light of day didn't penetrate the interior. She breathed in the musty air and listened, both hoping and fearing that she would hear Mantia's painful moaning. *I should find Samuel and ask how she's been today,* she thought. Then she felt as if a flat board had struck her in the middle.

Of course Samuel wouldn't be here tonight. The fact remained that he *couldn't* be inside the stables finishing up the day's work. Where was he now, and what was he doing?

When she'd dropped off the letter, Brother Stephenson had been both comforting and cryptic at the same time. She couldn't get much information out of him at all. Yes, Samuel was still staying at that house. No, he hadn't lost his leg. Yes, the bleeding had stopped, but she'd have to ask the doctor about anything else.

It was the *anything else* that had her worried. At least Samuel hadn't experienced a turn for the worse, she figured. So far. And she still didn't know much about what his condition was in the first place. In the last twenty-four hours since she sent the note, could he have . . . ?

No, I would have heard about that.

Her feelings of love for Samuel welled up inside her, threatening to overpower her emotions and send her hands shaking. Once again she closed her eyes, forcing herself to break the connection. *He's alive,* she told herself. *And that must be enough. You must let him go.*

She shook off such dreary thoughts and focused on the task at hand. "It's dark in here," she said absently. She reached for the lantern hanging on a nail nearby and lit it, casting a glowing orb several feet around them. As she raised the light so it reflected down the corridor, Tabitha suddenly felt fearful of what lay beyond the edge of the light. What fears of the night—of life—might reside just beyond the reach of the lantern's golden circle?

Tabitha held the lamp in one hand and took Will's with the other. Summoning any last vestiges of courage for facing whatever Mantia's condition would be, she walked with Will, their footsteps echoing on the hardened dirt floor. At the end of the corridor, Dolores lowed moodily and scraped a hoof against the wall. Clucking from the chicken coop seemed to echo. The baas of sheep leaked mournfully through the walls.

But there were no neighs.

The two of them passed several horses, all of which stood in their stalls with an eerie quiet—the only sound the swishing of their tails. It was as if they knew they shouldn't make a sound, not while Mantia lay so ill.

When they reached the stall, Tabitha let go of Will's hand and unlatched the door. Slowly, she pulled it open, her heart rapping against her ribcage like some crazed blacksmith on an anvil. Mantia lay motionless on the floor. She made no sound. In the deep shadows, Tabitha couldn't see much besides the large bulk, so she held the lamp forward, throwing light onto the beautiful lines of the chestnut mare—first onto the infected, puss-filled gash on her hindquarters, then onto the healed leg sores and to the ribs that no longer jutted through the skin from starvation.

Ribs that didn't move. On a body that lay unnaturally rigid.

And glassy eyes that gazed sightlessly into nothingness.

Praying fervently, Tabitha stepped inside and placed a hand on the horse's side. Cold.

"Aw . . ." The single syllable caught in her throat as she stepped back into the corridor, hoping to close the door, to protect Will from seeing the dead body—the shell of what used to be Mantia.

"What is it, Mama?" Will asked, trying to lean past her. He jumped as high as he could but remained unable to see over the wall. "What?"

Tabitha kept her back pressed against the door and its latch. Samuel. She wanted Samuel to lean on. But he wasn't here and might not ever be. She had cut herself off from Samuel. It was no longer her right to pry into his affairs or ask for help from him. She had walked away from that possibility. She closed her eyes tightly, sending tears down her cheeks.

"Mama?" Will's voice rose with concern.

"Come here," she said, her voice dry and scratchy. She knelt before him and pulled him onto her lap.

"I'm not . . . sick," Will said with a touch of confusion.

"I know."

He yielded, resting his head against her chest. "What's wrong with Mantia? Maybe if I sang her a song . . ." His voice trailed off as if he already knew such an event wouldn't be happening.

Tabitha took a deep breath, let it out, then said, "She's gone, Will."

His head popped up, and his eyes drilled into hers. "No, she's not. She's in her stall. I saw her." He studied her face, a look of panic flitting across his eyes.

He needs me to be strong. Don't upset him. She closed her eyes, bade the tears depart, then opened her eyes. "Will, Mantia has died. She's in heaven now."

For a moment, she wondered if that were entirely true—did animals have souls? She certainly hoped they did; what kind of heaven would be complete without animals to love and cherish?

"She's . . . dead?" Will sat up fast and began shaking his head. "Oh, Mama! She died all alone, without anyone. She was hurting, wasn't she?"

Tabitha wanted to lie, to say that of course Mantia didn't feel any pain when she had passed. But as a mother, Tabitha couldn't pretend, even when her son looked at her with that pitiable expression that tore at her core. "Yes, she was probably hurting." Her throat felt as if it constricted tighter with each word. "Perhaps it's better this way. She's no longer in pain." But even Tabitha had a hard time accepting the idea that things were better now.

"What a terrible, lonely way to go!" Will said, drooping as his inner spirit seemed to collapse with sorrow. He shook his head and sniffed. "Oh, I wish we would have come earlier, Mama. Then maybe she would have been a *little* happy when she died. At least she wouldn't have been all alone." Tears coursed down his cheeks, testing the limits of Tabitha's resolve not to cry.

A brief image came to mind of Samuel lying in bed, alone.

I will not cry. I will not.

"Mama, she died, hurting, without any love medicine."

"I know, baby," Tabitha said, pulling Will closer—less for his comfort than to block his anguished face from view. She couldn't endure the look in his eyes.

Mantia. Dead.

Tabitha could scarcely believe it—or bear it. What was the point of saving the beautiful animal's life, of nurturing her, helping her heal, teaching and taming her, if she were to just die from some fool illness anyway?

Samuel has no "love medicine" either. The thought stabbed her like an arrow to the heart. *But I can't give it. I can't. Even if he deserves it.*

After a minute, she gently edged Will off her lap. "Let's go home."

"But—"

"There's nothing we can do right now. I'll make sure she'll be taken care of."

Will nodded glumly and stood. Tabitha made sure the stall door was securely latched—hoping no one would inadvertently disturb Mantia's final rest—then took Will's hand. She returned the lamp to its nail and extinguished it. Together they left the stables as they had come. Intermittently, Will swiped at his wet cheeks and sniffed hard.

They walked home, Tabitha trying to remain stoic. She squeezed Will's hand whenever he let out a particularly large sob, knowing all too well the pain and sorrow he felt, but denying herself the opportunity to experience similar feelings or even admit to them. Doing so would unleash the floodgates, and she daren't do that.

So she remained tearless.

She could feel her eyes burning red as they walked, mother and son, in the gray dusk. Normally Tabitha would have breathed in the cool evening air, reveled in the purpling, velvet sky.

Not so tonight. Instead of feeling refreshing, the chilled air seemed to bite into her skin. The dark sky, instead of seeming to be a soft blanket descending over the world, now felt like a coffin lid.

And still she would not cry.

When they entered the house, her mother was the only one still in the sitting room. She knew immediately that something was wrong. She sat bolt upright in the rocking chair then tossed her darning aside and hurried to them. "Whatever is the matter? You look as if you've seen a ghost."

Will's face twisted. "Mantia died, Grandma." His lower lip trembled. "She died without me there to make her feel better."

The gentle grandmother's eyes flew to Tabitha, who gave a curt nod and added stiffly, "Must have been a couple of hours before we got there. She's already cold."

Her mother ushered Will to the back bedroom, taking off his coat and fussing over him like a mother hen. In a daze, Tabitha registered a dim gratitude to her mother for taking Will as she walked to the wingback chair before the fire and sat down. She stared at the flames licking one another, listening to the crackling and the popping that sent sparks into the air. The gentle blaze seemed to have more life in it than she did.

Hollow. That's how she felt.

Yet not long ago, she had felt so wonderfully happy. Life had held promises of a wonderful future—the *Sentinel*, Mantia . . . Samuel.

All hanging in the balance in one way or another. Now Mantia was taken, a beautiful thread cut from the tapestry of Tabitha's life. Samuel might follow soon. The newspaper . . . she had the newspaper. But what did that matter when so much of her heart had been cut out?

I have no strength anymore. It's gone.

How quickly her happiness had faded, vanishing like the morning dew. And yet . . .

Her promise to Samuel echoed in her head. *I promised to let him carry some of the load. I gave up before even trying.*

She tried arguing with herself. How could she conceivably give him some of the load when *he* was part of that load as he lay injured and near death himself? Mantia was dead. What could he do for Tabitha about that now?

And yet . . .

The two words kept repeating in her mind. And yet . . . perhaps solving her problems wasn't what Samuel meant. Shouldering a measure of a burden didn't mean getting rid of the burden.

Mantia might be gone now, but the sorrow Tabitha felt was still a very real weight.

And Samuel . . . dear Samuel.

If he were here, what would he do? He would hold me close and let me cry. He'd make me feel better because I know he cares. He loves me. And oh, how I want to cry.

She stood and walked to the window in the round, turret-shaped side of the room, where she gazed out over the star-strewn sky. There in the distance were the rising walls of the temple—the place where so much of her life had been determined, including life-changing moments with each of the men she'd loved.

She turned away and hugged herself. Where was Samuel now? How was he?

A burning desire swept through her to know—to find out. And this time she allowed herself to feel the worry, the anxiety, the possibility of despair.

I have to know, because I still care. I have to hold his hand and be with him, whether he lives or no. I must be his "love medicine," and he mine.

She couldn't allow either of them to languish in pain, alone, as Mantia had done.

Tabitha went back to the wingback chair, from which she snatched her shawl, then swept out the front door and headed toward Brother Stephenson's home. She had made a promise to Samuel, and she intended to keep it.

CHAPTER 29

THE LITTLE HOUSE STOOD THERE, waiting for Tabitha to go inside. The dark of night surrounded her, broken only by the dotted lights of windows with candles and the brilliant constellations in the inky black sky. She raised her eyes to the brown railing of the balcony above the porch and then to the window, where brown calico drapes fluttered in a light breeze, backlit by a candle.

If I were to call his name, he could hear me, she thought, then imagined herself doing that, saying, "Samuel, it's me, Tab." Even at this distance, he'd likely be able to hear through the window. Maybe he could respond—perhaps step out of the window onto the balcony and smile down at her.

She shook her head. If he could come out and speak to her, he wouldn't be at this house in the first place. He would be back at Mrs. Mirkins's or working in the stables where he belonged.

A sad smile curved her mouth the slightest bit. Who would have ever considered the stables to be a place where Samuel *belonged?*

Was he awake now? In pain? Bleeding?

Dying?

She bit her lower lip—hard—to force back the emotion bubbling beneath the surface. *When I see Samuel, I'll allow myself to shed a tear. I will stay strong until then. I will* not *cry before that point.*

As much as she hated to think it, Samuel might not want to see her, not after her short—and hardly kind—letter. Not after she hadn't visited him. Would he be angry, so hurt that he'd turn her away? Or would he understand? She lowered her head, unable to consider the first option, even though it was the most likely.

The breeze picked up, blowing her skirts as she moved forward. She walked across the street and faced her fears by rapping soundly on the brown-painted door.

While waiting for an answer, she glanced over her shoulder at the construction site. The entire structure seemed enormous, and standing as it did atop the hill, almost anywhere she went in the town, the temple seemed to watch over the community like a glowing, ivory angel.

Please watch over me now, she thought, turning to face the door as the handle turned and the hinges creaked open. The door was pulled back to reveal a stocky man with a long, black mustache curling low on either side of his face.

"Brother Stephenson?" Tabitha asked hesitantly.

"Yes?"

"Good evening," she said, wondering if she should introduce herself. When she'd dropped off the letter, she might not have even mentioned her name. "I'm Tabitha Chadwick, if you recall."

"I remember," he said with a nod.

She gave a slight, if awkward, curtsy, not sure what the protocol was in situations like these. "May I see Mr. Barnett?"

"Sorry, but he can't have visitors right now," he said, making Tabitha's stomach lurch with worry. Maybe he'd requested not to see her after reading the letter. However, "visitors" was general and could mean anyone, and it could be just the doctor's orders. But if he wasn't seeing anyone, perhaps he was in poor condition. No matter how she looked at the comment, she couldn't find a way to interpret it that didn't make her stomach feel heavy.

"Is he *very* poorly off then?" Tabitha tried to sound matter-of-fact, trying not to betray the intense anxiety she felt as she awaited a response. She peered inside the tiny house, wondering if she could see something behind the man—perhaps Samuel was downstairs instead of in the upstairs room as she had assumed—but the room held no one else. A wooden settee and a cracked table made up the majority of the furnishings. The stairs on the far side must surely lead to the room where Samuel lay.

"Oh, he'll pull through, if that's what you mean," Brother Stephenson said.

"Thank the Lord," Tabitha said, letting out a breath she had been holding. It came out ragged, making her put a hand to her chest.

"That is, he'll live."

"What does *that* mean?" Just as relief was getting ready to wash over her, and to slowly release some of the knots she had been carrying around since she first heard the boom, she had to stave it off. She hadn't known much of anything about the explosion or the aftermath—only what she had seen and what Bishop James had told her.

"He may still lose a leg," Brother Stephenson said. "It ain't pretty, ma'am. Take my word for it."

Her cheeks felt hot now in spite of the chilly evening air. Again, images of Fred's blown-off leg flitted across her mind. But Samuel would *live*. What was a missing leg compared to life itself?

"I want to see him," she said with a boldness that seemed to jump from her skin.

"He's sleeping, I reckon. He sleeps a lot. Needs to, doctor says."

Tabitha reined in her nerves. *Patience is a virtue,* she reminded herself. But any patience she might have ever owned evaporated. "Then I'll wake him up . . . please?" She tacked the last on so it wouldn't sound too brash. She had strength right now to face Samuel. But she needed more strength to face Mantia's death, to mend fences with Mother Hall, and to make a life for herself there in Manti. That strength rested upstairs with Samuel. If she were to leave now, to stretch the silence into two days or three or four . . . she might lose the courage to ever return.

And then what? Anytime in the future when she had to face everything else, she might just crumple to the ground in a whimpering mass of womanhood, never to rise again.

Stephenson drew a hand down the sides of his moustache as he contemplated her request. "Doctor said he'd need his rest. Tomorrow they're decidin' whether to try keepin' his leg or just to cut it off now before it festers and dies on its own. Mr. Barnett remains rather weak. Lost quite a bit of blood, you know."

"Yes, I know." The man seemed to be on the verge of relenting. She took a half step forward. "Please, let me in." The man clearly didn't understand. She *had* to see Samuel. Snipping her emotions didn't work. The threads that bound them together were stronger than that, and right now they felt like the only thing keeping her alive.

I need him. I need to cry with him over the explosion. I need to see and hold his face. I need to tell him about Mantia and let myself cry into his shoulder about her death.

The thoughts brought her an increased sense of urgency, one that the portly gentleman simply wasn't going to quash.

"Well, now, I don't rightly know . . ."

"I have to see him," she announced, ignoring all convention. She pushed the door open and marched past the stunned man, who gaped at her forwardness. *Call me brash, then.* She paused at the base of the narrow staircase and looked over her shoulder at him, her hand poised on the banister. "Oh, and when the doctor returns, please place the blame for Mr. Barnett's early wakening on *my* shoulders."

With that, she lifted her chin in defiance and marched up the stairs, her heart speeding with each step that brought her closer to Samuel. First she saw the legs of the bed then a faded green quilt made with a chain pattern. A square of moonlight fell onto the blanket from the window to the east. She stepped higher, now able to make out the shape of a man beneath the blanket, and finally, after reaching the top step, Samuel's dear face and disheveled hair, his eyes closed to the world and possibly dreaming. Of what, she wanted to know.

A bandage with dried blood was wrapped around his head and partially covered his right eye, which was swollen, with purples and blues all around it. *We match,* Tabitha thought wryly, thinking of the fading bruises under her eyes.

Resting atop the quilt were his hands, callused with work and strong enough to control a wild horse, yet soft enough to brush away a tear, to hold her close in a tender embrace. He breathed deeply.

He doesn't look to be in pain, she thought gratefully.

She stepped forward, and a floorboard creaked, making her pause and hold her breath as Samuel turned his head to one side on the pillow. Should she speak or wait for him to open his eyes and see her?

She took a step, and another, then stopped. The creaking of the floor made him stir again, then blink. He blinked a second time and then a third, seeming to focus his eyes as if he wasn't sure whether he was awake or whether Tabitha were an apparition of dreams.

"Tab?" he said, sounding raspy and confused.

"Ye—s," she said, her voice breaking. She crossed the short distance and carefully perched at the edge of the bed. "Yes, I'm here, finally. I'm so sorry I didn't come before. I hope you aren't too angry with me."

"Not angry. Confused," he said.

And hurt, too, I'm sure, Tabitha thought with an ache. "I'm sorry I didn't come myself. It was cowardly to send a letter . . ."

"I've had a lot of hours to lie here and think about what you said. You were right to stay away. I don't want to make you suffer the way you did when your husband died."

Tabitha couldn't answer at first. Tears streaked down her cheeks, and for once, she didn't try to stop them.

Samuel took her hand with one good hand. "Why did you come now?"

She covered her eyes, the tears coming so hard now that she was unable to speak for a moment. When she lifted her face, she wiped the tears with the back of her hand. "I came to keep my promise."

"You . . ." Samuel's eyes narrowed, not understanding.

"I was wrong. I do need you to help carry my load." She shook her head and blinked, sending heavy tears into her lap. "I can't do it alone, Samuel. I tried, and I can't. I need you."

Samuel stroked the back of her hand with his thumb. His eyes looked full of moisture, but he didn't speak right away. "But I might lose my leg," he said. "And I'm deformed now—I have only one ear."

"I don't care," Tabitha said. "You're alive, aren't you? That's all I need."

"That's not all you need, and we both know it. You need someone to care for you. I don't know that I'll be able to do that. Even if I can keep my leg, I'll probably never be able to do hard labor again. Stick with me, and you'll be in for a life of poverty."

Panic pushed against Tabitha's chest, making it difficult to breathe. "Samuel, please . . ." Surely he wouldn't pull away now. "Remember what you said about bearing one another's burdens? I want to help carry yours, just like I'll let you carry mine. We can do it together."

"But how will I support you? Where can I find work for someone lame like . . . like me?" He looked over his wounded body and shook his head. "I can't do that to you. You were right before. You should have stayed away, Tabitha."

"Please call me Tab," she said. She tilted her head in consideration. "You know, I happen to be aware of a business in need of someone with a knack for fixing things. No heavy labor required. Just a lot of dedication . . . and a screwdriver."

Samuel laughed, the first sign of optimism in his face since the conversation went down this path. "Dedication I have. A screwdriver, too. Perhaps that might work."

"*Perhaps* isn't good enough," Tabitha said, gripping his hand tighter. "You have a promise to keep in return, Mr. Barnett." She leaned over and kissed him softly, then, still holding her face close to his, whispered, "And I intend to see that you keep it."

CHAPTER 30

Christmas Eve

WILHELMINA HALL WALKED THROUGH THE drifting snowflakes with a strange mix of heavy heart and anticipation. In one arm she held a package wrapped in bright green paper and tied with a red ribbon, a Christmas gift for young Will—a scarf, mittens, and a sweater, all made by hand.

In all his life, Will had never received a decent gift from her for the holiday. For six years the difficulty of spanning the distance to Logan was plenty excuse to send nothing more than a letter and two bits, at least in her mind. She couldn't bear to bestow much love onto the child whose very existence tore at her heart as a constant reminder of the death of his father.

Her son.

Snowflakes freckled the package, and Wilhelmina brushed them off to keep the paper dry. The graying light seemed to overtake the day rapidly, and for a moment, she wondered if Will would still be awake to receive the items she had spent hours knitting for him—the sweater was of light brown wool and had an intricate pattern of cables. She almost hoped he would already be in bed for the night, because the very sight of the boy made her ache.

Since returning with his mother last spring, Will had reopened an old wound. She avoided seeing him whenever possible, because Will looked eerily like his father at that age. He had Fred's six-year-old mischievous grin and mismatched teeth. When those grew in, he'd keep his father's cowlick over his left ear. Will shared the same shape of eyes, the same tilt of his head. The Hall family mouth. It all felt too much like visions from the past, mocking her.

But avoiding Will for months hadn't helped. If anything, she grieved for Fred more now than she had when they had arrived in April. Avoiding him had only made her miss her son more.

If only Will still had a father, she thought grimly.

Across the street from the Chadwick place, she paused beneath the boughs of a matronly willow. Golden light spilled from the windows onto the snow-covered yard out front. The glow silhouetted two figures, a man and a boy, laughing and playing in the snow.

From the delighted shrieks of joy, she could clearly tell that the smaller of the two was Will. He scooped up snow between his hands, formed a ball, and lobbed it smack in the middle of the other's back.

The man nearly lost his balance, catching it with a cane—which he looked far too young to be using—and spun around on one foot.

"No, you don't," came the mock-threatening voice. "You'd better watch out."

It was that Samuel Barnett man she had seen spending time with Tabitha, Wilhelmina suddenly realized. So he'd kept his leg, after all.

He limped a step or two, then went down on one knee, where he scooped snow between his hands. A second later, a much larger snowball than the first flew through the air and landed with a thud on Will's shoulder. The boy gasped with the shock and stumbled a step or two, nearly bowled over by the force. Then he burst out laughing.

Will ran forward and jumped onto Samuel from the side, knocking him down. Wilhelmina sucked her breath, expecting the man to cry out in pain or to reprimand Will. Instead, he rolled in the snow, tickling Will and chuckling heartily himself.

Would that Fred could play in the snow with his son, Wilhelmina thought, gripping the package in her arms. She squeezed it tightly to ward off emotion. Despite her efforts, hot tears filled her eyes and dripped down her cheeks.

She looked down at the gift. Will's sweater would have to wait until she could return without tears. She took one step backward and then another, still watching the two play. Turning on her heel, she gripped the package to her chest and headed quickly for home.

Her boots crunched in the snow, a loud noise that didn't come close to drowning out her melancholy thoughts. She imagined what it would have been like for Fred to grow up without one his parents. What a blessing it had been for Fred to have such a wonderful, attentive father, who had died only after Fred reached adulthood. Having only a mother would have been tragic, indeed. For both mother and son.

The idea struck her with force and made her brow crumple as she pondered it. She had never once considered what such a life must have been like for Tabitha. She looked over her shoulder, now barely able to make out Will's and Samuel's shapes in the darkening night.

Continuing to be so fiercely loyal to Fred's memory would only hurt Fred's son. And Will still needed a man in his life, a father figure.

And I suppose Tabitha deserves some happiness too.

The thought appeared in her heart with a suddenness that took her breath away. Wilhelmina stared at the snow, trying to grasp the idea. *Tabitha's a better woman than I had assumed years ago,* she admitted to herself. She smiled wryly, thinking of what kinds of problems the family might have had with Betty Hunsaker as a daughter-in-law. Perhaps Fred had known best after all.

She swallowed deliberately and kept walking, trying to rid herself of the intense feelings about to overwhelm her. *I must analyze it with logic,* she told herself. That was how she handled all of life's difficulties.

For months now, she had figured that if seeing Will was painful, then logic dictated she not see him. If she was to be true to the memory of her only son, logic said that there could be no one to replace him and that she could never allow herself to feel whole without him.

Her creed had always insisted that emotions were weak and that logic must rule.

But I've broken that creed, she realized. *I've let emotion blind me to the greater good.*

She took one last look over her shoulder and imagined the figures in the distance as Fred and Will, frolicking in winter play. It brought a rare smile to her face, and she wiped a gloved fingertip under her eye.

I was wrong, she thought. *So very wrong.*

With a sniff, she headed for home.

* * *

Samuel wiped the last round of snow from his eyes and raised his arm to shield himself from further onslaught. "Enough!" he said with a laugh. He rose on his hands and knees and pretended to growl like a dog then darted forward toward Will, who squealed with delighted fright and raced toward the front door, where he ran headlong into his mother coming out.

With an oomph, Tabitha caught him in her arms then quickly backed up. "You're soaking wet, silly boy," she said, swiping off the white stuff in long strokes. "Take off your boots and wraps and then go dry yourself by the fire." Watching the scene warmed Samuel head to toe in spite of the frost.

From where he was, still on his knees in the snow, he turned his head and looked in the distance where the figure of a woman slipped around a corner—a woman he could swear was Sister Hall. A few minutes ago, he thought he had imagined seeing someone under the willow across the street and now felt certain it had been Mrs. Hall watching him and Will.

Samuel reached for his cane and slowly made it back to his feet, careful not to slip on the ice. His right leg was still weak, and heaven only knew whether he'd ever get full use of it again, but at least it was still there and he could walk.

The front door closed, and footsteps sounded.

"Are you all right?" Tabitha asked quietly, coming up beside him. Her arms were folded tightly against the cold.

Samuel instinctively put an arm around her. "I'm quite well if you don't count losing a snowball fight to a six-year-old." At Tabitha's laugh, he leaned in and kissed her temple. She snuggled closer and rested her head against his chest.

In a spell, he would be leaving Tabitha for the evening and going back to the boarding house, to his empty room. What he wouldn't give to be able to stay with her every day, every night.

"It's icy on the roads," Tabitha said. "I'd better walk home with you."

He agreed with nothing more than a nod, not liking the situation but getting used to the extra help he needed to get around.

Tabitha lifted her head and looked up at him. "I know you don't like getting help for something as trivial as walking a few blocks."

"But we bear one another's burdens now," Samuel finished.

"And a promise *is* a promise," Tabitha said with a contented sigh as she leaned her face against his shoulder once more.

Samuel looked up at the stars, shining like tiny crystals scattered across a sea of coal. *Am I well enough to make her my wife?* The question had no simple answer, and he didn't allow himself to pose it often. But over the last couple of months as he healed, the question broke through the surface of his thoughts, forcing him to ponder it. Earlier today he had decided that tonight before going home he would do it.

He had already asked for her hand from her parents and from Will. *Everything is ready,* he thought. But after seeing Sister Hall a moment ago, he doubted whether it was the right time. *I don't want to wound anyone else through my actions.*

"You seem rather pensive tonight," Tabitha said, patting his chest. "Especially for a man covered in snowballs."

Using his cane, Samuel adjusted his position to face her. "Tab, there's something I have to do tonight."

A pleased smile broke across her face. She bit her lip. "Yes?"

Samuel's heart thudded in his chest, and he wanted more than anything to simply ask the question hovering on his lips. It would be so simple, and it would change the course of his future. But he knew there was one thing lacking.

Tabitha's eyebrows drew together. "*Is* everything all right then?"

"It will be, I promise," Samuel said with a reassuring smile.

"What do you need to do?" she asked. "You can't go alone, you know. I'm going with you whatever it is."

Samuel chuckled and ran a thumb across Tabitha's cheek. "Always the headstrong one," he said softly. He leaned in and kissed her cheek. "I love you more than you know, Tabitha Chadwick."

"And I you," she returned, raising a hand to cup his face. She studied his eyes, worry in her expression. "Samuel, what is it? What's wrong?"

He put her arm through his and carefully maneuvered along the footpath toward the road. "Come see."

They walked slowly, Tabitha making sure to pick the least slippery parts of the road and supporting his weight betimes. She must have been too wrapped up in attending to Samuel to understand where they were heading until they arrived.

Her step came up short as the realization seemed to dawn on her. "Mother Hall?" Her throat choked out the name. Her voice dropped to nothing more than a whisper when she added, "Why?"

Samuel couldn't answer her yet; he had to focus on his mission here before letting himself think beyond that. They made their way to the front door, where he rapped loudly three times. Tabitha's grip on his arm tightened noticeably as they waited for an answer.

It took a full minute before it creaked open and Sister Hall came into view, looking perplexed. "To what do I owe this visit?" Her typical challenging tone was unmistakable, but the abrasive edge, the obvious irritation, was absent. The woman looked tired and defeated—and somehow softer.

"Sister Hall," Samuel said. Again his heart sped up, thudding against his chest like galloping hoof beats. His mouth felt dry as he tried again. "Sister Hall, I have come to ask for your blessing . . . in taking Tabitha's hand in marriage."

Both women breathed in sharply and stared at him. Under other circumstances, the sight could have made Samuel laugh, but tonight, when his very future hung in the balance, he stood frozen, waiting for a response. What if Sister Hall said no? Would he move forward anyway? He prayed it wouldn't come to that. He also prayed that the woman would speak; she stood there silently, not moving a muscle for what felt like an eon.

Finally she made a single movement—she closed her eyes. To Samuel's surprise, the action pushed tears onto her wrinkled cheeks. She began nodding, first one long, slow nod, and then several after that, more rapidly, before she spoke, eyes still closed. "Yes," she said, her voice quavering. "You have my blessing."

She reached out to close the door, but Tabitha pushed forward and kept it open. "Oh, Mother Hall, thank you," she said, holding her arms out. She took the woman into an embrace—surely the first between them—and together they cried.

"I'm sorry, so sorry," the elderly woman said. "I just miss him so."

"I know," Tabitha said, holding her mother-in-law tight and crying into her shoulder too. "I never asked for any of this to happen. I'm so sorry."

"Tabitha," Sister Hall said, pulling back and wiping a handkerchief across her nose. "You don't know how I needed to hear that." Sister Hall tried to regain some semblance of composure. She withdrew a handkerchief from her pocket and dabbed at her nose with it. "Thank you for coming, Mr. Barnett," she told Samuel. "You are truly a good, honorable man." She pressed her lips into a tight line as if fending off another round of tears. Her chin trembled for a moment, but when she got control, she added, "Will you do one thing for me? Take care of her as Fred would have. And be the father to Will that Fred couldn't be."

Tears pricked Samuel's eyes now, and in a husky voice, he said, "I give you my word as a gentleman. I'll do my best to live up to your son's memory."

"Then that is all I can ask for," Sister Hall said. She wiped another tear with the handkerchief. "Merry Christmas."

"Merry Christmas," Samuel and Tabitha chorused in response. The door closed slowly and clicked into place.

In a sweet but powerful silence, Samuel and Tabitha walked arm in arm to the street and back toward her home. When they reached the willow, he stopped.

"Shall we make this a proper engagement, then?"

Tabitha looked overwhelmed by emotions. Instead of speaking, she nodded.

"I can't kneel very well," Samuel said, lifting his cane and letting it hit his bad leg lightly. "But I can mean every word when I say that I love you, Tab, and I want to spend the rest of my life with you. Someday we can go through those doors"—he glanced up at the rising temple—"and be sealed for eternity as well. If you'll take me."

"I'll take every inch of you, Samuel Barnett," Tabitha said, crying through her laughter.

"Even the inches with the bum leg?"

"You'll just have to accept that you're stuck with me," Tabitha said. "It would do you no good to try shaking me off."

"Like your father says, it'd be like trying to get a rattle off a rattler."

"Exactly," Tabitha said, stepping close.

Samuel ran his fingers through her hair and eased her face closer to his. Their lips met, and he kissed her deeply and with more emotion than he had allowed himself before. She would be his, and he hers. She had brought to life a part of him he thought was dead, and as they broke apart, he couldn't wait for the time when she would be at his side, making him feel alive for the rest of his days.

"You know, Tab," he said, holding her hands and resting his head against hers as they gazed at the temple, "I think I'll be perfectly happy being with stuck with you."

HISTORICAL
NOTES

BRIGHAM YOUNG COLLEGE OPENED ITS doors the fall of 1878. It began with bachelor degrees and high school courses, eventually offering grade school classes as well. During the time this novel opens, students met in the unfinished Logan Tabernacle.

BYC was not, as is sometimes assumed, the forerunner to today's Utah State University, which is also located in Logan. BYC came first, with the Agricultural College—the real forerunner to USU—being established in 1888. The two schools offered competing classes, which eventually led to BYC closing its doors after its 1926 commencement. BYC was located near current-day Logan High School.

While coal mining is a dangerous profession, the 1877 explosion in Coalville is a creation of the author's imagination.

The area now known as Sanpete County was originally called after a man called Sanpitch, who was the brother of Chief Walker, one of the friendly Native Americans who actually invited Brigham Young to settle the area. Eventually "Sanpitch" became known as "Sanpete."

The first winter for the original settlers of Manti was a brutal one. Some Saints built dugouts on the south side of what would later become Temple Hill, while others huddled close to one another in their wagons. Many of the cattle died over the winter, and those that survived were weak, most unable to do farm work.

That spring, rattlesnakes came out of the hill in droves, and the men spent days fighting them, as described in the novel. The settlers quickly found another location for their homes.

The hill became a popular location for children to play on throughout the year. In winter, children sledded down the hill, and in more temperate months, couples courted there. Collecting wildflowers was a particularly popular pastime. Children collected "pearl stones" just as Tabitha and her schoolmates did.

The Little Fort had walls made of the same oolite stone used for the temple. The walls were eight feet tall and two feet thick, with a three-foot-thick foundation. The fort was originally built as a protection from Indians and housed several cabins early on. It later contained a campground, the tithing office (which itself contained other Church administrative offices, such as for the bishop and temple superintendent), stables, granary, etc. Later, two other forts were built, one of which encompassed the area of the Little Fort. A historical marker, a remnant of a Little Fort wall, still stands at the corner of 100 North and Main Street.

The site for the Manti Temple was dedicated by Brigham Young on April 25, 1877. After that, major blasting, grading, and smoothing of the hill began, including the construction of the four massive terrace walls. Not until 1879 were the cornerstones set in place and dedicated.

No major injuries were ever reported in connection to the stone quarry or the rest of the temple construction. The only injuries recorded were all minor, such as a rock landing on someone's foot, as is briefly mentioned in the story.

John Parry was master mason of the Manti Temple and other temples. The Parry brothers had a stonecutting business that was heavily involved in temple building. The story about the Parry mules being missing and found already in place and ready to be hitched up is found in several records.

The terraced walls made the hill look like a fortress. When the temple was complete, Anton H. Lund, Manti Temple's second president, reportedly compared the building and its unfinished landscaping and terrace walls to "a fair maiden of his native land, Denmark, dressed in a beautiful silk gown, but with clumsy wooden shoes on her dainty feet" (William H. Peterson, as quoted by Glenn R. Stubbs in *A History of the Manti Temple,* 71).

The terracing was eventually ripped out in 1907, after which the hill was smoothed out and a grand staircase built from the street up to the west doors. The stairs were removed a few decades later when new improvements were made.

Much of the oolite rock used for the Manti Temple was blasted from Temple Hill itself, although some came from the Parry Brothers Quarry in Ephraim. By 1884, the year the bulk of the story takes place, the main walls were completed and the towers were under construction.

Maypoles (or "liberty poles") were popular in Manti at this time, and they were decorated in patriotic colors as described. May Day and maypoles have a long history and likely came to Utah via England, where Samuel would have been familiar with them, too. Since they were decorated in patriotic colors, I thought it likely that one would have been used for Independence Day as well as May Day. John H. Hougard, who appears briefly at the Independence Day celebration, was the mayor of Manti from 1881 to 1885. July 4, 1884 was really a Friday.

President Joseph F. Smith was the second counselor in the First Presidency at this time, and Church leaders periodically visited Manti. Once when Brigham Young came, the Saints created a floral arch for him to drive under, like the one depicted in the book. Canute Peterson was both the stake president and superintendent over the temple construction during this time.

The *Sanpitch Sentinel* is entirely a creation of the author's imagination. Manti's earliest paper, the *Manti Messenger,* didn't begin publication until 1893. The printing press in the book is modeled after the Stanhope press, which was invented in the early 1800s and had significant advances from previous presses. It's possible that Tabitha could have had access to a newer press, but since the *Deseret News,* based in Salt Lake City, was originally published by an even older press, I doubted that Manti, a much smaller community, would have had access to one of the fancier, steam-run presses that large newspapers in the East would have used in this period.

Theater was popular at this time in Manti, including Shakespeare performances and plays written by Sister Adela B. Cox Sidwell, an influential early resident of Manti. Other community events included debates, dances, and recitations, and many of them took place in the South Ward Assembly Hall. Benefit concerts to raise money for a final push for the temple fund began in 1886, a couple of years after this story ends.

Many people are under the impression that no wages were ever paid to the Manti Temple workers, quoting Brigham Young when he declared shortly after the site dedication, "Now, bishops, if any person should inquire what wages are to be paid for work done on this temple, let the answer be, 'Not one dime'" (see *The Manti Temple*, Manti Temple Centennial Committee, 6. Capitalization and spelling modernized). However, volunteer labor didn't last. When John Taylor succeeded Brigham Young as president of the Church, he determined that workers would be paid wages in cash. On May 21, 1878, new instructions were created, setting the pay rates for quarrymen, carpenters, and others. Labor tithing was still given as well, even by paid workers.

Cash was in short supply during this time. Church leaders encouraged members to donate to the temple fund in cash instead of in kind whenever possible to enable the temple committee to purchase construction supplies typically unavailable with bartered goods.

The city of Manti did not have a bank at this period. The law enforcement and jail systems were invented for the sake of the book, after the author did not uncover anything specific on how either functioned in the Sanpete area in the 1880s.

"A Folk History of the Manti Temple," a thesis by Barbara Lee Hargis, from which much of the information for this book was drawn, also includes a recipe for bear tallow ointment. I attributed the recipe, which was used by some early Manti residents, to Wilhelmina Hall.

On a Sunday in August 1928, a thunderstorm came upon the city of Manti quite suddenly, and lightning struck the southwest corner of the temple's east tower. Because the fire was so elevated, the people had a hard time fighting it—the water pressure was too weak. The fire burned for three hours but was eventually extinguished. Some said it was the slowest burning fire they had ever seen, and damage was minimal.

Eve Nielson, who was a young girl at the time, told scholar Hugh Nibley about her experience. He retold the story in his book *Temple and Cosmos* (see 29–30). According to Nibley's account, she and her family fearfully huddled together at home during the storm, looking out at the temple. As she clung to her mother, young Eve asked if the temple might be struck by lightning. Right when her mother started to assure her that the Lord wouldn't allow such a thing, the temple tower *was* hit, setting the east tower aflame.

Eve's father was part of the crew that went up to fight the fire, and when he returned, the children asked him why such a thing had been allowed to happen. He explained that during the construction, debate had gone on about whether to add a lightning rod. The decision was made against one, as they were certain that the temple would be protected. Eve Nielson reported her father as saying that the Lord had given the workers means to protect the temple, and since they neglected to do so, they had no right to expect miraculous intervention.

Following the fire, city water was connected to the temple grounds for emergency use, and a lightning rod system was installed. Which people involved with the construction were for or against a lightning rod is unknown to the author. As such, the representation of the debate over adding a lightning rod is invented.

The Manti Temple has a rich history and is often admired by tourists. Below is a favorite quote regarding the Manti temple, according to William Peterson (quoted by Stubbs, 74):

> "This is indeed marvelous," said an eastern tourist as he stood with a group of fellow tourists on bright angel point on the north rim of the Grand Canyon. "But have you seen the white temple on a hill near a town called Manti?"

ABOUT THE AUTHOR

Annette Lyon, Utah's 2007 Best of State medalist for fiction, has been writing for most of her life. While she's found success in freelance magazine work and editing, her true passion is fiction. In 1995, she graduated cum laude from BYU with a BA in English. Her university focus on 19th-century literature proved beneficial years later while writing historical temple novels. Her fifth novel, *Spires of Stone,* was a 2007 Whitney Award finalist.

When she's not writing, Annette enjoys spending time with her husband and their four children. She also loves reading, knitting, and chocolate—not necessarily in that order.

Readers may contact her via her website, www.annettelyon.com.